OF SAND AND BONE

OF SAND AND BONE

a novel

VICTORIA DOUGHERTY

OF SAND AND BONE

Published by Bloodwilde Press
Printed in the USA

ISBN (paperback) 978-1-955039-08-6
(hardback) 978-1-955039-09-3
(ebook) 978-1-955039-07-9

Visit the author at www.victoriadoughertybooks.com

The sound of your voice is sweet
Like the taste of date wine
And I, drunken girl, in a tangle of flowers
Live only a captive to hear it

— Egyptian love poem
c. 1300 B.C.

Prologue

Cairo, Egypt 1886

THE AIR IS STILL AS A PHOTOGRAPH. Nearly as hot as a stove. The sun is merciless, and the men in my vision fight to stand straight and move with fortitude under its tyrannical gaze. There are thirty or so, the lot of them British. I can tell by the uniform. The tall helmets that look as if they were shaped to the skulls of alien beings, the neat button-down shirts and utility belts. Criss-crossed leather straps across the chest, small buckled purses on the hip and canteens made of hide. The metal ones won't do in the desert. Their trousers balloon at the thighs and hug the calves snugly. Well-tailored. All of this military finery—in light brown with only a hint of green—is a notably elegant compliment to the ever-present sand. Death can be elegant, too, you know.

The commander has taken the time to groom this morning. He's used wax and curled up the corners of his mustache. Shaved his cheeks and chin so smooth that they shine. I've always admired that about the British—their attention to detail and decorum no matter the circumstances.

He paces nervously, then picks up a torch and lights it from a matchbox he keeps in his purse. He holds it high and away, keeping its unpleasant warmth at bay as he looks all around him, eager to hurry his men along. There are several desert tribesmen among them—at least a dozen—their bodies wrapped up in the indigo linens some of the more practiced desert wanderers wear. A few are sitting in the sand, their movements slow and their gazes disoriented. The ones who are on their feet are helping the British commander's men put the finishing touches on a tall stack of sticks and debris, all dry as dust.

They back away, and the commander, right there in the blistering heat of mid-day, puts the torch to the stack in several places. It takes only seconds for it to be consumed by flames.

A young soldier, barely eighteen by the looks of him, begins reading from the Bible.

"The Lord is my shepherd; I shall not want. He maketh me to lie down in green pastures; He leadeth me beside the still waters."

The commander gives a nod and his men line up the able-bodied tribesmen. They leave the ones in the sand alone. Some of those begin to weep into their robes, saying prayers in their tribal language. A tongue I, myself, don't know all that well, but I recognize a plea when I hear one. Especially one spoken in utter despair.

"He restoreth my soul: He leadeth me in the paths of righteousness for his name's sake," the young soldier continues.

The British face the tribesmen and draw their pistols. The signal from the commander comes almost immediately and the men fire, killing every single one of the robed men with shots to the head and heart. Even the poor wretches in the sand. Two by two, the soldiers lift the dead by their hands and feet, tossing them onto the pyre. When they've finished, and the desert men are burning—the black smoke rising up into a cloudless sky of aquamarine—they reload.

"Yea, though I walk through the valley of the shadow of death, I will fear no evil, for You are with me; Your rod and Your staff, they comfort me." The young soldier adjusts the

Bible in his hand, losing his place for a moment. His eyes search the page in a panic, before landing once more where he left off and giving an audible sigh. "I have set the Lord always before me. Because He is at my right hand, I will not be shaken." But his voice does indeed shake. The sweat pours from underneath his helmet.

The others, the ones who did the killing, stand at attention and salute their commander. A man I assume is his deputy—tall, clean shaven, with a large mole in the crease of his nose—raises his hand and the men draw their pistols once again. This time, at the commander's signal, they shove their barrels beneath their own chins and fire. They fall right to the ground, blood and brain splattering the sand. It'll blow away soon, get covered up like it was never there, once the desert winds start.

Only one of the commander's men is left standing—it's the young man reading from the Bible. He bites his lip and goes on, squaring his shoulders and putting his back into it. "Surely goodness and mercy shall follow me all the days of my life; and I will dwell in the house of the Lord forever."

The deputy raises his pistol and shoots him, watching the Good Book tumble into the sand, and the young man crumble on top of it. Removing a handkerchief from his pocket, the deputy wipes down his face and closes his eyes, taking a deep breath.

They don't waste time. The commander and his deputy throw this new batch of bodies onto the pyre. The corpses stare up into the heavens as if they're waiting for God to take them whole. Beneath them, many of the eyes of the tribesmen have already begun to boil and burst; flames licking from some of their sockets. The British commander and his deputy ignore the grotesquerie, but I can't. I watch the skins of these men crack as the fat beneath it melts, then starts to come away from bone. I know that inside them, their internal organs are heating up and will boil, too, then explode. As the muscles succumb completely to the fire, they'll dry up, wither, and burn away. The fire is hot, the bones will burn up, too, becoming black dust. I've seen it all before, having built my share of funeral pyres. Having been burned at the stake once or twice.

The commander takes a flask from his belt and opens it up. Likely whiskey. He offers it to his deputy and the man drinks, ever so grateful. He even laughs, and the men shake hands. I think they want to embrace, but they don't. Instead, the commander takes out his pistol and shoots his deputy directly in the heart. He drags the man's body to the pyre and tosses it up as best he can. The deputy is heavy for him, though, and the commander is already sun-whipped and shattered. He gets too close to the flames, his arm catching fire. Gasping, he beats at his sleeve, putting it out with his palm. When he's finished, he stares at his burns with a strange detachment, raising the charred fabric off the bright pink skin of his forearm. It's already starting to blister.

He takes out his flask once again and drains it, tossing it to the ground with a note of flair. Holding his pistol tight to his chest, the commander backs up, taking a good, hard gander at the pyre and the men whose bodies are being consumed by it. He breaks into a run and jumps onto the fire himself, screaming as he lands squarely on the blaze. His helmet comes off and his hair is all aflame in a poof. I imagine his nerve endings must be firing all at once, fast making his pain unbearable, because the commander wastes no time. He shoves his pistol in his mouth and pulls the trigger, putting an end to it all. An end to his hope of returning to England, of seeing his wife's hands dance over her piano keys after Christmas dinner, and an end to the terror. His terror that what they encountered in the desert could survive fire and sand and time.

"**There, there,**" my mother's voice says. "You can't be hungry again, can you?"

The room is dark and my tears have made the whole of my head wet. She lights a lantern and unties her nightdress, putting me to her breast. I'm not hungry, but I begin to suckle. It is awfully comforting.

I must have woken up screaming again. I've been doing that every night since I was born. Three weeks ago yesterday. Usually when I dream—especially so soon after a birth—I'm bathed in memories from my previous lives. I'm visited by my forever love, Nif, and we whisper to one another about how we can set about finding each other in this life. Perhaps discover a way we can leave clues that point us in the right direction. It is soon after a birth that dreams are all we have left. Our waking hours become consumed by our new lives and our memories of the past dissolve like sugar in tea.

Such is the life of a Nin'ti. And that's what I am, what Nif is.

We're as rare as angels or demons.

Born to live and die over and over again. Born to love only each other. Born to help God's human experiment endure.

Only, this time around, things seem different. I fear my dreams are firmly anchored in the present time and I'm watching what is, not what was. Nif's voice has come to me only once or twice since I took my first breath, and I wonder if he isn't absorbed by what I see, too.

"What I see in my dreams is death. Death in the desert," I tell him.

"Then we must go there," he finally says.

"There is a wind that speaks of anger in the desert. It will

make you bow so low that you will no longer be." I sing to myself, to Nif, from the *Songs of the Desert Wind.*

It's an ancient, epic song that could be sung for days without end. My father used to sing it to my mother, but only the more pleasant parts. The beautiful ones made of poetry. My first father to my first mother, I mean. They died long before the great kings of Europe and the Orient. Before Caesar. Before Moses.

"Leila," my new mother says. Her voice as cool and rich as fog.

I let go of her nipple and look up into her face. I love her eyes, black and wet like a London street after a heavy rain. I love her, so kind and strong. I wish I could speak to her, tell her what I see in my dreams before my memories up and leave me. I know she'd believe me; that she'd understand. Not all mothers would, but Llizabith Saber is different. Her rebellious heart, her Egyptian blood, her lyrical brain. She understands the truth of myths and fiction, knows the science in them.

I could tell her what I saw in the desert through my dreams. Something I hoped I would never see again. I could warn her. Warn them all before I forget.

Chapter 1

Cairo, Once More
Egypt, February, 1902

I STARTLE AWAKE as our train screeches to a halt. My neck hurts and I tilt my head ever so gently and give it a bit of a stretch.

"We there?" I ask Father.

"Just a caravan," he says, chewing on the yellowed ivory bit of his pipe.

Out the window, I see a group of men in striped robes and plain turbans as white as cotton balls. They're leading a herd of camels across the track and taking their sweet time about it. As the last of them saunters past, flashing a gap-toothed smile, the train wheels slowly begin to grind again.

"Another hour, I think," Father says. "Perhaps sooner if there are no more caravans."

I lean over and kiss his brow before reaching into my satchel, which sits on the bench next to him. I retrieve my journal, sitting down quickly and setting about writing down my latest dream before I forget it.

I could see the desert long and wide before me. The strong Sirocco wind was blowing hot and dry, reshaping the sandy floor. In a shallow gulley made by that very wind, I saw what looked like the top of a ball. The wind blew harder, meaner, and that's when I noticed it wasn't a ball at all, but the top of a skull with only one of the eye sockets in place. As for the rest of it—the cheeks and jaw were absent and the skull itself had a large, black fleck on one side, as if it had been burned by fire.

Macabre and lonely, the dream has an odd sense of familiarity about it. I put down my pencil and take a deep, quivering breath like I've got the vapors. Mother would have found that funny. Not the dream, which was unquestionably awful—the vapors part. She always made fun of women prone to histrionics and had even less regard for men who indulged the behavior.

"Get a hold of yourself," I say under my breath. "This won't do at all."

Leaning back, I close my eyes again, and whisper the Coptic Prayer of Thanksgiving, a soothing balm for my disquiets. Then I take in the fine tobacco and leather smells that all First Class cabins seem to share. Even here in North Africa, where nothing smells as it does anywhere else. Especially not London, which smells of cold rain and coal, perfumes and meat pies. Smoke and fine liquor in the places I'm not allowed.

North Africa, and especially her jewel, Cairo, smells of everything humanly possible. Spices and feces and fresh fruit and old sweat. Incense, dry air, animals, sticky honey, disease. I could go on. A cacophony of aromas I feared I might never breathe in again.

"All things are possible," I say out loud this time. "Who you are is limited only by who you think you are."

"What's that, dear?" Father asks, and I shake my head.

They're words from the Egyptian Book of the Dead. Words from my mother. My breaths are strong again just for saying them. Not a quiver among them. I bat open my eyes and watch out the window as the countryside begins to give way to a small tented settlement, where street merchants likely live, traveling to and from the city to peddle their wares. We're close. I glance over at Father and he senses my attention. He takes his pipe out of his mouth and blinks hard at me. I blow him a kiss I know he needs like medicine, and watch him turn back to the window. His mouth is set with the trace of a smile, and I feel a renewed confidence in our decision to return to this place.

It's funny how it all seems quite inevitable now. Our coming back to Cairo, I mean. When we left for London the year after Mother's death, it was meant to be for good. A fresh start for us both, in my father's homeland this time. A country of reason and refinement. Power. A place I did grow to love, along with a family who embraced me fully despite my Egyptian peculiarities. Maybe because of them. Father's family has always been an eccentric lot. Even Aunt Imogen, the most conventional of them, who lives for her gardening club and her art collection, nearly burst into tears as we said goodbye a fortnight ago. And Aunt Imogen never cries.

"Take care of him," she whispered, meaning my father. "He's never been the same."

I look over at him again, and know how right she was. Almost every good thing that ever happened to Father happened in Cairo. But it came with his greatest heartbreak. And mine.

"I've missed the palms," I say, and he smiles, his mustache a bit wooly and needing a trim. Wish I'd tended to him better before we left Alexandria.

He gazes out the window again and my eyes follow. The palm trees we both missed dot the track like random water spouts and give me such a rush of excitement that I nearly laugh out loud. We've been in a desolate stretch since we left Alexandria for Cairo, saying goodbye to a gaggle of my mother's relatives. There are bursts of flora and some green patches, but otherwise it's dry as bone. Even the square houses that start turning up as we near the outskirts of the city are the color of sand, blending into the landscape like chameleons.

"The castles the cousins and I built on the beaches of Brighton always reminded me of Egypt. They made me terribly homesick."

Father takes my hand and squeezes it. "Cairo is a wonder."

He can hardly get the words out, his eyes brimming with water. The smattering of square houses have given way quite suddenly to the dense and dusty architecture of what my late mother stubbornly called *Kashromi*, the Coptic name for Egypt's capital. The word also means "man-breaker"—ha ha. Very fitting for Mother, Father always said.

But it doesn't matter what it's called—we've entered Cairo at last. The walled city. Maker of dreams; keeper of souls. My heart beats loudly, musically, and my hands grow cold and damp. I put an index and middle finger into my mouth to calm myself, like I always did as a little girl. Like I still do from time to time, when no one is looking.

Father sees me do it and actually giggles. First time I've heard him do that since . . . well, since before. Makes me giggle, too.

"Cairo! Cairo!" I can hear the attendant calling, his steps thudding on the wood floor as he marches up and down the corridor outside our compartment. The car seems to come alive at once, like spring. Voices, shuffling of feet, a boisterous laugh from a big bellied man.

I join Father at the window. Moorish buildings and sycamore trees blink past us, until at last, in the distance, I can see it.

"Misr Station!" I say, reaching over and squeezing Father's hand.

A fine, fine building, also Moorish in style, but so obviously fresh as a baby, having been built only a few years ago. New and old, just like Cairo. Our new and old home. My mother's birth city and final resting place. Four years gone now, but it seems like yesterday sometimes. And forever ago others. God, I miss her.

"Busy as a bee!" Father exclaims, his eyes roaming the bustling platform. By the time our train shrieks all the way to a stop, I've already been active, getting our snacks and reading materials in order. Father can't take himself away from the window.

"I won't be carrying this for you like a servant girl," I tease, handing Father his copy of *Lord Jim,* which he holds to his chest like a babe.

I am devouring what he refers to as (ahem) "rubbish that would've made your mother's hair curl," and tuck the so-called rubbish sneakily into my satchel, disguised as a perfectly acceptable Thomas Hardy novel. In reality? Mary Elizabeth Braddon's horror stories. I love them and anything that involves ghosts, demons, devils, and whatever other other-worldly misfits and scalawags happen to scroll across the page. And regardless of what Father says, I happen to know Mother would have found them delicious. Under bare lamplight, she read *The Strange Case of Dr. Jekyll and Mr. Hyde* to me every night before bed when I was only seven. It was our secret.

"Hugo! Why, it's Hugo!" Father calls out, practically shaking with delight.

Hugo Hughes—"Uncle" Hugo—and his wife Clara are standing on the platform as if they've been waiting ever so long for us to arrive. Hugo's cheeks are red as cherries and Clara looks a bit wilted, but her joy at our arrival takes possession of her the moment she sees Father's arm flailing out the window, Homberg hat in hand.

"Hooly-hoo!" Father calls out to our friends, and I very nearly shriek with happiness.

Father and I rush out of the train together, practically

elbowing our way down the steps. I actually shiver as my shoes touch the floor of the platform. Father takes my arm and pulls me along, as if I'm one to dilly-dally. All around us are travelers, mostly British and European, as it's Friday. Every man has a neat mustache and is smoking. Hats abound, naturally. Straw boaters for the men and for the ladies, the ones with big, taffeta flowers that are a must for any fashionable tourist. Especially of the Thomas Cook variety.

But Clara and Hugo are not tourists, especially not the Thomas Cook variety. He wears a safari pith helmet, left over from his days in India, while Clara sports a straw beach hat that's overused, one a fashionable lady would never be caught dead in.

"Oh, dearest dear!" Clara Hughes says, squishing my cheeks as if I were still eleven. I can't bring myself to feel cross about it, because Clara is simply the most adventurous and fascinating woman, besides my mother, that I've ever encountered. It's no wonder she and Mother were the best of friends.

"All is right with the world again now that you're back. And don't bother saying it's only for the completion of the dam. We both know you belong here."

"Ah the dam. Finally, it can be completed without further incident now that you're in charge again, Floyd," Hugo says.

Apparently it's been muddled in inefficiency since Father left, which makes him feel quite good. While it's only just February and the opening of the dam won't be until mid-December, HRH the Duke of Connaught and Strathearn plans to be there, so it must open on time. And, in all honesty, while I don't much give a damn about the dam, Father needs a purpose besides me. Overseeing the final stage of the building of the near fabled Aswan Low Dam will hopefully keep him occupied and thinking about the future. He's always loved his work here and believes his obsession with engineering is a calling not unlike the calling of a priest or an artist. I quite agree in his case. He could never manage a house like his brother Andrew. It would drive him mad.

Clara takes my face in her hands again, but this time she does so gently, barely touching me. "You're so much like her," she whispers. "I think you have everything but her eyes. Those are explicitly yours and yours alone."

Green eyes. Greener than a lime. The only green eyes on either side of the family, I've been told.

"Having you here will be like having Llizabith with me again," Clara continues. "You have her spirit, you know. And, I suspect, her propensity for making trouble."

Clara winks like this information is just between us.

"I wouldn't say I make trouble, Aunt Clara," I tell her. "But it has been known to follow me around."

Our luggage, all new, big, and leather—Father wanted something that could take a beating—is taken off the train by Egyptian men in white robes and tarbushes. Clara begins giving them direction in her impressive Arabic, while I turn towards Father and Uncle Hugo, hoping to urge them along. I can scarcely wait another moment to plunge into the streets of Cairo again!

"My dear, I hope you'll accept my pardon," Uncle Hugo says, putting his furry lip to my hand. "A gentleman should always properly greet a lady first, but the mere sight of your father made me feel a good twenty years younger! Such is the spell a true friend casts."

"Not at all," I tell him. I take Father's elbow and now I'm the one doing the pulling.

We walk through Misr Station, all gorgeous and electrifying. I'd only noticed the sultanic flourishes of its neo Mamluk architecture when I was a girl, but now I can detect a wink towards the Modern Style, too, and I love it. Makes me feel as if all of me is being welcomed back.

As we spill out onto Ramses Square, a musical racket of chants, footsteps, arguments, and laughter comes at us. The clim-clam of camels moseying along and the elegant trot of horses pulling a carriage rolls in the background like percussion.

"It's like nothing at all has changed," Father marvels. He walks on, as gape-mouthed as a first-timer.

"It hasn't been all that long we've been gone," I tell him. "I'm sure the pharaohs think the same when their spirits come down from the heavens to visit their pyramids."

He holds me close and squeezes my shoulders. "You and your ghosts."

One thing, of course, has changed irrevocably, and I know it's on his mind. He's wondering how we'll ever live here without my mother. Unlike me, he doesn't believe in ghosts. To him, gone is gone.

"Nothing ever really leaves here, darling," Clara says, patting my back as if she knows where my head has gone. "Such an old city, and an even older desert filled with phantoms."

Hugo's brougham pulls up and the men in tarbushes go to work again, loading our bags up top and bowing deeply, then helping us ladies inside the carriage. I get side-glances from all of them, a firm reminder that, here in Egypt, I'm not quite Egyptian enough for the Egyptians. They can look all they want. The desert has always felt like home to me, and my blood is every bit as old as theirs. *Older*, my mother would have insisted.

Only one of them looks at me not only as if I belong, but with deep affection. It's Horus, Uncle Hugo's coachman.

"Little Leila," he says, utterly breaking decorum. "You've come home to make more mischief for me, I see."

"You're hardly one to talk," I tell him.

It was Horus who once drove me into the town center when I was barely tall enough to see out the carriage without standing. And he did it knowing full well I was determined to sneak into one of my mother's incendiary feminist readings—where children were most certainly not allowed. The adults were required to make a big stink out of it, of course, but they were all just blowing smoke. Horus was docked a day's pay, which was snuck back to him by my mother the following week, once things had settled down.

I give him a wink and he flinches in horror as if it's the evil eye.

Inside the carriage, I feel like I'm back in London all of a sudden. It's a new one, with plush, creamy velvet and gravy-brown tassels all over.

"Ach!" Clara waves her hand and gives one of her famous eye-rolls. "A gift shoved down our throats by Hugo's grandfather. It was after one of the cousins came to visit. Clearly he complained about how he was brought about town. The old rig was just fine if you ask me."

"Hmm, just fine, yes," Hugo says, though it's quite plain he enjoys his new toy. The old rig was only a buggy.

"It's very handsome," I whisper to him, and he takes a puff off Father's pipe to keep from smiling too broadly, then comments on how fine a tobacco my father has brought with him.

While I've never minded roughing it at all, it is lovely to sit in comfort and get reacquainted with Cairo. I lay my arms on the window ledge and balance my chin on my hands, enjoying the street circus.

We pass men playing big bass drums hung around their necks. They're singing a song, but I can't make it out. One of the many folk songs sung on the streets as often as small talk is exchanged.

Men, and even some women, carry baskets on their heads. But it's only the men, all pouch-bellied, who sit sprawled on rickety chairs, smoking hookahs and watching the crowds.

Their heads are wrapped in thin, white linens that have all seen better days. They sit playing dominoes on stone tables that look as if they were dragged in from the pyramids.

A small wooden Ferris wheel, cranked by hand, is set right in the middle of the road, forcing us to go around it. Only about four benches on it, each fit for one, rocking and jerking with every turn. Makes the riders—men, of course—chuckle. When each of them reaches the top, they spit over the side, prompting a strong rebuke from Horus.

Lines and lines of merchant stalls, their proprietors dressed in skull caps and tunics striped like pajamas. Each and every one of them has a bushy mustache as thick as a fur collar. Except for one. He is clean shaven and catches my eyes as we pass. He looks right at me like he knows me and holds up a small statue barely the size of his hand. It's a rather distinctive looking thing, and I notice its lion's mouth straight away, along with its eyes, which feel as if they've caught my gaze and won't let go. I raise my head up and clutch the frame of the window, trying to get a closer look.

An ox cart passes between us going in the opposite direction and I strain to keep my sights on the man, but it's no use. By the time the carriage has passed, the merchant is gone and I feel as alone as I felt on the day Mother died.

Chapter 2

A love poem, a promise

THERE SHE IS, pride of place above the mantel in Hugh and Clara's home on Zamalek Island. In a portrait by Lawrence Alma Tadema, sat for on a visit to London some fifteen years ago, when I was just a babe, my mother stares back at me with that look of hers. The one that says, *I dare you*, but in a way that makes you want to go on whatever adventure she's been cooking up. She wears a dress the color of peaches, and has lips of hibiscus, skin the shade of a light mink stole, but with cheeks painted to flush like an English rose—which, of course, she was not. We look like we could be sisters, she and I, except for the eyes.

Llizabith Saber Wellington. Her name is engraved on a small gold plaque that's affixed to the bottom of the frame, also gold. God bless her soul.

"You know, Hugo," Father groans. "For a man who's made Cairo his home, you live like a Londoner."

It's true. The Hugheses' place is all high-backed sofas and crystal chandeliers, as if ready to receive the Queen. Not unusual for the residents of the pastoral hamlet of Zamalek, but unusual for the likes of the Hugheses.

"A man always brings the comforts of boyhood with him as an exile, I suppose," Hugo says with a playful shrug. "Even if the exile is self-imposed."

"And all of this is as fresh as baked bread," Father teases.

"Not a hint of your boyhood. I suspect your grandfather was as disapproving of your furnishings as he was of your carriage."

He glances at Mother's portrait then looks away. But I don't think it's because he can't bear it. His shoulders are square and there's a sprightliness to his movements. He, too, feels a thrill from her image. As if she's visiting us, alive and healthy.

"What are you chuckling about?" he asks me. I didn't realize I was.

"Just feeling a bit of excitement," I say, my hands dancing about my face as I talk, as they're apt to do.

"Live like a Londoner – ha," Clara sniffs. She faces my mother's portrait and takes out a handkerchief, shining the gold plaque emblazoned with her name. "Cairo is more modern than London these days. At least in certain circles. Less so without our Llizabith, but she did leave her mark."

Modern is the kind way of describing my mother, though I know Clara means it with great admiration. Rebellious is the less charitable way. Whatever the case, once you met her, you tended not to forget her. For Father, the eminent Lord Floyd Wellington, meeting my mother was a seismic event on par with the eruption of a volcano. And I know he's thinking about it right now. I can tell by the look on his face. Faraway. Happy. Lost in a memory that almost feels unreal now.

My memories of her have a similar quality. Yet, somehow, the stories I hear about her from others still feel immediate. Like they happened yesterday, or could happen again tomorrow. Like the one about how my parents met. I prefer my father's version to my mother's. Not because they differ so much on the details, but because of how she changed his world—gave him a completely different way of looking at things. I like to imagine it in my mind in bed when the Sandman won't come.

"Good afternoon."

A British officer, and lieutenant general by his insignia, stands at Hugo and Clara's door, which was left wide open so the servants could carry in our heaps of things. Balding, but not a gray hair on his head, he stands erect, bowing slightly as he greets us.

"Lieutenant General!" Hugo says. "Come in, Al, come in."

"Al" is Albert Blackwood, apparently, and Uncle Hugo seems to like him a fair bit by the way he introduces him. All smiles and outstretched hands.

"And this here is my dear friend Lord Floyd," Hugo says.

"Ah, Lord Floyd Wellington," the Lieutenant General says, as if he's been hearing about Father all his life.

"*Saber* Wellington." Father emphasizes Mother's name the way she always did.

Lieutenant General Blackwood doesn't seem to know what to do with that, so he merely smiles and nods. Father, in taking my mother's name as part of his own, has gotten used to raised eyebrows.

"I know we'll be seeing each other at the club tonight, but I did want to stop by to welcome you personally to Cairo and to Zamalek."

"And I thank you for that, Lieutenant General," Father tells him. "This here is my daughter, Leila."

"How do you do?" I say, and he smiles warmly.

"Well," he says. "The last thing we needed was another beautiful girl on the island. The young lads have enough distractions as it is."

That gets a knowing chuckle from everyone, and makes my cheeks burn hot and awful. It's a good thing I didn't inherit the skin of an English girl, otherwise I'd look like a ripe cherry.

"Oh, don't worry," I tell him. "We won't be on Zamalek all that long."

"Yes," Father chimes in. "My daughter and I plan to move into my late wife's family home as soon as it's livable again, which should be in the next fortnight, I hope."

The Lieutenant General takes a deep, solemn breath. "I heard about the fire, and your father-in-law's tragic death."

"I thank you," Father says graciously.

There's an awkward pause. In truth, my grandfather's death was a tragedy for no one. It's a sin to think ill of the dead, I know, but Ashraf Saber was a mean drunk and habitual carouser. A true black sheep in an otherwise fine family. I can't help but think that it was God's will that he burned down the top floor of his house and took himself with it. At least now Mother's family home can be filled with those who loved her.

"Father's fixing the house up quite a bit," I say, breaking the silence, to everyone's relief, I think. "It'll have electricity and everything. Even a rooftop garden for me to grow and tend. I can't imagine a home without a place to put my hands in the soil."

"And such a fine house it is," Clara chimes in. "A gem in the midst of Old Cairo, and being restored to its rightful glory, all while becoming utterly modern. Like Cairo itself—poised to take charge and be at the center of the world again!"

The Lieutenant General tips up his extrusive cleft chin. "Quite true, Mrs. Hughes. The house indeed seems much like Cairo. Brought up to modern standards, yes. And by an Englishman, of course."

"Er, we should all start getting ready for the evening, should we not?" Wisely, if a bit clumsily, Hugo changes the subject. Aunt Clara sees herself as an Egyptian nationalist and doesn't approve of the British occupation.

"Aunt Clara," I say. "You will help me pick out a dress for tonight, won't you?"

A final nail in the coffin of the previous line of conversation, thank goodness. Though in truth, Aunt Clara is the last person anyone wants to help them pick out a dress.

"Why, I'd love to," she says. "So many new people for you to meet! It's as if Cairo has shed a layer of skin since you left."

"Indeed," I tell her. "Most of my friends from here go to school in England now."

Aunt Clara rolls her eyes and puts her hands on her hips.

"Well, I can tell you that many families, new and old, are quite happy with the Tawfiqiyya School, and I'm sure you'll be quite happy there, too."

"Well, I'll be tutored," I say. I can't help but throw her a teasing smile. "And by mostly Egyptian scholars whom Father has retained. There's only one Englishman among them. Besides," I whisper, "I hear the headmaster at the Tawfigiyya School is as English as the English come."

Aunt Clara pinches my arm. "Oh, you!" She says.

WE HAVE A LOVELY WALK to the Khedivial Sporting Club. Carved out of the Botanical Gardens, it's a lush oasis in our desert city, and I breathe in the fresh, leafy scents of one of my favorite places as a girl. It's where Mother and I would play tennis, ride horses, and swim all in a single day.

Lieutenant General Blackwood is waiting for us under an acacia tree at the end of a walkway near the entrance of the grounds. He escorts Father, the Hugheses, and me out onto the courtyard patio, which is as full tonight as I've ever seen it. So full that couples begin to spill out into the gardens as guests continue to file out from the Lida, a fine clubhouse that horseshoes the deck. The Lieutenant General offers me a wicker chair, but I decline. Too much sitting the past fortnight. He signals one of the servants to fetch us some drinks and they arrive as if by magic before we can properly say our first *hellos*.

Old friends of Father's draw in from every corner and we are practically swarmed by *welcomes*. Pats on the back for him and stares of disbelief at me.

"My heavens, you've grown up," I hear over and over.

We are regaled with stories of what's been going on since our departure, but they're mostly for Father's sake, as they revolve around the dam and politics and the Shepheard Hotel. Those were purely adult topics for me when we were living here before—ones I only understood through the gauzy-eyed view of a child.

I'm increasingly squeezed out of the group that's gathered around us, and for the first time feel like a stranger, unsure of what to do with myself.

"Come," says the Lieutenant General as he offers his arm. I'm not too proud to admit I'm grateful for his attention. He walks me over to a man with a very brightly patterned waistcoat, who sports quite possibly the furriest mutton chops I've ever seen.

"Dr. Davies," the Lieutenant General calls. "May I introduce you to Lord Floyd's daughter, Leila?"

"Dr. Alfred Davies?" I inquire. "The archaeologist and scholar? I understand you'll be responsible, in part, for my continuing education."

Dr. Davies nods with a slight bow.

"Dr. Davies has only recently come to Cairo with his son, and works at the new museum being built by the Italians," the Lieutenant General informs me. "It'll be quite the place to receive your education."

"It's all chaos and clutter yet," Dr. Davies says. "But at least our offices are finished. And she is a beauty, I might add."

"I've read of it, yes. I'm so pleased our Pharaonic antiquities will be getting a place of their own," I tell him.

"Indeed," he says, then shakes his head. "Forgive me. You do look just like the portrait of your mother. The one at the Hugheses'. My wife, well, she admired your mother so."

He says this with such a tender warmth, and I sense we'd both like to continue in this line of conversation, but we're interrupted by a pleasantly plump woman whom Lieutenant General Blackwood cannot hide his distaste for. She's of the sort who always appears out of breath and in a tizzy about something, and she waves her handkerchief at us as if we're set to run away before she can reach us.

She gives us what I assume is her usual preamble judging by the look on Dr. Davies's face. It's all about how utterly exhausted she is from the duties of being the wife of an army officer, which is what many of the married women here are, although they don't appear to be nearly as put out. When she finally notices me, she asks what I'm doing just standing there and tells me to fetch her a drink.

Dr. Davies looks down in embarrassment and the Lieutenant General bites down on his lip in fury. I'm liking him better and better all the time.

"Girl, I told you to fetch me a drink," the woman says— speaking slowly as if I'm an idiot. "I'm blistering in this heat!"

The gentlemen are about to speak up, but I beat them to it.

"Um, well, I am a girl," I tell her. "But not that kind. I'm not a servant. My father is a member."

"Mrs. Watson," the Lieutenant General says, "this is Leila, Lord Floyd's daughter. They'll be the guests of honor at the club dance tomorrow evening."

"How do you do, Mrs. Watson." I extend my hand, which she stares at with a ripe mixture of confusion and discomfiture.

"And you're an . . . ?"

"An Englishwoman," the Lieutenant General says. "Well, not quite a woman yet, I suppose, but awfully close."

I glance over at Dr. Davies and he winks at me.

Just then Father approaches us and the Lieutenant General makes the proper introductions. This is a welcome development for Mrs. Watson, since she can go about doing what makes women like her feel most at ease—figuring out who is who and to whom.

"You must be related to the Duke of Wellington," Mrs. Watson charges.

"A rather distant cousin," Father replies with some detachment. "I see you've met my daughter, Leila."

Flustered once again, Mrs. Watson sees a friend and excuses herself, huffing and puffing, waving her handkerchief. The woman must be quite used to people trying to make their escape when they see her coming.

Lieutenant General Blackwood takes this opportunity to bring my father aside and inaugurate their discussion about the completion of the dam and the various pageants that will surround it. Apparently his wife, who is presently in England, will have a heavy hand in planning many of the formal events.

"Miss Leila," Dr. Davies says. "Mrs. Hughes has told me an awful lot about you. About both you and your father, actually. She tells me you have an interest in the historic, and the occult."

"I wouldn't say occult, exactly," I tell him. "I am a Christian woman."

"Of course, I didn't mean at all to suggest otherwise. I should have chosen my words more carefully."

"Not at all," I say. "I wasn't offended—just trying to be clear, so you wouldn't misunderstand."

"You are a rather mature young woman, I see."

"My mother always said I was the oldest soul she'd ever known." I smile at him as he takes two lemonades from a passing servant's tray and hands one to me. Cold and tart with much too much sugar, but delicious.

"Would you like to see something?" he asks me.

Reaching into his breast pocket, he pulls out an amulet. A gold oval engraved with two interlinked circles, and a red stone at the center. It's old and beaten, but so lovely. Simple in the ways of a great poem, and I cannot adequately describe the sensation I experience just looking at it. As if it holds a treasure of secrets for me alone. Dr. Davies places it on his palm and holds it out to me. I touch it, tentatively at first, then pick it up, feeling a peculiar urge to kiss it.

"It's beautiful," I whisper.

"That's a raw ruby in the center," he tells me. "Some of the locals call it a bloodstone when it's in this state, but it's not jasper, which we would commonly know as bloodstone."

I turn it over and Dr. Davies steps closer.

"You see the markings?"

I nod. "It looks terribly old."

"Thousands of years, I'd say."

"Thousands! Yes, now that I look at it, how can it be anything other than ancient? Is it from the time of the pharaohs?" I ask, although I'm quite sure it's not.

"Doesn't seem to be," he confirms. "It's quite a curiosity to me, I have to say."

"It's in remarkable condition. Is this something you found on one of your expeditions?"

Dr. Davies straightens up and puts his hand behind his neck, giving it a rub. I recognize the look in his eyes. It's a flash of grief I've seen in my father's eyes many a time.

"You might say that," Dr. Davies says. "It was years ago when I was helping uncover the tomb of Ptahmes in Saqqara. Newly married and barely out of University. A Bedouin woman I encountered was wearing it, and I traded my watch, my sandwich, a bottle of good gin, and a hair comb for it. Gave it to my wife after she gave birth to our son."

"I'm sure she treasured it."

"She did, I think. Never took it off."

Clearly he means, never took it off until the day she died. I wonder why he didn't bury it with her, the way Father buried Mother with every love letter he'd ever written to her.

"Do you know what those markings mean?" I ask him. "They look like hieroglyphs, but they're not Egyptian. They look almost like they're in motion."

"You can read Egyptian hieroglyphs?"

I'm about to reply in the affirmative when Father comes up to us, a bit sozzled by the looks of it.

"And the written Sumerian," he adds, before disappearing back into a sea of lively exchanges.

"You are a marvel," Dr. Davies says. "Just like your mother."

"You knew my mother?"

Dr. Davies shakes his head. "No, but I've read her work. Her poetry and articles on womanhood. They weren't just for women, you know."

I think I'm going to have to peel the grin from my face.

"But as for the markings on the necklace," he tells me. "I've no idea what they are. They're from no known language, ancient or otherwise. Quite a mystery. What do you suppose it says?"

I look carefully at the amulet, my finger riding the lines of the two interlinked circles that surround the ruby, making it the center, like a red star. I turn it over and do the same on the markings there, the ones that look like dancing hieroglyphs.

"It's a love poem, I'd say. A promise."

Alfred Davies smiles. "I'd like to think so."

WHILE MY BED at Uncle Hugo and Aunt Clara's house is as comfortable as a cloud, I can't seem to fall asleep. It's the amulet, I think. And talk of my mother. So much of my early life in Cairo catching up with me. I can hear Father snoring, although he's in the room next door and there's a wall between us. He only snores when he's been drinking, but I can hardly fault him for tying one on our first night back.

Taking a deep breath, I close my eyes and fold my hands across my chest, like a mummy. I begin my nightly ritual by saying my prayers—for the health and well-being of my father, for Aunt Imogen, for Clara and Hugo—then tell myself the story of how my parents met. As I imagine my mother and father—young, eyes vibrant and hopeful, just starting their lives—I can already feel a sense of peace settling over me. Works every time.

Father had come to Egypt as an engineer to help repair the Delta barrages. But, on only his second night in Cairo, he met my mother at a reading arranged for the intellectual class at the Shepheard Hotel. The Shepheard is where everyone goes. But had he known it was a *feministe* reading by a *feministe* Egyptian writer, he would have never gone, naturally. Such is the trickster nature of destiny, isn't it? At least that's what my mother always said.

Mother was scarcely twenty and dressed to the height of fashion—she was all glossy black hair and eyes that night. Her long mane pinned up under a hat, of course. She read aloud from a long article she'd written for *al-Fatah*, the leading women's journal in Cairo—secular, obviously. It touched on everything from women's seclusion to education and travel. She led with a passionate discourse on unveiling, and concluded her lecture by taking off her hat and letting down her up-pinned hair, shaking it and allowing it to flow thick like oil all the way past her posterior. Scandalous behavior for the British let alone your average Egyptian girl. Even a Coptic one. But she was anything but average.

I don't know how many times I've heard my father tell that story. Always chewing on his bottom lip like he's daydreaming about having met a mermaid. How he shouldered through the crowd to meet her, insisting on taking her for tea to further discuss her ideas. They became engaged that night, and by the time they married a few months later, Mother had convinced him to add her name to his own, urging him to introduce himself as Lord Floyd *Saber* Wellington—a title that embarrassed him while mother was living, but one that he now relishes.

My eyes flutter as I start to drift into my own dreams, my own stories, and I hear a voice as warm as a fever.

"Ah'kwarah'a," he says.

"I was born for you," I whisper, before the Sandman takes me.

Chapter 3

The Hanging Church

I PUNCTUATE the last sentence describing my most incredible dream with a rather florid exclamation point. *After he finishes his words of love, describing every part of me as if he himself were my maker, he takes my hand to his body, as bare as on the day he was born, and puts it to his beating heart!*

I take a deep breath, letting the words fill me. It's just before dawn and a faint glow has touched the horizon. I shut my thick, leather-bound little dream book and latch it closed, snuggling it like a lap dog.

I do love dreaming of love, though it is so secret a pleasure that I'm always a bit hesitant to write down what I've seen in my sleep. But it's too beautiful a vision to leave only to memory. Father is good about respecting my privacy, so it should be safe. If he ever did dare to open my diary and read about the things that come to me in the night sometimes, he might die right there of a mixture of shock and embarrassment. As it is, he thinks I only dream of deserts—those eerie dreams I do tell him about. The ones about an endless sea of sand and of storms and burning skulls. If he knew about the others . . . well, maybe he wouldn't be as traumatized as I think. He does, after all, tell me I'm my mother's daughter.

Quickly, I spring off my bed and go behind a rather elaborate Rosewood screen to dress. But I don't put on a dress. I don the simple clothing of a male servant. Not the red robe and tarbush of a man, but the light dove gray frock of a boy, complete with a white turban that disguises my hair quite nicely.

Checking myself in the mirror, I'm pleased to see I look like any old Babu or Akiki—at least at first glance.

While I did my share of climbing out of windows when we were living in Cairo last, I admit I'm a bit out of practice. As I shimmy off the ledge, I nearly slip off the trellis twice, but then I find my footing and manage to make my way down from the Hugheses' second floor without incident. Never occurred to me that having a bosom—even one I've done my best to bind—could be such a hindrance to a simple descent from a window.

I brush the dust and dirt from my hands and smooth my gown a bit, but just as I look up from my costume, I see another creature of the dawn. Nearly causes me to yelp in surprise. Just across the back garden is a young man climbing out a window, this one on the ground floor. He jumps over the ledge with the grace of a panther and fixes his collar. As he pivots, I notice his shirt is open all the way down, exposing a chest as white as moonlight! A girl who can't be much older than I am leans out that window and kisses his cheek all sweetly while he's buttoning up! Then he turns from the girl and goes right into a trot, hurdling over the row of bushes separating the girl's yard from the Hugheses'. That's when he spies me! Up closer, he's all sandy hair with an inquisitive arch to his brow. He stops and tips his head as a rather shrill woman's voice calls out in the dark—"Get back here, you scoundrel!"—then he gives me a nod, and puts his fingers to his lips in a *shhh,* and begins running off in the direction of the street.

It takes me a moment to remember that I'm dressed as a servant boy and that he probably feels his secret is quite safe with me. And mine, it turns out, with him. I'm finally able to let go of the breath I've been holding. While it wouldn't do for a young man to go sneaking about at the crack of dawn, a young woman doing the same is nothing short of an outrage. Even if certain social allowances are made for British citizens who live in foreign ports. And for Egyptians who are half British. It's one of the benefits of a neither here nor there life.

I look back at the girl's window, and there she still is. Ignoring me entirely and looking out at the greenway where her young man is no longer. She's awfully pretty. The English rose type who looks ethereal and clever all at once. I'm almost tempted to go to her. Make a friend, perhaps, and partner in crime. But that wouldn't do. Besides, she doesn't look like she much wants a new friend right now. She looks sad. Perhaps she knows her brash young man will do her wrong.

It's hard to get the young lovers out of my mind—so eager to risk themselves for love, so romantic—and they stay with me as I make my way to the road.

Ah, but there's Horus, who takes all of my pensive thoughts away with one look.

"I was hoping you would change your mind," he says to me in Arabic.

"Liar," I tell him.

I climb up and sit next to him, where a servant boy belongs. Horus looks me up and down and shakes his head.

"Don't I look marvelous?" I say.

"You look like your mother."

He *hmmfs*, snapping the reins and making a clicking noise at the horses, which they dutifully seem to understand. Away we go, rumbling down the road towards Cairo center like a father and son off to do the bidding of their master.

By the time we arrive in Coptic Cairo, the sky is red with early morning. Most of the street lights are still lit, but one by one the lanterns outside homes and cafes are being extinguished as residents begin the rituals of a new day. Horus eases the carriage to a stop and I look up at two white bell towers set against the bloody sky like sharp canines.

"I have so missed this place," I say.

"And I'm sure it's missed you, but you could have waited for one of your cousins to take you. A girl should never be out in Cairo on her own, even if it is for a spiritual purpose."

"I like to be in Cairo alone," I say. "And I need to do this alone."

Although I insist that I'm trying to stay in character, Horus ignores my resistance to his chivalric overtures and helps me climb down from the carriage. To an observer, we must look positively ridiculous—a coachman treating a servant boy like a lady!

"I'll be back here in an hour," he tells me. "Don't make me have to come in after you."

He urges me through the iron gates, waving me along like he's in a big hurry. I know that he's not, but he knows that I am. I'm dying to see it again—The Hanging Church. To pass through its doors and behold the *haikal*—the main altar screen made of ebony inlaid with ivory and carved into Coptic crosses. To watch the golden early light beam in through the high windows, to honor the icon of Mary, as my mother did every morning. This was our place, hers and mine.

I jog past several palms in a narrow courtyard that ends at a staircase leading up to the entrance, and I stop for a moment and take it all in. Our spiritual home. A third century church inspired by the Blessed Mother and built atop the Roman Fortress of Babylon; its nave suspended over a passage—hence, why it "hangs." Though the façade from this vantage point is new, there's something preternaturally timeless about the place. Otherworldly and magical. As if the mother of Christ could appear at any time—and it is said that she has on at least two occasions.

With a certain degree of reverence, for both my history and the one of this structure, I climb the steps and enter a further small courtyard that takes me into an outer porch that's a thousand years old. It's from there that I enter the church.

My first thought is that it's smaller than I remember it. When I was a girl, it seemed positively enormous. But today, I feel that I'm in an intimate space, like the great room for a close but wealthy family. The details of this place, however, I've kept in perfect memory. It's all lacey wood and marble just as it always was. Mosaics and stained glass, red carpets, painting after painting. I sit in a pew and look to the twelve pillars that represent the apostles. All white, except for one. That one is black and meant to signify Judas. It's always seemed like such a sad pillar to me.

I unwrap my turban, letting my hair fall down my back, then I fold my hands and close my eyes tight.

"Mother," I say. "I'm home."

Then I startle at the sound of a dramatic gasp and look up.

"Hello!" I say, my heart giving a deep *bum-bum* that I swear echoes all around us. "Father Joe, it's me, Leila."

He blinks his eyes and his whole face opens up in an expression of pure joy.

"Leila! Goodness, I thought you were . . . as if she . . . your mother . . . my how you've grown up!"

I can hardly breathe, I'm so happy! I jump up and rush to Fr. Joe Saber, who clasps my hands. His are so warm—always have been.

"Father and I have moved home," I tell him. "I was so hoping I would see you this morning!"

"Such wonderful news! I heard talk of your plans at Christmas, but I didn't dare believe it would really happen."

"I am sorry," I say. "I should have written to you about all this. I meant to, wanted to so many times. It did all happen rather quickly, but that's no excuse."

"You don't need an excuse."

"But I do. The truth is I wanted to take our old life here by surprise. Makes it feel easier somehow to start anew. I mean, without . . ."

"Without your mother."

I nod and swallow the tears that threaten. I feel his soft finger tuck my hair behind my ear.

"I'm just happy you're back," Joe says. "And don't much care if you announce yourself with bugles or whisper in like a soft wind. As long as I get to hear that honeyed voice of yours again, and to watch your hands waltz in step with your sentences."

I put my hands back at my sides, giggling, and Joe steps back, taking me in whole. Poor man raises an eyebrow at me, and I look down. I've completely forgotten about my appearance.

"Forgive my dress, it's just that—"

"You needn't explain," he says, chuckling. Then he lowers his voice to a whisper, even though no one else seems to be around. "Your mother used to go about Cairo dressed as a boy all the time. Slipping into cafes and smoke shops, playing street games with the urchins. Said it was the only time she felt truly free."

Little Joe, as my mother called her younger brother, shakes his head. "And it's no surprise you would follow in her, er, footsteps. But you really can't allow yourself to be spotted by the faithful like this. I'll be saying mass in under an hour and people are going to start coming in."

"Of course," I say, twisting my hair up and wrapping it in the turban again. "Better?"

"It'll have to do. Now tell me, what brings you back to Cairo?"

"The dam. That's the excuse at least."

"An important excuse. The dam is to your father what going to mass is to people like you and me. And how is your father?"

"Still fragile sometimes, but his spirit is getting strong again. We've practically only just arrived and already I notice a difference in him. I think he'd like very much to see you."

"I wish that were true."

"It is. No, it really is. He loves you, but you know how he's always felt about our more unconventional convictions. The church part is fine—Father still considers himself a Christian, regardless of how tenuous his beliefs are."

Fr. Joe takes a deep breath, his eyes misting with regret.

"I should have never told him she appeared to me."

"Don't be that way," I tell him. "It was a great comfort to me. Because, you see, these past years she's seemed farther and farther away from me by the day. But not now, not here."

I can't help it. I start to cry. The first time in a long time. Father Joe takes me in an embrace, like he used to do all the time when I was little. "Don't worry," he says. "You'll see your mother again soon. This, I promise you."

"I wish I could believe you."

Fr. Joe places his soft fingertips on my forehead, stroking it gently, just like he would if he were trying to help me fall asleep.

"You don't have to believe me," he says. "You just have to have faith."

I STAY WITH FR. JOE until it's almost time for mass, watching him prepare the altar with the reverence of a surgeon minding his hands as he cuts into a sleeping child. We agree to get together properly once Father and I have moved into our house, and he promises to bring his sticky and delectable *konafa* for dessert.

After that, I just can't help myself. I go wandering around Coptic Cairo, through its churches and mazes. It's a quiet, spiritual place, a deep breath in the heart of an old metropolis that thrives on chaos. The most likely place in Cairo to find an actual ghost, I think, but I see nothing of the sort. Only a small group of black robed priests who seem to float by me, one of them offering a paternal smile. And a young lad, also in servant's attire, who assumes I'm one of his own. I'm a full half hour late meeting Horus, and he actually huffs like a bull, offering what can barely be described as a greeting. He continues his huffing nearly all the way back to Zamalek.

"If your father catches you," he says.

"But I was at church!"

"You went wandering alone! A girl should always be accompanied by a protector."

"But you're my protector," I tell him.

All his fears are for naught, though, as I'm able to slip into Hugo and Clara's house the back way while they read the paper on their sun porch. The early risers walking about simply assume I'm a servant boy, just as the boy in Coptic Cairo did, and everyone inside the house, including Father, just figures that I'm sleeping in.

I pretend to do just that for much of the morning, while actually reading *Eveline's Visitant*, a most delicious tale of romance, murder, and a ghost who is as seductive as he is dangerous. The story prompts me to reread my summation of the dream I had last night, and I can't help but wonder if I'm not the victim of an unnatural seduction myself.

I haven't been able to stop thinking about the young man in my dream. His hair is dark, with soft curls. Eyes closed as if he's dreaming of me, too. A neat, pink line of a scar on his forearm. But he's not Egyptian—this I know. In fact, he's nothing like anyone I've ever met.

The only true respite I've had from him since awakening was at the Hanging Church, when I was praying, and communing with my late mother. Even when talking to someone as dear to me as Fr. Joe, seeing him for the first time in years, I found my mind drifting, thinking about a touch, a scent, a whisper. I fear Cairo's ghosts are not merely passing through me, but are intent on taking me whole this time. And what's worse, I welcome them, pulling them close, and never wanting to let go.

"Darling!" Aunt Clara's voice trills through my door and is followed by a quick rap of her knuckles. "Won't you join me for a walk?"

Downstairs, I'm greeted with an eager smile from her and a croissant from a new French bakery. Aunt Clara then offers me the paper, which I devour.

"It's nothing but young Turks and nationalists today," I say. "This Mohammad Gamal fellow is quite the rabble-rouser, with his marches for Egyptian independence."

"And his handsome young face. All the girls your age just swoon for him." Aunt Clara refreshes my tea and rests her face in her upturned palms, like a girl. "Cairo feels as if it's being reborn and it's so exciting! Truly the perfect timing for your return. As if it's been waiting just for you."

After breakfast, we stroll around the gardens, and I make notes of the flora I intend to raise once we move into our family home. We run into old friends here and there, but mostly pass strangers. Plenty of Egyptians, too—well-to-do ones, not merely servants to the British merchants and military. And plenty of new arrivals to Cairo. They're new to me at least, and mostly British, with a smattering of international folk. Infants of her rebirth, Aunt Clara says. We stay on the grounds until the hustle and bustle begins to thin, right around tea time, which finds the four of us—Father, Uncle Hugo, Aunt Clara, and I, chattering like warblers in their parlor. Eating baklava and English sandwiches as if the two go together.

Aunt Clara sneaks me a glass of sherry, just as we slip upstairs to dress for dinner. We're heading back over to the Lida this evening to be properly reintroduced into Cairo's international society.

"A young woman should feel a bit loose when she goes to a party in her honor," she tells me with a sinful little snicker. "But only a bit."

Chapter 4

A Gentleman He Is Not

IT'S HALF DARK when we approach the sports club, and the windows of the Lida are aglow. We're all dolled up to the nines, and my heels clack on the harlequin tiles as we enter. I can't help but steal a glimpse at myself in a long mirror in the foyer. "Lord, I do look all grown up tonight," I say under my breath, echoing Aunt Clara's sentiments when she joined me in my boudoir earlier—plying me with yet another glass of sherry. And she did insist on helping me choose my gown, which I resisted at first, but then she went ahead to my wardrobe and pulled out a dress of lilac that just happens to be my favorite.

"Oh, you must wear this," she said. "It was your mother's best color as well."

I had my choice between two pairs of cream and lilac slippers—footwear being an indulgence of mine, I admit with some, but not enough penitence—and picked a pair with a good sized heel, which I now regret.

We enter the celebration with the Hugheses leading the way, Aunt Clara like a busty figurehead on a ship's bow. We're bombarded by a jam of the aforementioned newcomers to Cairo, who are curious about the infamous Wellingtons. *Saber* Wellingtons. I'm relieved to see Dr. Alfred Davies standing next to a circular banquette of gold velvet and make a beeline straight for him.

"If it isn't my new student," he says.

I curtsy. "And the eminent Dr. Davies here to save me from tedious chatterers!"

But before we can even say two additional words to one another, that church bell of a woman, the endlessly breathless Mrs. Watson, marches up to us, greets me perfunctorily, and turns the whole of her attention to Dr. Davies.

"It's that son of yours again," she says.

Dr. Davies looks beyond her and into the crowd. "Ripley? Where is he?"

Mrs. Watson makes a fish-face that would make a starchy spinster proud.

"How on earth should I know?" she says. "In any case, it's not about where he is but what he's doing!"

"And what is that?" Dr. Davies inquires.

Mrs. Watson folds her arms across her chest, and gives a look betraying the fact that she's not as thick a woman as she appears to be. There's a bright light in that head of hers after all. That light, unfortunately, goes out as quickly as it was lit, and her lesser nature takes hold of her again.

"Edna," she tells him.

"Edna? Your daughter?"

Mrs. Watson nods.

"What's Ripley doing to your daughter, Mrs. Watson?"

Mrs. Watson is aghast, and this time her face contorts into a chewy mass of emotions—anger, insult, mortification, excitement, and if I'm not mistaken, a trace of a crush on Dr. Davies that she's doing her best to repress.

"Nothing! I assure you," she says in that panting voice of hers. "It's what he'd *like* to do, Dr. Davies." Her eyes widen. "And would you speak of the devil!"

Just then we're approached by a young man whom I can only assume must be Ripley Davies. He comes up, one hand in his pocket, fair hair neatly slicked back with a lightly fragrant Macassar oil. Neat and confident in a black tailcoat trimmed in velvet, the younger Davies stands with his shoulders square, but loose, as if he's had a couple of glasses of sherry, too. He's a bit older than me, I'd guess, as his face is clear of the spots that usually mock the faces of young men my age, and he wears the bare minimum of a smile. The kind that only turns upward on one side. I discover that I've unconsciously mimicked his expression, and quickly adjust my countenance.

"Good evening, Mrs. Watson, Dad," Ripley says. He turns to me and takes in a breath, deeply, looking me over. The smile on the one side of his mouth falls away, and I sense a queer sort of intimacy in the way he regards me.

"And, Miss . . . ?" He holds out his hand to take mine, and the moment I place my fingers in his, I feel the strangest sensation. A warmth in the center of my left palm that grows hotter until it's almost painful.

"Good evening my foot!" Mrs. Watson says, with real venom this time. "This young man has been hanging about the windows of chaste and unsuspecting young women!"

My palm goes cold and my jaw about falls to the tips of my lilac shoes as I realize this must be the same young man I saw early this morning coming out of that English girl's window! An English Edna who Mrs. Watson claims as her own! I must say, he looks quite different now, and not just because he's dressed for a party. He comes off as a proper gentleman, which I know very well he is not! His eyes widen a bit as he notes my reaction, and I probably ought to look away but I don't. They are a most striking brown, his eyes, with deep amber rivulets in one, and ruby veins in the other. They look at me boldly, and it's as if he has no other features all of a sudden. Neither hair, nor skin, nor fine clothes. Those eyes flit over me, and I don't know what he sees, but one thing is plain: he doesn't recognize me from this morning. Not surprising as I was dressed as a boy when we met, if you can call it a meeting. As I shake off his stare, I grow increasingly aware of my advantage over him. I know him, but he doesn't know the first thing about me. It gives me a rather criminal feeling of power that I should be ashamed of.

"Edna's window?" Dr. Davies says, luring us both back into the conversation.

"Certainly not!" Mrs. Watson insists. "But I have it on trusted word that someone has said he's been showing an unwholesome interest in more than one of our daughters here tonight, and perhaps more than one window."

Ripley takes a step back, and it's quite rich of him to feel so affronted.

"Are you sure it's Ripley?" Dr. Davies says. "As far as I know he was dead asleep last night."

I press my lips together in a smirk and catch Ripley's eyes again. He seems confused at my expression and raises an eyebrow at me, but then turns back to Mrs. Watson, eager to defend his honor.

"Mrs. Watson, I assure you," he starts to say, but Mrs. Watson cuts him off.

"I didn't see him per se, but I'm sure it was he. Who else would be so bold? My woman's intuition told me this boy was a troublemaker since the time he pushed my Edna into a fishpond!"

"But Mrs. Watson, we were only three," Ripley says. "And truth be told I don't remember the incident you speak of at all. And neither does Edna."

"But do you remember ducking right into the bushes when you heard me calling after you last night? You didn't come even when I demanded that you do so!"

"Dad!" Ripley exclaims. "This is not at all what Mrs. Watson seems to think . . ." But now it's his father who cuts him off.

"Er, but you say it wasn't Edna's window, and that you weren't the one who saw him," Dr. Davies says. "So, which window, Mrs. Watson, would you be referring to? And who, specifically, saw my son wandering about in the night?"

Mrs. Watson gets all flustered and begins babbling, but Ripley Davies interrupts her this time.

"Please forgive me, Mrs. Watson, should have asked sooner. But was your daughter harmed in any way?"

The woman wrinkles her nose like a King Charles spaniel.

"Edna? Heavens no!" She gives her back to Ripley and addresses Dr. Davies. "I assure you, there was no actual contact between the two of them whatsoever."

It's now my turn to raise an eyebrow, and I do so at Ripley, who gives a firm shake of the head.

"Well, ah, Mrs. Watson," Dr. Davies says, "if it wasn't Edna's window, and you say there was no contact between Ripley and your daughter—in fact, Edna's not involved in any way—then I fail to see the problem."

Boxed in, Mrs. Watson is uncharacteristically quiet, though her mouth remains wide open.

"Mrs. Watson," Ripley says, with a good deal more contrition than he feels, I'm sure. "I'm afraid there has been a misunderstanding. You see, I was out and about last night. Couldn't sleep a wink. But I was just having a bit of a stroll is all."

"A stroll!" she says, finding her voice again and using it like a whip. "Did you not hear me calling your Christian name?"

Ripley smooths his hair, which didn't need any smoothing, and considers this.

"I think I did hear someone. But just then I saw poor Mrs. MacDonald's little poodle who'd gone missing and I dove into the bushes right after it."

"Did you indeed?"

"Sadly, the little dog got the better of me."

"I'm sure he did!" Mrs. Watson spits. "This is by no means finished. I'll be keeping an eye on you." She looks him up and down before stomping away, leaving thoroughly unsatisfied, but unable to make a bigger stink out of the situation without pulling her daughter into things in a most unbecoming way.

"Son . . ."

"Dad, really, that woman is the worst. And I wasn't hanging about Edna's window quite as she says. I was having a stroll and Edna called me to her window and . . ."

"Ripley! Ah-hem." His father purses his lips and holds out his hand, indicating me. "The Wellingtons have arrived in Cairo."

Ripley seems befuddled by that information and cocks his head. He blinks hard and forces a smile—at least what constitutes a smile coming from him, it would appear. That one side of his mouth simply goes up higher, while the other remains stubbornly in place.

"I'm so sorry," he says. And, at last, we're able to conclude our introduction. He takes my hand, this time with a sweetness that I can't deny. My mouth goes a bit dry, as my palm begins to warm again, prompting me to remove my hand from his rather abruptly. Wish I hadn't, but I couldn't help it. I suppose it's for the best, given his character, or lack of it. I don't want him to think I'm like the other girls whose windows he haunts.

During this admittedly awkward exchange, Dr. Davies waves to my father, who comes straight away, taking two glasses of champagne from an overly-zealous waiter. I think Father and Dr. Davies must have become properly acquainted at some point today, as they practically seem like old friends.

"Lord Floyd and his Leila, I'd like to introduce you to my son, Ripley."

Ripley bows, and Dr. Davies accepts a glass from my father.

"Lord Floyd," the doctor says, "I've been eager to get your attention since you came through the door, but it being your night, in your honor, I demurred."

Father is clearly tired of small talk and seems happy at the prospect of a conversation of substance. "I think I've earned a little time away from the crowd," he says.

"Son, would you be so kind as to mind Leila, while Lord Floyd and I have some man talk?"

Now, this ought to be interesting. Father throws me a glance of apology and Ripley agrees to this arrangement, naturally, and doesn't seem to mind having been stuck with "minding" me. The two widowers walk off in the direction of the bar.

"Oh, good," I say, once I'm sure we're out of earshot. "While they're having man talk, I can have girl talk with, um, Ripley is your name, isn't it? Tell me, what do you think of the Persian embroidery that's been all the rage on dark dresses this winter?"

Ripley Davies ignores my cheekiness and goes right to the heart of the matter. I have to respect him for that.

"What were all of those looks you were giving me for?"

"Looks?"

"Don't play coy, *Lady* Leila."

If that's how it's going to be, then fine.

"Well, if you don't mind my being direct," I say, "it's just that I would hardly call what you were doing while crawling out of Edna Watson's window 'strolling.'"

For the third time since we met, really only minutes ago, Ripley Davies appears utterly dumbfounded.

"You were there?"

"Don't you recognize me? You looked right at me. But I suspect that, like our esteemed Mrs. Watson did yesterday, you mistook me for a servant."

Now it's the fourth dumbfounding.

"That was you!"

"Hmm."

"Dressed as a boy?"

"For comfort at such an early hour. Corsets give me a devil of a time. And so do shoes with a heel. Do you mind if we sit?"

Ripley eases me onto the velvet banquette, then takes a seat next to me. He leans back, folding his arms over his chest like I'm the one who's inappropriate.

"Do you always walk about dressed as a boy, spying on people?"

"Spying! I was doing no such thing!"

"What would you call it then?"

I narrow my eyes at Ripley Davies, having no intention of letting him try to turn the tables on me.

"Do you always crawl out of young women's bedroom windows with your shirt undone?"

"Shhh!"

"Are you afraid of Mrs. Watson all of a sudden?"

Ripley leans in closer to me, and then inclines back, as if thinking better of it. Somehow, this offends me.

"It's not just about me, you know," he says with a lowered voice. "Edna's a decent girl—a lot better than her mother at any rate—and it would be cruel to destroy her reputation for sport."

"I'd never do that," I tell him. "I could have ratted you out after all, and I didn't."

Ripley Davies softens, those eyes of his glittering under the light of the chandeliers.

"No, you didn't. But you should know—it wasn't what it looked like."

"It did look pretty bad."

"Looks can be deceiving. Look at you."

Touché.

"And why, if you don't mind my asking, do you go about in the early morning hours dressed as a boy?"

Only one of the male persuasion could possibly ask such a thing and genuinely have no idea.

"It's fun, of course, and allows me to do things I can't do in a skirt. My mother used to do it all the time."

Ripley Davies nods his head, as if it's all starting to make sense to him now. "Yes, of course, your mother," he says.

"And what is that supposed to mean?"

"Nothing," Ripley says. "Well, not nothing. My father told me a good bit about her, is all, and gave me some of her essays to read. Ones my mother had been particularly taken with."

My throat gets a bit gummy and now I'm the one who needs a minute.

"What did you think of them?"

Ripley smiles an unguarded smile this time, one without any of the usual stone fence that manners can erect between two individuals. And it's not a one-sided smile either. It's full-on, with both corners of his mouth going up most pleasingly.

"They were true."

"True?"

"Yes," he says. "Every word she wrote was honest. I suppose it's why she was so controversial."

"Is that how you see her? As a controversy?"

"No," he says. "I see her as an original, but the two often go hand in hand."

A twiddle of treble notes begins to play and our eyes, Ripley's and mine, follow the sound to a baby grand piano, where a well-dressed Egyptian man has sat down to play songs from *Véronique*. All at once, it's as if everyone in the room begins to sway, and one by one, couples pair off to dance.

Maybe it's because we've been talking about my mother, and this is definitely something she would do, or maybe it's because I just want to see another look of amazement on Ripley Davies's face, but I stand up quite suddenly and offer him my hand.

"I haven't danced in ages," I say to him. "Won't you?"

Ripley Davies laughs and shakes his head at my unconventional offer, but it's clear he's not a bit surprised by it.

"It would be my pleasure," he says, rising up to a full head taller than me. Don't know why I didn't notice his height before. Must be the casual way with which he holds himself, leaning on his hip with the one hand in his pocket.

While I'd like more than anything to kick off my slippers and dance in my stocking feet, there's no way I'm going to allow myself to be even that much smaller next to him. I grit my teeth as we begin to step and twirl, but soon forget all about the pinching of my toes. Ripley Davies, typical of the gal-sneaker type, knows how to dance.

It's on our second turn around the room that I notice none other than Edna Watson. She's behind a large palm with that mother of hers and it's clear they're having quite a row. What's more, Edna's not even dressed for a party. I wonder if she hasn't come to have it out with her mother, all be damned. Ripley notices her, too, though he turns away quickly.

"There's your friend," I say.

"Who?"

"Edna Watson. The one you pushed into a fishpond."

Ripley is saved by a change in tune, which signals a change in dance partners. He and Lieutenant General Blackwood gracefully switch partners, as Ripley takes the hand of sweet girl no older than twelve. Her first big dance, I imagine—she's watching her feet and counting under her breath. Ripley catches my gaze one last time before spinning the little miss towards the window.

"You've met Ripley Davies, I see," the Lieutenant General says, with just a hint of slyness. "I was just having a rather fascinating exchange with his father."

"About archaeology?"

"Yes, that, and about uncovering more recent lost histories."

"Oh? Such as what?"

"It's just a hobby of mine, I must emphasize. I like mysteries and consider myself a bit of an amateur sleuth. My wife calls me Inspector Bucket."

"I do see some similarities," I tell him. "The honest appearance, for instance, although you're a bit younger than Inspector Bucket. And I don't recall Mr. Dickens describing his character as being such a good dancer." The Lieutenant General gives up a wide, open-mouthed smile and leads me into a Feckerl, in which we twirl for eight dizzying, merry steps. He is a wonderful dancer; I wasn't just throwing compliments. Even better than Ripley Davies. We float about the room together, easily managing both a Viennese waltz and a conversation.

"I must say, Lady Leila, whoever taught you to dance deserves a commendation. It's rare a young woman of your age is able to move with such skill and confidence."

I try to resist the urge to giggle at the praise, but fail. Instead, I lead the conversation back to where it started.

"What types of mysteries do you take it upon yourself to investigate, Lieutenant General?"

"Well, there are the more notorious ones. I admit to having a fascination with the Ripper."

"Jack the Ripper?"

The Lieutenant General nods.

"I've read just about everything I could find on the Ripper," I tell him, "though don't tell my father that. He thinks my interest in such things is unbecoming of a . . ."

"Lady?"

I don't mean to burst out laughing, but I can't help it. "Heavens no! Unbecoming of a serious intellect, Father would say."

Lieutenant General Blackwood's expression betrays a genuine warmth behind his very proper comportment.

"Your secret is safe with me," he says. "You know, I've interviewed just about everyone involved in the case, even a young lad who was only seven at the time Annie Chapman was killed and claims not only to have heard her cries, but to have seen a man coming away from her body."

"Extraordinary! What did he say?"

"Are you sure you want me to continue? It's rather morbid."

"You're being very polite, Lieutenant General Blackwood, but do go on."

"He said he watched the man dip his fingers in Ms. Chapman's blood, then paint the wall with it. After, he quite calmly took out a handkerchief and wiped his hands. Despite it being such a memorable scene, the only thing the boy remembered about the man was his eyes. Not his height or weight or even clothes. They were aflame like ginger—the eyes of a demon, he told me."

My mind must have wandered away for a moment, as the next thing I know, Lieutenant General Blackwood is leaning over me, his face right in mine.

"Are you alright?" he asks me.

"Fine, yes, of course," I manage. "Children have such vivid imaginations, don't they?"

"Indeed."

"Tell me, do you believe he is or was a physician, the Ripper?"

Lieutenant General Blackwood licks his lips and his eyes quickly scan over the crowd as if he's looking for clues right here. "No," he says, quite definitively.

"Neither do I," I tell him. "The cuts were too savage for a surgeon—even if they were quite precise and clearly orchestrated by a man who understood how to make death come about quickly and decisively."

"You're a very perceptive young woman, Lady Leila. Another skill beyond your years."

"Just Leila, please."

"Leila, then. How would a young woman on the cusp of sixteen years know about the distinctions between the cuts of a surgeon and the ones of a murderer?"

I consider this question for a moment, and then answer the best way I can.

"I once watched a surgeon cut into my cousin's throat when she couldn't breathe. She'd dipped a strawberry in honey, and somehow that caused an allergic reaction, making her tongue swell. That surgeon then placed a metal tube into the cut he'd made, allowing the air into her lungs. Saving her life."

"I see," he says.

"He did it elegantly, but with a steely sense of purpose. A nobility, you could say." I think of the Ripper's unfortunate victims: Mary Nichols, Elizabeth Stride, Catherine Eddowes, Mary Kelly, and Annie Chapman. Throats cut, bodies mutilated. "Those women, there was no nobility to the way they were cut down."

"No," the Lieutenant General agrees. "But that still doesn't answer how you know about the cuts a murderer would make. Are they the same as someone who cuts, say, in self-defense, but nevertheless kills rather savagely as a result?"

They are not the same. I know this from the very core of my being, though I have no idea how I would explain it to Lieutenant General Blackwood. Especially since I can hardly explain it to myself. It's as if I've seen such murders up close, or been the victim of one. I've felt this way since as long as I can remember.

"I suppose I only know such things from my imagination, Lieutenant General," I tell him. "I have quite an active one, just like that little boy who thinks he saw the Ripper. Tell me, do you have any idea who could have done it—if not a surgeon, I mean?"

The Lieutenant General takes a deep breath and shakes his head. "Not at all. I will say that I don't think Scotland Yard has either. Their list of suspects is rather flimsy if you ask me."

"So, you're not close to solving the Ripper case?" I tease.

Now it's the Lieutenant General's turn to laugh. It's the sort of laugh that comes from a man who knows how to laugh at himself, which is something I greatly appreciate.

"I, my dear, was never even on the case. Just a hobbyist as I told you. But one with a friend or two in Scotland Yard. Maybe one day I'll pick it up again."

The song ends with a dramatic tickling of the piano keys and Lieutenant General Blackwood bows to my curtsy.

"It was an unexpected pleasure," he says.

"The pleasure was all mine, and I do hope we can pick up our conversation again soon."

"I would be delighted," the Lieutenant General says.

We both exit the impromptu dance floor to explore the outer edges, where people are chatting and drinking. The Lieutenant General invites me into a conversation with another officer and his wife, but I excuse myself, feigning hunger. Instead, I walk all about the room looking for my former dance partner, but Ripley Davies is nowhere in sight. And neither is Edna Watson.

Chapter 5

The Bug of Antiquity

MAYBE IT'S THE SHERRY on an empty stomach. Or the dancing in a pair of shoes that I swear were designed for a lady who would only ever wear them whilst lying down. Whatever the case, I can't stand being at the party any more, literally, and don't have it in me to repeat, yet again, the story of why we've moved back to Cairo, and what we've been doing in the four years we've been gone. The latter question is usually from homesick ex-patriots who wish to hear any news of our King's country—from the way the weather's been to how a pound note feels in one's hand.

I make my apologies to Uncle Hugo and Aunt Clara, and ask them to bid my father a good night for me. He's in a rather animated conversation with Dr. Davies and a pair of Egyptian engineers, so I don't wish to intrude. The Hugheses insist on having Horus walk me home, but I insist on going it alone.

Despite so much talk of the likes of Jack the Ripper, I make it to the Hugheses' house without incident and fall into bed after the bare minimum of a toilette. My breath slows, my mind clears as if swept by a diligent maid. But soon, the empty room that housed my thoughts becomes filled again. Not with images from my day, my life, but with a foreign world that has always inhabited my dreams. A world of people and histories that I can't possibly know, but who feel as intimate as my own beating heart. I hear a laugh, and a voice as devoted as a caress.

"It always takes you time to warm to me, you know," he says.

"You're one to talk."

"Oh, no. I always love you from the first."

Tonight I don't see him, but hear only his voice. Yet, he's here. So close that I long to fling myself into his arms. To stay in my night world and never wake up. But for the first time, I feel as if my lover and I are not alone. There's another soul watching us, waiting.

"Nif," I say, calling the name of the one I love. "I'm scared."

I'VE ALWAYS been an early riser, but in Egypt particularly so. Perhaps it's because morning is the most pleasant time of day here. The air is thin and clear and has a freshness to it.

Zamalek makes the morning all the better, with its banyan trees and figs and date palms. I stop to finger the leaves of a fragrant eucalyptus, and it shivers as I approach. Must be a light wind.

"Good morning."

I turn to see Ripley Davies standing there in a pale blue striped shirt and cap, a towel thrown over his shoulder. His eyes look molten in the morning sun, and there's a wistfulness to them that's at odds with his swaggering demeanor. They make me like him more than I thought, and more than I'd like.

"Going for a swim?"

"Would you like to join me?" He flips the towel over to his other shoulder quite playfully, but his eyes don't change.

"Not in the winter morning chill, thank you."

Ripley holds up his hands. "It's rather balmy in Cairo—even

in winter. And I've swum in the Cornish sea, so the pool here feels like a warm bath."

"Well, having grown up here, I could never quite get used to the cold of England. Even on the beaches, I tended to just piddle around in the sand while the others took a dip. Besides, if I climb in the pool, some people might feel the need to climb out."

"Nonsense," he says. "Only the people you don't want to swim with anyway."

"Like Mrs. Watson?" I say, crossing my arms.

"Precisely like Mrs. Watson."

"Well, she's probably not the only one. I'm sure you know the club only takes British members and no Egyptians are welcome to actually live on the island, unless they're servants, of course."

Ripley leans in a bit, conspiratorially. Not so much as to be improper, but enough that I can feel his warm breath on my cheek.

"I do know," he whispers. "And I also know you're a full member just like I am and are more than welcome to live here. Besides, everyone knows all about you. Your genius father—a bit of a mad genius, but a genius nonetheless. And your mother . . . well, I find her a bit difficult to explain."

"I'm sure Mrs. Watson could think of plenty of words to describe her."

Ripley laughs. "And you seem to have charmed the entire party last night, even Lieutenant General Blackwood. They're not just talking about you because you're . . ."

"Difficult to explain?" It's quite hard to explain to someone like Ripley Davies, who has always fit in, what it's like to endure stares from both sides of your heritage.

"I think it's your eyes that confound them at first," Ripley tells me. He takes my elbow and we begin walking down the garden path. "No Egyptian I've ever seen has green eyes, let alone ones that are positively luminescent. Not even the most green-eyed Briton has eyes quite like yours either, come to think of it. You're confusing to the military folk, too, as you're the daughter of a gentleman, as well as a rather famous—or infamous, depending on whom you talk to—Egyptian intellectual woman."

"Well, you can name it, but you don't have to experience it, do you?"

Ripley Davies's mouth turns up on one side into that half smile again. "Oh, boo-hoo."

"Excuse me?"

"Egyptian you may be, but you're a good deal higher up on the food chain here than I am. Your father is one of the wealthiest men in Cairo—or anywhere else he goes—and your mother was from one of the most prominent families in all of Egypt."

"Well, you're not the one mistaken for being a servant, are you? Anyone standing a mile away would know you're English."

Ripley stops, but doesn't let go of my elbow. He doesn't actually pull me closer, but it feels that way.

"Leila, you're Lord Floyd's daughter and everyone knows it—and the ones who don't get schooled awfully quickly. And I should point out that the Egyptian servants who bring Mrs. Watson her drinks and her linens are the same ones who serve you. Are you honestly expecting me to feel sorry for you because of a looksie or a silly woman asking you to fetch her a drink?"

I take my elbow from his grasp, but can still feel the ghosts of his fingers. "Well, that was pleasant until it wasn't. Good day, Mr. Davies."

Then I attempt to walk past him, but he blocks me!

"Wait. Please."

"I will not."

He leaves me no other choice but to give him a push, but as I do so, he clasps my hand, pulling me towards him!

"I'm sorry. Leila, I really am sorry," he says. "I was teasing. I didn't mean to offend you."

And I really should retrieve my hand and keep walking, but I have a few things to tell him myself.

"You know, you have a lot to say about other people's perceptions given that you don't seem to care one wit about the perception you give regarding your so-called friend, Edna Watson."

Ripley Davies swallows good and hard. "I told you, what you saw yesterday morning . . ."

"It's not merely about yesterday morning. You and she just happened to disappear from the party at the same time last night. I doubt I'm the only one who noticed."

A bare line of a smirk paints his mouth and it's infuriating!

"Well, I'm sorry I left your party—I really am," he says. "I wanted to stay and talk to you more than you know. But I didn't go because of Edna."

"I don't care that you left my party!" I rip my hand right out of his and place it on my hip.

"Well, I care," he says. "Look, won't you reconsider and come to the pool with me—we could talk about it there."

You see, this is what really gets to me about young men like Ripley Davies. They seem so sincere, and yet their behaviors betray them. And it's really unfair that on top of being so casually handsome, he has those eyes, which seem tender and honest, as if they're just for me. I remind myself that he's probably skilled at making lots of girls feel that way, and press my lips into as thin a line as possible.

"It's kind of you to invite me," I say with not one bit of sincerity, "but I still must decline. I'm going into the city."

Now Ripley Davies narrows his eyes in judgement, like he's my custodian.

"You're not going without an escort?"

I nod that yes, of course, I'm going without an escort.

"That's a terrible idea," he says.

"Who says? It's my home, you know. I was born here, and you've only been here, what? A couple of months? Besides, I've already been to the city. By myself, mind you, and it was a very good idea."

I leave out the fact that, on my first solo venture into Cairo proper, I was dressed as a servant boy. Today, I wear a simple summer frock the color of lemon cream and a hat with fresh pink roses.

Nonetheless, Ripley's look of judgement falls away, replaced by a shameless expression of mischief. I'm suddenly made quite aware of how a respectable girl like Edna Watson can find herself acting on some stupid impulse.

"You wouldn't mind if I joined you?"

I take a deep breath and expel a most unladylike huff. He's got me over a barrel and he knows it. While it would be unpardonably rude for me not to accept his invitation, I could get over that bit of convention. But there's the hidden threat that he could casually mention the fact that I've gone off to Cairo entirely by my lonesome. To the Hugheses, to my father. He might even let it drop that this is something I've done once before, and dressed to hide my sex, no less.

"I don't mind," I tell him, although I realize as I say this that it's actually true, and this incenses me further.

The afternoon is likewise complicated when Ripley and I run into his father just outside the gardens. He also happens to be going into the city, and not only offers us a ride in his carriage, but also invites us to join him at the new museum. As much as I'm annoyed that my day has been entirely hijacked by the Davies men, I welcome an addition to our party of two for obvious reasons. Besides, I find Dr. Davies to be delightful and his work fascinating, so I can't feel too sorry for myself. He's been charged by Gaston Maspero, the Director General of the museum, with preventing the illicit trade of Egyptian antiquities, which must be quite the undertaking given the thriving black market. So thriving, in fact, that priceless objects are often traded right on the street in full view.

"Have you seen the new museum yet?" Ripley asks, as he helps me into his father's carriage. "I mean on your previous jaunts into Cairo?"

I ignore his baiting comment and turn to his father. "I admit I've been dying to see the future home of our greatest legacy! It's as pink as a piglet, I hear, and as grand as an opera house."

"Indeed, it is," Dr. Davies says. "And just about finished. Although I must say, now that it's nearly done, it seems it's taking forever to finish-finish. The Italians were all industry when she was going up, even ahead of schedule, but now there's all sorts of details that have yet to be tended to. Faucet handles, trim, half the door knobs are still missing."

We discuss the particulars of this new museum, and the delicate matter of moving all of the precious antiquities from the royal palace in Giza without damaging or losing any to plunder. The time goes quickly and enjoyably in conversation, but I find myself distracted by the knee of a certain Ripley Davies, which keeps bumping into mine every time the carriage hits a knot on the road, which is often. Each time, Ripley catches me in his gaze, even if briefly—in those luxurious eyes of his—and the last time the carriage jerks, when we come to an abrupt halt at our destination, he holds me there.

I'm vaguely aware of Dr. Davies saying, "Thank you, Akhem," to his driver, as he climbs out of the car.

"Ah, my dear," Dr. Davies says, and I break away from Ripley's stare at last.

"Yes?"

I notice Dr. Davies has been reaching his hand out for me and I mutter an apology.

"The ride into Cairo can be rather hypnotic," he says, and both Ripley and I chime in, agreeing wholeheartedly, and, I fear, a bit too enthusiastically. I try not to pay any attention to Ripley as we enter through the back of the museum, and luckily, given the magnificence of the building, that's not too difficult to manage.

The interior is grand, like a cathedral, with high ceilings and part of the roof done in glass, creating an atrium. There's stone and marble and arches, and some of the largest artifacts from the royal palace have already been transferred and installed. The colossal statue of Amenhotep III, his wife, Tiye, and their three daughters stands as centerpiece in the main hall, and makes me feel as if I've entered a temple. Other New Kingdom statues have been put in place as well, but most of those are still covered in tarps.

"There are forty-two rooms on the ground floor alone," Dr. Davies says. "Currently, I'm trying to arrange for the safe transport of an extensive collection of papyrus and coins. There's been a great deal of decay over the past two millennia and we must be ever so careful."

"I can imagine," I say.

"Wait until you see the sarcophagi," Ripley tells me.

"Mmm," his father assents. "Moving those is going to be quite the production. Last time we tried, word got out and we were nearly set upon by a particularly insidious black market ring."

"How awful," I say.

We arrive at Dr. Davies's office, tucked well behind the main hall, and he produces a rather elaborate ring of iron keys, each one more intricate than the next. But before he can conclude the process of distinguishing which of those keys will open his office door, we hear a loud clamor inside. Startled, Dr. Davies drops his ring of keys, but as he bends down to pick them up, Ripley goes and twists the knob, which isn't locked after all, and bursts into his father's office.

Inside is a young man about Ripley's age. He's African, with a long neck and nearly blue-black skin. By his features, I'd guess he's from Senegal—all high-boned and glossy as polished ebony—but his nose doesn't fit at all. It's rather small and a bit pointed, almost like my Uncle Andrew's nose. And he's not dressed in the Moslem way. In fact, he wears the casual shirt and trousers of an Englishman, although one who looks as if he's had a rough night of it.

On Dr. Davies's large mahogany desk is a broken magnifying glass, and in the young man's hand is the amulet Dr. Davies showed me on my first night back in Cairo. He glares down at his hand with a pronounced look of horror, then all of a sudden leaps up onto Dr. Davies desk, the glass crunching beneath his sandals. He then jumps to the floor, and bullies his way past us—nearly knocking me down in the process! Ripley tears off right after him, chasing him into the main hall, as Dr. Davies and I rush to follow them.

Right there, at the feet of Amenhotep III, Ripley reaches out, grabbing the African by his shirt, and pulling him down onto the floor. They roll about and the amulet flies from the young African's hand, skittering across the tiles and landing on the toe of Amenhotep's wife. I scuttle after it, and manage to scrape it up, handing it back to Dr. Davies gingerly. He holds it to his breast and exhales, then turns back to the brawling young men on the floor.

"Stop this instant!" he calls out. "Ripley Martin Davies!"

Ripley does indeed stop, panting heavily, but he keeps the African pinned to the floor. Dr. Davies walks over and looks down at the intruder, scrutinizing his face.

"I know you," Dr. Davies says, and this does not appear to be good news to our would-be thief.

"Don't be afraid," Dr. Davies assures him. "I won't be calling the authorities. Not if you join us in my office for a few minutes."

"Dad!" Ripley says, but his father shushes him.

The young man glances over at me and above him at Ripley. He doesn't appear eager to be joining any of us anywhere, but nonetheless, he nods.

"What are you waiting for, son, get off the lad, won't you?"

Ripley does so, reluctantly, keeping his eye on "the lad" the whole time.

"Come, come," Dr. Davies says, and the African rises up from the floor, smoothing his shirt and pants. We all follow Dr. Davies back to his office, Ripley and I trailing at the back. Once there, we're instructed by Ripley's father to sit on a worn leather sofa. Ignoring the rubble on his desk, Dr. Davies sits down in his chair, placing his elbows on the armrests and folding his hands. It's strange that I feel a bit like a girl who's been called to the headmaster's office, even though I've done nothing wrong.

Dr. Davies continues to stare at the prowler, but I can't help but notice that instead of staring back, he stares past Dr. Davies, eyeing with marvel a large glass case suspended behind the doctor's desk. It's filled with smaller antiquities—everything from hand tools to arrowheads to fertility dolls—and is quite an eclectic menagerie of historical curios.

"Tell me, why not the roasted nuts and the apple?" Dr. Davies inquires of him, as he gestures towards a small table littered with food. "You're clearly hungry and the trinket could have just been shoved into your pocket."

The African does glance longingly over at the food, and then shakes his head. "I wasn't here to steal anything," he says. "I just wanted to look. I saw that trinket hung over the picture of the lady and I wanted to see it better. I reached up onto your shelf for the magnifying glass, but it slipped from my fingers. Then you came in! I clutched the amulet on instinct and ran. I wasn't going to take it, though—at least not on purpose. I swear it!"

"Do you honestly expect us to believe—?"

"Ripley. Hush!"

"Dad!"

His father gives him that look that fathers give their sons, and Ripley does hush, though unhappily. He looks over at me and I shrug.

Dr. Davies returns his attention to the young African man. "I believe you," he says.

"What?" Both the young man and Ripley exclaim.

"I told you, I've seen you before. You followed me from the Royal Palace last week. And from the pyramids a few days before that. Why?"

Still quite frightened, the young African doesn't seem to know what to say, and I can't say as I blame him. The penalties for thievery can be severe depending on the accuser, and Gaston Maspero, the General Director of the museum, if he had his way, would slay by his own hand anyone who ever dared to even touch one of his precious artifacts.

Finally, the African steels himself, squaring his shoulders and taking a substantial breath. "I'm just interested," he says.

"Interested in me?"

"No, I mean, yes. I'm interested in what you do."

A slow grin spreads across Dr. Davies's face, as if a suspicion of his has been confirmed.

"You're interested in archaeology?"

The young man nods.

"I see. In that case, I wonder if you wouldn't like to make a little coin? Learn a little about your interest while you're at it."

Now it's my turn to glance over at Ripley, who looks a bit stupefied. He makes no effort to interfere in his father's engagement with this possible thief, however. I get the feeling he's used to his father's eccentricities, and has long ago learned that resistance to his whims is futile. Then I look over to gauge the African's reaction. There's an excitement in his eyes, and a quiver in his lip. Damn if Dr. Davies hasn't called this one.

"Well?"

"I'd like that very much," the African stammers.

"I figured you would. And what, may I ask, is your name?" Dr. Davies inquires.

"Cornelius P. Neville, sir."

Dr. Davies cocks his head and taps his finger on his thigh. "What does the P stand for?"

"Pissarro."

"Like the painter?"

Cornelius P. Neville nods. "Exactly like the painter," he says. "He was an acquaintance of my mother's. Gave her a beloved dog."

"You get more interesting by the moment, young man," Dr. Davies tells him.

Cornelius P. Neville gets up and leans over the desk. He begins picking up the broken shards of magnifying glass, but Dr. Davies shoos him away.

"Never mind that," he says. "The custodial staff can take care of the mess."

Dr. Davies opens the top drawer of his desk and plucks out a leather pouch that chinks audibly. He digs out a couple of coins and indicates for Cornelius to hold out his hand, which he does.

"An advance," says Dr. Davies. "I'd like you to get something to eat and meet me here first thing in the morning. You'll need a full belly for what I've got in store for you."

Cornelius P. Neville clenches the coins in his fist, which he stares at with a certain degree of wonder.

"What are you waiting for?" Dr. Davies asks, and the young African nods to him, then, tentatively, to me and Ripley. He backs out the door slowly, but spins around when he bumps into a column and runs toward the exit.

Dr. Davies turns to me and Ripley. "And that goes for the two of you as well. Go on and enjoy the rest of your day in Cairo, but be sure to get a decent night's rest and plenty of sustenance. I'll need all three of you here come morning for a three-day excursion. Lord Floyd has entrusted me with enhancing his daughter's education, and by Jove, I will do that and then some."

"Did you honestly just bring that Cornelius character into your employ?" Ripley marvels. "He broke into your office, and I don't care what he says, he took mother's amulet and attempted to abscond with it!"

"Yes, I suppose he did. But then, here it is," Dr. Davies says, dangling the necklace from his finger. I watch it swing back and forth and have a hard time taking my eyes away from it, if I'm to tell the truth. I glance at Ripley and notice he's rather transfixed by it as well.

"I don't imagine you noticed," Dr. Davies tells his son, "but to your average thief and black market dealer in artifacts, your mother's amulet doesn't have that much to offer. For one thing, it's not even Egyptian, and Egyptian relics are all the rage. No," he continues, as he looks about him. "There are many other pieces in this room alone that he could have gotten a much higher price for."

"Perhaps he didn't know the difference," I say.

Dr. Davies rests his knuckles on his hips and sighs. "Oh, he knew. And certainly anyone who's bold enough to break into the museum to rifle through what I've got here in my office would know the difference between an Egyptian artifact and something from another era, a different region. I can assure you his would-be customers would know—if he had any; which I'm quite certain he does not."

"And what is it exactly that you have in store for Cornelius P. Neville—assuming he shows up tomorrow," Ripley inquires.

"Oh, he will. I know a man bitten by the bug of antiquity."

Ripley chuckles a bit and folds his arms across his chest. "Takes one to know one, does it Dad?"

"Indeed. And tomorrow's activities are sure to put him in permanent thrall."

"Sounds intriguing," I say.

"It is," Dr. Davies crows. "After a few bits of business here at the museum, we're going to Thebes!"

A thrill rushes through me. I haven't been to Thebes since I was a little girl, and it had seemed then like a place of magic. It's temples, harbors, palaces, and markets, all jutting out of the desert floor like the skeleton of a god!

"The desert is a place of sand and bone," I say. "I remember my mother telling me that, as we walked through the Temple of Karnak."

"Of sand and bone," Dr. Davies repeats, caressing every syllable. "Yes, the desert is that."

He closes his eyes and folds his hands at his waist, then licks his lips. "My name is Ozymandias, King of Kings; Look on my Works, ye Mighty, and despair! Nothing beside remains. Round the decay of that colossal wreck, boundless and bare . . ."

"The lone and level sands stretch far away," I finish.

Dr. Davies blinks and open his eyes. "Somehow I knew you would know that poem."

"It's one of Percy Shelley's most famous. And a rather evocative contemplation on the fall of civilizations."

Dr. Davies nods. "And on the hollowness of even the greatest human endeavors."

"No," I say. "On the ineptitude and vanity of poor rulers!"

I didn't mean to be quite so strident in my response, and don't even know where such a sentiment came from. But there it is, and expressed with a vehemence as hot as a crime of passion. I feel Ripley's gaze again and turn to him. His eyes bore into me, making me forget to breathe.

"You have an inborn comprehension of the desert, my dear," Dr. Davies whispers. "Of its wins and losses throughout history."

"Yes," I say, but not to him; to Ripley. "I do."

Chapter 6

The City of the Dead

AS RIPLEY AND I exit the museum, we're immediately set upon by the usual pack of Egyptian boys, who make it their business to seek out those they believe to be tourists. They spin about us like whirling dervishes. "I say matches," they tell us, assuming every foreigner to be a smoker.

"I say, get yourselves a treat," Ripley tells them, flipping a coin into the air. It lands several feet away from us, and the boys scamper after it, giving us our chance at escape.

Ripley takes my hand, pulling me into the maze of lanes off Tahrir Square, and there is a thrill to being swept into the Cairo street circus by him. His wonder at my home city's every peculiarity and whim touches me, fueling my own excitement and making me delight in everything anew. We run past a snake charmer parading one of the longest cobras I've ever seen, and a tumbler who encompasses us in a dizzying turn of cartwheels.

"Strawberry! Strawberry!"

Strawberry sellers in February are quite insistent, and I have to pull Ripley away from them.

"They look delicious," he says. "I'd like to buy you some."

He really does know so little about the way things work around here.

"Well, it's kind of you," I tell him, "but I must warn you

that they moisten the strawberries in their mouths when they become dusty—which is often."

Ripley takes a second look at the truly succulent-looking berries, noticing the very lack of the film of dust that covers just about everything else on the streets of Cairo. He looks up at the seller, who gives a wide, gap-toothed smile and gestures towards his offering.

"Right," Ripley says, wrinkling his nose, then crossing over to another vendor. One who sells prickly pears. Ripley buys us each one, and pulls a brand new Swiss army knife from his pocket, proceeding to peel the spikey fruit. It's a wonderful poppy red on the inside, which I prefer to the orange and yellow ones, even if they taste equally sweet and refreshing.

"There's something about the red ones, isn't there?" Ripley says, as if reading my thoughts.

He cuts a piece of the fruit and puts it to my lips. Without even thinking, I accept his intimate gesture. Feels natural between us somehow.

"Mmm."

A small morsel of the fruit tumbles off my tongue and Ripley catches it in his hand. He eats it himself and smiles.

"What?"

"I like the way you make that sound, that's all. Makes me want to feed you again."

I'm not accustomed to feeling embarrassed and I don't like it on most occasions. Though I resent the flow of blood to my cheeks that Ripley's touch initiated, and his comment exacerbated, I'm also warmed by it. He lifts another slice of fruit to my mouth and I bite into it, finding myself caught once again in the rich hues of his eyes.

"You were right," he says.

"About what?"

"Coming into Cairo is much more fun than going swimming."

His voice is as sweet as pudding. Only the vaguest notion that he's the same young man I saw crawling out of a girl's window hangs in my memory, disturbing me from time to time, like a poltergeist. I try to keep it in mind, to keep my head about me. Ripley's sense of adventure, however, is infectious, and the way he looks at me, how easily we fall into one another's eyes, is bewitching.

He takes my hand and we wander down any street that strikes our fancy, being led by our interests and the pleasure of discovery. Of sharing a laugh over an alleyway where nothing but taxidermy is for sale—alligators, ostriches, a baby hippo of all things. As we emerge onto a small square, the offerings become more varied, and in some cases, more bizarre. Whips, tarbushes, Syrian picture frames done in mother of pearl, wedding lace, balloons, exotic birds in cages, narcissi, carnations, roses of all sorts—even black. At the center of this market is a small leopard in a glass box, as if to demonstrate the rarified tastes of the merchants and their ability to obtain the unobtainable. All the holy mess that I'd missed as I walked the more orderly streets of London.

"Hey," Ripley says, and I look up from an embroidered pile of coverlets, each one more brilliant than the next.

At first I think he's diverting my attention to a pen of baby piglets, but I quickly realize that's not it at all. Down the row of stalls, all the way at the end, we spy Cornelius P. Neville.

His dark face etched with a look of raptness, he stands in front of a merchant, negotiating a sale. We watch him remove some coins from his pocket—the very ones Dr. Davies gave him. He drops them in the seller's palm, but instead of getting his supper, as Dr. Davies had instructed him to do, he takes a small statue from the man.

A bird's head.

A lion's mouth.

A strong and lean body with clawed feet clutching a flower.

The very statue I saw on the way back from Misr Station when we arrived! I look up at the seller, and it's the same one as well. Clean shaven, unlike the rest of them, and a pair of wide-set eyes that find their way to me.

"That statue," Ripley says.

"You've seen it before?"

Ripley nods.

"Come on, let's follow him," he says, as Cornelius makes off in the direction of the Citadel, walking at a clipped pace.

We begin our pursuit, but before we turn the corner, disappearing into yet another warren of streets, I look back at the stall where the young African had purchased the odd sculpture. The seller is gone. In his place is an old woman with a beaded scarf over her face. A Turkish angora cat walks about on the seller's table, sitting right down at its center as if he owns it. The cat trains his eyes on me as if I'm the only person in the market.

"Leila, come on," Ripley says.

Something makes me want to stay here and try to find the merchant, but stalking our would-be antiquities thief and his curious statue takes precedence. Ripley and I try our best to blend into the spectacle of hagglers, game players, and street magicians that swarm around us like agitated bees, but I can't help thinking our formality alone makes us stand out. Cornelius isn't expecting to be trailed, however, so that does give us one advantage. We follow him to the edges of Old Cairo, and it's not long before I realize where he's headed.

"The City of the Dead," I say.

Ripley looks at me strangely, as if he has no idea what I'm talking about, and I realize that for someone like him, who has spent most of his time either at archaeological sites or on the garden island of Zamalek, the rest of Cairo is a bit of a mystery. There are Britons who've lived here for years who've never made their way to the City of the Dead.

"It's not as ominous as it sounds. Or maybe it is," I tell him.

We shadow Cornelius into the Southern cemetery, where, upon entering, a white swallow swoops down out of nowhere, nearly clipping my hair. I somehow manage not to yelp. Its wings flap with a forceful grace as it lands on a green tombstone scratched with Arabic graffiti. It stares us down, and Ripley and I look briefly at one another before continuing on.

"Ominous indeed," Ripley says.

Up ahead, a sleepy dog snorts and adjusts his head on the sun-warmed gravestone where he lies. He sniffs and growls lazily at us as we walk by, making the place seem a little more ordinary. But only a little.

"It's over a thousand years old," I explain. "And it is, in fact, a massive burial ground that is home to the graves of Cairo's most illustrious and historical elites, as well the most common of its commoners. Everyone is equal in death."

We stop, hiding behind a rather large and elaborate tombstone, when Cornelius bends down to dig a stone out of his sandal. He stands abruptly when he finishes and looks back in our direction, then tucks his statue firmly into his trousers, as if for safer keeping. Once again, he begins weaving his way through the center of the graveyard, now heading towards a menagerie of lanes lined with tomb structures the colors of sand, mustard, and red clay. We lower our voices to coarse whispers and continue in our pursuit.

"Why is there laundry hanging between tombstones?" Ripley asks.

"Well, the City of the Dead is also, to a growing number of Cairo's citizens, a place of residence for the living."

"You can't be serious?"

As evidence, a gangly child runs out from one of the lanes, kicking a ball made of twine. It hits the door of a mausoleum, and a woman in a headscarf peeks out, castigating the little rascal.

"My God," Ripley says.

"It used be that just the gravediggers and tomb custodians lived here," I tell him. "But with Cairo growing so quickly, others have begun to move in as well. Bakers, servants, and the like. Even some stalls and little shops are springing up in the hawshes."

"Wouldn't it be sacrilegious to have commerce going on in the actual tomb enclosures?"

I shrug my shoulders and observe as the woman in the headscarf hangs a prayer rug from the mausoleum window and begins to beat it, dust billowing all about.

"Christ did drive the money-changers from the temple, it's true, but the people who find shelter here are poor and have to get their wares someplace. Do you really think God would mind?"

"I suppose not," he says.

We try to remain a good distance behind Cornelius so as not to be spotted, at least not quite yet, but it's difficult to keep him in our view with all the tall tombs and headstones about. The further we go into the oldest part of the necropolis, the more it feels as if we've stepped into a Cairo that's more legend than true history. Like a painting based on an artist's macabre imagination. Yet strangely, Cornelius Neville seems as if he belongs in this place. As if he belongs in any place of times past, where the dead and the living exist side by side.

"Looks like he's going into that mausoleum," Ripley says. "You're sure people actually live in those?"

"They're better built than a lot of the newer houses in the city center," I say. "Made of stone, with walls as thick as the trunks of oak trees, and grand wooden doors that keep out or invite in the sun; I imagine that once one gets past the idea of sharing a living space with a few corpses, the prospect of sleeping in a tomb isn't so bad."

"I suppose you're right. Not like I haven't slept in my share of tombs. Par for the course when you're the son of an archaeologist."

Ripley cocks his head and squeezes my hand, which I realize he's been holding all this time. I feel a very warm rush from the top of my head to my toes but I let him pull me gently along, concealing us behind a rather weathered series of prominent grave markers. Ones engraved with an illegible Arab scripture that has been worn down to almost nothing over many hundreds of years.

The mausoleum Cornelius entered belongs to a once important Moslem family, it would appear. By its decaying grandeur, I would guess it is a family that died out some time ago. It is at least as old as a millennium and has windows with wooden shutters that look as delicate as spiders' webs. Ripley and I sneak closer and try to look through the slats of one of the shutters. Inside, there's a large stone tomb of the sort that could fit several cadavers. There's also a mat and blankets in the corner, plus a small table with unlit candles. It's definitely inhabited.

"Should we knock on the door?" I whisper, but just as I do, Cornelius Neville comes flying out of the door with a pointed dagger in his hand!

I gasp and Ripley immediately gets out in front of me, nearly hissing at the young African like a vigilant jungle beast! It's an extraordinary and primitive gesture, completely at odds with his usual comportment. Even Cornelius, who's the one with the weapon, steps back, clearly stunned by such a display. Stunned, but undeterred. He holds the dagger with the confidence of a fighter.

"It's you," Cornelius manages to say. "You've come after me."

Ripley is not backing down. He takes another step closer to the young African, as if entirely unafraid of the knife being brandished at him.

"Not on purpose," I explain.

I run out from behind Ripley, inserting myself squarely between the two young men. Not sparing a moment, Ripley grabs me by the arm and pulls me so forcefully to him that I feel like a rag doll. He then pushes me off to the side, where I spin and stumble, steadying myself against a small palm standing vigil outside the mausoleum. Despite the discombobulating attack upon my person, I'm able to catch a look at his eyes. The brown of them churns, while the amber and crimson threads have become like raging rivers.

"We were just walking about Cairo," I call out. "And we saw you buying that statue. You see, I've seen it before and want to talk to you about it."

Cornelius takes a deep breath and flits his eyes at me for just a second, before training them back on Ripley. He, too, seems to have noticed the change in Ripley's eyes, and narrows his own in consternation.

"You can put the dagger away," I continue. "We're not here for anything else, I swear it. Please Cornelius. This is all a misunderstanding."

For the first time since our discovery, the tension in the air seems to break a bit. Cornelius's grip on the dagger slackens and Ripley's posture softens. I step close to him and place my hand on his shoulder.

Cornelius cranes his neck and looks the both of us over. A keen observer this one is. Slowly, he puts out his other hand as a peace offering and begins to pull back the dagger.

"What do you know about the statue?"

"Nothing," I say. "I just saw it a few days ago, when I first arrived in Cairo. That man who sold it to you; he had it, and was holding it up, looking at me. I was hoping you knew something about it."

"And you?" Cornelius asks Ripley.

Ripley shakes his head, a faraway look about him. "I've only seen it in my dreams."

Chapter 7

A Very Ugly Story

"**T**HE SELLER CLAIMED it's thousands of years old," Cornelius tells us.

He rolls the statue out of the worn swatch of linen the seller had wrapped it in and places it on top of a little table next to the big stone tomb. He gets busy lighting a fire, searing his finger on bits of kindling that give out a burst, and swearing in French with the vociferant flair of a native speaker. Apologizing profusely, he invites Ripley and I to sit on a pair of wildly colored pillows, which we do. These are firm and well made. He starts to make tea, as Ripley and I ogle the statue.

"It's not Egyptian," Cornelius says. "Not even early Egyptian, I'd say."

"No, clearly not," Ripley concurs, as he stares into the big, round eyes of the sculpture.

The violent nature of our encounter outside of the mausoleum has largely faded, just as a ghost would through a castle wall. Especially, as we have all turned our attention to a shared interest that has the curious makings of an obsession.

I reach out to take the statue into my hand, but Ripley grips my wrist. "Don't touch it," he says.

"Why? Was it something in your dream?"

"Yes. No. I don't know. Just, not yet, alright?"

And while I do want very much to take the statue into

my hands, Ripley's warning is so heartfelt that I feel obliged to honor his simple request. I do scoot closer to the figure, though, noticing the tiniest fleck of red—probably paint— around its mouth.

Ripley turns to Cornelius. "What else did the seller tell you?"

The teapot the young African has suspended over the fire starts to whistle and he pours us each a cup filled with fragrant leaves. He's generous with his supply, I notice, although he doesn't appear to have all that much tea left. He then serves us with more than a modicum of ceremony, putting out sugar in a small, copper dish, a single napkin—worn all over, but free of holes—and a serving spoon.

"He told me the most remarkable story about it," Cornelius says, in a whispery voice made of thirst and awe. "I know to take their stories with a grain of salt, but his was fascinating, and this sculpture—well, it is unlike anything I've ever seen. And I've seen quite a bit in my twenty years."

He takes the statue in his hand, confidently, despite Ripley's warning to me. "He says it was made long before any civilization that we know. In the time of a great people who were buried in the sand."

"Like a desert Atlantis," Ripley says.

Cornelius nods, the tip of his burned finger touching ever so lightly the flower clutched in the statue's talons. "But it wasn't made by them, exactly. He said it was made by an ancient tribe of prophets. He told me they lived apart from the settlements in the earliest days of the desert. In fact, they lived outside of time and space. Their only real connection to the human world is that they were charged by their god with protecting what he called Nin'ti."

"Nin'ti." Ripley lets the word curl about his tongue and I say it silently to myself. Makes my heart beat a bit harder, louder.

"They're beings," Cornelius continues. "Human, for the most part. Destined to be born and to die over and over again. He said this tribe made the first Nin'ti from this statue the way God made Eve from the rib of Adam."

"For what purpose?" Ripley inquires.

"He didn't say, but as strange as this may sound, I believed him."

"Does this god of theirs have a name?" I ask.

Cornelius leans in to us, as if telling a most valuable secret. "He called it, 'the Unknowable One.'"

"How very cryptic," Ripley murmurs.

"And accurate. At least in terms of the way we've come to understand God," Cornelius says. "I was rather gripped by the fact that these ancient prophets—ones who were conceived in myth long before the Jews, the Christians, and the Moslems walked the Earth, would have initiated the concept of a single god, a unifying entity."

Gives me a shiver when he puts it that way.

"What about you?" Cornelius turns to Ripley. "You say you dreamt about it. What did your dreams tell you?"

Ripley leans back against the tomb and takes a deep drink of his tea. He closes his eyes. "In my dream, I'm holding it. I mean, it's me, but it isn't me. Hard to explain. I don't look anything like myself and yet I'm unmistakable. And the statue is hot. Not like a hot kettle, more like a current that runs through every part of it and me."

Ripley opens his eyes and looks my way. "Have you ever dreamt of it?"

"I don't think so," I tell him.

But I've dreamt of so many other things. Of vanished people, of lost deserts. I want to tell him, but I don't. Not here. Not in front of Cornelius.

"And you," Ripley says to our new African friend.

Cornelius shakes his head and holds the effigy to his breast.

"I never dreamt of the statue, but I knew from the moment I laid eyes on her that I would buy her when I could. It was the third time that seller offered her to me. He said many had offered him a good price, but that he would sell the statue to me and me alone. It's nonsense, of course. I didn't believe that part."

But as I study Cornelius Neville's expression, I think that perhaps he did.

"Will you bring the statue tomorrow?" Ripley asks him. "I'd like my father to have a look at it if you don't mind."

"Your father is a great man," Cornelius says. "And a good one to boot. No, I don't mind at all. I wasn't intending to leave her behind here anyway. There's a lot of petty thievery in the City of the Dead and most recently a gruesome murder."

"How ghastly!" I exclaim.

"Cornelius," Ripley warns.

"No, I want to hear!" I turn to Cornelius. "What sort of murder, and who?"

Cornelius looks to me and nods, a deep breath filling his chest. "A young woman's body was found in a rather unholy state. Mutilated, they say."

"Mutilated? In what way? Ritualistically, like by a cult?" I make the sign of the cross, and kiss the tips of my fingers, sending a blessing to the poor woman's soul.

"Cornelius," Ripley interjects. "I think this is a conversation we might save for another time."

"Oh, please," I tell him. "I'm nearly a woman of sixteen! One who hardly needs you to act as my protector."

"Well, I'm nearly a man of nineteen, and while you're in my company I am your protector."

"Well, if the way you protected Edna Watson some nights ago is a demonstration of your skills in this regard, I'll take care of myself, thank you."

Ripley looks as if I have struck him. Cornelius looks back

and forth between the two of us, and I'm too ashamed to look at Ripley, having insulted his character like that, and in front of a stranger.

"I am sorry," I say. "Cornelius, would you go on with your story, and please, don't leave out any details. I feel it's important somehow."

A silence falls between us all, and I don't know what to do.

"It is a very ugly story," Cornelius whispers, and I'm so grateful he broke the ice. "Strange and diabolical. A bit like this statue."

And there it stands, commanding all of our attention again. Looking bigger than it is, suggesting a latent power that is yet to be discovered.

"Perhaps you should tell us the story, after all," Ripley says.

Cornelius takes the deepest of breaths and closes his eyes. He places his hands on his knees.

"She lived with her family, in a crypt only a short walk from here. I didn't know her name, but she always greeted me with a smile. A sad smile, but not hopeless. Then I didn't see her for a few days."

"Had she been abducted?" I ask.

Cornelius shakes his head.

"She was found nearly sliced in half. In an empty tomb in the Northern Cemetery. It's fairly populated there, even at night, and no one heard sounds of a struggle. A baker thinks he might have seen her walking with a well-dressed gentleman."

"What a horror," I say. "We've heard nothing about such a thing!"

"I scour the papers every morning due to all the antiquities thefts," Ripley tells him. "And there's been no mention of such a wicked crime!"

"Well, it's been kept inside the community here, for the most part. You see, her behavior and late nights out would bring shame upon her family. Some would see her manner of death as a logical conclusion to the way she lived her life, and by extension to the way in which she was reared by her parents."

Ripley stands up and paces about the floor.

"But that's terrible," he says. "If she was poor, she was no doubt doing whatever she could to survive. Her death deserves to be acknowledged and her murderer brought to justice."

Cornelius's wry smile is not without sympathy for the girl. "Nobody likes the poor, Ripley. Not even the poor themselves. And few people have any real compassion for the choices people with few choices are forced to make. Unless it suits them, of course."

"Do you really believe that?"

Cornelius places the statue back on the table and picks up his tea. He looks long and hard at Ripley Davies. "I didn't grow up poor, you know, but my family's finances fell into a terrible state after my mother's death. I've been on my own since then. I can tell you I felt no sympathy for the poor when I wasn't one of them, and don't feel much more now that I am. All I want is to get away from them if I'm to be honest."

"That's a terrible thing to say."

"It's the truth," Cornelius tells him.

"Then you're no better than the people who would take advantage of you now that you're down on your luck!"

"Ripley!" I admonish.

"I'm sorry," Ripley says. "It's not my place to say such a thing. Especially to you, Cornelius, and when I am not poor and never have been. I just can't stop thinking about that girl is all."

I think none of us can. The grotesque and ungodly manner of her death, the mystery surrounding it.

We finish the tea in silence, each of us in our own world of thought. Ripley slices up our extra prickly pear, but neither he nor I take of it. We leave it for Cornelius, who intended to go hungry in order to buy that statue.

"I'll see you tomorrow," Cornelius says, as we get ready to go back to Zamalek. He's clearly excited about our coming adventure, just as we are. "And I'll bring her."

"You keep calling the statue a her," Ripley says. "I have to say, as I look, I can't tell what it is."

Cornelius laughs. "Well, I can't either, but the seller was sure it is a she, and I rather like to think of something so savage in appearance as female."

Indeed, the bird's head and lion's mouth are a formidable fusion. Only the talons clutching the flower give the sculpture any gentleness of heart.

RIPLEY AND I leave Cornelius and the City of the Dead by late afternoon. We walk for a good long time, hardly speaking, and shaking off thoughts of a poor girl's murder and an ancient statue that beguiles us all.

In Old Cairo, Ripley flags down a buggy and we climb in. Despite the mysteries that fell upon us throughout the day, the fade of evening into night brings a new mood, a different set of obscurities. As gas lanterns start to glow, the city of Cairo looks to be lit by a thousand candles held in vigil. The Southern Cross stands above the Nile like a beacon, and a feeling of being one with all the things God made comes over me.

I turn to Ripley, and he takes my hand. He holds it gingerly this time, not in the firm way he gripped it when we were snaking our way through Old Cairo. His thumb rides down the length of my index finger and my lips tremble, my breath hitches. Despite my best efforts, he makes my skin feel tender all over, my heart beat faster.

"They say on the Nile, nothing can be believed or depended on," I whisper.

"Who is they?"

"Egyptians, I suppose. My ancestors."

Ripley smiles and looks out onto the ancient river.

"The Nile, forever new and old: Among the living and the dead: Its mighty mystic stream has rolled."

"Henry Wordsworth Longfellow."

Ripley nods. "Forever reinventing herself. Always murmuring the tales of our first civilizations to anyone who will listen."

"Did Longfellow say that, too?"

Ripley shakes his head. "I did."

The moon has risen, her light glowing upon the surface of the river Nile like the stars above us. The sky and the river; each infinite in their own way. The heavens like God Himself, and the Nile . . . well the Nile is perhaps like man, made in His image. And Ripley and I. Suddenly, I don't know where we fit into all of this.

"You called me a snob, earlier today. When we first ran into one another on Zamalek," I say.

"I did not. I merely meant . . ."

"You were right." I take my hand away from his and place it on my lap. But I do look at him. I will not be a coward. "When Cornelius told us about that girl—I felt so much for her, for her family. But part of me also thought it was right that they bury her manner of death along with her. Not that she deserved her fate, but that it wasn't surprising such a thing would happen to her. It's a terrible way to think—as a woman, as a Christian. And quite typical of the Egyptian elite, of which I am one as you pointed out. Except my mother—yes, she was as high born as they come, too, but she wasn't like that and she would have been ashamed of me for thinking about a woman that way."

"I doubt it."

"You didn't know her."

"Did she not write 'We cannot change the circumstances of our birth, but we have it within us to change our minds. It is the spark of divinity God gave us'?"

"So, you've not only read my mother's work, but put it to memory?"

"Some things she wrote are hard to forget."

I tear my eyes away from Ripley and scan the city that made my mother into who she was.

"Sometimes I fear I'm forgetting her. That I can't become what she would have wanted of me."

Ripley leans in close, putting his cheek to mine and looking out onto Cairo with me. "Perhaps you were meant to be something else."

He nuzzles closer, his breath warming my earlobe. The sincerity of his touch is at odds with the furtive way in which he crawled out of Edna Watson's window.

"Won't you look at me?" he whispers.

If I look at him now, I'll let him kiss me—I know it.

"Can we just watch the city together?"

"Yes."

And so we ride the rest of the way back to Zamalek in silence, our bodies fit together like spoons. Our eyes dance over the lights and shadows of one of the oldest cities on earth. Our ears tune in to the music of laughter and conversation that flows from nearly every doorway. Ripley scoots away from me for propriety's sake once we arrive on the island, but the spell that our adventure has cast over us remains. It was a day that started out in suspicion and annoyance, and for good reason, I remind myself. The Ripley Davies who would stand between me and a dagger, and dream of a statue that speaks to us both is still the same Ripley Davies who, by all reasonable accounts, is showing most improper attentions to Edna Watson. And I won't be played.

"Won't you walk with me for a while," he asks, as he helps me down from the buggy.

"No," I say, and it takes just about all of my will to deny him. "We have quite a day tomorrow, and I'll see you then."

"Yes, you will," he tells me.

Chapter 8

In the Valley of the Kings

RIPLEY, CORNELIUS, Dr. Davies, and I board our train at promptly 7:00pm, having very nearly been late, as Father insisted on seeing us off. Dr. Davies had asked a visiting photographer, one who'd come to take archival pictures of his various artifacts, to take one of us outside of the museum, and the man certainly did take his time about it, making us stand there posing for much longer than we'd expected. But after an endless day spent running a labor of errands for the director-general of the department of antiquities—all in anticipation of Dr. Davies's mere three-day excursion to Thebes—I admit that it was fun to commemorate the occasion.

It will be left to The Great Maspero, as he is called (often with a note of sarcasm), to shepherd into the museum a collection of coins from the royal palace, when it's plain he would much prefer to be joining us. As a protest, he refused to be photographed, saying he much favored having his portrait painted and by a proper artist rather than snapped by some plebeian.

"Gaston Maspero, while enormously popular among museum keepers and collectors, has a rather delicate reputation among the rank and file workers at the various digs in and around Luxor," Dr. Davies explains.

I know exactly what he's referring to but is too polite to say outright. The Great Maspero has been known to resort to

torturing captured grave robbers, and while his brutal meth-
ods have recovered numerous important finds, they don't sit
well with everyone. My mother considered him a vile and
wicked man, even if a necessary tool against the plunder of
our heritage.

"I, myself, am happy to no longer have to listen to his
rather *afternoonified* French accent," Ripley tells us with an
eyeroll.

"But he's a brilliant man," Cornelius counters. "The
third volume of his *Histoire Ancienne des Peuples de l'Orient
Classique* is the definitive modern history of Egypt, Chaldea,
Syria, Babylonia, and Assyria. There's nothing even close to
it!"

Cornelius, I did notice, attended to The Great Maspero's
minutiae today with a degree of zeal that only the most passionate student of archeology could muster.

"Quite true," says Dr. Davies. "You should try reading it,
son. You'll see Maspero's not all bad."

"Not to you, Father, but to just about everyone else. And
by the way, I have read his *Histoire*, and yes, it is brilliant. I
don't deny his genius, I just don't wish to be in his company."

Ripley can't stand the way his father's employer talks to
people he considers below himself, which is just about everyone. I rather like that about the young Mr. Davies, and admit
that I enjoyed watching him treat The Great Maspero in a
rather republican manner that got on the Frenchman's last
nerve.

And I was more than impressed that Ripley, with the
blessing of his father, invited Cornelius to stay with them in
their sleeping compartment for our journey to Luxor. We will
all of us now arrive refreshed in the morning, and ready for
our adventure—whatever that may be. In the meantime, we
make ourselves comfortable in a small seating area adjoining
our night-time quarters. Ripley is kind enough to jimmy a

stubborn window open for some fresh air. He then sits down next to me, rather close.

"A light breeze makes for a pleasant addition at this point in the evening," he says to me. It's a rather simple line of small talk and yet somehow it feels to me as if he means something else entirely. Something tender and voluptuous.

"I often find myself thanking God for the month of February in Egypt," Dr. Davies says, oblivious to the way his son is regarding me.

Cornelius, on the other hand, appears perfectly attuned to the undertones in Ripley's and my every exchange. He looks on with unmasked amusement.

"I have a tremendous surprise for you all, once we arrive," Dr. Davies tells us. He knots his hands together and leans in to me conspiratorially. "Your father was rhapsodic when I told him, and it's the single reason why he was willing to part with you. 'A most momentous development in Leila's education,' he said."

Perhaps for Cornelius's sake, he begins to deliver for us a thorough and animated history on Thebes—or Waset, as the ancient Egyptians called their imperial city, and as Dr. Davies continues to call it. He details its expansion in the Middle and New Kingdoms, how it grew into the largest city in the world by 1500 B.C., and its plunder by the Assyrians in 663 B.C.

He next expounds on the majesty of the Valley of the Kings, which sits on the western side of the Nile, about three miles from Thebes and its temples. I have a deep suspicion that he plans on taking us there, and thrill at the prospect. I've never been to the burial ground of Egypt's ancient kings, and distinctly remember throwing a fit as a child when I was told it was not a place for little girls. I was forced to stay behind in Thebes with a governess, while the adults got a personal tour of the open tombs by the attending French archaeologists.

"Ripley has always loved the desert, haven't you, my boy? Clean and dignified, you call it. Perhaps you'll feel even more at home in Waset than you do in Cairo."

"You feel at home in Cairo?" I ask Ripley.

"In the desert, yes. I always have."

Once again, I feel as if he's communicating something secret just to me, and my cheeks flush under his gaze.

"Looks like you got a bit of sun today, dear," Dr. Davies says, appraising my change in color. He stretches and gives a most exuberant yawn. "My sincerest apologies, but I fear I must excuse myself. I've been up since well before dawn."

"Will you not have supper before you retire, Dr. Davies?" I say, happy for the switch in topic away from me and my cheeks. "If not in the dining car, then here. I've brought some of my Aunt Clara's Koshari."

I jump up and pull a small, leather carrying bag from our luggage rack. It contains a veritable feast of Egyptian goodies which I extoll the virtues of to Dr. Davies.

"As tempting as it sounds, I'm absolutely knackered," Dr. Davies assures me. Of course, he promptly changes his mind upon spying some fresh *basbusa* that Horus's wife made. He takes several of the rosewater flavored biscuits, along with a tray of tea with him into his sleeping compartment, and bids us goodnight with a full mouth.

Ripley, Cornelius, and I waste no time digging in to Aunt Clara's bounty. Her efforts at perfecting the Egyptian national dish of rice, vegetables, pasta, and legumes is clever and loaded with a most un-English amount of garlic. Though I had nothing to do with making the food, I take a certain pride in watching Cornelius pick off every last piece of rice, every fleck of herb stuck to the side of the tin in which I brought our communal meal.

"I've so missed eating with my hands," I say, peeling off bites of bread and dipping them in a bowl of *baba ganoush*.

Ripley follows my example, sucking a smear of aubergine off his finger.

"Why do Egyptians pronounce *baba ganoush* with a K at the end?" Ripley asks me.

"Why do the English put a silent 'gh' in so many words? Like thorough."

"Or thoughtful," Cornelius adds.

"Or tough," says Ripley.

"But the 'gh' isn't silent in tough," I point out.

"Isn't it though?" says Cornelius and we all laugh.

Ripley yawns, unfolding much like his father, and Cornelius follows in contagion. He curls up on the bench, leaning his head against the window. Within a minute he's got a light snore going.

"Am I really so boring?"

Ripley shakes his head and smiles. "Poor Cornelius helped unload some rather heavy stone palettes today, and as for me, well, I was up most of the night."

I try my best not to show that I rather like the way Ripley's fair hair has fallen in a light curtain over one eye.

"And why is that?"

"Excitement about the day, I suppose."

"Surely you've been to Thebes with your father since coming to Cairo."

The one side of Ripley's mouth turns up as it's apt to do in that way of his. "Actually, no. We've been so busy—what with Father being nearly hounded to death by Maspero—that, until recently at least, I've spent most of my time on the island or on the route to the museum."

"What? No dazzling nights at the Shepheard?"

"A few of those, too," he admits.

"Well, I won't be offended if you wish to nod off for a while, like your father and our new friend here."

"Are you sure?"

"Positive," I tell him.

As I stare out the window into the dark, and my companions sink further into a state of oblivion, I find myself becoming hypnotized by the shuffle of the train wheels. My eyes open and close with some effort, and my breath turns sluggish.

It feels as if I do not sleep, but I go in and out of dreams, sometimes sitting up with a start, having been jarred out of my doze by that voice in the night which usually speaks to me of love. But not this time.

"Stay close to me," he says in warning.

"I cannot help but be close to you," I tell him. "I love you. I've always loved you."

"Then do not leave my side tomorrow."

"Why not?"

"Because he's there."

I jerk awake with some violence to find Ripley staring right at me with a most peculiar look on his face. Like he's known me my whole life.

"Perhaps it's time for all of us to retire," I murmur.

He nods and I stand up, holding the rail as I make my way to the door of my compartment. Before going in, I turn around once more. Ripley is still watching me, and for a moment I nearly ask him to come with me into my sleeper! I pivot back to my door, jiggling the handle until it finally gives way and I'm able to close myself off in my compartment. I sit down on my cot, gape-mouthed and utterly appalled at myself, praying he hadn't read any of what I was thinking. *Oh, but he did,* a voice within me says. *He knew exactly what you were thinking.*

WE DO NOT GO to Thebes, just as I suspected, but immediately are taken by buggy some three miles from where the Temple of Amun at Karnak sits, across to the western side of the Nile, where lies the Valley of Kings.

Cornelius is agog at the dramatic cliffs that hide the sacred tombs of the pharaohs, and I can hardly say I blame him. They rise up high and red in the morning light. I would be as mesmerized as he if it weren't for the powerful bodily awareness I have developed of one Ripley Davies. I do attempt to make small talk with him, trying to pretend that our strange exchange the night before never happened. It's difficult for me, as it feels as if something deeply suggestable occurred between us, even though it didn't.

I prattle about the weather, like an idiot. How it's a chilly morning, but one that'll give way to a warm, although not hot, day, thank goodness. How soon the days will become stifling again, and even the light floral dress I've packed for a casual day at an archaeological site will feel like a heavy blanket. Ripley says almost nothing, tacitly agreeing with me by a nod of the head, while Cornelius and Dr. Davies dive knee-deep into a philosophical conversation; one about the spiritual elements of these most barren cliffs which stand before us in the western desert. They're becoming thick as thieves, those two.

"Alfred!" A young, mustached gentleman exclaims, waving his hat about like a maniac. He trots over to us as we step down from the body of the carriage.

Dr. Davies introduces us to one Howard Carter, who has been appointed to the position of chief inspector of the Egyptian Antiquities Service. He's in a demonstrably buoyant mood, shaking Dr. Davies's hand with great vigor and moving on to Cornelius and Ripley with no diminished enthusiasm. When he comes to me, he bows, all smiles, and makes warm reference to my father.

"Tell me," he says, facing us all. "Are you ready to enter into the ancient world?"

⋯⊰◈⊱ ⊰◈⊱⋯

CARTER WALKS with the conviction of man who has heard God speak to him personally. Long, decisive strides, and arms that move through the air as if he were wading through water that's waist-high. We all have to turn on the steam in order to keep up, as we follow him down a dry, dusty road leading past several tombs. They sit like open mouths at the base of these golden cliffs; the unknown beckoning us into the unknowable.

All around, there is the industrious quality of an ant hill. Workers push wheelbarrows filled with debris and hidden pieces of antiquity. They whistle, hurry, call out to one another – sometimes in camaraderie, other times in rebuke. There is a happiness in the air that comes from being part of an important endeavor that will be talked about for years to come. All of this due in no small part to Howard Carter who waves us along as we round a curve. There, we see a small wooden sign staked into the ground. It reads: KV45.

"Come this way," Carter whispers, as if he might awaken these dead kings.

Around a jagged slab of limestone is a shaft in the hillside. Carter leads us right up to it and reaches into a metal bin resembling a washtub. From there, he retrieves a torch that he lights with a match struck hard against his belt. He enters the shaft and we trail behind him like ducklings, Ripley Davies sticking so close to me that we bump one another every few steps. It's cool, dark, and claustrophobic in here, and the going is slow.

"I discovered this only a few days ago," Carter says. "And you're the first, besides the men working for me, to see it."

"Are you saying you've unearthed a new king?" Ripley asks.

Carter shakes his head. "Not quite a king, but a noble. A man named Userhat, who was the Overseer of the Fields of Amen. But the tomb was reused, I believe, during Dynasty 22. About a third of the chamber is filled with debris and has been heavily damaged by flooding, unfortunately."

"But the mummies are still there!" Cornelius exclaims. "In their original place?"

"Indeed, and it's where they may remain. I don't know if it'll be possible to remove them at all. Not without damaging them irreparably."

"What about other artifacts?" I ask.

"We'll have to see, of course," Carter says. "There are fragments of canopic jars among the rubble, but like a lot of these tombs, it's been stripped clean of much of the treasure."

"But for men of our interests, gold is not the only treasure to be found," Dr. Davies says, just as we finally enter the tomb chamber.

It stinks of dankness and limestone and decay. On the one side of the chamber is a mound of rubble composed of silt, rotted wood, what look like various tools, and what are certainly human and animal bones. Carter shines the torch on the less ravaged part of the chamber, revealing a colorful wall of hieroglyphics that nearly takes my breath away.

"We are the first in thousands of years to see this," Cornelius whispers, his lips quivering with an awe that touches me.

I tap his shoulder and point to a depiction of a jackal-headed Anubis crouched at the foot of a large scale. "Here is a spell for the weighing of a heart against a feather. If the heart equals the weight of the feather, he may pass through the *Duat*, or underworld, and into the afterlife."

"You can read this?" Cornelius asks me, and I nod. "Could you teach me?"

"Of course," I say. "You'd pick it up in no time at all."

"I see you were right, Dr. Davies," Carter says. "These are indeed the right young people to bring into this new discovery. But I'm afraid we can't stay long. The debris is unstable in here, and made more so by the beginnings of my excavations."

In a state of wonderment, we file out of the chamber and through the shaft again. Back in the sunlight, it feels as if, in the short time we were gone, the morning has grown considerably warmer. It may be a hot one after all. Carter leads us to Seti's tomb, which was discovered some eighty years ago and has been fully excavated. It's brightly lit with torches and as grand as I've ever imagined. Chamber upon chamber of breathless Egyptian art, with a full depiction of the night sky upon the ceiling. Bright colors all around us and enormous columns of limestone covered in various incantations. Far more beautiful than the tomb of Userhat, but far less of meaning to me, I must say. Userhat's final resting place feels as if it belongs to us now and always will.

"When the Italian archaeologist, Belzoni, discovered this tomb, he found some of the artists' paints and brushes still on the floor," Howard Carter tells us.

At the far back of the tomb, past the burial chamber, we come upon a small room that Carter explains was once used for nonessentials that the king might want, though not necessarily need, in the afterlife. Baskets and such. This is where Carter has made his field office.

There's a proper desk at the center, and a large trunk next to it. In the corner is a pile of pillows, typically Egyptian and dyed in flamboyant hues. We each take one and make ourselves relatively comfortable on the floor. Howard Carter and Dr. Davies lean against the desk.

"I think you've given me the best day of my life," Cornelius says to Carter.

Carter smiles, folding his arms across his chest. Ripley and I meet eyes, and he elbows Cornelius, nudging his daypack with the toe of his shoe. The young African nods and clears his throat.

"I was wondering," he says, "if I might show you gentlemen something? Get your professional opinion on a find I made yesterday."

Both Carter and Dr. Davies tip their heads in interest; Dr. Davies with a note of pride about his newest protégé. His eyes flitting to both me and Ripley first, Cornelius reaches into his daypack and removes the statue from it. He unwraps it delicately from its linen and holds it up for the archaeologists to see.

"May I?" Carter says, and Cornelius hands him the effigy. Howard Carter takes a deep breath, his eyes wandering hungrily over the statue's every feature. "Extraordinary."

"I—we—were hoping you'd know something about it."

"Yes," I say. "The three of us have taken quite an interest in it, as it seems to have caught each of our attention independently."

"The mystic draw of the ancient," Dr. Davies says. "Happens all the time."

"So you do think it's ancient?" Cornelius sits up on his haunches, folding his hands before him as if in prayer. Dr. Davies looks to Howard Carter.

"I would certainly say so," Carter says, handing the statue to Dr. Davies for further inspection.

"It was common for ancient cultures—the Sumerians and Egyptians and the like—to invent such odd creatures, of course," Carter continues. "Mixtures of various animals, like the lion and the bird here on this one. Often they were meant to depict gods, or beasts favored by the gods in some way, ones who may have been tasked with something great. But this, I've never seen anything quite like this, I must say. It has nothing of the sort of lanky but powerful figures you might see among the Egyptian artifacts, for instance. Nor does it quite resemble in style what other ancient societies in the region would craft. It looks surprisingly contemporary and ancient at once. Realistic in its approach."

"Perhaps it's from the same peoples who made that necklace of yours, Dr. Davies," I say. "There is a similarity in aesthetic, I think. Both contemporary and ancient, as you said."

Ripley's father reaches into his breast pocket and pulls out the amulet, and I must admit I nearly gasp as my eyes catch it in the light of the torches. The raw ruby at the center appears simultaneously red as blood and transparent. The interlocking circles, almost three dimensional in form. Like the statue, there's a sense of movement about it, as if it never seems to be truly still. A fierce flurry of butterflies flap about in my belly and I feel Ripley's arm brush my side, but don't dare to look at him.

Carter takes the necklace from Dr. Davies and examines it carefully under the light of a large hanging lantern. "Hold on," he says with a certain eagerness. Reaching down, he unlatches the trunk next to his desk and begins carefully digging about in there. Removing several well-wrapped items, he places them delicately on the floor. He then lifts a sturdy something wrapped in a heavy swathe of cotton fabric. By the strain on his face, it looks heavier than its size would imply. Reverently, he unwraps it, revealing part of a tablet of some sort.

"Looks like a piece of the Ten Commandments," Ripley says.

"It's definitely official," Carter tells him, his eyes going over the fine engravings on the small slab as if he's looking for something specific.

"Most writing of ancient times was inscribed like this,"

Carter mumbles. "At least anything of real importance. Certainly there was plenty of writing going on in civilizations of old—among the elites, mostly, since literacy was a rare art—only much of it will have been lost."

"Hmm," Dr. Davies hums in agreement. "In the earliest times such things were painted on walls, floors, pieces of wood perhaps. Whatever was handy. Papyrus, maybe. That came about around 3,000 B.C."

Carter nods and hums back absently, until his eyes bulge and he looks as if he's going to jump into the air.

"Ah, I knew it," Carter says. "Right there!"

He lays the tablet on his thigh and unhooks the lantern, holding it up and pointing to one of many tiny symbols engraved into the stone slab. Right there, at the end of a line, is what appears to be the exact symbol of interlocking circles found on Dr. Davies's amulet!

"You found this here?" Ripley's father marvels.

"No, not even close," Howard tells him, waving away a tiny swarm of flies which seem to have developed an affection for his lantern. "This was found in Tripolitania by some day workers."

He turns back to us. "A rather unglamorous fact of an archaeologist's trade is that he gets many of his finds by accident. From local trinket sellers like our friend Cornelius did, or from other archaeologists."

He holds up the amulet as evidence and hands it back to Dr. Davies.

"Looks quite different than Egyptian writing," I say, scanning the tablet. "Or Sumerian. I mean, it looks a little bit like each one, don't you think? Do you suppose it could be even older?"

"Older," Carter says in contemplation. "There's no evidence there was any sophisticated culture before the Sumerians, let alone one with writing."

"Then how do we explain this?" Cornelius asks. He glides his finger over a few of the markings on the tablet, circling the head of what looks like an owl.

"That's a good question, young man," Carter says. "And one any archaeologist worth a damn should always remember to ask."

We walk about the Valley of the Kings for a couple more hours, before Howard Carter arranges a buggy that takes us back to Thebes. There, we wander the Temple of Amun, and through the Great Hypostyle Hall, with its columns—over a hundred of them—telling the story of creation. At least according to the ancient Egyptians. I branch off from the others, in need of solitude, I suppose, and circle the sacred lake where the Egyptian priests used to bathe to purify themselves. Crouching at its side, I dip my fingers into the waters, gliding them along the surface. When the waters still, Ripley Davies's reflection comes into relief. He's standing behind me, with a most concerning look on his face.

"Leila," he says. "I think someone's following us."

Hopely, Virginia
Present Day

I WAKE UP WITH A HOWL AGAIN, from a dream that feels like a memory. That's the worst part. I was running away from someone this time. Someone I never ever wanted to see again, but I don't know who that someone could be. Whoever it is, though, it's someone I know. That's what makes me shiver. From outside I hear a snore as loud as a lawnmower. It brings me back to here, to home.

So I pull aside the Dora the Explorer curtains my mom made for me when I was still watching that show—like years ago—and look out at the trailer next door to ours, just to make sure everything is as it should be. Two Russians live there—a man and a lady—all tatted-up almost head to toe. The windows are still dark and they're probably asleep. They drink a lot and are dead to the world most mornings, especially this early. Mom says they're involved in "one helluva batshit crazy love affair." She always follows that up with "like I should talk."

I guess what she's talking about is my dad, who I haven't seen in the four years since my seventh birthday. That was when he and my mom got in a huge fight and both fell off the wagon for a few days, nearly burning Granny Dora's house down. Granny told them some changes were going to be made and were they ever! Dad went away to God knows where, mom got sober again, and we moved from Granny's almost burned up house to here.

It's funny, whenever I think of my dad, what strikes me most is how much I don't miss him. Even if he never beat me or anything. Never said a mean word to me either.

I close my curtains up so no one can look in, and then grab my diary off a stool that I use as my bedside table. I open it up and start to write in those pictures again. The ones I see in my dreams all the time. Simple and graceful lines that come together to look like birds, zig zags, fish, and all sorts of shapes. I finish with a pair of circles that overlap in the middle. Without thinking about it, or why, I lean down and kiss them.

"*Ah'kwarah'a*," I whisper. It's a word my imagination must have made up and shows up in my dreams a lot. Granny Dora says I have the biggest imagination of anyone she's ever met.

There's a knock at my door and it could only be one person.

"Hi, Ever," mom says, sticking her head in. "You having nightmares again, baby?"

I shake my head. "Just strange dreams," I say. It's not entirely a lie. Some of my dreams are scary, yes, but some are wonderful. And I love the picture language they show me.

My mom comes full-on into my room and sits down on my bed next to me. She's wearing a pink uniform that matches my Dora curtains and she looks pretty. I tell her she'll get lots of tips today.

"What's this?" she asks me, picking up my diary. "More of those funny cartoons you like to draw?"

"They're not cartoons, they're writing."

Mom giggles in that way the men around here seem to like.

"What kind of crazy person writes like this?" Mom likes the word crazy and uses it a lot.

"An ancient person," I tell her. "Like the Egyptians in that book Dr. Neville sent me."

"So, these crazy things are Egyptian, huh?"

"No," I say.

She hmmfs.

"Well, speaking of crazy things, the Nevilles want you to come see them in Charlottesville again for a few weeks once vacation starts. Seems like that's becoming a yearly thing, I guess."

I already know and I'm so excited. Mickey and I have been emailing back and forth about it, making all sorts of plans. That is, until my teacher caught me using a computer at school for "non-school related communications."

"They're home for the summer again this year," Mom says.

She shakes her head, rolling those big, blue eyes of hers. Pale blue, like the sky, whereas mine are the brightest green you'll ever see.

"When you're together, you and that boy of theirs, you don't seem to want to be around anyone else. Been that way since the day you were born. I think if it weren't for the fact that those Nevilles spend so much time living in foreign places, I couldn't get you to stay here with me at all."

"They live in a place called Cairo, Mom." I glance down at the worn and marked up map lying next to my bed. Mickey gave it to me before they left at the start of the school year. It was so I'd always know where he was and could picture the places he was telling me about.

"Except that Dr. Neville spends a lot of time far deep in the desert, digging around in that old city he found."

"It's called excavating, Mom. He's an archaeologist. Like five generations of his folk have been archaeologists, too. His great-great grandfather started it all—and in Cairo, more than a hundred years ago."

Mom "hmmfs" again, like this is the first time she's heard

about Cairo and archaeology, and is doubtful about the existence of both. She looks down at my dream writing and cocks her head.

"Well, if these are sentences, what do they say?"

"You want me to read it to you?"

Mom nods.

"I'm not sure what all of it says, just some. I forget some-times after I wake up."

"That's all right."

I look down at the page and run my finger along one of the images I drew—the head of an owl. My finger circles around it in a way that seems familiar. Like I've watched someone else do it just like that. Déjà vu is what Granny Dora calls it.

"There is a wind in the desert that speaks of children," I begin. "Ones here and ones we will make. One day, the desert again will be filled with our numbers. We will be as many as the tiny crystals that lie in these sands."

"How nice," she says, smiling.

"That's not all," I tell her. "It is then the executioner will rise up again from the pit in the desert's stomach. He will come to claim what he was denied."

When I look back up at Mom, she looks like she's swal-lowed a bug. "Real nice," she says, then clears her throat. "But I've got to go to work." She pats my leg and moves a chestnut curl from my forehead, before kissing me there. "Don't open the door for anyone until Silvia gets here. She's got a soccer game at ten, but should be back here by noon. You can entertain yourself inside until then."

Mom stands up and moves aside my Dora curtains just like I did. She takes one of those deep breaths of hers. "We've got to get out of here," she whispers. Then she walks out of my bedroom, stomping through the kitchen and out the front door.

By "here" she doesn't just mean our trailer.

Between Craysville and Graymare, Virginia, are two small towns named Heavenly and Hopely. They are neither, according to Mom and Granny Dora, but Hopely is where we live and it's not all bad. I mean, it's not fancy, that's for sure. A lot of creaky old houses with red dirt driveways. Little kids running around in diapers and nothing else. At our place, it's just me and my mom, but I'm well out of diapers. And our driveway is filled in with loose gravel and looks nice enough. The trailers out here are better than the houses, everyone likes to say so. It's not always true, though. Silvia's trailer is infested with cockroaches. "Too many kids and too much good food," Silvia always says. Her mom does make the best enchiladas in the world.

Now, where Mickey lives in Charlottesville—he's got a paved driveway and a brick house that's not creaky old, but beautiful old, with polished furniture and pictures on the walls. When I visit him, I like to pretend that I live there, too. The Nevilles always make me feel welcome, like I belong, and I'm not some charity case they picked up.

And that's the thing. I feel like I do belong there. It's not just because of Mickey, although he is my best friend and has been since the day we were born, just like my mom said. On the same day and in the same hospital no less! After that, we lost touch and didn't see each other again until we met at Jamestown on our second grade field trip. Granny Dora took me, and there was Mickey with his dad standing right in the middle of the original first English fort in the New World, watching a lady dressed in old time clothes pretend to churn butter.

Dr. Neville recognized Granny Dora right away and Mickey and I both swear we knew the other from somewhere, too, although everyone said we hadn't seen each other since the hospital, and there's no way we could remember that.

But I know I recognized Mickey. It was like I'd been waiting for him all that time, and I knew—just knew—I'd see him again. And he recognized me, too.

Chapter 9

Fears of a Trampled Heart
Cairo, 1902

W E HAD ONE MORE DAY of enchantment and shadows in Thebes. Of feeling the eyes of a phantom upon us. That flicker of movement in the corner of an eye, the sound of footsteps. No one there when you turn around. Yes, I felt it too, although not as keenly as Ripley. This sensation of being stalked seemed to disappear entirely as we returned to the Valley of the Kings to bid *adieu* to Howard Carter. We boarded the night train to Cairo without further incident.

"I wonder if it wasn't just a thief," I tell Ripley, as we arrive at the Shepheard Hotel the evening after our return. "You do, after all, cut the figure of a very fine tourist."

Ripley smiles. "Perhaps."

But I can tell that he doesn't believe it for one second.

We're helped out of Uncle Hugo's carriage by a white-gloved Egyptian, who Horus disapproves of judging by the sucked-a-lemon look on his face. It's me, Aunt Clara, Uncle Hugo, Father, Ripley, and Dr. Davies tonight. We bid Horus a good evening, for now, and I take Father's hand, squeezing his fingers affectionately.

"I'm inclined to think it was one of those black market scoundrels, who want to find out when the next large ship-ment to the museum takes place," Aunt Clara says.

Dr. Davies finds this a reasonable hypothesis. "You

wouldn't believe the lengths to which they'd go! Probably thought we were arranging to have something brought from Luxor!"

Dr. Davies, himself, detected no surreptitious behavior while we were walking about Thebes, but takes his son's suspicions quite seriously. He must, given the responsibility he holds for so many precious antiquities.

We climb up the stairs to the entrance of the hotel, where a set of strikingly tall twins in tarbushes open the doors with a bow. The lobby, filled with ancient-Egyptian-inspired statuary and English-inspired wicker furniture welcomes us in. Between the two great granite pillars that resemble those of the temples in Thebes, we are greeted by an elegant concierge with a permanent look of pleasant surprise etched upon his face. The men are promptly taken to the "long bar," which is only for chaps. Ripley looks back at me once, and I wave, twiddling my fingers at him.

"Its barmen are the souls of discretion, I hear," Aunt Clara says with a titter.

We women are escorted out to the terrace, where we're fanned by smiling servant boys and offered a selection of refreshing beverages.

It's my first time coming to the Shepheard as a bona fide young woman; one allowed all—or most—adult privileges. As a girl, I'd simply run around here playing hide and seek with my friends, an international assortment who are now in Zurich and Paris and London, or danced about like a fairy on the enormous Persian rugs. Gloriously oblivious to the fact that anyone who's anyone comes to the Shepheard. Today, I look about and see lots of rich Americans, along with the usual top tier of British and French officers. Whereas once, The Shepheard only offered the wonders of imaginary play, I now see it as a place of dances and evening gowns, where deals are forged and histories are made.

The terrace, once an agony for me, where I was compelled to sit still while I dutifully drank my strawberry-lemonade, is quite different, too. Now that I've been invited into the ranks, I'm privy to conversations, not to mention able to get a sip or two from Aunt Clara's gin and tonic. And she's in fine form tonight—excited about a coming trip for which she has finally been able to find a suitable guide. She downs her first G&T, then orders another.

"It will be quite an effort to make our way to the central Sahara, my dear, but well worth it!"

"Seems awfully remote," I say, feeling a strange sense of dread all of a sudden.

"Ah, but it's the volcanic summit in the Tibesti Mountain range! Of course it's remote, and that's the point! Hardly been explored at all, except by a few local tribes. And soon . . . by Hugo and myself!"

"You're right, naturally," I say. "I've seen drawings of them and they do look very ominous!"

"Like one of those scary stories you love could take place there." Aunt Clara pretends a shiver. She will no doubt come back with some delicious tales of her own.

"But I'll miss you terribly," I tell her. "Who else will feed me sherry until you return?"

"Oh, I think one Ripley Davies would feed you anything you like."

"Aunt Clara!"

"The men may be deaf and blind to the spells of young love, but I am most certainly not."

"Hardly love," I say, unable to meet her eyes. "Besides, Mr. Ripley Davies seems to have a reputation for spreading his young love around to a variety of girls."

"Is that so?"

I nod with a bit more certainty, reminding myself that boys like Ripley are quite expert at making a girl feel like she's the only object of their affection. The past few days have obscured that point, I admit, as Ripley and I have gotten closer, drawn in by a rather deep and dark common interest, but being back in our own milieu has given me a cold glass of water to sip on. And I intend to take several gulps.

"What girl anywhere within a thousand and one miles of here could possibly be as lovely and quick-witted as you?" Aunt Clara says, palming my cheek. "Besides, a place like Zamalek breeds gossip. Trust me, I've been the subject of truly preposterous stories on several occasions. That I danced naked in the moonlight around the Sphinx at Giza! Or that I had nearly my whole person painted in henna by a priestess in the blue city of India!"

I place my hand on my hip and give her a look she knows well from my mother. "Aunt Clara, you did dance naked in the moonlight around the Sphinx and have your body painted in henna at Jodhpur."

Aunt Clara bites her lip and a perfectly wicked grin sneaks onto her face. "Well, that, yes. But I danced for my husband, after all. And as for the body painting . . . I did that for me!"

I don't mention, of course, that I'm the one who happened to see Ripley in a compromising situation. While I know that some young men have a need to sow their wild oats, and I'm sure many of those turn out to be fine gentlemen eventually, I'm not the type of girl who allows herself to lose her heart to one.

"Ripley's a wonderful young man," Aunt Clara says softly. She pats my hand the way my mother would have done. "I know these things."

WE'RE JOINED by the men and go to dinner in The Grill Room, taking our seats under an extravagant Moorish chandelier. It glows almost as amber as the streaks in Ripley's eyes, light glittering over us from a lace trim of patterns cut in its bulbous copper body. Aunt Clara makes sure Ripley is seated next to me, and the young Mr. Davies looks me over and smiles with a deep swallow.

"What?"

Ripley shakes his head.

"No, really," I tease. "You've given me your opinion on all manner of things since we've met—from my choice of dress to what I should or should not be affronted by, so do tell."

He folds his hands in his lap and blinks his eyes. "You look lovely, is all."

And now I'm the one swallowing, with an awkward half-smile pasted upon my face. I manage to thank him and then promptly stare straight ahead, my eyes fixing on a cameo pin Aunt Clara has stuck to a bow on her ample bosom. It's not the first time I've been given a compliment, for heaven's sake.

"I didn't mean to make you feel uncomfortable," Ripley murmurs.

"Don't be ridiculous."

"Then won't you look at me?"

And I do. Part of me wishes I hadn't, because whenever I do look at him—really look at him, into his eyes, it's very difficult for me to look away.

"Better?"

"Much."

"A commission on yellow fever in America has announced that the disease is carried by mosquitos!" a well-oiled Uncle Hugo announces. "Anyone who's spent five minutes in India knows those wretched little monsters carry all sorts of deadly maladies. No need for a commission on that for the love of God."

This begins an uproarious conversation about the American President Theodore Roosevelt, who is generally thought to be a showboat and a vulgarian—as most Americans are. Only he more so.

I don't think one way or another about Teddy Roosevelt, but I am glad for a vigorous discussion. Ripley thinks the American President is just marvelous, and is admiring of his can-do attitude. "He's a conservationist," he exclaims. "That alone should make him a hero at this table."

Although it doesn't.

I watch with some degree of admiration as Ripley makes his point further, expanding upon President Roosevelt's time with the Rough Riders in the Spanish-American war, thus cementing his status as war hero and putting a final nail in the coffin of the grumbles that he's all swagger. Ripley is exuberant and won't be deterred, gesturing with a grace that I envy. While I talk with my hands quite a bit—especially when I get excited—my motions tend to get unruly, even wild sometimes, while Ripley's hands move with an elegance that mirrors his dancing.

But as I watch him, I find my attention being drawn beyond him, to a table for two. There sits Edna Watson, watching him as well. She's seated across from a gentleman who looks to be a bit stiff, from where I'm sitting, and she glances quickly away when our eyes meet. I keep tabs on her throughout dinner, discretely of course. Can't help it. A peep her way through the potage St. Germain course. A quick turn of the head when the Langue de Boeuf à l'Italienne is served. I walk right by her when I get up to use the lavatory just after dessert, and notice she does look up at me as I go by, though I can't quite read the emotions behind her expression.

As the table is cleared, and glasses of a rich, honey-colored Armagnac are served, the conversation turns to a Greek string quartet that was apparently a favorite of Father's and the Hugheses way back when. This very quartet is performing a concert at the hotel tonight, and Dr. Davies seems quite keen on the event as well. "Jolly" he calls it.

"Oh, my dear," Father says. "I do recall you've had your fill of string quartets."

"There are quite a lot of them in London. I was rather looking forward to getting away from them."

Aunt Clara, now fully in her cups, seems to find our exchange hilarious. She dabs at the corners of her eyes with her napkin.

"Well, go on then," Father says with a hefty exhale.

I admit I'm relieved that Father's released me from my obligation to join the most adult adults in what sounds like a slightly less than dreadful performance, at least for a modern woman of my age. I can now look forward to a pleasant ride back to Zamalek alone.

"Ripley, you will be kind enough to escort Leila home," Aunt Clara says with an undisguised smirk!

"Happy to," he says. "I mean no offense when I say I wasn't particularly looking forward another string quartet either."

He turns to me with a most expectant look on his face, and I hope to all heaven that my own look doesn't betray what I'm really feeling. That what my heart of hearts wants even more than to have a solitary ride home is to remain in the company of Ripley Davies.

IT'S STRANGE. We speak not one word on the ride back to Zamalek, a carriage ride through Cairo at night is a seduction all its own. The winking of the stars above us, gas lanterns lit and extinguished like the bellies of fireflies, the whispering of the Nile. My pride flows out of me like blood being let. Even my fears—those of a trampled heart, of foolishness—seem to have taken a seat in a corner somewhere and dozed off. There's just the quiet, the jostling of the carriage, Ripley, and me.

On a dimly lit street, our carriage comes to a halt. A horse as golden as jewelry rises up on his back legs under the single light of a lantern. He seems to be dancing for us, braying, shaking his head each time he lands.

Ripley tears his eyes away from the spectacle and catches mine. I see myself reflected in them, with the shadow of the magnificent steed casting over my face like a phantom, making me look half-woman, half-beast. It is only a moment or two that we hold each other's gaze . . . and then, we find ourselves . . . holding each other. Ripley kisses me anywhere my dress is not. On my neck, my ears, my wrists and palms, and finally, my lips. I have not been kissed before tonight, obviously, and yet I know his every touch and where it will land next. And I wait for it, breathless. I long for more of him the way the wind longs for a full and leafy tree in the spring, the way the ocean seems to hunger for a storm.

My hands wander his face as we kiss, my fingers grip his hair. Ripley breaks from me gently, takes my palm again and kisses that, too. His shirt is unbuttoned all the way to his vest and I do not know how he could have become so disheveled. I wonder, briefly, if I was the one who opened his shirt so, or if he did it to himself. The question leaves me entirely as Ripley takes my hand and places it on the bare skin over his heart. I feel it beating, just as I did in my dream. It's as if all of time has stopped.

"There, there, boy," a man says in Arabic to his golden horse. He clucks his tongue and whistles.

From the driver's seat, I hear Horus compliment the man on his beast, telling him he's never seen his equal. The men exchange a series of pleasantries. But all that matters is the feeling of Ripley's heart beating in time to my own. The pulse in my fingertips like a low harmony.

The carriage starts to move again, but for a long time, we do not.

It's only when we arrive at Uncle Hugo and Aunt Clara's, and Horus comes to help us down from the passenger car that we return somewhat to ourselves. Ripley has re-buttoned his shirt, but while Horus is no fool, he doesn't even appear to give us a sideways glance. He stands aside and lets Ripley walk me to the door.

"Goodnight," I somehow manage. I hardly sound like myself.

"It was," Ripley says. He takes my hand and kisses it, releasing it back to me as if setting free a balloon.

It's now that Horus does take his cue to intervene. He clears his throat in a loud, long note that almost sounds like a growl. Ripley gives me his one-sided grin and bows. I return with a shy curtsey, barely able to put up a smile. My breath is still on the wild and rough side, I notice. I just hope Horus doesn't.

"Between two worlds life hovers like a star," Ripley says softly.

I finish Lord Byron's words. "Twixt night and morn, upon the horizon's verge."

Hands in his pockets, Ripley Davies begins his short walk home.

My walk is even shorter, as I only have to go through the door. In a daze, I enter Hugo and Clara's house. I'm not even sure I bid goodnight to Horus. I wrap my arms around myself like it's Ripley still holding me. All over, I start to shiver.

"Oh, Mother," I say, looking up at the portrait of her. If she were here, I could tell her everything—even about my dreams. And she'd have so much to say! On Ripley, me, tomorrow, the statue. She'd dab her thumbs at the tears which are threatening to fall, but haven't yet. I won't let them. She'd say a prayer with me to help set my head straight.

Expelling a few good, sharp breaths, I clench my fists quite hard and run up the stairs to my room. I cannot be with my mother right now, but I can inhabit her. Unbuttoning my evening gown, I strip myself of each layer, hanging them over my dressing screen. I lean over the large copper bowl with a sizeable ankh engraved in its bottom—Aunt Clara's touch— and pick up a pitcher of cool water, pouring it over my neck and hair. Makes me gasp. After toweling off with some vigor, I dress in the clothes of a servant boy again, wrapping my damp hair up in a long, white linen cloth.

At my bed, I stuff the covers with a few extra throw pillows to make them look—at first glance—like the sleeping form of a young woman. I know father or Aunt Clara will want to have a peek at me when they come home.

No need to shimmy down the trellis this time as nobody's here. I march down the stairs and out the back door, stopping only to take a good, deep breath. The night air has become almost cold.

The back gardens of the houses are dark and still, and I make my way through them, climbing over stone fences when necessary—they're not very high. Only a few gardens down, I'm caught in an exquisite bouquet of some early-blooming Jasmine. I cannot help but sink to my knees next to the flower. I run my fingers through the supple skin of her petals, feeling her thrill to my touch. Back in England, Aunt Imogen always told me that her flowers seemed to look to me like they would to a mother. I suppose she was right, and in this moment, I miss England for the first time. Not England, exactly, but Aunt Imogen's garden. My garden, it became. The way the flowers seemed to turn to me whenever I arrived. As happy as I have been to be back in Cairo, I'll never feel truly at home until I can have a place to make things grow for my own sake. I remind myself that our house should be ready for us in the next few days, and make a vow to begin shopping for the right seeds and bulbs tomorrow.

A murmur of voices catches my attention, and I crawl to the base of a short, stone fence. It wouldn't do for me to be caught creeping about on the island in the middle of the night, so I place my fingers on the top of the wall and inch my face up, so I can get a look at who and where the voices are coming from. In the next garden over is a small gazebo, white as a tooth. The sort of place where lovers would come for a clandestine rendezvous.

And yes, there is a pair of lovers there. A young woman with long, sandy hair—I can only see the back of her head. She's holding the hands of a young man, who stands under the cover of shade made by a bright half-moon. She's whispering to him, nodding her head, then she gives a rather vocal giggle and he shushes her. At that moment I feel a decided chill of recognition, and a name comes to my lips.

"Edna," I say.

Edna Watson pulls her young man out of the shade, and the tips of my fingers dig so hard into the grout that one of my nails splits down to the quick. Yes, it's Ripley. Of course it's Ripley. Who else would it be?

Ripley, who pulled me through the maze of streets in Cairo and fed me prickly pear. Who kissed me like a lover and held my hand to his beating heart. Who looked at me like I was made of his dreams.

Ripley, who quoted Shelly and Longfellow and Byron and my mother.

That same heart of mine, the one that beat in time with his not thirty minutes ago, booms sluggishly in my chest. It actually does hurt—a lot. My hands feel all cold and my temples begin to throb.

The tears that wouldn't come before. The ones my mother's

soft thumbs would have stopped. Those now pour down my cheeks, burning. I feel like a fool dressed in a servant boy's clothes now. A fool fooled, who was intent on fooling others. Stupid me.

Drying my tears with my tunic, I stand up from behind the short, stone wall. I watch Ripley and Edna Watson walk out of the gazebo and then out of my view. They don't see me.

Cairo at night is no longer a lure for me, and the Hugheses' house, a place soon to be filled with people who actually care about me, is the only place I want to be. At first my steps are tentative, weary, like the first few cranks in the turn of a locomotive wheel, but in no time at all, I break into a run. I jump two stone fences and gallop out of the back gardens and out onto the street, where I don't really care who sees me. It just feels so good to move. I race past several gas lanterns, hitting each one with my hand, reveling in the sting. I dash past the Lida and into the public gardens, my heels hitting the walking path with a hard, hypnotic rhythm. I close my eyes for only a second, blinking away fresh tears, but in that brief interlude of blindness collide with someone on the path, and find myself tumbling into the grass.

I sit up, breathing hard. My turban has fallen off my head, and my hair spills all over me. I watch the man I ran into scramble to his feet, his silhouette suggesting youth and vigor. He glances back at me, perhaps to make sure I'm alright, and then freezes entirely.

"Leila?"

"Co-Cornelius, what are you doing here?"

Cornelius P. Neville walks to me, and holds out his hand, helping me from the ground. "I, um . . . please," he says. "Don't ever speak of this. I'm not supposed to be here."

"I won't, but why are you here? Is it to see Dr. Davies?"

I haven't seen Cornelius since we parted ways at Misr

Station, just after our arrival back from Thebes. But I know Dr. Davies will be expecting him to report to work as his assistant come tomorrow morning.

"No, not Dr. Davies," he says, seeming rather embarrassed. "I came to see you."

Chapter 10

A Serious Young Man

THOSE CRIMSON AND AMBER veins in his eyes seem to glitter and rustle like a river. The brown of them—brown like soil, like chocolate, like a fawn—churns slowly. In his eyes, I see my own. So green as to be otherworldly, as my mother used to say. My most recent mother, as good as my first. Our eyes, Nif's and mine, reflect infinitely in one another's, like we're between parallel mirrors.

"Always," he tells me.

"An always is always the most important thing of all."

My eyes flutter open and I lie in my bed bathed in contentment. The clock on my mantel ticks the seconds away, and the sounds of the street circus below come into relief. A man blows a piercing whistle, then berates his camel; a woman, his wife I assume, calls him an idiot and tells him to hurry up; a bell rings, and a rickshaw shuffles by. All of them announcing early morning in Cairo.

For a moment I think I'm still back at the Hugheses, but that's not so. Now I remember. I'm in my mother's old bedroom; my bedroom now. In our new old house that Father has re-done. I snuggle a gold-threaded quilt embroidered with lotus flowers and white-feathered ibises, breathing it in. Smells faintly of orange and the vinegar water it's washed in. Like everything always did in my mother's family home. Like it does now, again. At least that's a comfort.

I hate myself when I'm like this—wrestling with the melancholy that settles upon me every morning when I first wake up. When I'm pulled from my world of dreams and back into my life.

"For the love of all that's Holy," I say to myself just as my mother would. "He isn't worth your grief."

Don't know why I keep dreaming about him, then.

Struggling out of bed, I place both feet on the floor, with a thump-thump.

"That's it—be a bricky girl."

I do my toilette and get dressed in a jiffy, escaping my bedroom and climbing the stairs to the roof, which always cheers me up.

At the edge of our rooftop, I put my hands to my hips and look out onto the channel between Old Cairo and Roda Island, breathing in the mucky, humid air of the Nile. This, I do love. I place my foot upon a short iron railing painted a glossy black and feel like a queen. The railing runs along the perimeter of the rooftop, giving it something of a regal air; a crown atop our three-story home. At the south end is a long bench of juniper with a coffee table in front of it. That is topped with a silver tray which holds a bowl of Ful, pita bread, and tea, of course. A typical Egyptian breakfast. Horus's wife, Ahura, gives us a delicious array every morning, although it looks as though Father never quite made it up here before he left for work. Must be grabbing his breakfast with Lieutenant General Blackwood again.

I ease myself down onto the bench and pour some tea. As always, everything seems better, happier, from this rooftop. I suppose it's always been this way, even before Father's improvements.

The only good memory I have of my grandfather, the notorious Ashraf Saber, happened on this rooftop. On one of the few times when he was neither drunk nor ornery in my company, he took me up to the roof of this house and we looked out onto Old Cairo together.

"Our family helped build the Church of St. Sergius in the fourth century," he told me. "Right on the spot where the Holy Family rested at the end of their journey into Egypt."

Although he was not a religious man, he did have a great interest in history and would've made a fine scholar, at least according to Mother. That is, if he hadn't been consumed by his vices.

We talked a great deal about history, my grandfather and I on that day, if I recall. While he wasn't the best storyteller, he did have a memory for details, even after years of drink. I remember thinking that maybe he wasn't so bad after all.

Of course, by the end of that pleasant afternoon, his mistress had come to call, and he sent me away with my governess. Upon our return, much later in the evening, we found him naked and unconscious at the foot of the stairs in the great room. He was snoring loudly, using one of my dollies as a pillow.

Seems almost funny now.

This house has a distinctly different flavor now that he's gone. While most of the furniture and art work is the same—father made sure to honor both the generational and historical features of the home—the mere fact of my grandfather's absence has made it a place of comfort. The modern amenities Father added, electricity being the most crucial to our convenience, have certainly helped in that regard. But my grandfather's death, despite the gruesomeness of his end—being burned alive in his bedroom—has given this place a new life. Perhaps the way a fire breathes new life into a forest. I only wish my mother could see it. Especially this rooftop, which had to be completely rebuilt.

Father made it to accommodate a rather substantial garden, and already some sturdy-looking green sprouts have broken through their soil, promising to bring us orchids and roses, a plethora of herbs, celery, asparagus, a variety of peppers, and even a Venus flytrap, just for fun. Two large pots hold a lemon and a pear tree, respectively, and I hope to cultivate some figs as well.

"Soon, we'll have a jungle on top of our very own home!" Father says nearly every time he comes up here.

I hear footsteps coming up from the house, but I don't have to turn to see who it is.

"Good morning," Cornelius says. He holds in his hands the substantial book on hieroglyphics that I gave him, and appears ready to begin today's lesson.

I prepare for Cornelius a small dish of Ful, and I must admit the stew smells heavenly, even if I don't prefer to eat quite so early. The aromas of cumin and garlic and lemon are top-of-the-day smells that, in my opinion, are only rivalled by the smell of frying bacon.

"Security at the museum has gotten much tighter," Cornelius tells me between bites. "Three collections have been successfully transferred from the palace since I started, and Dr. Davies is sure that a prowler has been watching the place, squatting behind the bushes near a service entrance and smoking hashish, judging by the litter he's left behind. The guards know me, of course, but even Mr. Carter was detained and had his pockets searched."

"Howard Carter? He's back in Cairo?"

Cornelius nods.

"Been back and forth from Thebes quite a bit, and currently staying at The Shepheard. Ripley and Dr. Davies had dinner with him just last night."

The hair on the back of my neck does stand up at the mention of Ripley Davies, and it's as if I can all of a sudden feel the soft touch of my cotton dress upon every inch of my skin.

"I imagine the Davies men are themselves quite busy, what with all the back and forth from the Royal Palace at Giza," I mention, casually.

"I suppose you would know that for yourself if you were speaking to Ripley," Cornelius says. "And neither of you would have to go through the indignity of having to fish for information about the other."

I don't mean to huff, but I do. I haven't spoken to Ripley in over a month, having managed to avoid him when I'm at the museum for my lessons, as he's been busy cataloging a rather large collection of pharaonic jewelry that remains at the royal palace.

And yes, Cornelius is right. I was fishing, and not only am I embarrassed, but hate myself for putting a friend in such a position. He works for Dr. Davies, after all, and he and Ripley are chums. Not to mention the fact that sometimes I get the feeling that Cornelius feels a little more for me, perhaps, than the simple affection one has for a new comrade. I admit that my own feelings are not exactly clear either. I, too, feel a deepening of emotions for him. One I can't quite put my finger on. Problem is, I can put my finger on what Ripley Davies stirs within me quite easily. I hate myself for that, too.

"Perhaps you should talk to him," Cornelius says, softly.

"No!"

"Leila, I don't know what he's done to trouble you so, but I've seen nothing in my experience of him to indicate an absence of character. It seems to me the two of you should clear the air—to be able to move on, if nothing else."

"Do you want me to move on from him?" I ask. Maybe I shouldn't have.

Cornelius looks deeply into my eyes, his like two perfect discs of volcanic glass. "Yes."

He leans back, appraising me. "But I won't come in second place."

I feel a foolhardy urge to take his hand, and place my hands in my lap in defense of such a yearning, folding them firmly together.

"I could never stomach making you second place," I tell him. "I just wish I understood myself better. I used to think I did."

"You will again, I'm sure."

Cornelius holds out his hand, and I swallow quite hard. I buckle and place my fingers in his, accepting his tender offer. He takes them very gently and bends over, kissing my knuckle without ever taking his eyes from mine. It does make me blush. That must mean something. "We haven't known each other very long," I tell him. "But I feel somehow that we were meant to meet. I hope that means something to you."

Cornelius smiles, which he doesn't do nearly often enough. Not because he isn't full of humor, although he did come off that way at first. No, Cornelius Neville is a thoughtful young man, and a man to be reckoned with, I'm learning.

"It does mean something to me," he says. "And yes, I am very sure we were fated to meet."

There's something of a racket on the stairs leading up from our third floor and I know it's Father and not Horus by the slow, determined rhythm of the way he takes that narrow staircase, and also by the way he stops and swears midway through, thinking I can't hear him.

"You forget something?" I call out.

Father emerges from the open trap door, replacing his hat, and rolling his big, grey eyes like he does when something's afoot.

"Don't get me started," he says, swatting the air. "It's the usual skilamalink that's got Sir John mad as hops!"

Cornelius raises an eyebrow at me.

"Sir John Aird's company is the main contractor of the Aswan Dam," I explain to him.

"Red ashlar granite," Father grumbles.

"Supply problems again?"

Father doesn't need to speak his reply—his face says it all.

"I'm sorry my dear, but I must go down to Aswan for a few weeks."

I fold my arms across my chest in solidarity with his frustrations, but really, I'm not all that upset at this news. I could use some time away from Cairo, and by extension the specter of one Ripley Davies. "I'll start packing us up."

Father deflates like a bicycle tire. "I'm afraid I've already arranged for you to stay with the Davieses in my absence."

Honestly, I just about lose my footing and fall to the floor. "The Davieses!"

"The dam is a bore for a young woman, and I won't have even a moment of time for you. If I don't get things back on track and right soon, there won't be a grand opening of the dam come December!" He raises a finger in the air like a flagpole and cannot stop shaking his head. "And I will need you to check on the house, after all. The lights still aren't working on half of the second floor and you'll have to liaise with the electrician for me."

I stomp my way towards Father with my arms tightly in place under my bosom—although not in solidarity now. In utter fury.

"But why the Davieses?" I say. "Can't I stay with Aunt Clara and Uncle Hugo for heaven's sake?"

Father tugs at his mustache. "Well, you would do under normal circumstances, but they aren't back from the Central Sahara yet."

"But they were supposed to be back last week!" I say.

"Indeed, but they've been delayed."

Deep breath. Try not to look so sour.

"Well, this is just awful," I say, and catch Cornelius eyeing me with a note of judgment splashed with mischief.

"I'll still come visit you," he says. "We can have our morning tea with the Davieses on their veranda."

I've known Cornelius relishes a challenge from our first meeting, but this is the first time I've noticed he's also the type who enjoys putting two scorpions in a glass together. "Won't that be marvelous," I say.

"Most of our friends live on Zamalek," Father says. "You certainly won't lack company, so I don't know why you're so confounded."

"I'm not confounded," I tell him. "I just don't wish to leave our house. We just moved in!"

"Well, you can't stay here alone, either, and it's only for a short while."

I begin stacking the dishes, just to have something to do.

"What on Earth will I do on Zamalek, anyway—especially while staying with strangers."

Father huffs, and I deserve that.

"They're hardly strangers," he says. "Dr. Davies is one of your tutors, and you traveled with them to Thebes, for goodness sake."

I let go the stack of our plates and am grateful they don't break into pieces.

"That was only for a couple of days," I grumble.

"Days, weeks, what's the difference in the grand scheme of things? Besides, Lieutenant General Blackwood indicated to me that he could use some help with a somewhat obscure tribal language—perhaps Toubou in origin. Naturally, I recommended you."

That, at least, might take up some of my days. "Toubou. Hmm. Don't know how much of a help I'll be. Tedaga or Dazagra? Keep in mind my knowledge of both languages is pitiful. For what have you offered my services, exactly?"

"The Lieutenant General may have stumbled upon some information regarding the lost regiment of '86. A Toubou man, Dazagra, I believe, had something of a story to tell and even mentioned the name of Hawkins, who was the commander in charge of the missing men. His story was transcribed—phonetically, of course, and Dr. Davies has been asked to find a translator."

"The lost regiment of '86?" Cornelius says. "Aren't they said to have disappeared without a trace?"

"Hmm," Father acknowledges. "Scouts from the regiment, actually. About twenty men were sent to spy on some of the desert tribes after there'd been skirmishes in the area. They simply vanished, including Commander Hawkins. Lost in the Central Sahara along with several of our Toubou friend's tribesmen."

"And this was near where Aunt Clara and Uncle Hugo went?"

"Well, my dear, the Central Sahara is a vast region, so I'm not really sure how one would define near."

Father eyes my Ful—hardly touched. And now I've completely lost whatever small appetite I had. "Here," I tell him, and he digs in.

"But you had the right idea," Father says between bites. "You do need to go downstairs and pack some things for us both for our respective decamping. Cornelius can escort you to Zamalek, then."

"I hardly need an escort." I glance over at Cornelius, whose eyes are boring straight into mine. "But will be delighted for the company."

Although very little about this delights me at all.

Chapter 11

IT IS UTTERLY STRANGE and awkward to be moving in and about the Davieses' house while Ripley and his father are at the museum. Of course, it'll be downright knotty once they return this evening and we're all forced to behave like everything's just lovely.

It's a good thing Cornelius has been given the day to help me settle in, otherwise I fear I wouldn't at all feel able to get comfortable and would likely spend the day baking out on the veranda. At least I'd have my horror stories. While I've finished with Mary Elizabeth Braddon's eerie tales, my late grandfather had Bram Stoker's "Dracula" in his library, and I've stowed it away in my luggage. Been dying to read it for years, and being at the Davieses' is the perfect time, since Father has strictly forbidden it.

"Certainly looks like the house of two bachelors, doesn't it?" I say.

Cornelius chuckles and shrugs. I suppose compared to his tomb house, the Davieses' place is the pinnacle of luxury. It's not that it isn't an interesting home, and certainly the house itself is spacious and fine. But the decor very much has the flavor of Dr. Davies's office at the museum. The furniture is simple, sturdy, and there's not much of it. Just a sofa and table, a chair, lots of bookshelves. Pieces of antiquity litter the mantel and every single shelf the way shells do at my cousin's house in Brighton. Everything from fat and bawdy goddesses to chips of ancient pottery. Each piece seems to burn with meaning, and is sure to be accompanied by a long story. The only anomaly is a small, oval picture frame that rests at the center of the mantel. It contains a photograph of a woman I assume to be Dr. Davies's late wife. She's a fair and pretty woman, holding a baby who is so obviously Ripley. Looking at her makes me terribly sad, but I can't seem to stop. Ripley's mother and Edna Watson could be sisters.

"Perhaps you should give this place a woman's touch?" Cornelius says.

"I will not," I tell him. "I'm merely a visitor, and I intend to behave like one."

CORNELIUS TAKES MY HAND and guides me to the sofa, a well-worn but handsome piece with a russet herringbone weave that's embroidered with peacock feathers. We sit.

"Leila," he says. "I suppose I should have told you before, but Ripley has asked me to inquire of you as to why you've shunned him."

"Has he? And how do you feel about being our intermediary?"

"Well, I'm curious, I admit."

"Can I ask you something?"

"Of course."

"I don't quite know how to phrase this, but you see, you have me rather curious as well."

Cornelius gives me that look of his, the appraising one, and I have the distinct feeling that he knows something of where I'm headed with this.

"I've never quite met anyone like you," I start. "I've met

people from Senegal, of course, all of whom were creatures of contradiction, I might add. But I think you're the most contrarian of contrarians."

Cornelius smiles as if it's the best compliment he's ever received. "How so?"

"Well, for one, you're obviously high born for—"

"For being an African?"

My eyes flutter to my lap in a brief and unholy wave of embarrassment. "Yes."

"Thank you for not insulting me with a denial."

"I didn't mean it to offend you. Will you let me finish?"

"I'm not offended," Cornelius says.

"You see, that's exactly what I mean. You carry yourself with a very peculiar sense of pride. You walk about the City of the Dead with as much ease as you've shown among the British occupiers here. It's a rather rare trait from what I've seen, being able to move freely among both paupers and peers of the realm, so to speak."

Cornelius inches closer to me, and if it were any other man doing so I would find him forward and tell him as much.

"Leila, you're a woman of strong beliefs."

I nod. "A Copt from my head to my toes."

"You believe in the one true God who sent His son."

"I do."

"I believe in God, too, more or less. And that I am but a single tiny player in a vast history that is infinite."

"So, it's not pride that drives you, but humility. Is that why you love archaeology so?"

Cornelius takes a deep breath, a bit like an old man remembering an unrequited romance, which is funny with him being so young.

"I love the simplicity of it. The connection it gives me to all things that were, that are, and I presume that will be. It is, for me, I imagine, what heaven is for you. A promise that life continues, that it will repeat ever more. That I have a purpose, a role to play in our human drama."

He puts out his hands and rubs them together. "On a more immediate plane, I love the way the dirt feels on my fingers and between them. The way it gathers under my nails; I relish the hunger and thirst that visits me when I've been so absorbed in another time that I forget to sate myself."

"You sound like a priest," I tell him. I can't help but lift my hand and place my palm gently upon his cheek. "Like my mother's brother, Joe."

The front door opens in a surprise burst and there stands Ripley. His face falls and his eyes widen—a gaze that grips me from within. I rip my hand from Cornelius's cheek and my own cheeks burn. Cornelius stands, but appears perfectly unruffled as usual.

"You have exquisite timing," he says. "I was about to pry out of Leila why she's so cross with you."

Both mine and Ripley's jaws practically unhinge.

"But now that you're here," Cornelius continues, ignoring our gape-mouthed mugs, "you can do that for yourself."

Without another word, our contrarian friend waltzes right out the door, closing it and leaving Ripley and me alone!

"Well, I suppose I should unpack my things," I say with a bit of a stutter. I rise slowly from the sofa, not knowing quite what to do with myself.

Ripley Davies narrows his remarkable eyes, the ones I've been dreaming about almost every night. His fine, arched brows nearly meet. "Why won't you talk to me?"

It seems to be a dizzying day of direct questions and answers from the young men in my life.

"Look," he says. "I didn't mean to offend you when, well when I kissed you, but you certainly didn't seem to mind it at the time."

Ripley Davies has the opposite effect on me as Cornelius

did a few minutes ago. His forward gesture, the fact that he dared throw our kiss in my face, makes me simmer with fury. Without a word, I walk over and slap him outright. He barely moves, as if he expected it.

"You think you can just have me because my mother was modern, is that it?"

"What in the devil are you talking about?" Ripley takes one good stomp towards me and I startle. He comes so close, practically nose to nose with me, until all of his face is a blur, but for his eyes.

"You're the one who stopped talking to me!" he says, seething.

"Because I won't be played for a fool!"

"And neither will I!"

A soft but insistent knock interrupts our hot-blooded exchange, but Ripley doesn't move. He remains, his face inches from mine, his diabolical eyes hypnotizing me where I stand.

"Aren't you going to get it?" I whisper, and he parts his lips and inches even closer. For a moment I think he's going to kiss me again, but then the knock comes louder, more adamant this time, making it clear that our visitor knows someone is home and will not be ignored.

I nearly wilt when Ripley steps back and tears himself away from me, then discharge a breath that could've blown out a candelabra. But my relief is short-lived when he opens the door to find none other than Edna Watson standing there, her face drenched in tears!

"Oh, Ripley!" She sniffles, and I just about want to pick up one of the many artifacts lying about and throw it at her!

"Edna, I . . ."

"Goodness," Edna gasps, her eyes darting in my direction. "I'm sorry. I saw you come home and I didn't realize you had a guest."

"How do you do?" I say. "I don't think we've been formally introduced."

Ripley steps back and allows Edna to enter his house, which she does with rather hesitant, unsteady steps.

"Edna, this is Leila Wellington. Lord Floyd's daughter," Ripley says. "Leila, Edna Watson. Her father was my mother's cousin."

"It's good to finally meet you," Edna says. She seems about ready to extend a hand, but then her entire façade crumbles and she dissolves into tears right there on the spot. She leans in to Ripley, and he walks her to the sofa, easing her down. I pull one of Aunt Clara's rather bold-printed Indian handkerchiefs out of my sleeve and dangle it before her. She takes it, and blows her nose.

"Thank you," she says.

"It's no bother," I tell her. "If you'll excuse me, I'll leave the two of you to your business."

"No!" Ripley says, and Edna looks up from Aunt Clara's handkerchief.

"I mean, you can trust Leila," Ripley tells her. "And I think, perhaps, another girl's perspective might be helpful."

Now, I wish I'd actually hit him with something much harder than my open palm! Does he really expect me and "cousin" Edna to discuss him while he stands here? "Excuse me?" I say.

"Ripley, yes!" Edna exclaims. "I think you're so right! Leila may have a unique perspective on our predicament."

"I don't think I would at all," I start to tell her, but Edna springs up from the sofa with an expression of such hopefulness on her face and she actually takes my hand! She's a tall girl, and looks down a good half-head at me, making me feel at a disadvantage.

"You see," she says. "I'm terribly in love."

It honestly feels as if the wind has been knocked out of

me, and I have to fight back the urge not to burst into tears myself. I tilt my head to catch a view of Ripley. He's still next to the sofa, arms folded, his eyes flitting from me to Edna and then back to me again, where they stay fixed.

"And Ripley, well, we've known each other for so long, and he's been so good to me," she goes on to tell me. "But increasingly I feel that things are hopeless."

"I'm sure that's not so," I manage.

"Oh, but it is! You don't know my mother, and you don't know Mohammad's family."

I wrench my gaze from Ripley Davies and look right at Edna, into her eyes of bluebell blue.

"Mohammad?" I say.

"Mohammad Gamal," Ripley answers.

"The Egyptian Nationalist?"

Edna nods furiously, dislodging several tears that had been dangling at her chin. They drop onto her breast like rain. "You know him?"

"Well, no," I say. "Know of him. Everyone in Cairo knows of him, though."

Mohammad Gamal—young and brash. Touted in the papers as an activist from an old Alexandrian family, who came to Cairo to start a revolution. He's the one Aunt Clara thinks is so handsome and she wanted to find some way to introduce to me, no less!

"You're in love with Mohammad Gamal?" I say incredulously.

Edna continues to nod. She rubs her eyes and swallows her tears.

"Only my mother wants me to marry a man from the British consulate. A nice man, I suppose. And Mohammad's parents, well they won't be moved at all on account of the fact that I'm not a Moslem. I've offered to convert! But they won't even agree to meet me!"

Edna's head falls onto my shoulder and her entire body quakes with sobs.

"I see," I say.

I pet her head gently and meet Ripley's eyes, which have a bit of an 'I told you so' look in them. Not too much, though. Mostly, his eyes are soft and seem to show genuine care.

"This man from the consulate, was he the man you were having dinner with at The Shepheard some weeks ago—the night I saw you there?"

Edna looks up from my shoulder, takes a deep breath and smiles a bit sheepishly. "I see," I say again. Seems all I can say.

"How do you fit into all of this?" I ask Ripley.

"Not much at all," he tells me.

"Nonsense!" Edna says. "Ripley has been my prince. If it weren't for him, I could hardly see Mohammad! Ripley has snuck him onto the island more than once, so that my love can come to my window late at night."

"Dressed as Ripley," I say.

"Yes," she says, glancing between him and me. "It's given Ripley a good deal of trouble with my mother, and um, other people, I think. Once, after he and Mohammad switched clothes to throw Mummy off the scent of blood, poor Ripley had to climb out my window half dressed!"

"Did he?" I say.

"But it's not at all as improper as it sounds! Not very, anyway," Edna Watson says with a marked English blush. "Mohammad just comes here so that we can talk and hold hands. Make plans to be together. He has been ever the gentleman towards me."

Edna turns from me and walks dazedly back to the sofa, sinking down—her despair threatening to overtake her. "But it's hopeless. Mohammad's parents feel he's disgraced them by falling in love with me, and his uncle has even threatened violence!"

I want to tell her that I'm sure it's not quite as bad as that, but it probably is. Still, I find myself giving her hope. "My mother's parents were unhappy about her running off and marrying my father at first."

I try to sound encouraging, but the fact is, no matter how different my mother and father were, they didn't have the added complication of religion between them. Although my father was an agnostic by nature, he did convert from his Anglican to my mother's Coptic sect to help quell the uproar their marriage had caused in the Saber family. By and large, it worked. Of course, my father's title didn't hurt things.

"So, you think things might settle down with our families? Mohammad is very pig-headed, you know," Edna says with affection. "He intends to do as he pleases, and says he can hardly argue for Egypt's independence if he's not willing to assert his own."

"Seems you've found yourself a unique young man," I say, and mean it.

I notice Edna has calmed down considerably. Her face is still abloom with red blotches, but her eyes are dry and her voice is steady and stronger.

"I would so like you to meet him," she says.

Well, never in this universe did I figure I'd be making friendly plans with Edna Watson by the end of today—or any day for that matter—but I tell her that I'd like that. I admit that the prospect of meeting *the* Mohammad Gamal is a pleasing one, too. Trouble attracts trouble, Aunt Clara would say with a wink.

"You'll be terribly fond of him, I'm sure of it," Edna tells me. "Ripley is."

In my peripheral vision, I see Ripley Davies standing by the sofa, watching me. I don't dare look, as I know for a fact that my expression will betray me and I'm not ready for that sort of exposure. Not yet.

But what I am or am not ready for becomes a moot point as Edna begs our pardon. She goes to take a moment in the bathroom, just to splash her face with some cool water and make herself presentable. While she's so engaged, Ripley and I find ourselves alone again. It is difficult to explain what comes over me as we stand there, many feet apart, yet feeling as if every part of us is touching. It's like we're on the verge of entering into one another and it's an overwhelming sensation, yet one as familiar as the urge to sleep or awaken. To breathe.

I hardly notice when Edna comes back in the room, and am vaguely aware that she excuses herself, rather awkwardly—our fault, I think—and goes out the door.

We are alone now—truly alone in the house—Ripley and I. A stir even stronger than on the night we kissed in the carriage has taken me over. For the first time in my life, I'm frightened, genuinely frightened of what I might do. Because I know that no matter what it is, it won't be enough. It'll never be enough.

"I know you," I whisper. "I've always known you."

Chapter 12

Nearly As Old As Time

RIPLEY IS ON HIS KNEES before me. I don't even remember how he got there. I just know I never want him to break away. His hands roam under my dress, caressing my legs over my stockings, while my fingers run through his hair. I feel his breath hot at my belly.

"You've been a stone in my heart." He speaks into the light fabric of my dress. "Do you know how many times I almost came to your house? To shake some sense into you."

"I hated you bitterly," I say.

He laughs and kisses my middle. "That's why I didn't come. Your pride wouldn't have let you hear the truth from me, you know."

Ripley leans back on his heels and looks me up and down. His hair is tussled and sweet, sticking up all over. His skin ruddy and warm. Rising up, he combs his hair with his fingers and shakes his head. "We should sit down," he says. "I have so much to tell you."

"If you don't mind," I say. "I would prefer to stand."

I don't think I could sit close to him right now without wanting to be in his arms. Ripley seems to understand this. He folds his hands in front of him and pushes his thumbs together as he takes a moment to collect his thoughts.

"Leila," he says ever so softly. "I'm so glad there's no more misapprehension between us."

I swallow hard and agree.

"I-I . . ."

"What is it?"

"This is difficult to say. I don't want you to think ill of me, but I must tell you this. I must—*we* must know."

"Ripley, you can tell me," I say. "You can tell me anything."

Ripley nods and takes a full breath.

"I had the most terrible dream. Terrible and beautiful all at once."

An almost unbearable urge to go to him comes over me; to put my hand upon the bare skin of his chest once again and feel his heart beating. To explain how my nights haunt me. "What happened in this dream?"

Ripley glances out the window with the most obvious sense of longing etched on his face. He does it as if to reassure himself that there's a common world out there of normal concerns. Taking meals with family and finding shelter in small acts of love and meaning. Nothing, more or less. I know that feeling very well. He runs his fingers through his hair once more, and begins to pace about the room.

"What's strange is that I didn't even remember having the dream, but I must have woken up in the night and written it down, because in the morning, there it was. A description of it next to my bed, written in my hand."

"It's not uncommon to forget a dream," I say.

"No," he agrees. "But that's just it. I don't know if it was a dream at all."

A lump comes to my throat and I find it difficult to speak. "What makes you say that?"

"What I wrote was so specific, some of it was written in verse—and I don't write poetry. I read it, obviously," he says, casting a brief smile in my direction before becoming solemn again. "Some things I wrote I should never tell you, at least not until . . ."

"Until what," I whisper.

"Until we're wed."

Ripley pinches his eyes shut and shakes his head. When he opens them again, he trains them on mine, and it's as if I've been given a window into the soul of an angel. A window of stained glass and prisms of light. That should be a ridiculous notion, and yet there it is, a feeling as true as the blood that runs in my veins. He comes towards me, taking my hands into his, and I feel a deep and painful burning at the center of my left palm. Like I'm holding fire in my hand. Makes me gasp.

"What are we," I say, and don't even know where that question came from. I've never thought of it, until now. Yet it's always been there.

"I don't know," he answers.

The front door latch jiggles and Ripley and I step apart quickly, my fingers still tingling from his touch. The burn in my palm fades, but doesn't leave me entirely. It sits with me stubbornly, like an old wound. I watch Ripley take his thumb to his palm and rub it deeply, as if he felt it too.

Dr. Davies shoulders his way into the house, carrying a rather large leather tote under his arm. He's distracted and mumbling to himself.

"Ah, there you are, son. I was hoping to find you here."

"Sorry, Father," Ripley says. He shudders a bit, like he's shaking off a portentous intuition. "I should have told you I was leaving the museum. Um, Leila had some questions about settling in that Cornelius couldn't answer."

"Hmm, yes. And you are settled in, are you? Good," he says, not waiting for my answer.

Something that looks bronze and exceedingly old, perhaps a platter of some sort, begins to slide from his tote, which Dr. Davies is holding at an awkward angle.

"Allow me to help," I say, taking the tote from him just as the artifact begins to fall out. Ripley catches it.

"What on earth is this?" he says. "Wasn't at your office this morning."

"No, no, it most certainly wasn't," Dr. Davies tells us. "It was sent to me by the Hugheses—a most fascinating relic from their excursion."

"So, you've heard from the Hugheses?" I ask him.

"In a manner of speaking, my dear. This artifact does imply they're having a most productive and intriguing journey."

He runs his hand over the back and takes the platter from his son, carrying it to a small games table that sits under their parlor window. Dr. Davies steps back, stroking his mutton chops.

"It's a bronze breastplate that's in rather poor condition," Dr. Davies tells us. "Warped by volcanic debris."

"I didn't know there were volcanoes in the Sahara," Ripley says.

"Mt. Koussi in the Tibesti range. No known historical records of an eruption there, but you'll find a thermal area on the southern side of the mountain."

"And you say the Hugheses brought it back?" I look at the blackened thing, twisted on one side, and an odd sense of familiarity comes over me. Not a pleasant one.

"Didn't bring it back, no," Dr. Davies tells me. "Had it sent. The Hugheses appear to have been detained."

"They are in a rather far-flung part of the world," I say, pointing out the obvious. I suppose I mention it to comfort myself, as I don't like that Aunt Clara and Uncle Hugo are late coming back from such a place.

"Hmm." Dr. Davies nods. "Political instability and a rather harsh climate have limited field access to the area. As far as we know, no one has ascended the highest peaks of the range. One of the loneliest places in the Sahara, they say."

Ripley takes the breastplate into his hands and holds it up to the light. "No Englishman has ascended it, but surely locals have, at some point during the ages."

"Perhaps," Dr. Davies says. "Whatever the case, it's going to take a tremendous effort to clean this up without damaging it further. I suspect it was once quite handsome, as ancient military armor tended to be."

"Military armor!" I say. "How ancient do you expect it is?"

Dr. Davies runs his fingers along some crusted black deposits affixed to the center of the breastplate, perhaps to a design of some sort.

"Oh, quite ancient," he says. "Perhaps nearly as old as time."

A VERY ENGLISH supper of roast chicken with mashed potatoes and gravy is prepared for us by the Davieses' girl. It's comforting to eat hearty, simple food as the three of us find ourselves preoccupied by the artifact. And two of us find ourselves preoccupied by each other. Ripley and I slip our shoes off under the table, and I place my feet on top of his. A soft and cherished gesture. It's an agony not to be able to hold one another. For me to have to wait to hear what he has to tell me. By the time a berry trifle is served, we're sitting in silence, apart from the occasional acknowledgement of how nice the food has been.

"I do have to meet with Lieutenant General Blackwood this evening for a sherry," Dr. Davies says, consulting his pocket watch. "Good Lord, with all this business about the Hugheses' artifact, I nearly forgot."

"Is it about the translation he'd like me to have a look at? The one regarding the lost regiment of '86?"

Dr. Davies scrapes the bottom of his dessert dish with a spoon.

"Actually, it's a purely social call, but yes, yes, he will like you to have a look at that translation. I don't think there's much to it, if I'm to be completely honest, but it's a priority for the Lieutenant General for obvious reasons, and he would like to make certain he has the proper meaning in order."

"I'll be honest," I tell him. "I'm not sure how helpful I'll be. I'm not exactly fluent in Toubou languages—just seem to have picked up a sense for them as a girl. My mother had a Toubou maidservant for a time."

Her name was Fada and I remember her well. Deep set eyes so black as to be violet. I felt those eyes on me whenever I was in her presence. Regarding me with a mixture of affection and suspicion.

"Didn't know there was a Toubou community in Cairo," Ripley says. "I guess there's a community for every sort of person here, though."

"There isn't, as far as I know," I tell him. "Or anywhere else apart from the expanse where the Toubou roam. Fada had come to our family during a time of famine in her region. She never seemed to adapt to a settled life, though, and one day, she simply left us."

Dr. Davies licks a last smear of cream from the corner of his mouth, dots his napkin along his lips and sits back.

"Fada. Fascinating," he says. "Well, whatever the case, I'm afraid you're all we've got in terms of a translator. But I am optimistic. Your father thinks very highly of your linguistic abilities."

Dr. Davies excuses himself from the table, and makes his way to the door, grabbing a light overcoat. But as he turns to bid us a goodnight, a look of dawning realization comes over his face.

"Oh, dear," he says. "This won't do at all, will it?"

Ripley stands and goes to his father. There is an authority in his demeanor that I hadn't noticed before. He walks straight, with his hands at his sides, and wears a decided look upon his face, as if all traces of his boyhood have left him.

"It will do fine, Father. You go right ahead and have your sherry. I'll make sure to lock Leila's door for safety's sake."

Dr. Davies clears his throat and lowers his voice. "Are you quite sure? It wouldn't do for anyone to know the two of you were left on your own here. Without a chaperone."

"Are you going to tell them?"

"Heavens no!"

"Then we've got nothing to worry about."

Dr. Davies hems and haws a bit, but it's clear he's going to give in. A nice sherry with Lieutenant General Blackwood is too tempting an outing for him to miss. I feel a flutter of nerves in my stomach and my palm begins to grow uncomfortably warm again.

"Goodnight, Dr. Davies," I say, and he waves and smiles at me most affectionately, although he does look back once before crossing the threshold onto the streets of Zamalek.

Ripley watches him saunter in the direction of the Lida, and waits until he turns a corner before shutting the door. He then comes around and faces me.

"Leila," he says. "We should go upstairs."

"If you wish," I tell him. I am free of any constraints, social or religious. Because it's as if whatever is between us is Holy, made by God Himself.

I begin to ascend the stairs, moving in a dream. One of my dreams—the ones that seem so real as to be whispering to me of parallel worlds. The dreams Ripley started to tell me about before his father interrupted us. Ripley is behind me, and his step, too, is as soft as a wisp.

At the top of the stairs, I proceed down the hallway, to

the room where Cornelius brought my things. My luggage remains stacked in the corner by a vanity, the only feminine piece of furniture in the house.

There is a staleness to the room, as if it hasn't been used, not for months, but years, and yet it's well-appointed and pleasant. A watercolor of Heraklion hangs above the head-board of my bed, and the thin, minty-hued quilt that rests on top of the mattress has settled in like a second skin.

I expect Ripley to come up behind me, wrap his arms about my waist and plant soft kisses on my neck. His name is on my lips when I hear the door to my room close and the lock click from the outside.

"Ripley! What are you doing?"

I spin around and go to the door, fiddling with the knob, but it's locked up tight.

"It's for the best," he says. "You know it's true."

"I want to see you!" I say, smacking my hand against the dark wood frame. "We've been apart for all these weeks!"

"I want to see you, too," Ripley says. "But I need to talk to you of things that shouldn't be said face to face just yet."

I lean my forehead against the glossed wood of the door, so smooth as to be slippery. I turn about and slide down until I'm seated on the floor leaning against it. I kick off my shoes once again. "Alright."

I can hear the floor creak on the other side of the door as Ripley crouches down. "Leila," he says, softly. "Can you hear me?"

I tell him yes.

"I think, perhaps, I should read to you what I wrote in the night. I could never say it as well. In truth, even if I could, I'm not sure I'd have the courage to put the words together as I did while I was sleepwalking. I must presume that's what I was doing, because the me on this paper is the me of my dreams, and not the man you've come to know. Not exactly, anyway. But our feelings for you are the same. Our character is the same."

I feel lightheaded now. Anxious to hear what he's going to tell me, but frightened, too. Not of him. Of *this*. Of learning something of him and myself that is perhaps best unknown.

"Go ahead, then," I say.

There is a long silence between us. Feels long, at any rate. Finally, I hear the crinkling of a paper being unfolded. Ripley shifts his weight as he inclines toward the door and begins to read.

> *The first time I touched you, unfettered, your body painted in the hues of the desert, with the stories of your heart meandering down from the nape of your neck to the supine bones of your legs . . .*
>
> *A finger trailing your every curve, my finger.*
> *Lips kissing over the whole of you, my lips.*
> *You had undressed me, my bride. Your eyes had drunk of me, my skin plain, with no story. Only the scars of my battles.*
> *My story had been told as I promised myself to you. From my tongue, my throat. As the moon rose and the sun set in glory. As the stars emerged from the darkness to glitter over us, a rain threatening with God's magic.*
> *But I did not finish my story.*
> *I told you, then, of my love for you. How it came to be and that I had waited for you. Watched you walk through your days, and struggle through your trials. Wander alone in the desert until your body burned with fever.*
> *But I did not tell you how long I had waited.*
> *Not merely a lifetime, our life together. Your first.*
> *I had waited another life before. And another, and another.*

My palm burns so badly that I break into a sweat at my brow. I squeeze my hands together and put them to my lips, biting down on my knuckle.

"Do you feel that?" I ask him.

"Yes. The burn. I awaken to it every morning."

"What is it?"

"Don't you know?"

I shake my head, even if he can't see me.

"It is what bound us as man and wife once, I think. At least that's what my dreams tell me."

A hot ember, dropped in each of our palms by a priest. Our love seared into us.

"Yes, I remember now," I tell him. "I dreamt of it, too."

MICKEY SQUINTS one eye nearly shut as he draws me. It's hard to stay still and not laugh, but he gets so serious whenever he picks up his pastels and goes to work on that thick, creamy paper his mom buys for him. Laughing seems wrong somehow, like laughing in church.

"Almost done," he says, and those eyes of his—so dark and filled with ribbons of red and gold—look as if they might catch on fire. Like a piece of coal.

Finally, he stops and holds the thick paper out in front of him, and I'm dying to see what he drew!

"Ready?" he asks me.

I nod, pressing my lips together so I don't giggle. Slowly, really milking the drama, he turns the paper around.

I can feel my mouth fall open, my breath float out of it the way smoke used to from my Granny Dora's mouth as she daydreamed out the window. What he's drawn is so perfect. Like a photograph, only finer. Because Mickey knows me better than a camera ever could. He gets the wave of my hair just right, the cowlick at my widow's peak. And all of the streaks of light brown and chestnut and rust that come together so that different people often think my hair is different colors. Mickey gets the curve of my lips right, too—full, but not as full as his, and with what my granny used to say was "a smile that made it clear I didn't like to smile for just anybody." But it's my eyes that he gets right most of all. Not just the shade of green, which he nailed, but how deep that color goes. Makes me feel a little self-conscious to know that when some people go on and on about how weird my eyes are, they kind of have a point.

"It's amazing," I tell him.

"You think so?"

I hold out my hand and Mickey gives the drawing to me, so that I can get a good, close look.

"What's that?" I ask him.

Above the stretched-out collar of my t-shirt, there seems to be a line-drawing of some sort.

"Is that supposed to be a tattoo?"

"No. I mean, I don't know. I just thought it belonged there."

"Looks like hands."

"It is. Palms up like they're holding your neck and head."

"It's nice, I guess." I look at him, cocking my head. "Well, you always say an artist can do whatever he wants, so it's your vision."

There's a groan on the stairs, and Mickey jumps into his bed, while I slip out the French doors onto his little balcony.

"Be careful," he whispers.

"I'm always careful," I tell him, as I climb over to the other little balcony that comes off my room, the guest room. But all the Nevilles call it my room now regardless of who they've got staying overnight when I'm at my mom's place in Hopely.

I manage to crawl under my covers just as the door to my room eases open, quiet as a breath. A sliver of light from the hallway reaches all the way to my open French doors.

"I can't believe they're actually asleep," Mickey's mom says.

She tip-toes into my room and closes those doors.

"Wouldn't do if Ever went sleepwalking again."

Both Mickey and I sleepwalk, or so we've been told.

She comes over and adjusts my blankets, kissing my

temple, and then goes back to Dr. Neville and kisses him. They close my door as softly as they opened it, and whisper to each other as they walk down the stairs and back to the living room, where they like to sit up and talk.

I lie in my bed a good fifteen minutes until it feels safe to go out into the hallway. Then I make my way, all sneaky, down to the kitchen, which is at the back of the house, facing out onto their yard. The Nevilles' house is big, so they won't be able to hear me from where they're sitting.

It's not like the Nevilles' mind me going down to the kitchen—"Our house is your house," they tell me every time I stay with them. But they're big believers in kids getting a good night's sleep and say it's important for our physical and neurological development. And I don't want to disappoint them by going against their rules.

It's just that I get so hungry when I'm at their place, on account of their food being so good! Only today, Mrs. Neville—I guess I should call her Dr. Neville, too, but it's just too confusing—made a batch of vanilla cupcakes with chocolate chip cookie dough frosting that are just to die for! I only ate one of them after dinner, because I didn't want to look like a pig, and now they're sitting there all lonesome on the kitchen counter like they're just begging me to pay them some attention. Which I do. I promise myself that I will only eat one, but then I go ahead and eat two, and one more after that.

From the corner of my eye, I catch Calixto, the Nevilles' Angora kitty, rubbing his side along the door frame and looking back at me like he wants me to follow him. Mrs. Dr. Neville says Calixto never pays anyone outside of the family any mind except for me. When I come over it's like no one else exists.

"Alright, I'll play," I whisper to Calixto.

His tail, fluffy like a fox's, but white as angel food cake, almost seems to wave me along, as if saying, *well, come on then.*

I follow him into Dr. Neville's study, which is maybe my favorite room in the house. Big bookshelves, back lit, that reach all the way to the ceiling, which is just high enough that even Dr. Neville needs a ladder to get to the top shelf. And Dr. Neville is tall! But it's not just books he has on those shelves, there are old trinkets and artifacts from all the digs he's been on, and also from the expeditions of his forefathers. Fertility goddesses, ale pots, tools, daggers, all sorts of things, interspersed with a couple of Mickey's trophies for sports and school stuff.

Dr. Neville's most prized relics, however, aren't displayed on his shelves. Those he keeps locked away in a deep drawer in this big old antique desk that's been passed down in his family since the early 1900s. It was willed to his great-great granddad by an English archaeologist who worked at the Museum of Antiquities in Cairo back then, and gave Dr. Neville's ancestor his first job in "the family business" as the Nevilles like to call it.

It's such a beautiful desk. It sits in the middle of the room, all dark wood and polished to such a shine. On its corner is a framed picture of Mickey and Mrs. Neville, those wild, dark brown curls of hers getting blown by the wind, and Mickey looking up at her and laughing. They look like coffee and cream next to one another, and are standing against the back-drop of the super modern new Grand Egyptian Museum in Cairo. It's huge and looks like a giant slab of steel with a pyramid wedged into it. But it's cool, I have to say. It's really cool.

Behind that picture is another photo, also framed. This one is crazy old, though. Dr. Neville says it's from 1902. In it is a slender, young black guy (who's Dr. Neville's great-great grandfather), the English archaeologist who gave him the desk, that archaeologist's son—a handsome blonde type who looks like that old actor when he was young, the one from "Titanic." And there's a girl in it, too. A pretty, young Egyptian woman in a summer dress. None of them are smiling—the way people never smiled in photos back then—but they've got this look of pride on their faces, like they just got some good news. They're standing in front of the old Museum of Antiquities, which Dr. Neville prefers to the new one, and says is colored as pink as my lips.

Calixto does a figure eight around my legs and rubs his cheek against my shin. He jumps up onto the desk and meows right at me.

"No," I say.

But he keeps on staring.

"It's not right," I whisper.

The cat jumps from the desk up onto the shelf where Dr. Neville keeps a whole row of fiction books about Cairo: "Sugar Street" and a bunch of other Naguib Mahfouz novels, as well as other books by different authors, both old and new: "The City of Love and Ashes," "The Stream of Days," and "The Woman of Cairo." I've read most of them. But the one I'm looking for is a tall, hard-cover graphic novel called "The Shadow People." It's about the golden age of archaeology, which was going on right about the same time the old picture on Dr. Neville's desk was taken. Dr. Neville says archaeologists are all shadow people, who follow history around, always one foot in the past, one eye on what was. Talking to ghosts.

"You're an evil spirit, you know that?" I say to Calixto. "Even if you're very cute."

I scratch Calixto under his chin, then take "The Shadow People" off the shelf. And I know I can't blame that hairy, white creature for what I'm about to do, even if I'd like to. I guess I knew I was going to come in here long before I snuck downstairs for cupcakes. I open the book and slide a brass key a bit longer than my middle finger out of a pocket on the inside of the cover. Then I jimmy the book back into its place.

I walk around the desk and sit down in Dr. Neville's chair, a black Aeron that feels light as air and spins around. Carefully, I stick the key in the lock of the deep drawer in the old desk, and turn it, hearing it click twice. Sliding it open, I take a deep breath before I look inside.

"Okay, that wasn't so bad."

At the bottom of that drawer is a statue, wrapped in a soft, almost furry piece of cloth. My hand is shaking a bit and I grip my wrist to steady it. Counting to three, I reach down and pinch my fingers around a corner of the cloth and slowly unravel it, careful not to touch the effigy, as Dr. Neville calls it.

Bird's head.

Lion's mouth.

Large talons gripping a flower.

"I'm not going to touch it," I tell Calixto. "Not after last time."

About a year ago, when I came in here to have a look at the thing, I remember reaching into the drawer as I did just now. Only that's the last I remember. I woke up on the floor of Mickey's bedroom some time later, without a stitch on and shivering in the air conditioning. The palm of my left hand burning like I'd stuck it over a lit candle. Mickey was still asleep, so I grabbed one of his t-shirts, threw it over my head, and snuck back into my room. There, I shivered under my blankets until dawn, but not because I was cold. I was freaked out and tried every way but Sunday to recall even a sliver of memory about what I'd done in the time between putting my hand on that statue and waking up on Mickey's carpet. I got nothing. I couldn't even tell Mickey about it as much as I wanted to. He would've told his mom and dad for sure, and what were they going to think?

I jump at the sound of a cling-clang-thunk and shoot Calixto an evil eye. Stupid cat knocked over one of Mickey's trophies! It's a lacrosse trophy that now lies on the floor, the golden body separated from its base.

"See what you've done?" Calixto seems to shrug, almost smiling at me in that diabolical cat-way of his.

Down the hall, I hear the Nevilles start walking in this direction and now I wish I could pick up a part of Mickey's broken trophy and chuck it at that feline. I bite down, doing my best not to breathe too heavily, and crawl under the desk, wrapping my arms around my knees.

It's Dr. Neville who comes in first, his hard-stepping unmistakable. He huffs and, if I could see him from under here, I'd bet he was shaking his head.

"Calixto!"

Stupid cat runs out of the room as Dr. Neville's hand comes down into my view and gathers up the pieces of trophy.

"What is it about Calixto and this room?" Mrs. Neville says, coming right in after him. Her step is as light as her kitty's.

"He's an old soul, that cat. Seems this house if full of them."

The big old desk creaks as Dr. Neville leans on it, his bare feet crossed at the ankles, heels digging into the Persian rug. I glance over at the drawer where he keeps his effigy and notice I left it open! My mouth pops wide and I almost gasp out loud, which would for sure give me away. Right then, Mrs. Neville steps up next to Dr. Neville. She leans in and kisses him in that way that I know is going to last at least a good few seconds, so I reach over and close the drawer carefully, praying it won't squeak or anything. It doesn't, thank God.

When the Nevilles finally finish their kissing, Mrs. Neville pulls away, stroking her husband's cheeks, and reaching down to take his hands. They pick up wherever it was in their conversation they left off, and I'm so relieved I could lie down and seep into the rug like a spilled root beer. I can't seem to make any sense of what they're talking about at first, until I realize it's me.

"Gifted as hell," Dr. Neville says. "I think Bonnie realizes that."

"I hope so," Mrs. Neville says. "And she seems to be warming to the idea of letting us take Ever to Cairo come fall. God, it would be great for her. The International School has an incredible languages program, and given her talent for picking right up on linguistic patterns . . ." Mrs. Neville snaps her fingers and Dr. Neville "mm hmm's."

My stomach nearly drops right out of me, through the rug, and straight down to their basement. I cup my hand over my nose and mouth, trying not to breathe so hard.

"Yeah, but let's not get too invested in that. Bonnie's been a bit erratic lately."

Mrs. Neville lets go of a sigh. "Oh, Neil, I hate to even say it."

"You're wondering if she's using again."

I hear Mrs. Neville swallow, as I go from panting all excited to forgetting to breathe at all.

"Hard to say," Dr. Neville says. "But I don't think so."

Thank God.

"Look, after what happened to Dora, I think we can cut Bonnie a little slack for being uneven. I mean, that woman was a handful, but she was stable, and she was always there for her and Ever. It's going to be a rougher road for them without Dora."

Granny Dora. I do my very best to chase her out of my thoughts and lock my mind up tight, but she always seems to slip back in. I miss her and it's awful what happened. Most of all because we don't really know. During a weird cold snap on Whitney Mountain, Granny Dora went wandering out in the night in just her pajamas, which was only an old heavy metal concert t-shirt and undies. She died of hypothermia about a mile from her boyfriend's house, and he says he didn't even know she was coming over.

It's all so strange because Granny's feet were practically raw from running so hard over rocks and sticks, like she was being chased by a wild animal. In the end, she crawled behind a bush and tried to cover herself with leaves to stay warm, but it didn't do her any good. It haunts me that she would've rather died freezing outside than gone back the way she'd come, taking shelter in her nice, new, warm trailer. She'd left the door wide open and the TV on, with a small can of chili taken down from her cupboard and a saucepan set out onto her electric burner. I think about those little details a lot.

"What is it?" I hear Mrs. Neville say. "You holding back on me?"

Dr. Neville takes a deep breath and I hear him crack his neck.

"It looks like Ever's father has come back in the picture."

"Hunter?"

I sit up tall and just about bump my head on the underside of the desktop.

"He's taken up with Bonnie again," Dr. Neville tells her. "And I think she's hopeful about their getting back together."

I haven't seen my dad in over five years, and, as far as I know, Mom and Granny hadn't even heard from him! Unless they were keeping him from me. Mrs. Neville starts to pace back and forth in front of the bookshelves, and I wish I could join her. I've got the urge to move and think. And scream.

"I'm surprised Ever hasn't said anything."

Well, I would if I'd known, I want stand up and yell! And Dr. Neville tells his wife as much.

"Bonnie said Hunter wants to keep things quiet at first. See how things go between them this time around, and then get to know his daughter again slowly, since he's been away for so long."

"What's he been doing all this time anyway?"

"Apparently, getting his life in order. According to Bonnie, he's got a really good job. He apprenticed with a master carpenter and can build just about anything. Has more work than he can handle, she told me."

Mrs. Neville stops pacing and goes very still. There's a stretch of quiet between them that lasts a little too long to be comfortable.

"I've always had a bad feeling about that man," she finally says.

"You and me both."

"Those eyes of his. It's like they're on fire," Mrs. Neville whispers. "The way he looks at Ever."

Dr. Neville pushes off from the desk and starts to lead his wife out of his study.

"You think, now that he's back, Bonnie will be more likely to let Ever come with us to Egypt? She does have full custody. It's her decision, right?" Mrs. Neville asks.

"Hard to say," he tells her, but I can tell in his tone that he's thinking exactly what I'm thinking. Even though my father hardly knows me, and even though back when he *was* around he spent most of his time either pissed off or high as a kite, I get this weird feeling that he didn't come back for my mom at all. I never thought he liked my mom very much, to tell you the truth. Not the way she liked him.

There's this horrible pit where my stomach used to be before it fell into the Nevilles' basement. Because I think I know why he came back.

He came back for me. Only me. And somehow, I always knew he'd do that.

When I'm sure the Nevilles are in their living room, again, I walk back upstairs. I don't go into my room, though. I tip-toe into Mickey's and crawl into his bed, wrapping my arms around him. He's deep asleep and so warm he almost feels feverish.

"Mickey," I whisper. "He's going to try to keep you away from me. But I won't let him."

I cuddle closer, spooning him like I did when we were kids. "You were born for me. I'm sure of it."

Chapter 13

"**I**T'S ACTUALLY quite accurate," I tell Lieutenant General Blackwood.

He sits perched on Dr. Davies's desk, holding a feline figurine about the length of a good-sized thumb. It's one of many little relics strewn about the office, and he massages it like a worry stone.

"There's only one reference that's truly beyond me, otherwise the translation is plain and straightforward." I've read the Toubou interpretation he wanted me to have a look at several times over now, searching for anything that might have been missed regarding the tribesman's encounter with the missing regiment of '86, but as Dr. Davies suggested was the case, there simply isn't much there.

I hand him back the document, transcribed phonetically from the spoken Toubou, and he adjusts his reading glasses.

"You're referring to the part about the fire fruit," the Lieutenant General says, rifling through the pages. "Our translator thought it was a food of some sort."

"So you say, although my instinct is that it's not an accurate translation. A bit too literal, although I will tell you that while I don't think fire fruit is actually fruit, I don't know what else it would be either."

I stand up from Dr. Davies's leather sofa and point at

the phrasing in question. "Look, right here, the tribesman appears to tell a story about encountering a man with fire fruit. Your translator seemed to believe the commander of the lost regiment ran across such a man while in the company of the tribesman, and that he appeared to be a trader of some sort."

"But you do not."

"I can't be sure, but my mother's Toubou maidservant, Fada, was always telling me stories—various myths her foremothers told her. One in particular was a myth that involved a rather sinister premonition about a being who was half man, half immortal. She said if you encounter such a man, a man with fire fruit—you're doomed."

It's a story I will never forget. Fada seemed to tell it to me and me alone. As if I should avoid the man, that he was coming for me, specifically.

"Hmm. It's just a superstition then," Lieutenant General Blackwood says, folding up the document and tucking it into his breast pocket. "Like breaking a mirror, or if a black cat crosses your path."

"Something like that."

"Well, then, I'm afraid this was indeed a fool's errand. The only information this newly uncovered encounter with the lost regiment of '86 seems to provide is that the tribesman who met with the commander believed the regiment was cursed in some manner."

"That's one way of looking at it," I tell him.

"Do you know of another?"

"No," I say. "But I would certainly wonder why the tribesman would have believed the commander and his regiment were cursed. Is it something they said or did? A person they met or a place they visited? It seems, at least in the way he answered your translator's questions, that the tribesman was avoiding telling you something directly and instead talked of this myth—the one of the half-immortal with fire fruit, whatever that is."

Lieutenant General Blackwood chuckles at this with deep amusement. "Leila, I must say that any discourse with you, whatever the topic, is never a bore. You see things few people would notice."

"The lost regiment of '86 is hardly a dull matter."

"Indeed," the Lieutenant General says. "But it is a dead end. I'm afraid the Sahara is a bit like an ocean. Once you are lost in it, you tend to be lost forever."

I think of Ripley and his love of the desert. The dreams we both have of its expanse and what it might mean for us.

"I hope you're wrong," I say.

The Lieutenant General stands, gaining several inches on me.

"Will you be staying until Dr. Davies and Cornelius come up from the work room? They'll be bringing that ancient artifact—speaking of things lost and found in the desert."

"As fascinating as it sounds, I'm afraid not. Lord Cromer is expecting me in an hour and our Consul General is not a man to be kept waiting."

I escort Lieutenant General Blackwood to the side door of the museum and bid him a good day, wishing we could have continued our conversation, given our mutual love of mysteries. But I'm rewarded with another conundrum when Dr. Davies and Cornelius arrive back at the office just as I return, carrying his precious artifact, all swaddled in suede wrap, as if it were a new babe.

"Wait until you see it!" Cornelius says. "It's spectacular."

They lay the artifact on Dr. Davies's desk and unwrap it with a child's excitement. Dr. Davies's face is alight with pleasure at its unmasking, but I step back and gasp when I see it.

"Looks to be the mouth of a snake," I say.

It's a snake that's a fraction of a second away from sinking his fangs deep into someone's flesh. There's a great deal of motion in the way the image has been amalgamated onto the twisted and dented metal breastplate. Quite different from the unnatural poses of so many ancient figures. It's a simultaneously hypnotizing and deeply unsettling image, like the remnants of a horrible nightmare. My nightmare.

"Are you alright?" Cornelius asks me.

He's been watching me intently as we stand over Dr. Davies's desk, ogling the ancient relic.

"I'm fine." Not completely true, but true enough. I look down, attempting to command my trembling hand to stop. It's no use, so I place it behind my back.

"How old do you expect it is, Dr. Davies?" I ask.

"Oh, very old. First Dynasty at least." Dr. Davies brushes fragments of rubble from the forked tongue of the leering reptile. "It's looking quite splendid, to my surprise."

"Never seen snakes represented in quite this way by the Egyptians," Cornelius observes.

"No, but plenty of snakes in Egyptian art and hieroglyphs," Dr. Davies says. "In fact, there's a representation of a snake on the very front of the pharaohs' crown. It's also the symbol of the goddess Wadjet of Lower Egypt."

"So, this could be from before the unification of Upper and Lower Egypt?"

"It's possible, although that would put it pretty deep in the ground. All in all, it doesn't fit in anywhere neatly, but we have to start somewhere."

Somewhere, according to Dr. Davies, is sometime roughly over five thousand years ago and in a rather distant and inaccessible region.

"And this was found near a mountain range in the Central Sahara," Cornelius says. "Debris uncovered in a landslide. Seems rather far for an Egyptian to go."

"I'm not saying it's Egyptian for certain, just that I can't think of what other culture it could possibly belong to. Egyptians had the Nile, don't forget. They could travel quite far south if they wanted to."

"Except this was found nowhere near the Nile."

Dr. Davies scratches his chin and removes his spectacles. He blinks hard and rubs his eyes just as hard.

"Ah, but where there are people, there are people's things. This could have come into the hands of a desert tribesman and traveled quite a ways from its origin. Any ancient nation that had a vast trade network could find its belongings falling into the hands of any number of people, don't forget."

"You're right, of course," I say. "But doesn't this, too, remind you of that stone tablet Howard Carter showed us? The one with the odd writing? There's no writing on this, but it is a bit like your necklace as well. At least in terms of the sense of animation that's brought to every stroke of line on this piece. I mean, it is possible that with all the digging that's been going on in and around Egypt that remnants of other distant cultures are being unearthed. Ones that have yet to be discovered."

Dr. Davies cocks his head and puts his spectacles back on, squinting at the artifact. "I do see what you mean," he says. "But in the absence of any proof of such missing cultures, we must try to see if artifacts such as this one could possibly belong to one of the civilizations we already know. The Egyptians, the Sumerians . . . peoples such as these had rich and varied traditions, after all, that we're only just now starting to get our arms around."

"Indeed," Cornelius says. "There is a repetitive quality in nature—even human nature, isn't there? The Aztecs, who had never seen the Egyptian pyramids, and knew nothing of them, did build their own on the other side of the world, albeit several millennia later."

The door squeals open and Ripley enters his father's office

seeming rather out of breath. "Mohammad is outside of the museum preaching independence to a gathering crowd," he informs us.

I am, quite frankly, relieved to have my attention drawn away from the ancient breastplate—which makes me feel more ill at ease for every moment I continue to examine it. And I do thrill to the idea of hearing Mohammad Gamal speak again. We've all become quite friendly with one another over the past fortnight—meeting in the old city and helping the lovers find precious time together. He's quite devoted to her, and it's warming to see, even if neither of their families have moved an inch as to their acceptance of the relationship.

"Mohammad Gamal. Hmmf. I don't see what the Egyptians would have to look forward to if they gained independence." Dr. Davies shakes his head as he covers the artifact once again.

"Sovereignty," my Ripley tells him.

"Egyptian sovereignty doesn't build dams, however, the British sovereign does."

Ripley puts his hand on his father's shoulder. "Tell me, Dad, if Britain lost sovereignty to a nation who built better dams, would you think we were better off?"

Dr. Davies raises his bushy eyebrows and bites down impishly on his bottom lip. "Depends on how they felt about archaeology."

THE SUN has already begun to dip her dome into the horizon by the time Ripley, Cornelius, and I meet Edna and Mohammad on Na Street. Edna tears herself away from her love, who is a vision in his "political garb," which consists of a handsome vest and pair of trousers the colour of an acorn. Our young men fall instantly into conversation about Mohommad's growing movement, while Edna clasps my hands and kisses me, talking excitedly about the crowds. Her face is still pink from yesterday afternoon, which we spent gardening and playing croquet on our rooftop garden. I'd told her to hold a parasol, but she'd have none of it.

"I have something for you," she says.

Edna bites her lip and reaches for Mohammad's case, in which he keeps flyers and other informational papers meant to further his cause. She opens the flap, pulling out a beautiful, leather-bound scrapbook with the most extraordinary glass oval on its cover. In it, she has placed sprigs of lavender and rosemary, which I'd identified as my favorite pairing of English scents, a peacock feather, and a years-old newspaper clipping about an essay my mother wrote about the history of women in politics. There's a sketch of my mother's face done to make her look like Nefertiti.

"Edna, I don't know what to say." I trace my finger over the image of my mother and breathe deeply.

"I thought we'd make a scrapbook together," Edna says. "I did take the liberty of arranging the front cover, but if it isn't right, I won't at all be offended if you wish to change it."

"It's wonderful," I say. "I wouldn't change a thing."

Inside, Edna has inscribed both of our full names in her perfect hand, placing a photograph of herself and Mohammad beneath her moniker, and leaving room for one of me and Ripley.

"Perhaps we can begin tomorrow at tea? I could bring several items I'd like to place in it."

"Perfect," I say.

"What is this about tea tomorrow?" Ripley teases. "Are you neglecting your studies already?"

I swat Ripley with the scrapbook and feign great offense.

"I'll have you know I plan to be reading a thick volume about Heinrich Schliemann and his excavation of Anatolia all morning."

"Ach, the ancient Turks! Anything but the Turks," Mohammad says.

Cornelius bursts into a fit of laughter. "For this, we need libations!"

Mohammad throws a fist in the air and signals for us to follow him. He seems simultaneously exhausted and energized from his demonstration—which we missed by a hair, to my great disappointment. He and Edna fall into walking at a respectable distance from one another and Ripley and I try to maintain a similar decorum for their sakes, even if every part of my being is drawn to him like a bird is to the air. Cornelius, as always, moves seamlessly between us all, and greets passersby with a tip of his hat.

We slip behind a white spackled building with a decaying balcony and go single-file down a narrow staircase leading us to a most enchanting place. It's a dark café that sits in a basement with a low, blackened ceiling and is lit entirely by candlelight. Smelling of beeswax, ale, mold, and roasting meat—the latter smoking up from a small fire pit in the corner—the place feels positively medieval. Mohammad assures us that it's the best kept secret in Cairo and orders a round of homemade, contraband ale from a sallow-looking fellow with a big, round belly.

"You were marvelous today," the man says to Mohammad. He sniffs back a tear and bows. "Your money is no good here. Not this evening, not ever."

He claps his hands and orders a boy of his to run to the kitchen and fetch us some food and drink, then escorts us to the best table in the house. At the center of the action, yet far enough away from the smoking fire pit as to be enjoyable.

"Having spent nearly all of the afternoon marching

up and down the streets of Old Cairo, I can use a bit of arfarfan'arf."

All of us, minus Cornelius, have a giggle at Mohammad's choice of words."

"Arf, like a dog?" Cornelius asks.

"Arfs, in Britain, are half-pints of ale," Edna says with a titter. "I've been teaching Mohammad some of our more colorful euphemisms."

Said ale arrives and we each take a sip of the bitter brew, pretending, for the sake of the generous proprietor, to like it. It's utterly unpleasant in flavor, but makes up for that with the sense of esprit de corps it allows us. Mohammad is impressive at choking it down, even if he's not used to beverages that provide, shall we say, a bit of a kick. Although he is Moslem, and therefore not supposed to imbibe, his family, like most elite Moslem families I've known, is divided between those who truly don't drink any alcohol and those who pretend not to drink any alcohol. Mohammad, to his credit, has decided that he is neither.

"You have a pathological sense of honesty," Cornelius tells him.

"Pathological? This word means compulsive, does it not?" Mohammad leans back, as if contemplating himself. His substantial brows furrow—a canopy to his liquid eyes, as dark as fresh petrol. "And if you mean that I cannot abide a lie, then I think you're right. I feel a compulsion to honesty, even when it is a danger to me."

"Honesty, by its very nature, is dangerous. That's also what makes it so sublime."

Cornelius's eyes widen, the whites of them gleaming like pearls.

"Spoken like a son of Senegal," I say, and Cornelius and I burst into laughter at a joke only the two of us seem to understand.

Ripley narrows his eyes at us and drums his fingers on the wooden table. I touch the toe of my shoe to his. Even if I know Cornelius and I will only ever be friends, I can't quite explain what kind of friends we are, as I don't understand it myself.

"Perhaps we should play a game," Ripley says. "A game of honesty."

"I'm in!" Mohammad claps his hands with relish. "How do you propose we begin?"

Ripley tips his head back, leaning against the white-washed wall of our clandestine pub. He twirls a horn button on his vest as his mouth curls up on one side. "I'd say we should all answer a question. The most important question of all, I believe."

"And what question is that?" I ask.

Ripley turns to me, those eyes of his bright in the dimly lit room, like Mars in the night sky. "What or who is it you most love?"

The center of my palm begins to feel warm, as it did on the night when Ripley and I swept away all of our misunderstandings. Almost all of them, I note, throwing a quick glance at Cornelius.

"Ripley," I say. I kick him lightly under the table. I don't think I want to play this game.

"I think it's a marvelous idea!" Mohammad elbows Edna, and they each blush as if they've shared a kiss. "And I offer to go first."

He takes a deep gulp of his ale and an even deeper breath. Mohammad then folds his hands tightly, as if he's about to recite a poem. "First and foremost, I love Egypt. I love her heroic nature and what her many Kingdoms have brought us. Her struggles, I love them, too. Her noble intentions and courage, in casting her gaze away from her illustrious past and towards an uncertain future. I love the heritage she has given me, including formidable enemies, also Egyptian, who she has put in my path. Perhaps to keep me honest." He turns to Edna and takes her hand. "And I love that Egypt, in my passion for her, brought me to love, even if my love is not Egyptian at all."

Edna sighs a most girlish sigh, and brings Mohammad's hand to her lips. It is a moving sight, the two of them. A modern-day Capulet and Montague. I turn to Ripley and our eyes meet, taking refuge in what feels like a bottomless past we share, and an endless future. It's like nothing can keep us apart now.

"That was lovely," I say.

Ripley clinks his ale pot to Mohammad's. "And bold, my friend."

"Mohammad, my love," Edna whispers. "If it is Egypt you love most, and Egypt who brought us together, than I, too, love Egypt most of all."

Their lovemaking is interrupted by our big-bellied proprietor, who tops off our ale pots and places an assortment of nuts and dried fruits, along with flatbread and cheese, before us. An unexpected bounty for such an establishment, but then, what do I know of such places?

"Ripley, you should go next," Cornelius says. "Since you're the one who suggested the game."

Ripley nods, his eyes roaming over us all until they settle upon me once again. I am laid bare as everyone's attention follows.

"I'll go next," I stammer. Pulling my ale pot close, I look deeply into its contents. "I loved my mother."

I hear Cornelius snort.

"Loved," he says. "You said loved, not love. That's not the game."

I glance up from my ale pot, briefly, then let my eyes fall back into its comforting abyss. They're all looking at me, but it's Ripley's stare that feels as if it's going to pierce a hole through my head.

"Can I not love her the way Mohammad loves Egypt? For all she gave me."

"Not if you're to be honest."

I tip up my chin, releasing my ale pot and folding my arms over my chest.

"Well, then, how about you, Cornelius?" I counter. "You're going to say history, I'm sure. Or perhaps archaeology, which, by your definition, is no better answer than my mother."

Cornelius smiles. It's a wicked, little smile made of riddles. A quality I like most and least about him, the beast.

"I wasn't going to say history or archaeology."

"Then what were you going to say?" Ripley asks.

"Nothing."

"You love nothing?"

"No, I was going to say nothing, because what I love most is my secret and I don't wish to share it."

"But that's dishonest," I say. "And that's not the game."

"A secret is not a lie."

"Not fair!" Edna chimes in.

"Honesty often feels unfair," Cornelius tells us. "It's why people dislike it so."

A low chuckle comes from Ripley's side of the table.

"Then what about you?" Edna says. "You were going to tell us what you love, Ripley, before Leila's homage to her mother."

One can't help but smile at Edna. She has such a thoughtful, obliging nature, and her every word is sincere. She strokes my cheek, then gives it a sweet kiss. It's a gesture of friendship that touches me.

"What I love?" Ripley says.

I take a good, hard swallow of my ale and meet Ripley's

eyes. They have been waiting for me all this time, and quite nearly take my breath away.

"I love my destiny," he tells me as if it's he and I alone.

"But how can you love it if you don't know where it'll take you?" Edna says. "What if it's a terrible place where you find yourself bound to a rock with an eagle swooping down and eating your liver every day?"

"Ripley as the god Prometheus!" Cornelius exclaims.

Ripley entwines his fingers with mine. It is not the tender-hearted gesture we had witnessed minutes ago between the other lovers at the table. His hand grips mine, pressing our palms together as they grow hotter.

"Then I should savor the journey all the more, and the one with whom I am destined to travel it. My liver be damned."

The spell Ripley has cast on me is interrupted by a young man sitting on an ale barrel in the far corner of the room. He begins to pluck the strings of a lyre, slowly at first—*plung, plung, plung.* But soon his instrument begins to sing a classical Egyptian melody about the coming of a wind storm. It's a beautiful song that starts like a light breeze and picks up in tempo, becoming thrilling and dangerous.

From behind a violet curtain appears a ghawazee woman dressed in a scandalous garment made mostly of thin veils and tiny, metal bells. Her veils are of voluptuous colors, as overly ripe as her figure: ruby, yolk, moss, tangerine, plum. She spins about the room, her hands high above her head, winding like earthworms. Her hips shiver and her belly undulates as if they are not part of her body.

"Good Lord, what is that?" Edna gasps.

"It's a form of dancing."

"Dancing!" Ripley says. "Is that what it is?"

"It's been banned in Cairo for decades," Mohammad tells us, and Edna drops her shocked expression and begins to laugh.

"And do you dance this way?" Ripley asks me.

"Of course not. Not in public anyway." This answer delights Edna and makes poor Mohammad cast his eyes away in embarrassment. I lean in to the table as the young woman shimmers by, making my voice into a theatrical whisper. "My mother was quite fond of this type of dancing and did her best to get it un-banned, but to no avail. It is said that such movements give flight to feelings of reckless abandon and inspire rebellion in women and lust in men."

"How positively awful," Edna says through her giggles.

"I fear I can attest to the latter part."

"Ripley!" My cheeks burn, but this time in ire. The thought of Ripley feeling even the slightest craving for a woman other than myself . . . it . . . well, it's awful somehow.

"He's just being honest," Cornelius chides.

Ripley sweeps his hand across the table, knocking my reticule to the ground. He begs my pardon and, as he bends down to retrieve it, puts his lips briefly to my ear. "Only you."

"IT'S ONLY EVER YOU," he tells me, after we part ways with our friends.

We stand under the light of a lantern, waiting for Horus to fetch us and bring us home. The light is flickering over Ripley's face, making him look like a phantom from the underworld, and a handsome one at that. I hold the scrapbook Edna gave me to my breast, and think of how much I'd like to capture how Ripley looks right now inside of it, to have forever.

"I'm sorry," I say. "I know I was being silly. We were all just teasing, of course. I don't know what got into me. Half-naked women are a disturbance to anyone, I suppose."

Ripley steps closer and kisses my forehead. "You're a disturbance."

"To you?"

"Not just to me. To everyone you meet. To Cornelius."

I take one of my hands from its grasp on the scrapbook and place it on his shoulder. It's so strong and warm. My eyes follow the thick and graceful line of his jugular vein. They linger at his lips.

"Ripley," I whisper. "In the weeks when you and I weren't speaking, Cornelius and I did get close."

"Clearly."

"Perhaps your trust is a lot to ask when I've given you so little of mine."

"I trust you," Ripley says. "I trust you with my life."

The elegant trot of Uncle Hugo's Percheron can be heard all the way down the street. As it turns the corner and comes into view, Ripley and I step apart from one another. Horus's censuring eye falls upon us, and I give him a look that says, *yes, I know, not on a street, not even a nearly empty one,* then place my hands on my hips. Horus, the dear soul, winks at me. He's been our accomplice in helping Edna and Mohammad meet, and in allowing Ripley and me our own adventures. But even Horus, a hopeless romantic who still misses my mother dreadfully and would do anything for me, has his limits.

Ripley and I are silent on the ride back to Zamalek, but it isn't an awkward quiet. It's one made of unspoken promises. The ones I couldn't bear to offer in front of friends tonight, the way Edna and Mohammad did so easily.

The words "love" and "forever" stick in my throat like honey, harder to say than even lust and yearning. But they are there, sweet and persistent. They feel as old as time.

And then a chill rushes over me, and a feeling of dread settles in my gut. I don't know where it came from, breaking the spirit of wordless affection between Ripley and myself. Making the very air taste of a subtle toxin.

"Come to my room tonight after your father has retired," I whisper to Ripley. "Just to hold me until I fall asleep. I don't think I can bear it to be alone."

Chapter 14

Terrible News

NIF, *don't you feel it?*
    "*I feel nothing but you when I dream. And this body that's mine in this life—what a pleasure it is to use it to hold you like this.*"

I turn Leila towards him and hear her groan in her sleep. I open her eyes and gaze upon Nif. Fair-haired this time, but his eyes are the same. Always the same. I lift her hand to his face and trace his lips with eager fingertips. We kiss deeply and I feel soft hands roam over her body, my body. Not like Nif's calloused hands from his grip on his bow and arrow all those thousands of years ago.

She's much like you. How you were when we first met.
She is me. But he's nothing like you, and yet everything like you.
He is me, too.
Nif, you do feel it, don't you?

He waits a long moment to answer.

Yes. I feel it. Don't be afraid. I'm here and won't ever leave your side.
What is it?
I'm not sure.
But it is terrible.
Yes.
If there was ever a time for you to share your thoughts with me, it's now.

Nif unties the nightgown Leila's body wears. I cross my arms and grip the soft cotton, pulling it off entirely.

Whatever it is, Sherin, it's close and coming closer.

Then bring me close and closer tonight.

I'll bring you very close.

His hands caress my breasts and belly. It's funny, I've never thought of Leila's body as mine until now.

When we dream, we are who we were once and always, Sherin.

I ask Nif to love me.

They're not ready, Ripley and Leila. But they will be. Soon. When they learn who they are.

I awaken as a slice of morning light spreads across my bedding. I'm alone, but can still feel the impression of where Ripley slept, fitting his body to my own—although he did remain above the covers, while I was snuggled beneath them. He made it clear we would be as proper as we could be about things, considering, but seeing as I was rattled by an evil portent last night that I couldn't seem to shake, he was intent on offering me his comfort. My hand caresses where his knees had nuzzled mine, where his belly had given soft comfort to my back, where his shoulder had dug into the mattress. The mold of his figure in the coverlet is no longer warm, but the memory of being held by him as I slept is. It makes me wish it was like this every night.

The house is quiet. Rather strangely so. Dr. Davies is a maker of noise in the morning, a hard-stepper who makes no attempt at keeping his voice down and comments frequently on the news of the day. This morning, although it is most assuredly after seven already, the house has the stillness of a chapel. It may be that Ripley and his father have already left on an early call at the museum.

As I sit up, I notice my nightgown has come untied. Beneath the covers, it is bunched nearly at my waist and I blush at the prospect of Ripley somehow having known this. But no, he wouldn't. He slept above the covers, I remind myself, and I do tend to be a restless sleeper. One prone to tossing, turning, speaking out loud, and even walking sometimes. Good Lord, I hope I didn't do that.

Slinking out of bed, I tug my nightgown back into place. My skin feels especially sensitive this morning, like it does after a hot bath and a soft washcloth.

I dress and do a quick toilette, grab the copy of "Dracula" I took from home, and descend the stairs, expecting to find myself alone in the house. I am not, though. Ripley and Dr. Davies are sitting at the small game table by the window, both of them looking stricken. Dr. Davies's fingers are at his lips and Ripley stares down at the surface of the table until he hears the stairs creak.

He looks up at me, his jaw tense and his face devoid of his usual hearty color. I feel my stomach drop.

"Leila," he says.

"My God, what is it?"

"Leila . . . Mohammad and Edna. They're dead."

I feel the blood drain from my face in a violent deluge. My belly seizes, painfully, and I nearly double over.

"It's not possible," I say. Ripley rises up and rushes towards me, meeting me at the foot of the staircase and enveloping me in his arms. I feel his breath, slow and heavy at my neck, and somehow the rhythm of it, the very evidence of his life, quiets the thunder of my pulse.

"You'll need to sit down," he says. "I'm afraid this is not for the faint of heart."

"I'm hardly faint of heart," I tell him, but allow him to attend to me anyway, guiding me to the chair that he vacated.

"We just saw them last night," I stammer.

"It must have happened shortly after," Dr. Davies tells me.

I look back and forth between Ripley and his father. "What happened?"

Ripley crouches down onto one knee and takes my hand. Knowing just what I need, he looks deeply into my eyes, letting his own take me in. Bringing me to what feels like home.

"They were found in the rented room of a small hotel not far from where we parted ways with them. Edna had been—,"

"Ripley," Dr. Davies chides. "These are hardly details a young woman should be subjected to!"

"Dad, I have every intention of being gentle in my recitation of the events, but Leila needs to know what happened."

"With all due respect to both of you," I say. "While I'm grateful for your care in sparing my feelings, I want to know everything about Mohammad and Edna—and not gently. I assure you that whatever you're about to tell me, my constitution—both physical and emotional—can manage it."

My strident counter-position notwithstanding, I have to fight the tears that threaten to fall, because once they start, it'll be impossible to make them stop.

"Leila, perhaps Father has a point."

I square my shoulders and drop Ripley's hand. I do want to know—must know—and I don't know for certain why. But if Ripley tells me everything, I feel it will be clear. My whole being tells me this. It's as if what has happened to Mohammad and Edna has only one foot in what is taking place today, and another in the past. Our past. I whisper this to Ripley and his eyes widen, as if he, too, senses it.

He takes my hand once again, tracing his finger over my palm. He pulls me closer, and our free hands join our linked ones, making a white-knuckled mound radiating grief and fear and anticipation. He swallows, presses his lips together hard, and closes his eyes for a moment. When he opens them, he looks into mine, capturing me, comforting me, even before he speaks a single, terrible word.

"Edna's belly had been slashed from one end to the next by a very sharp dagger."

"Ripley, for the love of God!" Dr. Davies cries.

"Father please!" Ripley puts up his hand, imploring his father to let us be.

Dr. Davies looks to both me and his son. His face twists in confusion, his brow furrows. He rakes his fingers through his dense head of hair and slumps.

It is only then that Ripley turns his attention back to me. Fully, as if I'm the only person in the world. I nod, urging him to press on before I lose my nerve.

"She died quickly, though not instantly," he tells me. His words come at a slow, watchful pace. "That same dagger was plunged into Mohammad's lower abdominals and ripped upwards towards his sternum. He did not die as slowly, it would seem." Ripley swallows with a grimace, his eyes harden. "The police have decided that it was a murder-suicide."

"No!" I say, leaping up from my chair. "It was not." I begin to pace, my palms pressed against my temples like bookends.

"When we parted last night, everything was fine between them. Jolly even! Mohammad was going to escort Edna to a carriage and accompany her to the island before stepping off and allowing her to go the rest of the way without him. This is what they've done every time we've gotten together with them! And you know as well as I do that they'd never even consider getting a room together—and what reputable hotel would give them one regardless?"

Once I start, I simply can't stop.

"Murder-suicide, my foot! How long did it take for the police to come to such a ridiculous conclusion? All of five minutes?"

"That's exactly what dad and I were saying just before you came down. None of this makes any sense."

"What time were they discovered? We said our goodnights at just about nine, didn't we?"

"Midnight," Ripley tells me. "They were found at midnight. Apparently, other guests reported hearing strange noises coming from their room."

"And no one thought it the least bit odd that an Egyptian nationalist who has been splashed across every newspaper in town would get a room with a proper British girl? That's utterly absurd—especially when they've been planning their future with such care. Mohammad would never compromise Edna's reputation like that."

"It's all entirely, tragically odd," Dr. Davies concurs. "It has been suggested by the police that the forceful rejection of their union by each of their families was the catalyst for their horrible end."

"So, between nine and midnight they all of a sudden decided life wasn't worth living? That instead of defying their families with marriage, they would defy them with a bloody death—and after a lovely night out with friends? They talked all night about how they planned to make their lives together no matter what, didn't they Ripley?"

"Indeed. And Mohammad, who is brave enough to stage nationalist demonstrations and withstand death threats from not only strangers on the street, but his own relatives, would hardly take a coward's way out."

"Oh, good God," I say. "That could be it, couldn't it? His family. They're certainly powerful enough to sway a police investigation."

"Nonsense," Dr. Davies says. "Not such a civilized family as that."

"That did occur to me actually," Ripley says. "And to Mohammad. An uncle of his had threatened him more than once. Father, you know as well as I do that when it comes to honor, cultures in this part of the world have different ideas of what it means to act in a civilized manner. To them, defying your family can be the ultimate act of incivility."

"And punishable by death," I remind them.

Dr. Davies looks out the window, shaking his head. "Such a brilliant young man. And sweet young woman I might add. It was Lieutenant General Blackwood who delivered the frightful news to us this morning."

Dr. Davies pushes himself away from the table and goes to a sideboard, plucking his keys from an old clay bowl. "He and I were supposed to take breakfast together, but he had other things to attend to, as he's been selected as an advisor to the investigation. To look out for the interests of the Crown, naturally. He did ask, however, if—assuming you feel up to it—you would stop by and see him before lunch today. Since you and Ripley were the last to see them alive."

"Of course," I say, even if part of me wants to crawl back into bed and not emerge for a month. "Ripley, will you join me to pray before going with me to meet with the Lieutenant General?"

I feel the impulse to run headlong to the Lieutenant General's office, but a little voice inside me, perhaps my mother's, warns me to seek guidance first.

"Excellent idea, son," Ripley's father says. "You should take the day to tend to Leila."

A MORNING OF PRAYER was indeed helpful in smoothing the sharpest edges of our grief. A reminder that God had taken Mohammad and Edna to his breast, letting them into the gates of heaven no matter what preposterous notions of self-murder the police had about their terrible end. Christian or no, I've always believed deep in my heart that our Heavenly

Father takes all the good souls to live with him, and our friends were good to the core – this much I know. But the painful bruises left by their loss are great, and will continue to ache for a long time to come. This I know too.

It's why Ripley and I are determined to make sure Lieutenant General Blackwood has our full account of the hours before our friends met with their doom, and that he will pressure the police for truthful answers. If a member, or members, of Mohammad's family were in any way involved in this tragedy, there is still hope that the power of British Common Law will prevail over the sway of dynastic connections.

"Good morning," the Lieutenant General says, holding wide the heavy door to his office.

Yes, it is still morning, I realize when he greets us. Ten-thirty.

Ripley and I enter Lieutenant General Blackwood's office with heavy hearts. It looks much like I expected. Of wood and wicker, a Turkish rug, a picture of the King most prominently displayed behind his desk, along with Queen Victoria and Prince Albert on either side. Several military portraits are positioned underneath, but none that I recognize. Otherwise, it's neat as a barracks, with his desktop clean not only of dust but any nonessential.

"I thank you for coming so soon after hearing the news," he tells us. "I know they were friends and that you'd likely prefer to keep to yourselves on a day like today. But time is of the essence if a murder has taken place."

"So you do think it's murder!" I cry out.

"I did say 'if' Miss Leila. I make no conclusions about prospective criminal cases until I have all of the facts in hand."

"I thought you were only an advisor to the investigation."

The Lieutenant General gives me a wry smile. "Well, my recommendations have been known to have some influence."

He guides us to two rather small, but comfortable enough

wooden chairs with quilted green leather seat cushions. We sit and Lieutenant General Blackwood positions himself across from us, at his desk.

"Between ourselves, I think it would be irrational to pretend that the most obvious explanation for last night's tragic events would be that young Mr. Gamal and Miss Watson made the decision to rip one another to shreds," he tells us. "Especially when pistols and poisons are so easy to come by."

"Pistols and poisons notwithstanding, it would be irrational to think Mohammad would ever do anything to harm Edna," Ripley says.

"Or that Mohammad, who has never shown even the slightest inclination towards cowardice would find himself in sudden despair over a situation he never expected to change and he had every intention of defying," I add.

Without further ado, Ripley and I provide Lieutenant General Blackwood with every detail we can possibly recall from the night before. Even the bits of information—the café, the dancer—that don't particularly reflect well on us. To his credit, the Lieutenant General doesn't even flinch, looking on with the detached interest of a man studying his hand of cards.

"A game of honesty, you say." Lieutenant General Blackwood taps his index finger on his desk. "Young Mr. Gamal, the hero of the Egyptian Nationalist movement professes his love for Egypt over pints of ale and then . . . abandons his country only a couple of hours later?"

"Bloody unlikely," Ripley says.

"Or, as the Interior Ministry is inclined to see things, Mr. Gamal, an unhinged political activist in love with a young lady who is a distinguished citizen of the very empire he wishes his beloved Egypt to be free from, finds his heart and his ideology at odds and, in a moment of passion, kills his beloved, then turns his wrath upon himself."

"You can't possibly believe even a trace of that account," I say.

"Ripley, Leila, as I told you, my thoughts on the investigation have some influence, but this is a matter for the police, and the Queen hasn't kept her empire intact by interfering unnecessarily in what can be described as a family matter, if you get my meaning. The only reason I'm involved at all is because a British subject has been found dead. The problem is, when that subject is a young, unmarried woman discovered in a barely respectable hotel and under unwholesome circumstances, both the family of the young woman involved and the Crown are eager for the whole unpleasant episode to go away."

"Just like the young woman in the City of the Dead," I whisper.

Lieutenant General Blackwood leans forward and folds his hands, placing them carefully on the perfectly polished wood of his desk. "Say again?"

Ripley and I meet eyes. I can see the thought about that poor girl occurred to us simultaneously, as is happening more and more frequently of late.

"It's a friend of ours," Ripley says. "Cornelius Neville, who works as an assistant to my father. He's been staying in the necropolis and mentioned the murder of a young woman there—a grisly one, similar to Mohammad and Edna's except for the fact that she was alone. Not much was made of it, as the family would have been shamed by her late night activities in Cairo."

The Lieutenant General strokes his chin, his eyes trained on Ripley. "Does this friend of yours know any other details of this alleged murder?"

Ripley shrugs. "He'll be at my father's office right now, and we could send a boy to go get him."

"I would very much like to talk to him, but I'm afraid

that'll have to wait. I must leave here in a few minutes and go to the hotel where Mr. Gamal and Miss Watson's bodies were found. The police commissioner would like to meet with me later this afternoon, and I don't think I need to tell you that it's his hope to close the books on this case at that time."

I leap up from my chair, nearly knocking it right over. "He can't! Please, Lieutenant General, you can't let him close the investigation!"

Ripley stands as well, though his posture is far more controlled than mine. "Leila's right. It would be a great injustice, not only to those who cared about Mohammad and Edna, but to the Egyptian nationalists who idolize him. They will certainly not be content with closing the books on this case, and I can't imagine the Crown or the Cairo police would be happy with the sort of civic unrest that this could cause once word gets out."

Lieutenant General Blackwood pushes himself away from his desk and takes a deep, patience-inducing breath. He stands, appearing ready to excuse himself.

"I assure you both I have no intention of allowing the investigation to close until I've uncovered every possible detail that could unearth what happened between nine in the evening last night, when you last saw your friends, and midnight, when they were found by the hotelier. That being said, if we're unable to provide a convincing counter-narrative to the one the police are quite satisfied by, we will have no choice but to allow the matter to be resolved as the Cairo police sees fit."

"Lieutenant General, please," Ripley says. "Would you consider allowing me to accompany you to the hotel? There could be a clue that might be plain to me in a way that it would not be to you or the police. I mean, due to my presence during their final hours."

"Me, too!" I say, and both Ripley and Lieutenant General Blackwood turn to face me rather abruptly.

"The crime scene is largely as it was when it was discovered, and I'm afraid such a gruesome sight is not fit for a lady," Lieutenant General Blackwood says.

"Not to mention that both my father and yours would be aghast if they knew that either the Lieutenant General or I exposed you to something of that sort!"

Their fealty to convention, while understandable under other circumstances, is infuriating after what's happened!

"I'll decide what's fit for this lady," I tell them both. "I'll have you know that in addition to having a most hearty stomach, I have every intention of involving myself in all aspects of our friends' murder investigation and I won't hear another word in contravention to my wishes!"

"And I won't hear another word in contravention to my orders," Lieutenant General Blackwood says. "Look, the bodies have been removed in the most dignified manner possible. What's left is a bloody mess—and I mean that literally. Leila, your father—he's not even here to give his permission for such a thing, but he would hardly want you anywhere near the scene of a murder. Even the murder of friends."

"Lieutenant General, I beg of you," I say. "I feel I need to go. You see, I had the most troubling intuition last night on the way back to the Davieses', and a restless night of sleep. I wish I'd listened to that instinct and hadn't tried to chase it from my thoughts. If I had, perhaps . . ."

"None of this is your fault," Ripley tells me tenderly.

"None of this is anyone's fault except for the perpetrator of this horrendous act." Lieutenant General Blackwood folds his arms across his chest and gives me a look of pure intention. "And you don't need to torture yourself with needless trips to crime scenes that can only offer you more sorrow."

"Lieutenant General," Ripley says, casting a glance in my

direction. "I must tell you, I had the same intuition as Leila did last night. While I wasn't raised to give such feelings too much thought, I've been taking them rather seriously of late. I am young, I know, and Leila is even younger. I don't wish to cause her trauma any more than you do, but what if Leila's right? What if, somehow, she and I hold the key to what happened to Mohammad and Edna?"

Ripley comes to me and takes my hand.

"I'm sorry I didn't mention my own dreadful inkling last night. I didn't know where it was coming from and I didn't wish to upset you, especially since you yourself were so out of sorts. I didn't connect it to Mohammad and Edna until this morning, when we received the terrible news."

Ripley looks down at my hand and turns it over, palm-up. He stares right into the spot that usually burns and I feel it grow warmer.

"Lieutenant General Blackwood, I know this is more than an irregular request, and part of me hates that I'm asking. Will you allow me and Leila to accompany you to the hotel? I can't say it's anything more than a hunch, and in all likelihood we'll add little of value to the investigation, but surely, under these extraordinary circumstances, it's worth a try?"

Lieutenant General Blackwood walks to his window, looking out at the Nile. He looks visibly older than on the other occasions I've been in his company. The lines around his eyes are deeper, and there are more of them. His mouth, the way it has settled, is heavy with disappointment. In others, in himself, even in God, perhaps.

"Leila, Ripley, I've seen my share of horrors. On the battlefield, and on common city streets. I don't know which is worse. I can tell you without reservation that I am not a better man for having seen such things. My sleep is the poorer for it. My conscience is full of shadows. I don't wish that upon you."

"I wish none of this," I say. "But it has happened. As for my father, you're right that he wouldn't want me to see the scene of a murder, but he also wouldn't wish the heaviness of my heart upon me, the torturous images that my mind is conjuring. And I can assure you, Lieutenant General, that any pool of blood—brown and drying at this point—is no match for where my own imagination has already taken me."

The Lieutenant General's eyes soften a little, but his wisp of a smile grows sadder. "I have no doubt of the powers of your imagination."

"Then please, sir, let us come with you. Let us help put our friends to rest."

Chapter 15

Seeing a Ghost

TO CALL THE HOTEL where Mohammad and Edna were murdered "barely respectable" is giving it a compliment. The outside is a shambles, with crumbling plaster covering pock-marked brick that peeks out in large patches shaped like countries on a map. The only hint of a more illustrious past is a stone archway—possibly hundreds of years old—that leads to the front door. It is through there that Ripley, Lieutenant General Blackwood, and I enter.

The interior, consisting of only a small foyer with a desk—no chair—is at least tidy, and looks to have had a coat of whitewash put on the walls in the past decade or so. The floors are of mosaic tile in excellent condition and I don't know why that matters to me, but it does. Perhaps it's because I just want there to be some level of decency here, in the last place Mohammad and Edna will have seen.

A man I assume is the hotelier peeks out from the dark mouth of a staircase a few steps behind his desk. He nods at the Lieutenant General, and wrinkles his nose at Ripley and me, shooting us a look of stern judgement. Can't say as I blame him. Here we are, yet another odd young couple reminiscent of the two unfortunate souls who besmirched his establishment. He scampers over to us, handing the Lieutenant General a key, then leaves in haste, as if we are the ones who brought the specter of death here.

As we ascend the unlit staircase, a feeling of dread settles over me. While I am determined to have a careful look at the crime scene, I'm not at all looking forward to it. At the top of the stairs, Ripley, the Lieutenant General, and I enter the small corridor leading to the room where Mohammad and Edna were found. It's bare and reeks of abandonment. I hate every inch of it.

We walk as if we have joined a funeral procession, which, in a way, we have. At the door, the Lieutenant General bends down to pick up one of several taper holders, each fitted with a thick, white candle. They must have been brought here after our friends were discovered. He strikes a match and lights two, handing one to Ripley.

"Onward," Ripley says.

He puts his arm around me, and I'm grateful.

As the door opens, we all take an audible breath. The unpleasant smell of a liquor I can't identify—certainly not the ale of last night—drifts over to us.

Lieutenant General Blackwood steps inside, casting light into the room. The only other light comes from sharp, thin streams that burst out between the closed slats of a shuttered window.

I don't know quite what I expected, but it was not a neat room with a slender, single bed, fully made. A small, bad painting of The Mosque of Ibn Tulun hangs above the wooden headboard, its artless strokes visible from where we stand.

It is the floor that instantly sickens me once I allow my gaze to go there. I must have gasped, because both Ripley and the Lieutenant General look to me in concern.

There is so much blood. A large, tacky pool of it next to the bed, its edges dried. It swallows the prayer rug it is spilled upon, and I have a deep and instant suspicion that it is where Edna died.

"It's alright," Ripley whispers, and kisses my forehead. But I don't think he feels any better than I do. I grit my teeth and recover my composure, at least on the outside. I will not give either of the men any reason to insist I leave.

"That is where Miss Watson was felled," Lieutenant General Blackwood says, confirming my intuition. "If you look closely, you can see the spurt of blood that splashed on the coverlet, as well as the speckles that were strewn all over the area. She was stabbed with some force before she was . . . um . . ."

"Gutted," I finish.

"Yes. It would have been done by a strong man."

"And quite a determined one," Ripley adds. "Hardly a crime of passion or despair, is it? Seems more like one of hatred."

"You think someone could have hated your friends so much?"

"Or hated himself," I say.

The Lieutenant General shrugs and shakes his head. "If that were the case, I would think he'd do the honorable thing and kill himself."

I look to Ripley, and I can see he's thinking the same thing I am: Not if the killer would only be born again to begin the same unbearable cycle.

Our attention turns to a simple chair and table at the opposite end of the room. It is there we spy an empty bottle with no markings, presumably the source of the liquor and its subsequent pong. The chair's legs are covered in dried blood, and yet another large sanguineous oval lies beneath it. It would appear Mohammad died there, seated, struggling. Smears of blood paint the surface of the table, where his left hand must have flailed, while he tried to stem the bleeding with his right. Awful. The devil at work.

"He must have been tied to the chair as he died," I say to

Ripley. A tacky bile threatens my throat, but I'm able to keep it down.

Lieutenant General Blackwood cocks his head. "What makes you say that?"

"Because he would have otherwise crawled to Edna. At least to be with her—even if she was already dead."

"That's assuming he didn't kill her."

"We *are* assuming that, aren't we?" Ripley says. "Isn't that why we're here?"

"Go on," says the Lieutenant General.

"Look at the way the blood beneath the chair seems to flow away from it, towards where Edna would have been. Doesn't that indicate that he might have been kicking, inadvertently pushing the blood pool in that direction?"

"I had the same thought," Lieutenant General Blackwood tells me. "Although not until you mentioned the possibility of Mr. Gamal being tied. He was not that way when he was found, I should tell you."

"Wouldn't there be signs of bruising if he'd been tied?" Ripley says. "Has his body been examined by a physician yet?"

"That should be happening presently."

My eyes keep finding their way to the table top. Where, in Mohammad's dying moments, he had smeared his own blood. There is something about the curve of line, a purposefulness to the way the blood has been spread, a familiarity. I step as close as I can, without dipping my feet into the mess of death on the floor, and stand on my toes to get a better look.

"Ripley," I whisper.

He stands behind me, his breath ragged and disbelieving. Yes, he must see it, too. The coil, unmistakably serpentine. The larger, diamond shape reminiscent of the head, the open mouth about to strike.

Lieutenant General Blackwood comes next to us and, when he takes a look at the table top, his eyes widen and he staggers backward. His face goes bone white. "Good God."

Ripley and I are both rather stunned at his reaction. While yes, the image painted in Mohammad's blood is too uncanny for us not to notice—we had spent much time yesterday examining Dr. Davies' ancient breastplate. But to our knowledge, the Lieutenant General hasn't seen the artifact. Dr. Davies certainly hadn't shown it to Mohammad. I look once more at the table top to make sure I'm not imagining things. The proportions are just like the snake icon that had adorned a soldier's chest so many thousands of years ago.

"Could be a coincidence," I say with little conviction. I feel hot and cold all at once.

"It could not," the Lieutenant General murmurs.

"The shape of a serpent is quite common in ancient cultures. Just as my father said."

"What?" Lieutenant General Blackwood shakes his head, running his hand through his thinning hair.

"The ancient breastplate with the serpent," Ripley says. "The one father has been studying."

Lieutenant General Blackwood swallows hard, and, even from several steps away, I can hear the dryness of his throat. "Yes, he told me about the breastplate."

"But you haven't seen it?"

Lieutenant General Blackwood shakes his head. "Forgive me, but what does your father's relic have to do with anything?"

Ripley and I look to one another, utterly mystified.

"Quite a bit," I say. "Lieutenant General Blackwood, perhaps you should sit down. You look like you've seen a ghost."

"I think I have seen a ghost," he tells us.

Dazed, he wanders to the window and opens the shutters, letting the strong midday sun flood the room. In the light, the room of death looks obscene. Deceptively cheerful, as if this place is already urging us to move on from the tragic events that occurred here only a few hours ago. This reminder that Mohammad and Edna were still alive only yesterday feels abrupt and bitter, and brings a new wave of grief with it.

I dare to look down, taking in the blood pools in the full light of day. They look entirely different now that I can get a really good gander at them. The blood has separated, leaving a thick rim of dried blackness at the edges, and some yellow serum. There's a lumpy, congealed ruby island in the center of both pools. It reminds me of the jellyfish that float on the surface of the Pelagos Sea in the early summer, and this happy memory juxtaposed against this horrific event turns my stomach.

"Leila," Lieutenant General Blackwood says. "Do you remember when I told you about the boy who saw a man with fiery eyes rushing away from where Annie Chapman's body was found in Whitechapel?"

I nod, and glance at Ripley whose eyebrow is raised in interest.

"The smear of blood—the one the boy watched the Ripper make with Miss Chapman's blood. I left out a detail when I was telling you that part. A most curious one. See, it wasn't just any smear. It was an image he made with his victim's blood—one very similar to the one on this table."

"My Lord," I say. "I don't remember anything resembling such a detail in the reportage around the Ripper mystery."

"Wait a minute," Ripley says. "Are you talking about Jack the Ripper? *The* Jack the Ripper."

"Indeed," the Lieutenant General confirms.

"And you think whoever did this is copying The Ripper, duplicating the peculiarities of the crime?"

"Ripley, no one save myself and a handful of men at

Scotland Yard know about the serpentine smear of blood near Annie's body. Unlike your friend Mohammad, she couldn't have drawn it herself, as her throat was cut savagely and she would have died very quickly—possibly even by asphyxiation before being mutilated. So, yes, you remembered correctly, Leila, that there was no mention of this in the papers or anywhere else. The police always keep some details close to their vests in order to weed out the troubled souls who feel the urge to confess to crimes they didn't commit."

"Lieutenant General," Ripley says. "Are you saying that the only other living man who might possibly know of such an element of those dreadful crimes was The Ripper himself?"

"Possibly. Could hardly have drawn itself could it?"

"But it could hardly be drawn by anyone else either," I say. "The breastplate was only just discovered, and far from here, let alone Whitechapel nearly twenty years ago. The relic had no recognizable image until Dr. Davies very carefully removed the debris that had collected on it. By any reasonable assumption, no one has seen the exact figure on the breastplate for several millennia."

The Lieutenant General shakes his head and looks about the room. He rubs his chin and neck, blinking his eyes hard and good. "We've been spooked, of course. Happens all the time in murder investigations—particularly ones as wretched and gruesome as this. Coincidence is a common trait in the realm of death."

"This seems more than just a common coincidence," I say. "We all recognize the image. Good Lord, Lieutenant General Blackwood, you yourself looked like you were about to faint, and unless I'm greatly mistaken, you are not the fainting type."

Lieutenant General Blackwood emits a deep, dark chuckle. One laced with irony.

"Leila, Ripley, come, let's leave this place."

The Lieutenant General closes the shutters and ushers us out of the dreadful room, closing and locking the door behind him with a certain vehemence. He leads us down the corridor, to the top of the stairs, where he stops and turns to us. He takes a very deep breath and purses his lips.

"In Malaya, some years ago," he says, "the wife of a young lieutenant was strangled while she was out walking her spaniel one evening. Three people, all unknown to one another, described a man in formal dress fleeing the scene of the crime. He was said to have a long, white beard, and wore a large sapphire ring. The woman's husband, a man I knew, although not well, was one of the witnesses. He swore the man who murdered his wife was his father-in-law, and even described the deep engravings of a fleur-de-lis on either side of the sapphire ring. The same pattern imprinted on the young wife's neck. An open and shut case, wouldn't you say?"

Ripley and I nod.

"Only the man the witnesses saw, the man who was described in such detail, and, in the case of the bereaved lieutenant, by someone who knew him, wasn't there at all. He couldn't have possibly been, for he'd been dead for over five years. And had died shortly after attending the theater, and wearing exactly the attire that was described by stranger and kin alike on the night of his daughter's murder."

Lieutenant General Blackwood places his hand on my shoulder and looks at me specifically.

"Violent death brings violent thoughts. It awakens cruel spirits—mostly of our own imaginings. And yes, that young woman's father had been a vicious man. Had he not already been dead he would have indeed been a prime suspect. Even without the benefit of witnesses."

"You think the blood painting of the ancient snake at Annie Chapman's death and at Mohammad and Edna's is just a figment of our collective fantasies?"

The Lieutenant General looks to both me and Ripley this time, and with great purpose. "I do."

But I feel he's trying to convince himself more than us.

Chapter 16

Poor Mrs. Watson

MRS. **W**ATSON has been confined to her bed since poor Edna's murder, although no one but me, Ripley, Cornelius, and Lieutenant General Blackwood will actually call it that—a murder. Most everyone else simply changes the subject, feeling it's improper to speak openly of alleged suicides and the implied moral failings of anyone who would die by their own hand, let alone the hand of a lover, outside the confines of marriage and social custom. It's infuriating.

Despite the fact that I never did have much affection for Edna's mother, I have nothing but the most heartfelt sympathy for what the woman must be going through. Not only to lose her daughter to such malevolence, but to feel the cold shoulder of disapproval from her very community.

That's why, no matter that both Ripley and Dr. Davies have advised against it, I have every intention of paying Mrs. Watson a visit today. Even if she is still far from being in any condition to leave her bedroom, as I've been warned.

"To grieve a daughter is one thing, to grieve alone is another," I told Ripley. "And it's Saturday. What a torment it must be for her to hear children playing outside, people laughing."

"Then I'll come with you."

While I appreciated his offer, and Ripley really has hardly left my side since all of this began, I know in my heart that

I need to do this alone. Apart from Mrs. Watson's cool feelings toward Ripley after catching him outside her daughter's window, I think even without such unpleasantness between them that I am doing what is right. A woman like Mrs. Watson prefers the company of someone of her own sex at most times, let alone one like this.

I bid good morning to Ahit, Mrs. Watson's girl, and she welcomes me inside, albeit with some trepidation. Taking the tray of tea and biscuits I've brought, she resigns herself to my presence and leads me up the stairs. All along she whispers most distressingly about Mrs. Watson's mental state.

"One can hardly blame her," I say.

But Ahit seems to think that poor Edna's mother has entered a most unholy state beyond any level of normal bereavement. Naturally, she attributes this not only to the violent manner of Edna's death, but the grave and deeply wicked sins Edna committed. Ones that ensured her an immediate place in hell. While it pains me to hear such talk, knowing as I do how very untrue it is, I remain largely silent as Ahit speaks. She's a simple woman who would always take the word of the greater society over mine, and holds me in suspicion for being a friend of Edna's. In fact, I get the impression that her words are meant as something of a warning for me to mend my own ways.

Upon unlocking Mrs. Watson's bedroom door, Ahit places the tea tray on the floor and turns to go. I grip her arm and stop her.

"Why have you kept her locked in her room?" I ask in Arabic.

She tells me it was on orders of Mr. Watson, who has accompanied his daughter's body to England, where she will be buried. Mrs. Watson, apparently, was not considered to be in any shape to make the trip with him, and I'm horrified to think that she's being kept from her own child's funeral!

"She could not have gone. Not like this. You'll see," Ahit tells me. She twists her arm from my grasp and rushes down the stairs as if fleeing the scene of a crime.

As I listen to the desperate scamper of Ahit's footsteps, I am overcome by the terribleness of it all. The biblical scale of tragedy that has befallen the house of Watson. I ready myself to offer comfort, although the tea and biscuits I've brought seem such a small gesture as to almost be an insult.

I crank the door handle and crouch down to pick up my pathetic offering. A floral waft of the Earl Grey tickles my senses, and I hope against hope, as I push the door open with my toe, that Mrs. Watson will find the smell a comfort.

The sun streams in from a large picture window. Speckles of dust sparkle and dance in its beams. Somehow, I had expected the room to be dark, with the shades pulled—like the hotel room where Mohammad and Edna had been killed. Not far from the window is Mrs. Watson's bed. The covers are tucked under her chin and she wears a cap with lace trim over her hair. Her face is tipped towards the window and her eyes are open, but they don't appear to be seeing anything. She hardly even looks to be breathing.

"Mrs. Watson?" I say. "It's me, Leila. I've brought you some tea and biscuits."

I place the tray on a side table near her dressing area and pour her a steaming cup of Earl Grey in a porcelain teacup festooned with country roses. My hand shaking, I place a biscuit on the saucer and carry the refreshment to her night table.

Now that I can get a close look at her, I can see why Ahit did not wish to enter the bedroom. Mrs. Watson is bone white, like one of Dracula's wives, and bluish crescents cradle her gray, lifeless eyes. I sit at the edge of her bed and place my hand gently on her shoulder. She doesn't seem to notice.

"I can't tell you how sorry I am," I whisper. "But what I

can tell you is that Edna's soul is with God in heaven. This I promise you. No matter what the police are saying, I know that Edna was an innocent and I will do everything I can to help bring the man who did this to justice."

My words seem to have no effect on her, but I continue speaking anyway. I feel the need to let her know everything I know, especially since I was one of the last people to see her daughter alive, apart from Mohammad and the murderer.

"Edna loved Mohammad very much. I know you didn't think well of him, but I want you to know he fought for her. I saw the room where they died, and even as he sat tied to a chair, bleeding to death, he tried to reach her, to be with her."

I lean closer to Mrs. Watson and place my fingers lightly on her cheek. "Edna wasn't alone. She died with someone who loved her, who would have done anything to save her if he could. And she did not die in disgrace. I don't know how Edna and Mohammad ended up at that hotel, but I am sure they were brought there or lured there by whoever killed them."

I sit up and scoot closer to Mrs. Watson. I do my best to fluff her pillows and tuck stray, knotty hairs under her night cap. Dipping my finger into her warm tea, I dot some droplets on her lip, but she ignores them, letting them stream down her chin like tears.

Swallowing my own tears, I recite to her an Egyptian prayer for the dead. I do it for her and for Edna and Mohammad. For the Egypt that brought them together and carried them to the next world.

"May you be given bread and beer, beef and fowl, clothing and ointment, everything good and pure such as the souls of the blessed dead live upon."

Placing my thumb on her forehead, I make the sign of the cross and finish with a Coptic prayer. One of many said at my mother's funeral. "Let us ask God the Pantocrator, the

Father of our Lord, God and Savior, Jesus Christ. We ask and entreat Your goodness, O lover of mankind, remember, O Lord, the souls of Your servants who have fallen asleep. That Christ our God may repose all their souls in the paradise of joy; and we, too, accord mercy unto us, and forgive us our sins."

For the first time, Mrs. Watson displays a sign of life. It's a small sign, just the quiver of her eyelids, but at least it's something. Perhaps she did hear my prayers and they gave her some solace.

"I'll visit again, if you don't mind. Perhaps tomorrow or Monday."

I rise from her bed and take a rather exhausted breath. I am so drained of vitality that my legs move as if they're packed with lead. At her door I turn around once more, and jump when I see her. I had expected Mrs. Watson to be staring out the window, as she has been, but she is not. Instead, she is turned towards me, her eyes wide.

"Mrs. Watson," I say. "Are you alright?"

Her lips part as if she intends to answer, but instead she begins to hum a strange melody. It's an olden one, nearly resembling a howl, and it makes my heart flutter. Her mouth opens wider, and she begins to sing what I think are words, though in a language I cannot name. To my ear, it is a jumble of consonants that make no sense at all. But as she continues to sing the lyrics, I begin to understand. At first just a word or two, but then the whole of it. As if sensing my comprehension, she begins to sing louder, stronger.

There is a wind in the desert that bellows; there is a wind in the desert that wails in anguish.

There is a wind that speaks of ghosts and memories; there is a wind that sings your funeral song.

I can hardly move, breathe, think. My hand reaches behind me, searching for the door handle. I grasp it at last, jiggling it desperately until, finally, it gives way and the door opens. I back up, nearly tripping on my skirt as Mrs. Watson sits up, all the while continuing on with this song. A song I know. That I've heard in my dreams all my life.

There is a wind that divulges secrets and murmurs deceptions. It blows long hair wild, clawing skin from bone. There is a wind. There is a wind for everything.

I turn, stumbling until I find my footing. My feet barely touch the stairs as I descend them, passing a stunned Ahit as I rush out the front door without so much as a word.

⸻ ◈ ◈ ⸻

"I HAVE TO GET OUT of here," I blurt out before Ripley or his father can even utter a greeting. "I'm going to go see my father in Aswan."

Even I can see how jagged my movements are as I make my way through their sitting room, intent on going up and packing my things.

"Leila," Ripley says. "What on earth?"

As happy as I am to see him, even Ripley cannot console me. "Nothing. Everything. I just miss him and, with all that's happened, I think it would be best if I go."

Dr. Davies looks to Ripley in distress, and I let my face fall into my hands. I've made a mess of this already, I can see, and the two of them must think I need an alienist. Steeling myself, I put my arms to my sides, trying my best to keep my lips from quivering. Poor Ripley steps towards me, but I put out my hand for him to stop.

"You should never have let her go to that hotel with you and the Lieutenant General, for goodness sake!" Dr. Davies says. "A woman, particularly of Leila's delicate age, shouldn't be subjected to—"

"Oh, Dr. Davies, for the love of God, I've seen more blood and death than you ever will in your one measly life!"

I gasp and bite down. "I'm sorry," I mumble. "I don't know what came over me."

"Dad, if you'll excuse us, I'm going to take Leila upstairs."

I feel Ripley's hands upon my shoulders and know instantly how wrong I was. I walk into his arms, needing every bit of his comfort, and he holds me better than anyone ever could.

"Yes, yes, of course," I hear Dr. Davies say. "She needs to rest."

That's the last thing I need, I want to say. I breathe deeply into Ripley's chest, where his heart beats, wishing it could be bare and that I could feel the raw warmth of it.

Ripley stoops down and hooks his arm beneath my legs, lifting me up. He carries me up the stairs and takes me to my room, laying me down upon the mint coverlet. Sweetly, he removes my shoes and places them next to my bed.

"What happened?"

"I don't know."

He takes my hand and sits at the edge of my bed just as I had done to poor Edna's mother.

"I wish it was just that I was going mad," I whisper. "A frightened girl who has seen too much for her sensitive nature."

Ripley's finger touches the hollow in my neck and my whole body comes alive to him. "A sensitive nature?" he teases. "Hardly."

I tell him everything that happened at Mrs. Watson's, the whole story coming out in a torrent. He listens carefully, stroking my head, and holding my hand.

"I feel as if we're being haunted," I tell him. "Like the stories in my books."

He leans over and kisses me so tenderly. My temple, my cheek, my lips.

"What if we're not the ones being haunted, but those doing the haunting?" I whisper. "What if, somehow, all of this is our fault?"

Ripley unbuttons his shirt and holds my hand to his heart. I want to bore through his chest and hold it, red and beating, in my hands. I want to crawl inside him and shelter behind his bones. But his eyes give me strength. The rivers of amber and blood within them rush and glimmer.

"Then I shall make it right. If it's the last thing I do."

Chapter 17

WE SIT ON A BENCH carved with Moorish flourishes, Ripley and I. Our dahabya cruises gracefully down the Nile, her two white sails, one near the stern and the other near the bow, swell and wave.

"Is this how a guardian would hold his ward?" I ask Ripley. He's behind me with his arms firmly around my middle.

"I'm not actually your guardian," he says. "I'm merely traveling as your guardian. Making sure you arrive in Aswan safely."

"I still don't know how you convinced your father," I tell him. "Even if, although barely, you are a legal adult."

The truth is, there has been a maturity in Ripley that has changed him since the night we first met. The night he crawled out of poor Edna's window. He didn't so much as ask his father's permission to accompany me to Aswan to visit my father, but told him so. Dr. Alfred Davies didn't put up a word of opposition, despite how obvious the progression of our relationship has become.

Ripley booked us two cabins on the Dahabya Oriental, a lovely boat that holds ten passengers and more than twice as many crewmembers. All the comforts of The Shepheard Hotel and under a night sky, with a river breeze blowing through our hair.

It's late and the last of our fellow passengers have gone

below deck—stuffed from a grand, French-inspired dinner of quail and perch, and soused with wine and brandy.

"On the Nile, nothing can be believed or depended on, they say."

"Hmm. And who told you that?" I whisper.

I turn to him, nestling in closer, my hands gliding over the ripples of muscle and bone beneath the thin linen of his shirt. When he kisses me, it's as if we belong to each other like darkness to night.

"We should retire to our cabins," he says.

"I'm afraid to. I'll dream of you again."

Last night, our first night on the dahabya, Ripley and I had the same dream. In it, we were lying on a bed of soft linens the color of rose periwinkle. We were naked, he and I, my brown body painted in bold hues that told a story. Of a desert, of love, of hands at my collar, as if holding up my head. A child's face on my hip. And flowers. So many beautiful flowers the likes of which I'd never seen. It was something to behold, my painted body—a work of art that could have held its own in the Italian Renaissance.

As for Ripley, he was not painted at all. His beauty was as raw as an uncut gem. We were entwined, his body lithe and strong. His hair dark and curly. Yet it was him.

In the morning, we awakened in each other's arms. I must have come to his cabin, walking in my sleep, since I don't remember having gotten up at all. We were snuggled under the covers, bare-skinned, and I shudder to think that I might have gone to his cabin without a stitch on. Not because I mind if Ripley sees me. It's as if my body were his. But if I wandered elsewhere, per chance, in sight of the crew, I will be mortified.

Ripley was ever the gentleman about our strange predicament. He gave me his robe and turned away as I got up from his bed. Although my skin felt tender all over, much as it had on the night Ripley held me while I slept, that terrible night

Edna and Mohammad had been killed, I was quite certain my maidenhead was intact. I felt no other disturbance of my person. Only the ghost of his touch.

"We'll lock our cabin doors tonight," he says.

"Your attention to my virtue is almost funny given that the first time I saw you, you were sneaking about late at night." I stop myself from saying more, and shiver as I remember poor Edna kissing Ripley's cheek as he buttoned up his shirt. He'd been helping two lovers, now dead, spend a few precious moments together.

"Oh, Ripley." He holds me tighter and I feel him expel a deep, sad breath.

The night sky twinkles above us. The moon is bright, but not full. It's as if the view were an old picture that's been handed down to us from generation to generation for centuries. Maybe more. At least we have this.

"Do you know what I called you last night?"

Ripley nods. He takes my fingers to his lips. "You called me Nif."

"Nif." I savor the name on my tongue. "Why does it feel so good to say it?"

Ripley leans in and kisses my neck so softly. "I think it's what you've always called me."

"Nif," I whisper, and Ripley kisses me once more.

WE ARRIVE in Aswan nearly a full day early, and at sunset. The rocky shore is aglow in orange light. Father is unmistakable, even at a distance. He stands in a pale suit, waving his hat at us just as he did at Uncle Hugo and Aunt Clara when we arrived in Cairo, what feels like years ago now, but isn't quite three months.

"Oh, dear, your noses," Father says.

Ripley's fair English complexion was not made for the desert sun. His nose is like a cherry tomato, even if he did wear his hat every day during high sun. My nose is merely rosy-pink, although I hardly wore my hat at all.

Father shakes Ripley's hand, thanking him for his kind attention to me, and then kisses my cheek. He gives me a squeeze that's unlike him, and I can see how much he's missed me. Since Mother's death, Father and I have hardly been apart for more than a day.

"How's the dam going," Ripley asks.

Father takes the entire ride to the hotel to fill us in on that, and it's quite a saga. Between the usual mix of general incompetence and mild sabotage is the tremor of political infighting amongst British and Egyptian officials. All of this is wrapped in the Herculean task of achieving, and on time, what many have called an impossibility—the construction of the largest masonry dam in the world. Father is in heaven.

"I do apologize for the accommodations," Fathers says as we pull up to the Old Cataract Hotel. "Clara thinks it's . . . well, you can imagine what Clara thinks."

Can I ever. The Old Cataract was built by Thomas Cook for his European tourists, and Aunt Clara has been known to mock the place something silly. For its frivolity, its opulence, its Moorish pageantry. Can't say it's that much different than The Shepheard, but Aunt Clara forgives Cairo's premier hotel due to its cultural prominence and distinguished clientele.

"Have you heard from Aunt Clara finally?"

"Er, dear, why don't we get you and Ripley settled? The dining is quite good at the hotel, and we can get caught up over dinner. Ripley, I hope you'll do me the honor of a drink at the men's bar? I'm sure Leila will need plenty of time to get ready after a long day on a dahabya."

Apart from a bit of washing up and a change of clothes,

I need very little time to get ready for dinner. I am happy, however, for the opportunity to be alone while the men do what men do.

I go to my room and, once there, I remove the scrapbook that Edna gave me from my suitcase, and place it on the writing desk by the window. It's the one we were going to make together. I open it, transfixed by the photograph she placed inside the front cover. In it, Mohammad and Edna are seated beside one another, and Mohammad looks so confident, and she, so hopeful. Next to this bittersweet image, I have put a print of the photograph Dr. Davies had taken of me, Ripley, and Cornelius just before our excursion to Thebes. Such a happy, exciting time of new and old: places, people, adventures.

How quickly things change.

Instead of a keepsake made of fond memories, things that provoke smiles and cheery stories, my scrapbook has become something else. In it, I have pasted fragments of notes from my days at the museum, a newspaper commentary detailing Mohammad's last speech, a pressed poppy—one of Aunt Clara's favorite flowers, plus a picture of her and Uncle Hugo taken just before they embarked on their most recent journey to the Central Sahara. Aunt Clara is actually wearing one of her husband's pith helmets. I have also transcribed some of my most vivid dreams, drawing, as best I can (I am a competent, though not talented artist), the desert landscapes, the images painted on the body of the young woman who haunts my sleep, Dr. Davies's necklace, Cornelius's statue, and most recently, painted in red, like blood, the figure of the snake found near the bodies of Annie Chapman and our friends. Ripley has asked his father for a photograph of the actual artifact.

I am discomfited to recognize that just as the purpose of my scrapbook has changed, I have changed too. I feel like I've aged a hundred years or more in just a few, short weeks, and that others treat me differently as well. Or perhaps I merely find myself uncovering parts of my existence that have been unknown to me until recently. Ones that produce a veritable jumble of Leila that are akin to the stratigraphic layers of an archaeological excavation.

"No, not today," I say aloud.

My intention, after I extracted the scrapbook from my luggage, was to make a collage of our trip on the dahabya. But my heart is resolute in its feelings of uneasiness, and I close the book, my eyes lingering on the glass oval that Edna had populated with things that reminded her of me. Things she thought, rightly, that I would love. I cannot help but stare at the peacock feather, which, in an act of clairvoyance on her part, is symbolic of awakening, immortality, and resurrection, according to Dr. Davies.

Splashing some cold water on my face, and grabbing my reticule, I say *au revoir* to my scrapbook, for now.

A little walk will do me wonders, I think, just to clear my head and try to imagine something other than the dreadful end that met our friends, and the peculiar mysteries that feel as if they are closing in on us day by day, hour by hour.

So I leave the hotel to stroll the streets of this desert city. My feet step lightly on the dusty ground, making puffy little clouds float about the hem of my skirt, but instead of each step infusing me with a sense of calm and comfort, I feel lost. While I smile at a group of four boys who have attached a leash to an adolescent crocodile in a misguided attempt to take it for a walk, such street scenes—ones that would normally delight me—seem distant. Like I'm reading about them in a periodical.

It's only when I see a small shop selling linens that I'm stopped in my tracks. I can see that they're beautiful, of the highest quality. A cloth of lilac, dyed expertly, hangs outside like a flag. When I reach out and touch it, a strange current runs through my body.

"It's so very fine, no?" The seller takes it down and urges me to hold it, even offering me a decent price.

"I'm sorry," I say in Arabic. "I can't."

The current continues to course through me, and I push away the linen and exit the shop, dashing around the corner into an alleyway. I can hardly breathe. "Mama," I say out loud. I wish she could hear me. Leaning back against the outer wall of a small domicile, I fold my hands at my belly, waiting for the peculiar, electric sensation to diminish. It does, thank God. I'm able to take a few steps with a bit of confidence, and not feel as if I'm losing my mind.

Down the alleyway is a sign for a fortuneteller, and I want to laugh at my own folly. It's a homemade sign made from a piece of tin—no words, just a rough painting of a hand holding an eye on its surface.

"Oh, why not?"

My mother said they always tell you money is coming your way and that you're fated to meet a tall, dark stranger. I have no use for either, but after the strangeness I encountered at the linen shop, a little guidance – even if it all amounts to a "heap of nonsense," as Father would say – seems in order.

I walk up the slim, wooden staircase and stand by the door, shaking my head. This is ludicrous.

"Where's your sense of adventure?" I can practically hear my mother say. I raise my hand and give a tentative knock on the door.

Seems to be as quiet as a church inside, so perhaps no one is home. Silly idea anyway. I start to walk back down the stairs, when the door opens behind me.

"Lady?" A boy's voice says in Arabic.

I turn around and see a youngster no older than nine. He's awfully thin and wears a shabby, red tunic.

"I'm here to see the fortuneteller," I tell him.

"I am the fortuneteller," he says. "I welcome you."

Now I really do have to cover my mouth to keep from giggling. I don't wish to insult the boy, and he is, after all, just trying to make a bit of coin. "I'd love to. Thank you," I say. "Are your parents at home?"

He shakes his head and holds out his tiny hand, inviting me in.

It's a small apartment that opens up to a terrace equal in its size. There are lovely plants—all thriving—set upon a wooden guardrail. This overlooks a charming and narrow street, where children are playing ball.

The boy smiles at me sweetly, and gestures to a cozy-looking corner lined with woolen rugs and filled with soft pillows in bright, desert colors. His eyes are black, as black as an abyss, and unsettle me suddenly. I avert mine from his and inch up my skirt, doing my best to sit down. It's a bit rough in my summer evening dress, but once I'm seated on the pillows, and can stretch out a bit, so as not to be so pinched by my corset, I'm relatively comfortable.

"What would you like me to do?" I ask.

"Lie down," he tells me. "Close your eyes."

"You'd like me to have a nap?"

"I'd like you to close your eyes. And Lady, don't open them."

His rather bold directive gives me pause. I don't like not knowing what's going on around me. For a moment I consider making my excuses, but to deprive a child of limited means what may be his only customer for the day seems unkind. So I lie down carefully, as he asked, trying to make sure I don't wrinkle my dress. "Like this?"

"Yes," he says. I hear the soft thud of his heels as he walks out onto the terrace.

"Do not open your eyes," he says once more. "No matter what you hear."

"No matter what I hear," I repeat.

I don't hear much at first. Just the soft purring of a house-cat, and the distant ruckus of the children playing in the street. There is a hollowness to these noises, however, making them sound more distant than they are. As the minutes go by, they seem to float away like a feather on the wind. The boy, too, is quiet as a mouse, though I believe he's still present. I didn't hear him leave.

"Pardon me," I say, still keeping my eyes closed. "Are we going to get on with this?"

Not a peep. Even the purring has stopped.

"Boy," I call out. "Are you there?"

Something touches me and I startle. Perhaps it was the kitty. But no. I feel it again, and this time the current returns. My whole body thrums and I cannot stop it. Nor do I want to. In an instant, I feel as if I could take this place apart piece by piece and put it back together again. That I could lead a legion, start a fire with my fingertips. And then, as suddenly as the sensation came . . . it's gone.

"Your time is near," a woman's voice says.

I sit up, eyes open and wide, darting glances about the whole place. My heart is pounding in my chest. I appear to be alone. No boy, no cat. No sound at all. Getting up carefully, I smooth my dress, and take a few, deep breaths. "Hello?"

At least I can hear my own voice.

I get up and walk the sitting room to the edge of the terrace, where I look down on the now empty scene below. The potted plants rustle as if a wind has come, but there is no wind.

"Good Lord," I say. "Paranoia does not become you."

The sun is quite low on the horizon and I sigh as I turn around, eager to take my leave. My gaze drifts down to one of the plants, a bright yellow chrysanthemum. Her neck seems to strain as if to offer herself to me, and I brush my fingers along her petals.

"Lovely thing," I say. My mother loved chrysanthemums.

With a startling urgency, I feel compelled to look up from the flower, and when I do, it's as if I have been pushed against a wall. Because she stands not a few feet in front of me on the terrace, wearing a dress of green and gold thread that was her favorite. The one Father buried her in. Next to her is another woman. She appears to be wrapped in the lilac cloth from the linen shop below, arranged to fall over her shoulder like a Roman toga. I grip the wooden railing at the terrace edge and can feel it rattle, as if I could easily push through it and fall to the street. I lose my balance momentarily and gasp. Then I pinch shut my eyes. Can't be. I'm imagining things.

"Don't be a coward," I say, and open my eyes once again.

"Mother."

She's still here; she and the other woman.

"Leila," my mother says.

"It's really you." My lip starts to quiver and I simply can't hold back my tears. I don't even try. "Joe. He said you'd come back to me, he really did."

The other woman steps towards me, and I notice the warmth I feel for her. She reaches out, as if to touch me, but I don't feel skin against skin when her fingers graze my cheek. Only the current.

"Sherin," she says, and it's then that I know her. This woman's name is Miriam. She, too, is my mother.

My first mother.

Chapter 18

Mothers

"**Y**OU'RE VERY CLOSE, now, Sherin. Closer than you've ever been," Miriam says.

I let go of the wooden railing, and feel almost as if I'm going to float away. I reach out my hand, but then pull it back. I want to touch her again, but I'm afraid.

"Close to what?"

"Your destiny."

"That's rather vague," I say.

Miriam's lips move, but I can't hear her. She begins to fade, becoming almost translucent and I call out to her to stay. Her head and shoulders fill in again, but the rest of her remains spectral.

"What's wrong with her," I ask my mother.

"She's very old."

"Mama," I say, stepping towards them both. Llizabith's hands reach out for me, passing through my body.

"The feel of you," she says. "Your heart, your bones."

I can sense the current everywhere she touches me, her fingers caressing my innards. It is a most intimate and sublime feeling, and tears sting my eyes again.

"I wish I could taste of your tears," Llizabith says. She looks to Miriam, who is hardly there at all anymore. The wind blows across the terrace, and it feels as if it could easily blow her with it.

"The desert will come for you," she says. "Right now, it lives only in your dreams, but when it calls, you must go."

"Don't leave me yet," I beg her, but she does.

"Leila," Llizabith says. "You will accompany your father to London."

"Father's not going to London, and I thought it was the desert I was seeking. Or rather, it was seeking me."

My mother begins to fade, the way Miriam did. Her feet are almost vaporous, making it appear as if she's floating.

"I cannot keep you from him any longer," she says.

"Who?"

My mother lifts her hand to my forehead, her thumb at its middle and her fingers at my temple. It's not merely a current I feel this time, it's blow upon blow. To my face, to my body. A feeling of being drowned and of soaring into the air, spreading across the sky. It's a terrible thing. Then I see the eyes—the color of a blazing sunset. They bore into me. I clinch my eyes shut and can hear myself screaming. And when I open them again, my mother is gone. The boy, the fortuneteller, stands before me on the terrace.

"Where is she?"

"I told you not to open your eyes," the boy says. "But you didn't listen, and now, he will find you, and you won't be ready to end this once and for all."

"What are you talking about?"

The boy tips his head, his eyes full of scrutiny. "The one with fire fruit. He'll come again and again, until you stop him. If not in this life, then another."

⊹ ⊹

I'M DISTRACTED and jittery when I meet Ripley and Father back at the hotel. We're led to a table on the veranda, where it's not their custom to serve dinner, but Father has had it arranged for us.

"Could use a bit of air, don't you think?" he says. His eyes sweep over the vista.

It's an uncommonly beautiful night, with a big, bright moon that makes a gleaming gold ribbon on the surface of the Nile below us.

I'm dying to tell Ripley what happened at the fortune-teller's, although I can scarcely believe it myself. I pick at my food and Ripley throws wary glances in my direction. "Later," I mouth.

Father narrows his eyes at us.

"Weren't you going to give an update about Aunt Clara and Uncle Hugo?" I ask him, trying to sound light.

Father hiccups and takes an ample swallow of his wine. He drums his fingers on our table and seems reluctant to look me in the eye.

"What is it?" I say.

He clears his throat and finally does look up from his hands, his eyes landing on Ripley first, as if for reassurance.

"I'm sure it's nothing," he says. "You see, some of their party came back without them. It appears Clara and Hugo decided to go deeper into the mountain range. No one has been in contact with the Hugheses for some days."

"What do you mean 'no one has been in contact'? How could their people have just left them like that in the middle of nowhere?"

My heart starts to hammer again, while the rest of me wilts in exhaustion. This, on top of everything else!

"They didn't just leave them my dear. Some in the party did stay with them. It's just that not everyone wished to forge ahead as they did. You know the Hugheses. High adventure. Nothing is ever enough. I'm sure they'll come back with a novel full of stories!"

"We can only hope and pray!"

Ripley puts his hand on mine.

"Their guide stayed with them, did he not?"

"Yes, of course," Father tells us. "A most experienced man, they say."

My father fidgets, twisting his wedding band, and staring and Ripley's and my joined hands.

"Isn't there any way we could send someone after them—to check on their welfare?" It seems unbearable to me that we would simply have to wait for good news, or bad!

"Leila." Ripley grips my hand with some force now. "We could use a walk, you and I. Let's have a little sherry and enjoy the night. Worrying about Clara and Hugo, who have always landed on their feet, won't do any of us any good."

"I couldn't agree more," Father chimes in. "I have much work to do yet, but the thought of the two of you staying out and enjoying yourselves would please me to no end."

I'm about to object, when it occurs to me that I do indeed need to get Ripley alone and away from my father so that I can clue him in to what happened to me. Father appears content with Ripley and I spending so much time together, too, and in fact, is encouraging of it. This makes me happy, taking some of the sting out of my worry for Aunt Clara and Uncle Hugo.

"Alright," I say. "A short walk. But tomorrow, we must do something! There has to be a better solution than waiting."

"EXTRAORDINARY," is all Ripley can manage as I rush him towards the fortuneteller's place and explain, as quickly as I can, about what transpired there. The night is quiet now, the streets nearly empty. The little linen shop, where I held the lilac cloth that Miriam, my once mother, was wearing, is not only closed up, but seems to have never been. The stone abode it was housed in is dark and ancient-looking, as if it hasn't been used in generations.

"It was here," I say, gaping at a pair of worn, wooden doors. Ones that had been open and festive only hours ago. Now, they stand covered with sand dust, a spider's web connecting the handles.

"Come, let's hurry," I say. "The child fortuneteller's flat, it's this way." I take Ripley by the hand. We enter the courtyard, where the cluster of boys had been playing, and I nearly faint with relief that the sign—the tin one, painted with the eye in a palm—is still there at the base of the stairs. It's back-lit by two lanterns flanking a storage door behind the staircase.

"Leila, I believe you," Ripley says. "You needn't panic."

"But of course I'm panicking! How can I not when I seem to be losing the ability to distinguish between dream and reality?"

Ripley stops, pulling me closer, until I can see the amber and crimson veins in his eyes. "Perhaps for us, they are one in the same."

It is all of a sudden that I feel a terrible sense of vertigo. The courtyard begins to spin so violently that I dig my fingernails into the flesh of Ripley's forearm in a struggle merely to remain standing. My heart seems to slow, and I cannot catch my breath.

"Leila!" I hear him call out.

I lean against the outer wall of the fortuneteller boy's dwelling and slide down to a crouch on the ground. The sounds all about me—a rapacious fly buzzing near my ear, Ripley's sharp breaths, a throaty cough from an above window—begin to drift away just as they did on the terrace of the boy's flat. In a moment's time, all is silent, as if we are under water.

Behind Ripley, I see something glimmer in the lamplight. Ripley notes my alarm and spins around, just as a man with a sword attempts to take his head with it! I try to scream, but I can't! Nothing but hot air comes from my open mouth! Ripley—thank God—ducks and sticks out his leg in a movement of tremendous skill and grace, as if he's done such a thing a thousand times. The swordsman trips over his foot and tumbles, his deep purple robes flailing like sails. The sword flies out of his hand, soaring over us, and landing several feet away. Ripley wastes no time diving to the ground to retrieve it, while the other man scrambles for it on his hands and knees. He is fast, like a bug, this evil man; as strong and nimble as a horned viper.

But Ripley is faster. He swipes the sword from the ground, and rises up so quickly, standing ready to duel. The confidence of his posture is arresting—bold and valiant. As he steps closer to the fiend in purple, the man reaches under his belt and produces two daggers—one in each hand. He waves and slashes them at Ripley so savagely, forcing him to jump backwards.

I want to call out, tear at his hair and clothes, do something, anything, but it's as if I'm trapped in a bubble!

I can only watch, horrified, at the mercilessness of the man's motions, the hatred bleeding from his pores as surely as sweat. I have no doubt this is the one. The man who killed Mohammed and Edna! I know it as surely as I know God exists.

Chapter 19

An Old Enemy

A SHOT IS FIRED and I blink open my eyes. I find myself lying on the ground in a state of befuddlement. Images come to me in flashes. Of a sword, a man in purple. He and Ripley clashing, sword against daggers—stepping, spinning in a violent dance. I remember my vertigo and how I found myself gasping as my vision faded to black.

Not a few feet from my supine form stands a British officer, his hand high in the air. He holds a pistol.

"Leila," Ripley says, kneeling at my side. He's still holding the sword, and its blade drips with blood. "Are you alright?"

I nod and Ripley takes me in his arms, holding me tight. I smell the sweat from his battle with our attacker.

"Mighty God," I hear the officer exclaim. "What on earth was going on here?"

"We were simply strolling, and a man tried to kill me for no reason at all," Ripley says.

"Not everyone needs a reason," the officer tells him. "Still, I've never seen such a thing in this quarter!"

The officer hands Ripley his handkerchief, and that's when I notice the cut across his belly!

"I'm fine," Ripley says. He doesn't use the handkerchief for himself, but to blot my forehead. "I'm fast, you know. He was barely able to scrape me."

"Fast! Ripley, look at you!"

The officer takes a flask from his breast pocket and hands it to Ripley. "This'll do you some good. Both on the outside and the inside."

Ripley accepts his kindness. He unscrews the flask and raises it in salute, but gives me a sip first. I nearly choke on it—straight gin, for the love of all that's Holy. Then Ripley takes a good gulp. Lifting up his shirt, he swallows a deep breath and pours the gin over his cut—which indeed doesn't look too bad, thank the Lord.

"I must say, young man," the officer says. "From the looks of it, you are an accomplished swordsman. Where did you learn to handle your weapon?"

"It's, uh, not my weapon," Ripley informs him, as he returns the flask. "It belonged to our assailant, but I managed to get it away from him before he could do harm to the lady. *Lady Wellington.*"

This peaks the officer's attention, superseding whatever curious notions he might be entertaining about why we're out late, fighting with a madman. He crouches down, assisting Ripley in helping me up, and offering his apologies for my distress.

"I dare say, Lady Wellington, it's a good thing you've found yourself a competent guard." He looks Ripley up and down. "I might recommend an officer for such a task. In the future, I mean."

Clearly, he hopes to be fingered for just such an appointment. He tucks his pistol quite proudly into its holster. "Your, er, guard, could have been killed, and left you to your own defenses."

I smile at him demurely, or at least as demurely as I can manage. I thank him, and truly am grateful. His offer to walk us back to the hotel is accepted by both me and Ripley with genuine relief. A pistol is always better to have around than a sword—a point which the officer makes as he proposes to take the bloodied weapon off Ripley's hands. As he had already admitted that it didn't belong to him, Ripley agrees.

The officer takes a good long look at the crimsoned blade of the weapon. "Well, it would seem you taught him a lesson."

"Not enough of one, I'm afraid. Like me, our assailant was fast. I did manage a proper leg wound, so I imagine he'll be limping for quite some time. With any luck, for the rest of his days."

There's a loathing in Ripley's tone that strikes me. As if he's just tangled with an old enemy.

"With any luck, we'll never see him again," I say, although I don't have much hope of that.

The three of us walk slowly, silently, back to the grand entrance of the Old Cataract, stopping at the bottom of the staircase to bid the officer a good night. Plainly, he wishes to be invited in to meet Father, and I ask him to drop by tomorrow, which appears to satisfy him. He bids us farewell and I find myself beginning to shiver, as if all of it, everything that's happened this evening, has come back to visit me like a poltergeist. The way the aggressor's blade came within a fraction of slicing Ripley's head clean off; the way he moved with such intention; the way it had all seemed familiar somehow.

Ripley puts his arm about my waist and I lean my head upon his shoulder. Like this, we enter the grand foyer, which is nearly empty. It's lit dreamily by Moroccan-styled lamps, and we sit on a plush, red sofa. It feels good to rest, as I still feel winded and quite unlike myself.

Ripley takes my fingers in his. They're still shaking, and he brings them to his lips.

"It's been quite a night," he says, breathing deeply.

"And you're quite a fencer. I imagine you must have had an excellent instructor at one of your boarding schools?" I'm trying to be light, I really am. Take some of the burden of tonight off our shoulders.

"Not really," Ripley says, with no humor at all. "I've always known how to fight. From the moment I picked up my first épée."

I knew it was so.

"That man," Ripley says. "Did you know him?"

I shake my head.

"And you didn't see your mothers again? I mean, when you felt so woozy, and . . . well, you lost consciousness and looked . . . Oh, Leila, I was so afraid you'd never wake up."

He takes my face in his hands and kisses me, publicly. But neither of us care.

"Please, let's talk of this tomorrow," I say. "We could both use some sleep."

I don't wish to be asked any more questions, because I'd be no good at lying to the one I love. I'd have to tell him that I'm sure the man we speak of was our friends' murderer. That he meant to kill Ripley, but that I fear he was really coming for me.

"Tell me," I say. "Was he familiar to you?"

Ripley swallows quite hard. "No," he rasps. Of course, I know he's lying.

Eagle River, Alaska
Present Day, Sixteen Months Later

ON THE OUTSIDE of the outside of the outside. That's been my life for almost two years now. Here I am on the outside of the continental U.S., I might add, where we live on the outskirts of Eagle River, which is outside of Anchorage.

All I ever do in my spare time is think about Mickey and the Nevilles. Still.

I look up pictures of Cairo in books from the library, as we don't have any wi-fi, and Hunter—he wants me to call him Daddy—won't let us get any.

"We're doing this the old-fashioned way," he says. Books, not Google. Homeschooling with a wild grouping of off-the-gridders like us. He says it's kept him from getting back on drugs and it'll keep me on the straight and narrow as I head into the "rough patch years," as he calls them. Since I turned thirteen a few months back, he's been eyeing me like he thinks I might burst into flame. Hunter says I've probably inherited "the gene" by being the daughter of two addicts. "Being too close to all of her old friends and bad habits is what killed your mother," he keeps telling me.

"I never saw her with any of her old friends," I tell him. "Except you."

"She must have had a run-in with at least one of them, or she'd still be here."

He says it just like that all the time. Like it's nothing. Like my whole life didn't end with those words. And I didn't get dragged away in an airstream trailer for four and a half thousand miles, watching as the landscape turned from lush romance to science fiction.

It is beautiful here, don't get me wrong, but it was beautiful in Virginia, too. Softer back home, classical beauty is what Dr. Neville called it. Rolling hills and hay bales. Hot summers and rope swings that drop you into a cool river. A kind of ease and comfort that comes from living in a mild climate. Virginia is like the girl in the fairy tale, who's the prettiest girl in a small, provincial town. At least that's what my Granny Dora used to tell me when I was little.

Alaska. Well, if we're keeping with the fairy tale analogy, she's more like Maleficent. She's got a mean beauty. One that catches your attention and is hard to turn away from, but at the same time, harsh and unforgiving. Makes you wish you'd never met her. The terrain here could hide monsters of all sorts. Ones that lurk in caves crusted over with ice that comes in a rainbow of colors. Craggy mountains topped with a pointy shock of white. They seem to rise up right out of the water like a row of angry wizards.

Hunter feels right at home here. He says it's the opposite of the desert, which he hates.

"You've never been to the desert," I've told him. Lots of times.

"I've dreamt about it," he says, and that always gives me the creeps because I dream about it, too.

Hunter loves the grandeur of nature in Alaska. Makes a statement, he says. He's proud of the house he built with his own hands, and thinks I should be grateful for that. I guess I am. No more shabby, decades-old double-wides. We've got a nice, two-story cabin that's rustic and modern all at once. Cozy when he's not home. A twisted air of lonely and smothering when he is.

Speaking of, the door to my bedroom swings open after a quick knock. He never waits to hear me say, "Come in."

"Getting late," Hunter says, tapping his watch. Even that's old fashioned—the wind-up kind.

I nod and crawl under my covers. "Night," I say.

IT'S DARK when I startle awake, but it's not the kind of dark that promises dawn any minute. I switch on my reading light and look at my clock, also the wind-up kind.

1:10 am.

The dream I was having is already a fuzzy mess. Something about a cave in a dune. One of those old paintings on the wall, made by an ancient people. Tiny figures migrating from one place to the next. I think of Mickey and me. How he went all the way to Cairo and I migrated up north. Somehow it feels like we did it together, even though we've lost touch. Or rather, Hunter made sure we couldn't stay in touch by bringing us here and cutting us off from the rest of the world.

All is quiet, so Hunter must be sleeping. If he was still up, I'd hear the faint voices of the radio drifting up from downstairs. He likes listening to a station that's all about true crime stories, and when he stays up late, that's what he does. The good thing is that when he does sleep, he tends to do it hard. No snoring, just slow and deep big animal breaths. Like a moose. I would literally have to shake him awake if I needed to get him up for some reason. We're kind of alike in that way, he and I. That, and our eyes of course. They glow like glow worms, my mom used to say. Just in different colors.

I slip out of bed and look out over a field of fireweed that's a bright sweep of orange and yellow during the daylight hours. The night is awesome at this time of year, I've got to give it that. September nights are not too cold yet. Clear and sparkly. A shooting star cinches it for me, and I pull on the second-hand Ugg boots I bought with my gardening money, and my Navy pea coat and pom-pom hat. Even if I know Hunter will smolder with fury if he catches me sneaking out again.

Lottie, one of my friends from our homeschooling co-op, says I should be glad he doesn't yell or stomp around, like her dad, but I kind of wish he would. Hunter's the type who goes to stone, but his eyeballs blaze and quiver like he's about to blow into a million little pieces. Though he hasn't. Not yet, anyway. Last time he caught me after I'd snuck out, all he did was take away all of my books on archeology and return them to the library. Like I couldn't just have Lottie check them right back out for me.

All the same, part of me is scared to death of him, even if he's never hurt me or even threatened to. Another part of me is like, "bring it on." Sick, I know.

At my window, the crisp air hits me like a slap in the face. Hunter keeps the house pretty warm, just because he can. He likes to show me that he's got the money now for us not to have to worry. But I like to sleep in a cool room, so I always crack the window.

I slide it open all the way and mount my desk, climbing out, Ugg by Ugg. Scooching feet first down to the edge of the roof is easy, then I slide to the ground wrapped around one of our wood columns like a fireman down a pole.

The sky reminds me of a glass-bottom boat tonight, showcasing the depths of space. The aurora borealis shining above Mt. Baldy is a shade of green right out of *Star Trek*. This is the one thing I love about Alaska.

I walk for what's close to an hour, hiking just high enough that there's spots of permanent snow. It's in one of those that

I lie down and make an angel. Always lifts my spirits. Plus, snuggling in the snow feels pleasant and comfy. The temperate air wraps around me like a light sweater, although by next month this same air will be razor-sharp and cut in all the way to my bones. I turn my collar up, and, before long, I'm getting drowsy.

Sleep is my only true refuge anymore.

It's when I no longer need books on Cairo. I can go there on my own. I can shed my life in Alaska and slip into a sky of twinkling stars that drape across my shoulders like a coat of sequins.

My first glimpse is of Calliope, my daughter. She's been spending a lot of time alone with Mickey, while her husband camps in the desert, uncovering the secrets of the Rah'a. Today, she's taking Mickey's temperature, her fingers grazing his cheeks with the sweet grace of an artist's paintbrush. Slender, feminine fingers that have been kissed by months of summer. I watch Calliope's eyes narrow with weariness. Mickey's got a touch of the flu. He looks glassy-eyed and hot to the touch.

"One hundred and three point five," she says, as she shakes two yellow pills out of a white plastic bottle. Mickey swallows them with a sip of tea and mumbles about how tired he is. Even when his voice is weak and sickly, I can hear his soft accent. One that he's picked up like a silk shirt from his adopted home state. It's that of a budding Virginia gentleman.

My Calliope kisses his forehead, then places a cool, damp cloth over his eyes. She goes to the window and closes the blinds, shutting out the afternoon sun entirely. It's just after 4:00pm in Egypt.

"Sweet dreams," she says as she slips out the door, leaving it open just a crack, so she can hear him call out if he needs her.

Mickey's eyes are closed, and begin to oscillate with R.E.M. sleep.

"*Nif?*" I say.

"*I'm here.*"

"*I have a few hours, yet, until morning. My body is deep asleep.*"

"*So is mine,*" he says.

We soar up above the Nevilles' house, looking down upon Cairo. The smog, soft as cotton thread, floats above a large colony of square buildings, all in various shades of brown. Here and there, a mosque breaks the pattern, opening up like a lotus in mud. Further on, we see the sand and the pyramids and the desert.

"*You must escape him, Sherin.*"

I think of Roon's fiery eyes, boring into me from Hunter's face.

"*The irony is, he actually thinks he's doing what's best for me.*"

"*He's evil.*"

Nif knows I know this. I know it best of all.

"*Do you think when he dreams, he knows himself? The way we do?*"

There is a rumble in the afternoon sky above the desert. Like the beginnings of a thunderstorm. Nif's doing.

"*What if he knows himself even when he doesn't dream?*"

That is a horrible thing to contemplate.

"*I must show you something,*" Nif tells me.

The sky growls again, voicing his apprehension. I wish I could take his hand—I'm missing his body right now. But if we were in our bodies, we couldn't fly.

We glide over the sands we knew in past lives, then enter the region that was our home. The place from which our human lives came. What was the Rah'a. We pass Neville's excavation of the Palace City, a strange crater in the desert surrounded by a small village of tents. People working the site. I hear Neville's voice as he tells a young Australian something about the stratigraphic layers.

We go onward, Nif and I, to what we knew as the Slay Mountains. Black and ominous, an ancient volcanic range. I hate this place more than any in the world, and Nif knows this, too. It's where Roon—the man I was once promised to—and his men massacred our tribe. Where I learned of the horror that had befallen my sweet young brother, Salan— that he was tortured and left to rot in the sun, only because I had fled the Palace City, and left Roon. All those thousands of years ago, in my very first life—what should have been my only life, if fate hadn't intervened. We've lost so much in these mountains, so many times.

"Do you see it?" Nif asks me.

Yes, I do. A single lula flower, growing next to the guelta where Roon and his men had beaten and abused me, broken my bones and fouled my body. The day, I suppose, when we became mortal enemies—Roon and me and Nif. Even if Roon professed that he would always love me.

"How could it be?"

It was the type of flower I'd grown at my father's house. Then in the gardens of the Palace City during my time there. A purple flower with torn, yellow flesh and an odor that smells of heaven from a distance, but up close could give Durian fruit, with its hellish bouquet of sweaty feet, onion, and petrol, a run for its money. Roon called it a "hideous flower" back then.

"It's been extinct since the Rah'a was buried."

Nif and I hover closer, and the lula quakes. It's as if she's screaming, trying to tell us something.

"Ever!"

I wake up gasping. Hunter is shaking me.

"Get away from me!" I scream. "Don't you touch me!"

I sit up, pushing him away. Breathing hard and running

my fingers through my snow-wet hair. My hat must have come off while I was sleeping.

"Ever, you were having a nightmare," he says.

"What?"

"You fell asleep in the snow. 'Hideous flower' was what you kept saying."

I'm all soaked on one side, from where I've lain curled in the snow. My body has melted a hollow beneath me in the shape of a snail's shell. I glance at Hunter, but I can't bear his eyes right now. Those peculiar, bright eyes of his that resemble a sunset.

"Your eyes are the color of the Northern Lights, at least as they were last night." It's as if he sensed what I was thinking. I hate it when he does that. I look about me and see the sun inching up from behind the mountain top. I've been out all night.

"I suppose you'll be taking what's left of my books?" I say. It's the last punishment he could possibly inflict on me. He's already taken everything else. "For sneaking out again."

"No," he says. He rubs the back of his head, over that thick, wavy hair of his that's the color of peanuts sprinkled with Old Bay seasoning. "I thought I'd take you to breakfast."

I'd rather he take my books, but I don't say it.

"I don't feel well," I say instead. "I think I'm catching a cold."

Hunter looks down and picks up my pom-pom hat, shaking off the snow.

"Another time, then."

I nod.

He helps me up, holding my elbow, and it takes everything in me not to rip away from his grasp. I don't know why I've always hated his touch. Must be all of those years we spent apart.

"Give him a chance," Mama had implored me. It was only

a few days before she collapsed in the make-up aisle at the Hopely Pharmacy. "He worked so hard to come back to us."

"Not us. *Me*," is what I almost said. I'm glad I didn't. That would have hurt her, and those words would be haunting me right now. As it is, I'm glad the last words I said to her were *I love you.*

Chapter 20

NATURALLY, it was a surprise to neither me nor Ripley when Father announced that he would have to visit England right away, just as my ghost mother had said he would do. It's because of a stern rebuke from one of the financiers of the dam, and one who obviously doesn't know a thing about doing any sort of business in Egypt. This also meant Father would have to do that which he despises most in the world: press some parvenu for money.

What *has* been a surprise to me, however, is how these few weeks in London have been a welcome interlude, even if I hate to be away from Ripley. He wanted to come with us, of course, but I made it clear to him that I was set on following my mother's directive.

"She didn't say you must accompany your father alone," Ripley countered.

"True. Not explicitly. But I know it's what she meant."

The soft pad of his middle finger graced my bottom lip, and I told him I would go mad if he didn't kiss me.

He did, and with a great passion—the force of a tall wave crashing against a rocky shore. He did not argue with me further about my plans. I think part of him was quite glad that I would be safe and away from all of the strange business in Aswan and Cairo, even if he and I would be apart. Unable to touch, to kiss, to fall into one another's eyes. This business of spirits and spilt blood was one he hoped to investigate further, and without the distraction of having to protect the woman he loves.

Father, for his part, was actually quite relieved when I insisted on joining him on his travels. Despite his zeal for his work, being in Aswan without me had been a bit discombobulating for him. No one to tell him he needs to eat, or that his tie is crooked. No one to kiss his brow before he steps out of his slippers at night, and slides under his bed clothes.

Moreover, he was aghast that a sword-wielding stranger had attacked us! We told him nothing of the fortuneteller boy, of course, or of my mother, but we had no choice but to brief him about our encounter with violence. How could we not with Ripley wearing a long slash across his belly? The British officer who had intervened with a shot from his pistol on our behalf came by to meet Father on the morning following the incident, anyway. He kindly offered to watch over us during the rest of our stay in Aswan, and was a virtual shadow to Ripley and me as we strolled along the Nile, and visited the dam in the days leading up to Father's and my departure.

We had no more trouble, I'm happy to say, which we both attributed to the wound Ripley had managed to inflict upon our assailant. A leg wound that would surely be giving him significant trouble, and take him out of the business of murder for some time. At least we hope.

"Leila, dear," Father says from behind the door to my bedroom at Aunt Imogen's house in Piccadilly.

"Father, do come in, will you?" I tell him. He's always so formal when we're in other people's homes. Even family.

"Edward is quite anxious to see you," he says, slipping in and closing the door as if he's got a big secret.

Sir Edward Maunde Thompson, dear, dear friend of

Father's and the Principal Librarian of The British Museum, is giving me a personal tour today in honor of my sixteenth birthday. I can hardly contain myself. I've felt winded the past couple of days, and Aunt Imogen made me stay home and rest, which has been tedious beyond description. Her company is always lovely, don't get me wrong, but I'm unaccustomed to lounging about and being useless, which she insisted I do.

"And I've got something for you," Father says.

He joins me on the settee and takes his right hand from behind his back, revealing a leather-bound copy of Mary Shelley's "Frankenstein," a book I simply love.

"I believe hell has frozen over!"

"Leila, for goodness sake, watch your language!"

"No one can hear us," I say.

Secretly, father loves it when I cuss. Reminds him of mother, who liked to do it precisely because it was frowned upon—especially for women.

"I know how you enjoy such stories," Father says. "And I haven't seen you reading one in quite some time. Happy Birthday, my dearest."

"Thank you. As for my horror stories, I suspect my own life has offered enough excitement of late."

My little jest puts an uneasy smile upon Father's face.

"What is it?"

Father starts to chew on his bottom lip.

"I'm afraid I'll have to be traveling to the countryside ahead of you today. Andrew has asked me to join him for a bit of fishing, and to talk business about the house. Anyway, I thought you would want something to read on the train."

"Thoughtful of you," I say. "I'm glad you get to spend time with your brother, even if some of it will be spent on talking house troubles. Ah, the difficulties of the manor born." I wink at Father. "I'll miss you."

"I've got one more thing for you," Father says.

He takes his other hand from behind his back, this time presenting me with a letter.

"Is it news about Clara and Hugo?"

Father shakes his head and my stomach goes hollow.

"We'll hear soon," he says. "I'm sure of it. In the meantime, I think you'll be happy to read this." I look down at the letter and recognize the handwriting straight away. I can't help jumping up from the settee as if I've been stuck with a pin. It's from Ripley!

"It came just this morning, and I brought it right up."

I place it on the tea table, and have to pry my eyes away from it to give Father the attention he deserves.

"It's alright, I know you wish to read it."

Father stands and backs out of my room with a wave, telling me he'll see me at breakfast in a few minutes. I blow him a kiss and try not to look too eager to see him leave, but who am I kidding?

I open the letter with a fervor that makes my hands tremble and dampen, then put the folded paper to my nose and inhale deeply the smells of something Ripley has touched. There is the faint hint of a posy of Egyptian spices that lingers on it, as well as the bare whiff of the soft herbal soap that Ripley's father keeps in their home. Heaven on earth. I unfold the letter gently, so that I take no chance of tearing the delicate sheet of paper. The letter is dated only a few days after Father and I embarked upon our journey back to London.

Cairo, May 23, 1902
Morning
My Darling Leila,

The happiest of birthdays to you, assuming my letter
arrives in time. I so look forward to celebrating in person

with you sixteen years of a world with one Leila Saber-Wellington in it.

In the meantime, I'm realizing that whatever courage I summoned to allow you to leave here without me was an utter delusion. While I am happy that you are safe and away from the madness we have found ourselves entangled in here, I feel a bit helpless without an ability to at least look upon you.

I confess that my concerns for your welfare are not the only thoughts that intrude upon me throughout my days. And my nights. I should be ashamed that I start my letter to you in this way, instead of inquiring about your journey, and your reunion with your father's family. In my defense, the passage from Egypt to England is one I've undertaken before, and a visit to London, my birthplace, and even the pastoral beauty of the English countryside, seem rather common to me now. Like a dandelion.

You, however, are not common. I won't ask in advance for your forgiveness for my candor, I will only say that we both know you're as captive to me, as I am to you. While you would have given yourself to me, had I asked, I do not take your heart or your body lightly. It is everything to me.

Still, at night, I can almost feel you lying next to me, as if you slipped into my room during a dream. The way you did at our house, and on the dahabiya to Aswan.

I cannot be sorry for that.

What I am sorry for are that my words are so direct, and that I don't have the facility with language that my nocturnal self—the man who wrote so beautifully to you in his sleep—has been gifted with. My words are not poetry. They would seem lustful and basic to a stranger who knows nothing of my heart.

That very heart, however, is filled with a thousand poems of you.

Forgive me, I'll take up this letter again later . . .

Morning, May 24

Another day has passed and I'm coming to the realization that every day without you is a complete and utter bore.

Cornelius and I did Father's bidding at the museum yesterday, and that was at least a consolation. Our friend, as you know, is great company, and we are each vulnerable to a love of conversation. About histories, mysteries, and the grand tapestry of existence. It is why, I think, the three of us get on so well when we're together, and our bonds extend beyond the strange statue and what it has brought into our lives.

In that vein, I'm afraid I must give you news that you'll find distressing. News I learned of only a few minutes ago, and am still trying to absorb.

There has been another murder in the City of the Dead. Another young woman. Another family reluctant to draw attention to themselves because of shame. She was torn up, this one, just like the first girl. And like our friends.

Cornelius saw her this time. A scream awakened him at dawn, and he ran towards the commotion, finding a washer woman in great distress, and the horrid, bloody body laid out on top of a tomb, like a sacrifice. He could not get too close, as the girl's father was right on his heels, and took her into his arms, poor man.

There is something that our friend did notice, however. A smear of blood on the side of the tomb. Unmistakably the same shape we saw in the hotel room where Mohammad and Edna were massacred. The same form of the snake on the ancient breastplate that the Hugheses discovered in the mountain range, and sent to my Father.

Leila, it would appear I did not injure our foe to the extent that he could do no evil. I must point out, that the unfortunate girl whom he killed—and yes, I think we both know in our hearts that it is he—was a cripple. Even with pain and a limp, it would not have been exceedingly difficult for a man of his general strength and skill with weapons to overcome her.

I suspected from the start that the man who would have killed me is indeed the same man who so viciously slayed our friends, as well as the madman who is haunting the City of the Dead. I should have shared this with you sooner, but I didn't wish to alarm you, and I wanted you to enjoy your time in England with your father.

Leila, this new ripper—*or is he one and the same as the wicked man who stalked the night women of Whitechapel years ago?*—has a distinctive interest in us. A history that we cannot name. This belief is born of an instinct as plain and palpable as thirst. It simply is, is it not?

The only question is, what am I going to do about it? How am I going to find that man before he recovers sufficiently enough that he no longer merely seeks out the weak, but comes for more of the people we love?

I hate to end my letter on such a note. Especially when I began in writing to you of love. But you are mine, and I am yours. We must share everything, never hesitating to bring the other with us—even into hellish places.

I also tell you all of my suspicions now out of my own selfishness.

Leila, I want you to be afraid. To think carefully before you go anywhere, when I am not with you. When I can't draw a fist, a sword, or a pistol to protect you. Even if you are far away from the terrible goings on in Cairo. Something about these things feels ever-present.

I love you. And I love this old city full of angels and demons, if for no other reason than it is the place that made you.

Be careful, be well, be happy.

Yours evermore,
Ripley

Chapter 21

Death, It Calls

IT IS SAID, in so-called polite circles, that the stench of an Irishman is so beastly and repellent, that once you've smelt it, it will never leave your memory. Whitechapel, home to a glutted community of mostly Jewish and Irish immigrants, does indeed have a sticky pong that includes urine, vomit, cut-rate liquor, spoilt foods, and the long unwashed. Having spent so much of my life in Cairo, where the poor abound and are not as sequestered from the rich as they are in London, the smell neither surprises nor offends me.

But there is a particular quality to the poor of London that is indeed inexpungible from memory. Especially in the morning, when the streets are filling up—many of its residents just coming home from a long night. With their damp, grimy clothes and unhealthy complexions, chapped hands and rotting teeth, a quality of not merely poverty, but decay, envelopes their persons.

With the exception of the Jews, whose homes and persons are conspicuously tidy, the poor in Whitechapel appear broken and unloved. The dreary streets, full of litter and human waste, are flanked by ugly buildings, artlessly designed. At least the hotel in Cairo where Mohammad and Edna were killed had its flourishes—the ancient entryway, the mosaic tiles. Whitechapel is all square and brick, each house suggestive of a short, lumpy boy with filthy trousers and an abundance of spots.

As I round the corner onto Hanbury Street, a boney young man, no doubt an Irishman, and one who truly does reek of squalor, looks me up and down.

"Got a penny for a starvin' man m'lady?" he asks as he weaves towards me, clearly still pickled in ale.

It would appear my attempts at blending in by donning a simple brown cloak and bonnet from a second-hand shop haven't fooled him. He looks down at my shoes—a pair of leather ankle boots trimmed in burgundy velvet—and winks at me.

"Aw, come on," he says.

I shake my head and endeavor to bustle past.

"Excuse me," I say to a darkly-clad woman who is sweeping her stoop. "Would you know where the entrance to the yard of 29 Hanbury Street would be?"

She mumbles to me in a language I assume to be Yiddish, clearly not having understood a word I said.

"You one of those, are you?" The young drunkard chuckles, but his laugh doesn't quite reach his eyes.

"One of what?"

"You know 'one of what.' You want to see where Annie Chapman was butchered by Jack. It's not usual that ladies come for a look, I will say that."

The man takes off his sorry hat, scratching through an oily and abundant head of hair.

"Well, I'm a second cousin of the Chapman family and I've come to pay my respects."

"Second cousin," he says with some amusement. "I see. Well come along then."

As the young man beckons me, I start to wonder what I'm doing in Whitechapel at all. Father and Aunt Imogen would be aghast if they knew I left early for my appointment with

Sir Edward at the museum in order to come here. And it's not even like it's a fresh crime scene that could give me any clues as to the goings on of nearly fifteen years ago on these streets, let alone on the streets of Cairo today. It was just a feeling I had after reading Ripley's letter—even though he'd asked me specifically to be careful about where I go and what I do. A feeling I should come here—I *must* come here. And now, here I am accepting an Irish beggar as my guide through the mid-morning streets of the East End of London. I remind myself that my instincts rarely fail me, and I've spent countless hours alone in the chaos of Cairo.

"You got nothin' to fear of me, m'lady," the young man says.

"I'm not afraid. The Ripper's been gone for years."

"It's not only the Ripper you've to be wary of in these parts. But I'll take good care of you. It's what I do. I'm out every night makin' sure the ladies come home safe."

"Very kind of you," I say, as we turn onto an alleyway bordered by derelict wooden fences on both sides.

My guide stops to the left, jiggling two nearly rotted boards free. He bows and bids me to pass through his makeshift entry. The center of my palm begins to feel hot, and I ball and unravel my fist.

"What you waitin' for? This here's the yard of 29 Hanbury Street, where Miss Annie was found with her throat cut deep."

He points inside the yard. "She was lyin' next to the fence separating 29 and 27 Hanbury. Her head almost touchin' the steps to the back door there. Near on made it home, she did."

I duck and slip into the opening he's made for me. Once again, he follows.

"I beg your pardon," I tell him. "But I would like to say a prayer for my kinswoman."

This doesn't deter him. "Oh, I pray here every day, m'lady. Every day since they found her."

I do realize that, to the residents of Whitechapel, the Ripper murders are more than a sensational news story. Jack the Ripper preyed on their own, and filled their streets, already pitiable and dangerous, with the specter of horror and evil. I look at the spot on the ground where Annie Chapman fell, her body thumping against the fence and causing a neighbor to call out in concern.

"You must have been very young when it happened."

"Oh, aye. But you never forget something like that. Especially when you done seen the devil who did it."

I turn to my guide, as my jaw drops open. He stands staring at the same spot that had mesmerized me. For a moment, I see him as the little boy Lieutenant General Blackwood described. The one he spoke to shortly after poor Annie's grisly murder.

"That was you?" I ask him. "The boy who saw a man rush away from the scene?"

"Aye, it was," he tells me. "Only he wasn't rushing. He walked away from Miss Annie and past me like he was strolling. And when he looked at me, I knew. I knew demons are real and that I'd seen one."

"Eyes of fire. That's what you said, isn't it?"

"Aye. Almost like coal aglow, you know? Except more like the color of a-pricots."

"Apricots?"

"Mm. Never ate one, but always wanted to. I seen painted pictures of 'em though. You know, they was temptin', too, The Ripper's eyes. That I'll tell ya. The way a demon's eyes would be. Temptin' and beautiful. I still can't sleep at night from the nightmares. I just go out wanderin' from place to place on most nights. Walkin' the girls home, like I told ya."

He rubs his bloodshot eyes and sniffs. The smell of him may very well fade from my memory, but the pain and terror in his voice never will. It's still fresh, as if he saw The Ripper only yesterday.

"Seems like you need some sleep. Why don't you go home? I can make my way alone."

"Oh, no, I'll be walkin' ya," he says with a truly sweet smile. "I don't ever leave no lady alone here. Especially one who don't belong, and who ain't no cousin of Annie Chapman neither."

As we walk, I pepper him with questions about the man he saw, but having been so captivated by the killer's eyes, it's all he speaks of. While he does, his voice raspy and aquiver, I start to fade away, feeling like a ghost within my own life. A sense of dread stirs deep in my belly.

All at once, I can see the shadowy moments just before Annie's murder, as if they're right before me. The killer, dressed in shabby elegance, is talking to her. He turns, the way he did towards the young Irishman when he was a boy, and I, too, see The Ripper's eyes. The eyes of a burning sunset, of the ripest apricot. Eyes so deeply familiar that I nearly cry out.

The Ripper's hand, dark and slender, reaches out to me. I hear his breath.

"Help me," he says.

"You alright?" The young Irishman asks me.

I hadn't realized that I'd grabbed his arm, and I'm still gripping it as if it's a bannister and I'm in danger of falling.

"I'm sorry. I suppose it just got to me. Your story, I mean."

I realize I'm trembling, and my face feels cold as if all the blood has drained from it. A wave of nausea comes over me, but I continue walking to shake it off.

By the time we arrive at Whitechapel station, I am back to myself, mostly, though the young Irishman seems reluctant to let me go it alone. I assure him I'll be fine, but before I descend the stairs, I turn back to him. My strange daydream has me feeling superstitious.

"Have you got a mother or sister?"

He gives a sad, but resigned sort of smile. "I did. Not no more."

"Well, here then," I say, reaching beneath my musky old cloak and removing a gold cross with a pearl in the center—one Aunt Imogen gave me. I take his hand and place the necklace in his palm in such a way that no bystander can see. "Perhaps you can wear this yourself, to keep you safe, or give it to a sweetheart."

His sad smile becomes impish. "I don't know I should take this from you m'lady."

"You should," I tell him. He doesn't need much convincing.

"See, I knew you'd come," he says, lifting the cross to his lips and kissing it. "It's like I been waitin' for you."

It does indeed feel that way.

I AM UNCOMFORTABLE in my skin the whole of the way to The British Museum. Arriving in the West End of London, it is truly another world. Clean and regal, bountiful in patches of green. A well-dressed couple passes me by, the lady of the pair lingering in her stare. I feel vaguely affronted until I realize that I'm still wearing the tattered, second-hand cloak I purchased for my excursion this morning. I remove the garment and lay it over the top of an iron fence, looking upon it with some affection before leaving it behind.

I no longer feel a part of this world here, the way I did when I awakened this morning. Not since my vision of The Ripper speaking to me. As I look around me, it's as if I've just come to London, and it only looks familiar because of the many depictions I've seen of it in paintings and photographs.

"My dear Leila!" Sir Edward says, as he greets me at the

entrance of the museum. "Happy Birthday. My stars you've grown up!"

All perfectly straight middle part and squared-off beard, he looks exactly as he did when I last saw him.

"You are a sight for sore eyes," I say.

He blushes a bit and kisses my cheek. "And you are a vision."

As he leads me into the Great Court, he asks many questions about how we've resettled into Cairo, excited about our acquaintanceship with Dr. Davies and my subsequent involvement with The Egyptian Museum. I try to amuse him with talk about how the installment of the ancient Egyptian collection is coming along, what with all the drama about thieves and such, but can hardly concentrate on our simple conversation.

The eyes of The Ripper continue to haunt my every thought, seeming to watch me, and watch with me as I tour the many artifacts with our family friend. Sir Edward offers engaging commentary on every piece we encounter, but I'm barely able to take in the gift of his remarkable knowledge.

"Ah, the Elgin Marbles," he says as we come to the figures. "The last time I took you here, you inquired as to why the sculptor had made some of them without heads!"

He lectures me about the classical Greek sculptures, once a part of the temple of the Parthenon, but I am distracted to the point of madness. So many of the pieces in this museum feel immediate, startlingly vivid. As we meander past the Medieval and Renaissance pieces of the Waddesdon Bequest—broaches, chalices, sculpted beasts—even those are intimate, as if they've sat in my sitting room all of my life. Or another life.

"This pre-Colombian piece is a bit of an outlier," Sir Edward says, pointing to a pendant with a tiny crucifixion inside. "It was made in sixteenth century Mexico."

"Yes," I say. "It once included feather work, but that appears to be gone."

Sir Edward raises an eyebrow at me, and I feel the blood drain from my face once more. I have no idea where my comment on the artifact came from, as I've never seen it before in my life.

"Indeed," he says. "We don't know for sure if it included the feather work you mention, but if we compare it with other pieces from the time, you may very well be right."

Sir Edward's eyes brighten and he smiles at me with great enthusiasm. "Since you have clearly been studying the period, I do have an indulgence for you. Come, dear, something truly special."

He leads me out of the main hall and around corners, into a place of wood paneling and lower ceilings. We come up to a heavy door, and Sir Edward presses a button provoking a shrill buzzing noise.

A small, balding man with greased strands of hair combed over a skull as pale as a goose egg opens up, peeking his head out of the door. When he sees Sir Edward, he cracks a wide, yellowed smile and ushers us in as if we're late for a party. The room is little more than a white box about the size of an ample study. Three large, rectangular wooden tables are lined up in the center, and at least a dozen paintings, most of them still covered, are lying about.

"We've only just received this collection left to the museum by an American, of all people. Originally belonged to the relative of a conquistador."

The first painting I see is a religious painting of the crucifixion. Mannerist and covered in splashes of royal hues juxtaposed with the muted tones of earth and troubled sky. The piece is a stranger to me at first, but when I step close, and the balding man holds it up for me to see better, I feel an acquaintance with it that causes me great distress, like the vague memory of a traumatic childhood experience.

"This came formerly from the collection of one Álvero Romero Álvarez, a great-grand-nephew of Alonso Álvarez de Pineda, the conquistador who mapped much of the Gulf of Mexico," Sir Edward tells me.

"Do any of these paintings depict this Álvarez?" Part of me wishes I hadn't asked.

"No, unfortunately. But we do have a rather skillful portrait of his daughter from about 1612."

Sir Edward waves his hand and the balding man uncovers an oil on panel featuring a young Spanish woman dressed in deep, dark blue.

"Oh," I say, feeling my heart start to flutter.

"Gabriella Liliana Álvarez was her name, and I think this is the best work of a middling painter by the name of Emiliano Sanz." Sir Edward inclines towards the painting, then looks back at me. "I daresay, Leila. It would appear she has your eyes."

Gabriella's eyes, green as the feathers of a peafowl, are exactly like mine. They make me shudder as she stares at me from the prison of her canvas. But there's something else in that picture as well.

"What is that?" I whisper. I point, my finger shaking something awful, to a credenza depicted behind the girl. A vase of red lilies sits front and center on its top, and a figure peeks out from behind it. I step closer, and yes, it's just as I thought. There sits Cornelius's statue—the very one from the market!

"Ah, the figurine. No one here can seem to place it. Interesting story behind the girl, though. That, we do know. You see, Alvarez, her father, was a bit of a sluggard, who mostly squandered his fortune. One that was quite considerable, as you can imagine. He used his daughter, Gabriella, to help him swindle people by having her read their fortunes. Poor girl was thought to be mad, always walking in her sleep, and dreaming of strange histories. It was said when she touched the statue, she had visions."

"Visions, you say." My mouth goes dry as toast. "Whatever happened to her?"

"A mystery, really. One day, she picked up that statue and wandered into the jungle never to be seen again."

The pit in my stomach feels as if it's made of spiny coral. I recall the monstrous fascination I feel whenever I'm in the presence of the figure. The way it seems to call to me and caution me all at once.

"Sir Edward, my friend Cornelius bought just such a statue in a market in Cairo some weeks ago. How on earth do you suppose that statue ended up in Egypt?"

Sir Edward sniffs, folding his arms across his chest.

"Assuming it is the same statue, which I would be highly skeptical of. Could be more than one, you know," he says.

"There isn't," I tell him definitively.

"You know that for sure?"

"Yes. I mean, no. See, no one in Cairo seems to know where that statue is from, but they all agree it's very, very old. Much older than the Spanish conquistadors. Some seem to think it's older than time—well, that's the myth the trinket seller told my friend at any rate."

"The trinket seller! Dear girl, they're just trying to fill their purses and will tell you anything."

"I'm sure you're right," I tell him, though I know he isn't.

"Well, if you've developed an interest in old statuary, allow me to show something else."

As Sir Edward ambles towards one of the tables at the back of the room, he begins to tell me about the Aztecs, only his voice starts to garble. The room begins to spin, and I find I cannot catch my breath at all. Gripping the table, I lean over

Gabriella, looking directly into her eyes—our eyes. They're keen, and appear as if they're desperate to break free of her body. A body that looks frail, defeated. Her face, on the other hand, while plain, has a steely determination etched upon it, as if she's just made up her mind.

"Leila!" I hear Sir Edward exclaim. Then nothing.

Everything goes dark until my eyes flutter open again and I find myself lying on a day bed, the overcast afternoon sky beckoning me from a window. It's clear I'm not at the museum anymore, but I'm not too far either. The familiar houses of London's West End peer down at me from outside.

"Leila," I hear again, but it's not Sir Edward's voice this time. It's one I recognize, but can't name. A face comes into my vision.

"Dr. Birtwistle."

All white beard and cloudy blue eyes, my mother's London physician is looming over me.

"Edward brought you here straight away from the museum. It's something of a stroke of luck that I keep my surgery in my house nowadays, though it's a pity to have to see you again under these circumstances," he says.

I somehow muster the facility to ask him about his wife and children and grandchildren.

"Mostly good," he tells me. "My wife passed a couple of years ago, but I keep busy."

"My condolences," I tell him, and he smiles.

I endeavor to sit up, and Dr. Birtwistle puts his hand on my shoulder, easing me down again. "You're still pale," he says.

"Well I'm not going to get my blood moving again by lying about. I swear, you're as bad as Imogen."

Dr. Birtwistle chuckles. He rises and goes to a sideboard bedazzled by crystal decanters. He pours brandy into two snifters, before returning to the lounge he's consigned me to.

"I think we could both use one of these," he says. "Cheers."

I take a sip, but Dr. Birtwistle downs his in one gulp.

"Good Lord," I say. "Was it something I said in my sleep?"

Dr. Birtwistle shakes his head and excuses himself to pour another. "I always admired your mother's directness. She looked you in the eye and didn't mince her words. Yet somehow, she managed never to sound unkind. That's a rare gift."

"Yes, it is."

"I think of her often."

"As do I."

"Leila," he says, and I do not like the way he says my name this time. "Leila, I wish to tell you what I'm about to tell you in a way your mother would do."

"Tell me what, exactly?"

Dr. Birtwistle takes another swallow of his brandy. A big one. He takes a deep breath, the oily sweetness of the liquor coming at me like a gust of wind.

"Your mother always worried about you, you know. You are so like her in physicality and temperament."

"I've always considered that to be a compliment," I tell him.

"It is, yes, it is. I'm afraid I don't mean it as the sort of compliment I would like to be offering you, though."

I look down at my nearly full cup of brandy. Something tells me I should take a sip.

"What do you mean?"

Dr. Birtwistle puts his snifter down and places his hand over mine.

"How long have you been having these dizzy spells?"

"Not long," I assure him. "Only a handful of times, and usually when I'm under great duress. Dr. Birtwistle, I've always been healthy as a horse, but I must tell you that there has been a great deal going on in Cairo. And it's not just our fear for Clara and Hugo, and the stresses of Father's dam.

And well, today, this morning, was quite eventful, too, I might add."

Dr. Birtwistle nods and glances out the window before his eyes find mine again.

"Leila, I'm sure that your adventures are hardly helpful to your constitution. A young lady needs rest and a calming environment. I would most certainly urge you to spend the rest of your time in England with your hands in the soil, repairing the damage Imogen's black thumbs have done to the garden you made for her. Such a splendid one, I might add. Then, upon your return to Egypt, I would hope you'll spend more time at your sporting club and less time out and about Cairo." He takes an even deeper breath this time, holding it for a moment before letting it go.

"However, those are not the maladies I'm speaking of."

I take a gulp of my brandy and purse my lips.

"I'm concerned about your health." Dr. Birtwistle takes my hand. "Do you remember when your mother began having her spells?"

A cold prickle comes to my temples. I want to tell him he's mistaken. He can't imagine the disturbing and dangerous events I've been subjected to since returning to Egypt! Or the love I feel for a young man I may have loved for countless lifetimes! That, surely, would make even a warrior dizzy and weak.

"You think it's my heart?" I whisper.

Dr. Birtwistle nods.

"It's not."

"Leila."

"It's not. It can't be. I feel fine, I told you. And besides, I have too much to do—if you only knew how much! God will not take me before I can get it done—I know it."

Dr. Birtwistle rubs his cheek and blinks his eyes hard. "My dear, I've found in my line of work that God does indeed know what He's doing, even if His ways seem cruel and rash." He leans in to me and smiles. "Nothing can stop God's plans for your life."

"Isaiah 14:27."

My forehead grows damp as early morning moss. I can barely get my next words out, and when I do, my voice sounds weak and raspy. "If indeed there is any truth to what you suspect, is there anything we can do?"

"Pray," he whispers.

I nod, saying a silent prayer, reaching out to the spirit of my mother. I feel feeble all of a sudden. Not in my heart, though. More like my blood is draining from my body. It all seems surreal, as if we're not talking about me, but someone else. Some poor, unlucky girl we all murmur about after mass. *Such a tragedy*, we say, with an unmistakable tone of relief in our voices. Relief it isn't us.

"It's difficult to say how quickly you'll progress. I'm encouraged that you've only just begun to have episodes like the one today. In your mother's case, she lasted nearly five years from the time her first symptoms appeared."

"But I don't feel unwell," I say. "A bit of vertigo is all. Short of breath—and only when I've had quite a shock, or if I've been running about like mad trying to make sure Father takes care of himself. Honestly, it's nothing I don't recover from quickly!"

Dr. Birtwistle nods patiently, his crinkled eyes closed.

"Your mother recovered quickly at first, too. Later, not so much, as I'm sure you remember."

I do indeed. How pale she would go when her breath became labored. The way her lips would turn blue and her hands would quake. In her last few months, she would lie in bed for days, too weak to get up, and hating her body for betraying her.

"I have something for you," Dr. Birtwistle tells me. "From

her. She gave it to me on her last visit to London only a few months before she passed—to give to you in the event that she passed her affliction to you. I told her not to be morbid about it, but she was insistent."

Dr. Birtwistle gets up again and goes to his file keeper, its square drawers arranged alphabetically. He retrieves my mother's file, and plucks a letter from inside. I'm afraid to look at it, and no small part of me wants to get up and run out of here. Yet my eyes are drawn to the letter as if it holds the secret to my cure. For the second time today, I recognize the handwriting of someone I love and my damned traitorous heart begins to hammer. The envelope is thick and larger than a simple letter, with *Leila* written in big, looping letters on its back. My mother's friend and physician hands it to me.

"May I have a moment?"

Dr. Birtwistle blinks and smiles, then exits his surgery.

I do not rip open the envelope the way I did this morning when Father gave me Ripley's letter. This morning now feels like a long time ago. I stare at it, noting once again that apart from the obvious shock of this news, I feel absolutely fine, and rejecting the notion that my heart, beating so strong and steady in my chest, could possibly be on the brink of an extended collapse.

Bringing the envelope to my nose, as I did Ripley's, I smell nothing of my mother. The letter has, after all, sat amongst Dr. Birtwistle's files for years now. Finally, I open it up and look inside.

The first thing I see are several photographs, taken with a Bellows camera. The first is of what looks like an island, one with many palms. On the back, it reads simply "Niue," and I know immediately that it must come from Father's cousins, the Ogdens, who moved to Oceana with the London Missionary Society some years back. Another photo shows a small gathering of people, all seated and dressed mostly in white. The majority are British, with two, darkly-complected Niueans seated prominently up front. This photograph reads, "Baxter and Lavinia (Ogden) with the King and Queen of Niue." Yet another, a photograph that appears to have been taken just before a rather threatening storm, is of a rock formation extending out from the shore into the ocean. "The Arches of Talava," it reads. "Savage Island."

I put the photographs down in my lap, wetting my lips as best I can with my thirsty tongue. I could use another brandy, but I don't indulge. Flipping through the images once again, I remember that my mother had liked the Ogdens, and had mentioned as much to me when I was a girl. She said they were modern-thinking, which was about the highest compliment she could pay another.

Now, I stare down at the envelope with my name splashed across the back. Inside is a folded paper that contains the last words my mother will have conveyed to me while she lived, and the words her spirit clearly wishes me to know. I reach inside the pocket and pull out a single sheet of writing paper folded in half. Before unfolding it, I quiet my breath and check the beating of my heart yet again. Constant, normal, a bit restless perhaps. Displaying nothing of the gloom and doom Dr. Birtwistle believes it is burdened by.

At last, I open up the paper, preparing myself for one of my mother's long essays—ones she was famous for leaving for friends, family, and the occasional periodical.

Only there's nothing long about it. I stare disbelieving at the block letters—not even cursive—that she's left for me.

They read: If you are not dead by your eighteenth birthday, you must find your way to Niue. Yours, Mother.

Chapter 22

Secrets, Promises
Cairo, 1902

"HALLOOOO," Ripley calls.

From our open balcony above the ground floor, I hear the wheels from his carriage creak and rumble to a full stop in front of our home in Old Cairo. My damnable heart nearly skips a beat. He hops from the coach, and tut-tuts about how our Moorish windows are shuttered in anticipation of the afternoon sun, when afternoon is hours away yet.

"Silly man, we just got home. Of course the windows are shuttered!" Father says.

I dot a bit of rouge onto my lips, and rush out onto the balcony. Ripley and I both catch our breath. I'm in light green, a color he loves, and he's got on his usual shirt, waistcoat, and trousers, with his sleeves rolled up. We drink each other in.

"I had to learn of your arrival from a servant twice removed!" he shouts.

"Quit your moaning and get in here straight away!" I tell him. Hastening back inside, I practically glide down the stairs.

Moments later I throw the front doors open, making sure to fill their frame. I want him to see me and only me as I open my arms wide to welcome him. He runs to me, enveloping me in his arms and spinning me about. I'm filled with pure joy and feel better than I have in weeks. It's as if I can live forever.

"None of that!" Father grouses from the top of the steps. He rumbles down them, duck-footed. "And without even having sat for a cup of tea."

"Well, gracious me," I say. "By all means, Ripley, come in for some tea."

"Lord Wellington," Ripley says, holding out his hand. "So good to see you again."

"Likewise, son. I dare say, it's splendid to be home. My daughter's insistence that we depart a few days ahead of schedule was golden! Both of us were out of sorts while we were away. Even Leila, who normally flies about like a fairy, elected to spend some of her days in bed."

"Got ill, did you?" Ripley asks.

"Too much commotion," I say, waving my hand in dismissal and feigning interest in where Father's translation of Nietzsche's notebooks disappeared to.

The foyer is cluttered with luggage strewn over our cacophony of old Malmuk rugs, and a confetti of stuffed tapestry pillows litter the floor and sofas. Refuse from our travels sits on just about every surface of our sundry walnut tables, and Ripley smiles to himself, and remarks how somehow, everything manages to look just as it should be. He leans in close, inhaling my scent.

"Malmaison," I say in my most perfect French. I bat my eyes and he holds his belly as he laughs.

"Is that someone I should know?"

"Malmaison by Floris," I chide him, swiping at his shoulder with my fan. "The London perfumery. Top notes of cinnamon, cloves, and lemon. Base notes of cedar, musk, vanilla, and . . . something else. Can't remember."

"I smell the cloves," Ripley says. *And I smell you*, he

mouths. I thrill to be on the other end of his whisper, and take in the smell of his breath—mint tea and cardamom.

Crisply, I smile and clear my throat. "Father, would you mind? I'm going to take Ripley up to the library. We have much to discuss."

"No, no, go right ahead." Father shuffles to the mantle, and plucks his pipe from under an ornate candelabra that one of my great-grandfathers fashioned. His eyes widen. "On second thought," he says, "Why don't the two of you get reacquainted in the courtyard? Plenty of space and shade. Lovely morning."

"It's a beastly morning, but the courtyard is vaguely within earshot for you," I say.

Ripley follows me through the sitting room and out an arched doorway into our interior courtyard. The strong bouquet of my favorite exotic flowers, potted all about the perfect square of space, hangs heavy in the air. They threaten to overpower my lavish perfume, but I don't mind.

"I've ached for you," I say, wrapping my arms about Ripley's neck. Just touching him again is the best kind of medicine.

He kisses me in a way he shouldn't. Especially with Father just around the corner. I kiss him back, most certainly in a way I shouldn't. We move slowly, as one, drawn to a canopied corner, where we fall onto a long cypress bench.

"There are no words for how much I've missed you," he tells me.

I place my head on Ripley's shoulder and kiss him lightly on his neck, letting go of a deep breath very slowly, like I've been holding it for a long time. In a way, I have. All the way since Whitechapel and the painting at the museum and especially Dr. Birtwistle's surgery. I can hardly keep it all in my head, it's so much.

"What's wrong?"

"Nothing," I say. "What could possibly be wrong now that I'm home and you're with me?"

"Plenty," Ripley says.

A determined wisp of sadness comes over me and I chase it away, but it does not go unnoticed. I give Ripley my best smile. "Just long travels and a restless night of sleep."

Ripley caresses my hair and the slope of my back. I hum with contentment, squeezing him tight, dancing my fingers over Ripley's collar, before finally resting one in the hollow of his throat. Slowly, I sit up, stroking his face and loving him with my gaze.

"Close your eyes," I whisper.

"What's this about?"

"Just do it."

He does, and I stand up, my skirts rustling. This prompts him to open one eye and I place my hand firmly at my hip.

"Alright, alright." He closes it again.

I reach into my reticule, removing the gift I chose for him in London. Enfolding my hand around it like gift-wrap, I draw it out.

"Now you may open them," I tell him.

Sitting again, I hold out my clenched hand. One by one, I unravel my fingers. At the center of my palm is the gold locket I bought for him. Handsome and simple. Very fine, I think. A token of love from me that will far outlast our bodies and lives.

"Open it," I say. My voice hitches a bit.

There is a look of wonder upon Ripley's face as he takes the oval from me and unclasps it. His eyes fall on the inside left, where our names and the year are engraved in italic cursive. Beneath that is a large, green emerald, so close to the color of my eyes as to almost be indistinguishable from them. I want him to feel that he's gazing into them every time he looks at it. On the other side of this is a picture portrait of me, new and taken in London.

"It's extraordinary," Ripley says.

"You really think so?" I bounce on the bench with excitement as Ripley nods at me, swallowing an influx of emotion.

"So you'll never forget me," I say.

"Forget you? I plan to live my life with you."

"You never know what can happen." I shrug a bit, trying to seem nonchalant. "I mean, we might be separated again, like we have been these past weeks."

"You and I were not made to be separated for long. And we will never be separated again, if I have anything to say about it. At least not in this lifetime."

I take Ripley's hand in mine, holding the locket between them. Inclining, I turn them over, kissing them firmly at the wrist. When I rise back up, I can feel my eyes are moist, but hope against all hope that he believes it's from happiness. Because it is—in part anyway. The other part, I'll contend with later. When I'm ready to make sense of it all.

"I have something for you, too," Ripley says.

He retrieves from his pocket the ancient amulet his father bought from a tribal woman when he was but a babe. Ripley dangles it before me, and I can't help but to gasp.

"It's for your birthday, which I hated to miss. I wanted to take you somewhere special, and still plan to."

My lip trembles as he places the necklace around my neck, the bloodstone at the center of the amulet dangling over my heart. The iconography touches the skin of my breast, and I place my hand over it, shutting my eyes and trying to think of heaven.

"I couldn't," I say.

"I want to see you wear it and know I gave it to you, the way my father gave it to my mother."

I blink, a single tear rushing down the swell of my cheek.

"Won't it hurt him to see me wearing it?"

"It hurts him to carry it around for a ghost. And when he saw I couldn't find anything quite right for you, he offered it. Because it is perfect, isn't it? Like it was made for you and you alone."

I nod, sniffing back more tears. Leaning over, I kiss Ripley, soft and wet-lipped. "Perfect," I whisper.

There's another commotion at the front door, and we hear Cornelius greeting Father. His light step snaps across the tiles and immediately lifts my spirits, beating away nearly all of my more morose thoughts.

"Welcome home!" He sweeps into the courtyard, and I stand, wiping my eyes. Cornelius bends over and presses his lips to my damp knuckle.

"I should say the same to you," I say.

"I thank you and your father for letting me stay here. I would have liked to decline your offer when your telegram came, but to be honest, I was grateful for it."

I place my hands on each side of his face.

"There was simply no chance we were going to allow you to remain in the City of the Dead after a second murder. Especially when Ripley and I, and our friends, appear to be of special interest to the one we believe is responsible."

Cornelius nods to Ripley, and I bid him to sit with us.

"Besides," I say, brightening up. "This old house was sitting here empty and all alone while we were gone. A house needs company every bit as much as a person does, and so did my flowers."

I reach into a pocket at my waist and pull out a photograph, holding it up for Cornelius to see. He raises an eyebrow.

"Doesn't look like the England I've read about," he says.

I place the photograph in our friend's palm. "It's the Vaikona chasm on the island of Niue in Oceana."

Cornelius brings it close, delighting in the image. He

collects little drawings and artifacts of places he'd like to visit, having added many such items to Ripley's father's office at the museum.

Ripley leans over to get a look himself. It's a vivid photograph, taken in high sun. Craggy rock walls rise on each side of a glossy body of water so calm that it looks as if it could be walked upon. A sudden sense of foreboding strikes me deep in the chest as we study the topography. It's not the pain of a phantom memory, like the ones in so many of the desert dreams Ripley and I have shared. More like we're looking at a page of our fate. One that has yet to come.

"Our relatives, the Ogdens, moved there some years ago with the London Missionary Society," I say. "Maybe the three of us can go there one day and visit them."

I smile at Cornelius with genuine satisfaction, but become restless again almost straightaway. Standing, I stretch a bit and take out my fan, pretending to cool myself, when really, I'm just trying to give my hands something to do.

"Cornelius, you wouldn't happen to have your statue here at the house?" I blurt out.

"It's at Dr. Davies's office at the museum." Cornelius looks me over, and I realize I'm fidgeting again, gnawing at my bottom lip, too.

"Is this urgent?" he asks.

I stroke the amulet with my fingers and crouch down, lowering my voice, and steeling myself.

"I have something to tell you."

The bloodstone at the center of my amulet seems to warm with the intensity of my emotion. I don't look down at it for fear it might be glowing. My eyes pierce Ripley's, as my incredible story spills out of me like pennies from a jar. I tell them about the young Irishman who saw The Ripper as a boy, and of the vision I had of The Ripper himself. The way he reached out his hand and asked me to help him.

"Are you sure this wasn't a dream?" Cornelius asks. "A memory from a nightmare, or a daydream of sorts?"

I tell him that I am quite sure it was not. It was as if the present world and the spirit world came together for a brief time, yet I was the only one who seemed aware of it. Then I explain to them about the painting Sir Edward showed me in London— the one which depicted a conquistador's relation who was used by her father to tell the fortunes of wealthy patrons. And how Cornelius's very statue was posed behind her on a table!

Our friend's eyes widen and tremble; he puts his hand behind his neck, giving it a good, hard rub.

"It was said the girl had visions whenever she touched the figure," I say. "One day, she took it in hand and disappeared into the jungle. Never to be seen again."

"And you're saying you'd like to take it in hand," Ripley says, shaking his head with vehemence. "That seems like about the worst idea I've heard all year!"

I purse my lips, ready to stand my ground. I've been practicing what I'm about to say for days now. "I wouldn't do it alone. I'd want the two of you with me, of course."

Cornelius drums his fingers on the side of his neck. "Well, it is an intriguing prospect, I have to admit."

"Cornelius, do shut up," Ripley says.

"It is, Ripley. Don't deny it. And could potentially answer a lot of questions."

Including ones about my own predicted doom, although I don't dare tell them about that. Never would they ever— not even Cornelius—agree to my plan if they even suspected my health was in any way compromised.

"Ripley," I say. "You felt it, too—the draw of that statue. And how providential is it that that very painting would be shown to me in London? You know very well it could be the key to all of these mysteries surrounding us."

My brow is tied in a knot, my jaw set. I can feel the tension in my body as surely as I would in the atmosphere just before a flash of lightening.

"You said she had your eyes exactly, this girl in the painting," Cornelius says.

"It was as if I was looking in a mirror. Not the rest of her, obviously. She was very small, almost doll-like. But her eyes, yes, they were unquestionably mine."

I rise and pace to the center of the courtyard, glancing at a row of blood-red lilies, which stare us all down.

"If Leila's right," Ripley says. "And the figure could have a similar effect on her that it did on the Spaniard's daughter, then it's obviously a danger. I mean, look what it did to that poor girl, who was probably eaten alive by some beast after getting lost. Not to mention the detrimental impression an experiment like this might leave on Leila's psyche."

I fold my arms in defiance. "I assure you my psyche will be fine. In fact, I'll match my psyche with the two of yours any day."

Ripley rises up and comes to me, kissing my forehead. "Well, as endearingly stubborn as you are, I'm not inclined to have you meet your match in some ancient statue with numinous powers."

"I'm quite certain I won't," I assure him. "As long as we find an appropriate place to do this, I feel it'll all work out. A place where I couldn't go wandering about, and if I tried, well, that's what strong men like you are for, isn't that right?"

"Leila," Cornelius says. "Ripley and I would surely wrestle the statue from your hands, but we cannot control whatever ways it could damage you, assuming it is as powerful as we fear. And as much as I want to know what secrets that statue holds, I would forego those secrets for your wellbeing."

I do hate this talk of secrets, as I know they have a way of destroying hearts all on their own. *Soon, you'll know the worst of it*, I promise them silently. In the meantime, I will tell them everything my heart can bear. I take both Ripley's and Cornelius's hands and lead them to the far side of the courtyard. There, I detach myself from them and reach out to one of the red lilies, caressing its stem. The flower shudders as if the ground beneath it shook.

"Do you see these flowers? I grew ones just like them at my Aunt Imogen's and they thrived until Father and I moved to Cairo. I nursed them back to health these past few weeks in England until they were as perfect as these. I assume they'll start to wither again now that I'm gone. It's something that's always been a part of me, you know—my relationship with the soil and what grows from it." I tip my head, and realize I'm looking at the open flower as if it's the face of a loved one. "These same flowers; they, too, were in the painting with that girl who had my eyes. Do you suppose every seed she planted thrilled to her touch and attention like this?"

I reach down into a gardening basket, removing from it a pair of shears. I clip one of the red lilies from its stem and place it behind my ear.

"That statue belongs to me," I say. "It has always belonged to me. Long before that Spanish girl got her hands on it. I can't tell you how I know, because I don't know myself. I just do."

We stand quiet for several long moments, looking at one another, all of us wondering where this will take us. All of us knowing it's to a place of both darkness and light.

"I have an idea," Ripley says. "Cornelius and I are to accompany my father and Howard Carter to the pyramids later this morning. Why don't you join us at the end of the day at the museum? After you've had some rest. Father and Mr. Carter will be having a late supper at The Shepheard, and we'll have a good couple of hours alone, in the locked office of a museum surrounded by security. We can observe the statue some more, perhaps devise an experiment—safely!"

"Or you could come with us today," Cornelius says. "You'd have to get ready quickly, though, as Ripley and I are running late already."

I tap my toe as I pull the chain of my watch, releasing it from my pocket and checking the time. I've made it a point to get an hour's nap every day, as Dr. Birtwistle prescribed.

"As much as I'd love to, I have a good bit to do. Not to mention all the help Father's going to need. Do give Mr. Carter my regards."

"Won't you reconsider," Ripley asks. "I feel vaguely disturbed at the prospect of leaving you alone now that you're back in Cairo."

"I couldn't possibly leave Father when we've only just arrived back," I tell him. "I'll meet you at the museum tonight. Horus will take me. And I'll even bring dinner. Can't be communing with mystical statues on an empty stomach, can we?"

Chapter 23

Record Keeper

I **HEAR** a coarse whisper. It's not Nif's. This is from a froggy-eyed phantom with small hands, chapped from desert wandering. A voice that has never quite been able to reach me in my dreams. Until today.

"I told you if you kept her with you I would find you again." He grips the head of the effigy I hold. The one he gave me.

"It is you."

He blinks his eyes.

"And you're like me and Nif?"

"Not quite, my kitten."

He leans in towards my ear and begins to tell me.

"LEILA, DARLING!" Ripley's voice is distant and muffled at first. He taps his hand on my cheek, then shakes me until I blink open my eyes.

"As I live and breathe," I hear Dr. Davies say. He and Mr. Carter trot up to us on a pair of camels. "Is she alright?"

I can't help but to inhale a deep, gasping breath, as if I haven't taken any air in much too long. My fingers dig into the sand beneath me.

"Ripley? What are you doing here?"

"We should ask the same of you, my dear," Dr. Davies says, as he dismounts from his camel and comes to my side. "We spotted you at a distance, talking to a man in white robes. Ripley seemed to think he was a merchant of some sort. In any case, the man looked a bit wild, I must say. Turned on his heel and ran round the Sphinx with Cornelius in pursuit."

"Even at a distance, you did not seem quite yourself," Ripley says. He's leaning over me, his eyes searching my appearance for signs of . . . illness or madness, perhaps?

"Mmm, the sun is rather strong this afternoon," Dr. Davies says.

The sun is strong and I must shield my eyes as Ripley helps me sit up. I realize quite suddenly that I am not in a dream, but even more disturbingly, I am not at my home, where I had laid down in bed after helping Father make sense of our luggage. I look around, taking in not only the sun, but the sand, the taste of air dry as a husk, the golden-pink flush radiating on the back of the Sphinx, its head against the backdrop of a vast sky devoid of a single cloud. A profound sense of alarm takes me over, as I cannot think of one rational explanation for how I ended up here.

"The Sphinx, the pyramids," I stutter.

"Father, give her some water," Ripley says.

Dr. Davies takes a canteen from his saddle bag and hands it to his son.

"I'm afraid you've missed our excursion inside the Great Pyramid," he tells me.

Ripley puts the water to my lips and I drink thirstily, as if I haven't tasted a single drop all day.

"Yes, well, my misfortune," I say, cutting a smile into my face.

Cornelius comes galloping round from the other side of

the Sphinx and stops behind Mr. Carter. He dismounts and jogs over to us, crouching at my other side.

"He's disappeared," he says to Ripley. "But at least Leila seems alright."

"What do you mean 'disappeared'? How could he when there's nowhere to go?" Ripley demands.

"You can go look for yourself, but I'm telling you he's gone."

"Who?" I demand.

"The trinket seller who sold me the statue."

"The trinket seller? What would he be doing here?"

Cornelius reaches past me and picks up the bag in which he keeps the statue, retrieving it from the interior. I feel a very sudden and violent emotion about the thing—wanting it and feeling repelled by it all at once. I hear myself take an audible breath and bury my face in the front of Ripley's shirt like a little girl frightened of a monster in her wardrobe.

"You brought it with you?" I ask him. "I thought you were keeping it at the museum."

Cornelius and Ripley look to one another and our friend scoots back, pulling the bag with him, and placing the figure back from whence it came.

"Leila, you brought it here," Ripley says. "On our way back from the pyramid, we spotted you talking to the trinket seller. He seemed to alert you to our presence, and when you pivoted towards us, we saw you were holding the statue. Then you stuffed it back in the bag and promptly collapsed."

"Leila," Cornelius says. "Do you remember talking to him?"

"The trinket seller?"

He nods and I sniff deeply, trying to pull myself together. I search every part of my day, from awakening at dawn as our train pulled up in Cairo, to Ripley coming to our house and our exchange of gifts, to now, and not one memory of the trinket seller comes to me. Not even the ghost of a memory.

"No," I say, shaking my head.

Ripley squeezes my hand and pulls me closer.

"The desert sun can be pitiless," Mr. Carter says. He rubs his eyes good and hard, and impels his camel closer to us. "There are days when hours have gone by and I would swear it was only minutes. And the reverse, of course. I once lost half a week after being felled by the sun, though my men swore that I was walking around, going about my business."

"Mr. Carter," Ripley says. "Do you think you could do us the favor of going ahead and fetching us a carriage for our return to the city? Leila only just came from a long journey back from England, and I fear you're right—the sun was a bit much for her today."

"Yes, of course," he says, tipping his hat. "Lady Wellington."

Ripley assists me in standing up and I'm quite relieved that my legs are strong, and the rest of me seems to be in working order as well. I don't feel any remnants of sun sickness at all. No headache or fatigue or fever. I do my best to mask my continuing bewilderment with another smile, this one coming easier, and apologizing to all for being such a bother.

"Really, everyone," I say. "I feel quite well. In my excitement to join you all, I must have forgotten to eat. I'm sure when you came upon me I was just inquiring as to if anyone had seen you."

"None at all," Dr. Davies says. "We would have been the better for your company, had you made it just a few hours earlier."

"Yes, well, I tried my best," I say.

"No matter, you're here now and looking better by the moment, thank goodness. You did give us a bit of a startle,

I must say, but the Egyptian sun can't keep one of its own daughters down for long, can it?"

"Certainly not," I tell him, and this time with a bit more confidence. I am feeling strangely robust, at least in a physical sense.

"I really am alright," I whisper to Ripley, who is pinching his lips together in worry.

Carefully, we begin to walk. Cornelius takes the reins of the camels, and Ripley takes my hand again, guiding me. Up ahead, I can see Mr. Carter in silhouette, summoning a carriage driver with a wave and a clap of his hands. I knit my fingers through Ripley's and look back at the Sphinx. There, at its base, sits a cat. A Turkish angora as white as snow, who watches us make our way for a few moments, before losing interest and maundering away.

"Did you say *kitten*?" Ripley asks.

"I'm sorry? Oh, yes, a kitten, or cat. It's nothing."

"My dear, you missed a most intriguing story told by Mr. Carter," Dr. Davies says with renewed relish.

"He told us Herodotus was said to have visited a glorious and gargantuan chamber somewhere beneath the Sphinx here, although there's no other evidence of such a place." Dr. Davies says this in that way of his, as if he's lecturing to an unseen audience of rapt students.

"While it is indeed an interesting story, Father, Leila did just recover from a fainting spell."

"Nonsense," I say. "I could use a good story."

"Besides, the trinket seller could have disappeared into one of those chambers," Cornelius says, prompting me to squeeze Ripley's hand this time.

"I'd like to think so," Dr. Davies chuckles. "Be exciting, wouldn't it? Sadly, he probably just walked away, and the sun played its tricks on you, making him blend in with the sand. Could have been right in front of you and you didn't see him."

"Or he's being fed grapes by the goddesses in one of those palaces Carter described," Cornelius quips.

"Miss Leila, Mr. Carter told us Herodotus wrote of twelve subterranean palaces interspersed with terraces arranged around twelve halls—all intricately carved and built of white marble. The enormous chamber also included a labyrinth and a pyramid of great height—much like the pyramid we visited today. He was told the chambers were connected to the pyramids at Memphis by passages. Rather difficult to believe that one, given that Memphis is miles from here."

"Perhaps, but the existence of lost Egyptian records buried deep beneath this area has long been a myth among the northern tribes of Africa, and the Greeks believed that the builders of the pyramids had a library of other ancient civilizations," Cornelius says. "Ones that are thought to predate our Egyptians by many thousands of years."

"According to folklore," Dr. Davies says, "such a hidden library was presided over by a record-keeper, a demi-god librarian of sorts who not only guarded the great histories, but could influence them through supernatural interference. Of course, folklore, though quite illuminating, can be a bunch of bollocks."

"You say a record-keeper?" I ask. Ripley catches my eyes in his, and for a moment, I see a flash of warning in them.

Just then, Howard Carter approaches us, fresh from his success in finding us a carriage.

"My people believe in folklore," Cornelius says.

Dr. Davies smiles at Cornelius with both great amusement and gratification. "You hunger for the great unknown discovery, like Howard here," he tells him. "I must warn you that archaeology is a long, painstaking endeavor that is far more liable to go piece by piece like a jigsaw puzzle, rather than produce a royal flush of instant success."

To this, Howard Carter gives a rousing hoot. I let go of Ripley's hand, gently, and walk closer to the archeologist.

"Did this record-keeper have a name?" I ask Mr. Carter. "One apart from his title."

Howard Carter raises an eyebrow and nods his head. "He did indeed, Lady Wellington. It was said they called him Rin."

"Rin," I say, just to feel the name on my tongue. I am sure I have heard it before. Just as I am sure it is a name that Ripley has known, too. Maybe even better than I, and that suspicion makes a disturbance within me.

Chapter 24

The Effigy and the Truth

WE DO NOT talk of the statue for days—Ripley, Cornelius, and I. In part, because we're allowed little time together alone. Work at the museum is harried on the Davies end, and I've had so many claims made on me by Father that I've only been able to visit there for my studies. But there is another reason, too. I believe we have each been dwelling on what happened at the Sphinx, trying to sort out the various elements unfolding, and how they may or may not relate to the arcane statue that's bedeviling us all.

The last that was said of my mysterious appearance that day was in the carriage, after leaving Giza. And I cannot stop thinking about it.

"Your father's office was locked," Cornelius had whispered.

"Furthermore," Cornelius said, "I had wrapped the effigy in a shroud of suede and secured it in his desk. I have the key with me here, and the only other is at your house, in your father's safe."

"Could you have broken in while sleepwalking? Or had someone let you in?" Ripley asked me.

A reasonable question given the animated nature of our dreams. Only the guards at the museum, all of whom are well acquainted with me, told us they had no knowledge of my visiting the museum that day, and recall only having seen

Maspero coming and going. It is as if the statue was able to leave Dr. Davies's office on its own.

Since that night, my dreams have been more vivid than ever, telling wild stories of blood and raw power . . . and, on occasion, love. I wake up with sweat beaded across my brow, babbling in the language of my amulet, the language I spoke at the Sphinx just before fainting, according to Ripley. This morning I awakened in a particular state. My hands were fisted and my left palm was burning hotter than ever. Every part of me—joint, muscle, bone—ached. My mind was the worst of all, as my thoughts swirled kaleidoscopically with images of horror that were at once shocking and strangely common to me: severed heads with their eyes gouged out, women so violated as to be unrecognizable.

Right away, I took out my scrapbook, and wrote everything I could remember about that dream, even sketching some of the most evil and frightening visuals. Then I paged through the many entries I'd made about Herodotus's stories of subterranean palaces and passageways beneath the Sphinx. Of a record-keeper named Rin.

It is the name Rin that haunts me as I get ready for my excursion to the museum today. I leave quite early and without Cornelius, taking a simple buggy on my journey. It is an open one that allows me to feel a part of Cairo, rather than merely an observer. All the time, the desert, the statue, the name of the record-keeper, dance in circles through my every thought.

"You look a bit peaked, my dear," Dr. Davies remarks as I enter the atrium. "Perhaps you should have slept in. I didn't expect you here for another hour."

I look about and am glad to see that Ripley has not yet arrived at the museum. Such a comment would disturb him. I greet Ripley's father, and excuse myself as I turn away from him, pretending to fiddle with the contents of my reticule. In reality, I'm biting my lips and pinching my cheeks in order to liven them, not look quite as peaked as he observed.

"Cornelius should be here soon," I say, brightly.

"Ah, good. Ripley is gathering some maps for me, and will be meeting us at the station with them."

Dr. Davies looks me up and down again as I stride towards him, ushering past the large, dynastic statues of Amenhotep III, his wife, Tiye, and their three daughters, and to a glass case that he's been arranging with assorted artifacts, several of them from Howard Carter's expedition.

He must leave for Damascus this morning, tracking stolen relics which were plundered from Howard Carter's new discovery in the Valley of the Kings, and promptly smuggled out of Cairo.

"Scalawags," Dr. Davies mutters. He believes a special place in hell is reserved for antiquities thieves.

"A fortnight away from the museum is not what I had in mind right now. Neither is purchasing back items that I'd already bought."

"No, I should think not."

Dr. Davies puts his finger under my chin and looks me over carefully. "You do look better than when you first arrived, I suppose."

"Apparently a cool bath didn't do the wonders for my appearance I'd hoped it would," I say. "But I'm fine, and thank you for your attention."

He sets down the canopic jar he is holding. The thing, a jackal-headed Duamutef once critical to the ancient Egyptian mummification process, stares indifferently from its case.

"Good heavens," Dr. Davies laments. "I do hope you haven't been having nightmares the way Ripley has. Given what has gone on . . ."

Dr. Davies stops himself from mentioning Edna and Mrs. Watson, and I put my hand on his shoulder, assuring him that I'm only suffering from poor sleep. "And the fact that we'll all have to do without you for the next few weeks."

Dr. Davies smiles and pats my hand. He closes the glass case and seals it with a temporary fixative. Stepping back, he evaluates his composition of the display, grimacing at the missing pieces.

"Well, don't have too much fun while I'm gone," he says. "I do expect you to keep up with your studies, as does your father."

Cornelius bursts in from the side door, punctual as always, and bringing with him the vim of a high wind. He looks dapper. Dressed to take Dr. Davies to the station, he's wearing a pair of black and white pin striped trousers with a matching jacket and pale cream vest. An ensemble that his employer had made for him, and one that suits him admirably.

"Horus has taken up your luggage," he says to Dr. Davies.

"Ah, good. Kind of you, Leila, to send him over. He always knows the fastest routes."

"And has a talent for making anyone who gets in his way get out of it right quick. I think that's even better than a fast route in Cairo."

Dr. Davies chuckles, and it's nice to see it. He bids me goodbye, and bemoans Cornelius not being able to join him on his journey. The Great Maspero, having gotten wise to our friend's value, put his foot down and insisted he stay to help him, despite Dr. Davies having hired the African for his own use. There was never any question of Ripley going, as he said nothing would make him leave me right now. My general malaise, as everyone close to me calls it, has been an all too frequent topic of conversation. One that I know I will at some point have to address.

"You be careful," I say to Dr. Davies.

"I'll get him on the train, but after that, he's in God's hands," Cornelius jests.

"Given my heathen ways, He's likely to drop me like a hot potato." Dr. Davies pats the pockets of his coat and vest, making sure he's got his travel documents. He dons his hat, smooths his facial hair, and clears his throat volubly.

I watch him and Cornelius take their leave in a much improved mood, laughing and teasing Horus, who is skeptical of Damascenes as a rule and does not approve of any trips to that ancient city. Or any ancient city that isn't Cairo.

Then, I sit down at the feet of Tiye. Still drowsy-eyed from the cacophonous state of my sleep, I'm relieved to have a moment to myself in this place. The smells of new construction are all around me and I savor them: varnish, fresh wood, minerals, cleaning agents. Makes me feel more durable somehow.

"Lay your hands on it," I hear in that language of my dreams.

I must have fallen into a state in between wakefulness and sleep, and snap open my eyes, blinking away the fuzziness. There, in front of me, is Ripley. For a moment, I think I've imagined him.

"Leila," he says, every part of him an invitation.

"What are you doing here?"

"Did you not wish me to come?"

"It's all I ever wish for."

I reach out and touch the soft cotton of his shirt. "I'm much better today," I lie. "Like my old self again."

I stand and take his face in my hands, meaning to kiss him sweetly, to make up for my dishonesty. But Ripley anticipates me, pressing his lips firmly to mine.

"You're lucky no one's here," I say as we break.

"Luck is only part of it," he tells me.

Ripley reaches into his pocket and produces a Western Union telegram.

"What on earth?"

"Read it."

And I do.

DR ALFRED DAVIES CAIRO (EGYPT), JUNE 29 1902

BEING CALLED AWAY TO ASWAN ONCE AGAIN AND ASK IF I MAY THAT YOU KINDLY TAKE LEILA INTO YOUR HOME FOR THE DURATION AS I WILL NOT BE GONE LONGER THAN A FEW DAYS AND SHE WISHES TO REMAIN YOURS WELLINGTON (FLOYD SABER)

"This is dated two days ago."

Ripley nods.

"It was intercepted by Maspero. It would seem that, in his usual obsessive state, he forgot to give it to my father. He only gave it to me minutes ago, as I was returning from the station."

"Does this mean what I think it means?"

Ripley nods. "It would appear it's just us for a while. You, me, and Cornelius, of course.

"That scamp of a father of mine didn't say a word to me. Obviously thought I'd put up a stink like last time."

I step in closer and put my head on his shoulder, feeling the most wonderful sense of contentment. I smell the citrus of his cologne, comingled with the warm, musky scent that is all natural to him.

"I want you to stay at our house while they're gone," I whisper, swallowing so hard as to practically hear it echo.

He strokes my hair, resting his chin upon my head. "Your father would expect me to behave as a gentleman, and I intend to. At least until we can marry. We have time, you know. You're barely sixteen."

Ripley extracts himself from me and takes my hand, bringing it to his lips. He kisses my palm, in the exact place where it had burned so savagely last night, then looks up at me. "Your eyes, deep and ethereal. Green as a chrysalis." His lips part again, only this time, he bites softly in the same place where he kissed me. Then he takes my hand and puts it to his heart.

"Do you know what you do to me?" he says.

"Don't," I say.

Ripley furrows his brow. "Don't what?"

"Don't behave like a gentleman." I take his hands and pull him with me to the feet of Tiye, leaning against the statue.

I grip his waistcoat and bring him to me, kissing him. I know nothing but the scent of him, of us, the strong, safe feel of his body. Because when I'm with him, nothing feels like it could touch me or hurt me. Not the statue, not the killer in our orbit, not the killer within me, which seeks to weaken my heart and stop it from beating. Just as it did my mother's. Everything around us fades away. But as we press against the tall, stone base of the monument, my foot bumps an object, and a hard, heavy thump on the marble startles us both, bringing us back to our senses.

Still wrapped in each other's arms, we train our eyes on the floor, to the source of the thump. Damn if it isn't Cornelius's statue!

"Did you bring it here?" he asks me.

Stupefied, I shake my head that I did not. Ripley lets go of me and crouches down next to the figurine. It lies on its side, the lion's mouth open as if roaring at us.

"I didn't see it earlier. Cornelius must have left it here when he came to get your father." It's unlike him to just leave it out like this, and I sift through my memory of his arrival, trying to recall if I saw him carry it in and set it down. I would think I would have, for the love of God. I would think he would have said something if he had it with him, too.

"We should put it back," Ripley says. There's a strangeness to his voice, an urgency and depth that I only hear when I dream of him.

"Yes, I think you're right."

I reach for the statue, and as I do, Ripley does as well. But my fingers strike like a Cobra—I can't help myself! Our hands touch the figure at the same moment, and instantly my body stings with a wicked pain that is at once awful and glorious.

I hear a voice come from Ripley's lips. "Sherin," it says.

RIPLEY'S HAND is shaking, his eyes wide, searching my face as he begins to tell me what happened. My hands are shaking, too. My heart is pounding. But I don't feel weakened—not at all. In fact, I feel damn near like I could fly.

"I found myself on the floor," he says, pointing at the very spot on the marble where he must have awakened. "My body was vibrating like a ringing bell. One by one, my senses returned and my eyes were able to focus. Above me was Amenhotep III, his stone body backlit by the sun streaming through the glass ceiling."

"What then?"

"I hear my name, expecting it to be your voice, Leila. Or the other woman's voice—the one that echoes in my memory every morning when I awaken. But it's Cornelius and he comes to my side. Quite a bit of time must have elapsed for him to have already come back from the station."

That's when I see Cornelius, who is standing behind Ripley, nodding emphatically.

"I demanded he tell me before *who* goes there. You see, Ripley said, 'We must go back to the dunes, and get there before *he* does.'"

I shake my head. "You did? To whom?"

Cornelius raises his eyebrows and tips up his head. I look

to where he's indicating—it's to one of the statues of Tiye's daughters.

"You," he says. "Ripley said it to you. See, you were seated on her lap up there, clutching the statue as if your life depended on it."

"I was?"

They both nod.

"'*Nif,*' you said. '*Listen to me.*'"

Ripley reaches out and touches my dress, as if it's a strange thing to him. Perhaps he's remembering our earlier indiscretion and regretting it. I would hate that.

"This body will die soon," Ripley says. "That's what you told me."

"What are you talking about?"

I shrug away from him and turn my back to them both. I walk closer to Tiye, swallowing the breaths that are choking me.

"You said 'my present body will die, but I will not. And when your body dies, you, too, will live on to meet me in another life. But before we do, there's a more urgent matter.'"

"That's lunacy," I whisper.

"You edged off the monument and came to me using small steps, instead of your usual assertive strides. And you looked into my eyes with a love that rendered me unable to speak or move. A love not made merely of years, but millennia. 'You must give me a child,' you said."

I turn to Ripley, and startle, as he's standing much closer to me than I expected. Cornelius steps up, and the two men, my men, stand side by side in a union of concern.

"When you let go of the statue, it seemed to fall for a long time. It hit the marble floor at last, and when it did, it was with so heavy a din, as if it's made of iron, rather than clay. Then we felt it—the current. If Ripley and I hadn't remained standing, I would swear we'd been struck by lightning."

"My goodness," I say. "Could it have done to us something in the way of what it did to that conquistador's daughter?"

"Leila," Ripley says.

"The current—it didn't come from the statue. It came from you."

Chapter 25

Nin'ti, Evermore

"DO YOU REALLY THINK these spirits who inhabit you can see the future?" Cornelius asks.

We've removed ourselves to Dr. Davies's office, now that workers have begun to arrive at the museum. Ripley sits on the sofa, looking pensive. He says my name to himself, as if coming to a dreadful realization, then looks up, catching my eyes in his.

"I know we are conduits of the past," he says. "Although it's unclear to me what kind of relation we have to the future. We do, after all, exist in the present, obviously. I think I speak for us both when I say Leila and I don't yet understand our limitations, or our abilities in this regard."

"We?" Cornelius says. "Do you actually see yourselves as one with these entities—whatever they are?"

"Nin'ti," I say. "I think it is time we say it. Ripley and I are the Nin'ti the trinket seller told you about."

Cornelius exhales in a most animal way. "Yes," he whispers.

He is holding the effigy, as if reluctant to let it out of his control. I do not fear the thing anymore and don't believe it poses us harm—at least not on purpose. It is powerful, to be sure, and requires care in handling, but I'm coming to see it as a telephone of sorts. A way of communicating with the people we are at night, in our dreams, and perhaps the people we have been in the past. Ones like the Spanish girl in the painting.

Ripley glances at me, as if he's heard my thoughts. Normally, he would be on his feet with me and Cornelius, but there is nothing normal about him right now. I go to sit next to him, and he takes my hand.

"Whatever the meaning is behind what was said in the atrium, you can't be taking any unnecessary chances, go anywhere on your own from now on. 'This body will die soon' you said. Not if I have anything to say about it."

I cannot look at Ripley right now, and turn my attention to Cornelius, who is leaning on Dr. Davies's desk, arms folded, the statue in the crook of his elbow.

"Not to be a hoper," our friend says, "but I think it's worth considering that for a being—a Nin'ti—that has possibly been around for thousands of years, in one form or another, the concept of 'soon' may be relative. For her, the woman who calls herself Sherin, *soon* could be twenty or thirty years for all we know. I mean, why on earth would she insist you give her a child if she's not going to be around to raise it? And merely having a child takes time. An infant doesn't just appear."

I sit back, my index finger stroking the bloodstone at the center of my amulet. Touching it usually helps to calm me, but right now it doesn't. The pain made of my fate and my lies of omission only feels stronger. But so does the clarity with which I am increasingly seeing our situation.

"Ripley is right. They are not spirits who inhabit us," I say. "Any more than our souls are spirits. As for knowing the future, well, that depends."

"On what?" Ripley asks me.

I turn to Cornelius, my hands wet and cold. "You said that when you returned from taking Dr. Davies to the station, you found us holding the statue together, and you are absolutely sure that you didn't bring it into the museum proper and leave it on the floor next to the monuments?"

"Quite positive," Cornelius says. "I've examined the statue in the privacy of Dr. Davies's office a few times since what happened at the Sphinx, but I've always put it back in his desk and locked the door."

"And you're sure you feel nothing when you touch it? I mean, apart from feeling drawn to it?"

Cornelius takes the statue in his hand, tossing it from one hand to the other. "See?"

"Seems to me that we—the Nin'ti—engaged with the figure on purpose," I say. "In order to communicate with each other. When I reached over to pick it up, Ripley did so at the same time. Both of us rather aggressively I might add."

"I don't remember that at all," Ripley says. "The last thing I recall is looking down at it after you kicked it over. I was surprised to see it. Elated, if I'm to be honest. I felt the strangest excitement just seeing it lying there."

Cornelius caresses the head of the figure, his lips parted in awe. I know the look, having seen it on Dr. Davies's face so many times now. It's the wonder that a detective of history feels for any truly old thing that he holds in his hands. Only more so.

"You didn't seem like yourselves at all," Cornelius says. "It was like you were wearing the costumes of Ripley and Leila, but exuded a very different essence." He looks up from the effigy at me and Ripley, but the spell it has cast over him isn't broken. "I didn't understand a word that was said between you, as you were speaking in that old language, but it seemed terribly urgent. When I called out your names, Ripley looked up at me and let go of the figure. You know the rest. He walked a few steps towards me and said that we must get to the dunes before 'he' does. Then he knelt to the floor and lay down on it. On his belly, at first, then he rolled onto his back, as if stargazing."

Ripley blinks his eyes tight, like he's dismissing a terrible thought. "Is there something you're reading into what happened that Cornelius and I are failing to see?"

Now, my heart begins to pound. I take my head in my hands, knotting my fingers in my hair. On the verge of tears, I sniff deeply to keep them at bay.

"Leila, please," Ripley says. "If there's something troubling you, I urge you to share it. I'm sure it affects me as well."

"And me," Cornelius says.

I steel myself, biting down until it hurts, squeezing my eyes shut.

"It does," I whisper.

There's no going back now. I fold my arms across my chest and a shiver runs through me. I can see Ripley has the urge to hold me, but I don't want him to. I need to do this alone.

"Ripley," I say. "The Nin'ti—Sherin. She wasn't reading the future. She was telling you something we both—she and I—already know. Something she had the courage to tell you when I did not."

Now I reach out, and thread my fingers through his, not for my sake, but Ripley's. I look down at our entwined hands, and feel a trickle of cool sweat run down my temple. My mouth goes dry. It takes every ounce of courage I have to look him in the face.

"I saw my mother's physician when I was in London. He believes I have the same heart ailment that she died from."

"No," Ripley says. But the word is merely his last defense against the truth, I can see that.

"It's not going to kill me today or tomorrow. It'll take some time . . . a few years. If I'm lucky."

"He's wrong. This can't be."

"Ripley . . ."

He pushes me away and looks to Cornelius, who is no longer leaning on Dr. Davies's desk, but standing, as if ready to fight an invisible foe.

"I'm with Ripley," Cornelius says, slamming the figure down onto Dr. Davies's desk. "What does your mother's physician know? I've only ever known such people to be right half the time at best. We're better off taking bets on a game of dice."

"He's not the only one who said it though, is he? Sherin. She said it, too."

"She might just be repeating what your mother's quack said."

I crane my neck, feeling my brows knit together like rope. I look at the statue and, for a moment, I almost pick it up again. I think Ripley is tempted as well, but shakes off the inclination.

"You feel it's true, don't you?" he says.

I nod. Every part of him is stiff with shock. It is he who is usually comforting, protecting me, but right now Ripley is the one who looks fragile and needs my strength.

"Come," I say. We walk towards Cornelius, my heart still hammering from my terrible revelation.

"I've had some weeks to ponder my situation," I say. "I'm sorry she had to be the one to tell you, Ripley. In my defense, she remembers every moment she's ever spent with you, and in every incarnation. She knows better than I how such information should be shared."

I rise up onto my toes and kiss his cheek.

"Leila," he whispers.

Then I turn to Cornelius. "And she—my ancient self, I'll call her—clearly wanted you to know it, too. Wanted all of us to consider what we must do—what destiny has written for us."

"Don't we write our own destinies, as well?" Ripley asks. "There must be something we can do—I mean, just think of that mighty current we felt!"

"Maybe," I say.

"Leila, surely if what your body can produce has the ability to level us the way it did—course through our every vein and organ—then it can heal your heart?"

"Ripley," I say, bringing my face close enough that I can feel his breath, and he mine. "I hope so, I do, but the force you felt in my presence earlier—it may not be bodily at all. Our immortality—whatever that even means when it comes to Nin'ti—appears to be one of recurrence, not maintenance."

"Appearances can be deceiving," Cornelius says.

He reaches out and hooks his arm with mine as well, making a chain of us. It is a strangely powerful gesture. One that binds us, as surely as a vow. All three of us feel the might of our bond just now, as if it was always going to be this way.

"You must give me a child, that's all I know," I tell Ripley. "Tonight. Somehow I feel that we must begin all of this tonight."

"Tonight," he says. "This is lunacy. There's hardly enough time."

"No time for love?"

"That's not at all what I'm saying and you know it."

"What are you saying?" Cornelius asks.

"That I will not ruin you or give you a child until we're married—no matter how much or how little time we may have. No matter what extraordinary circumstances we're facing, we must not be tempted to let go of those things that give us grace."

I give him my most loving smile, the one that means the most to me, and comes not merely from my heart, but the core of my being. "I thought I was the one concerned with God's graces."

"Ripley is right," Cornelius says. "Despite our extraordinary circumstances, as you say, and what they dictate, we cannot act recklessly, destroying your lives in the process."

"God's graces are of utmost importance—especially now."

Ripley leans in, kissing my forehead. His lips linger there; his warmth almost makes me feel as if anything is possible. "A ceremony means something, especially to a Copt. Particularly to you, Leila, regardless of the imperatives we have been given by our Nin'ti selves."

"You're right," I say, squeezing us even closer together. "You give me courage, but more importantly, an idea. Something that might expedite things, help us work around whatever bureaucratic obstacles might get in the way of what we must do."

I rise up onto my toes again, this time kissing Ripley's lips. I would die if I thought I could never experience his kiss again.

"We must go to the Hanging Church," I tell them.

"**I CAN SEE** the attachment you have for this place," Ripley says. "If I had been raised with deep faith, I can think of nowhere—outside of meeting God in nature—that I would like better."

Ripley is right, of course, and it gives me pleasure for him to see what I see. The interior of The Hanging Church is not grand, like the Hagia Sophia or other great cathedrals that he has visited. The colors—red, gold, dark wood and light marble—make for an intimate setting.

"The lacey carvings in the wood remind me of the doilies my grandmother used to make, and subsequently place on any free space in her house," he continues, as if finishing my thought.

Cornelius lets out a laugh. "The lacey carvings remind me of what I think snowflakes must be like."

"That's only because you've never seen one," Ripley says.

Cornelius is about to retort, but instead looks past me, his mouth falling open.

"Leila?" I turn around to see my uncle in his black robes and qualansuwa, the customary hood and veil. As always, he looks as if he was born to this place. When he moves, the large gold crucifix on a chain about his neck jingles pleasingly, like a wind chime.

"My dear Joe." I introduce him to Ripley and Cornelius, and he greets us with his usual warmth, making me feel like everything will be alright.

"I've heard many good words about you both," my uncle says. "And am only disappointed that we have not met sooner."

"You'll have to pardon my urgency," I tell him. "If this wasn't of the utmost importance, I would never dream of being so boorish. Especially when I'm acquainting those I love most in the world. We should be having supper together, taking our time about it."

"Not at all," Joe says. "Life doesn't always allow for leisurely association. But if I may impose on you all—while we might not have the time, today, to get to know one another through a meal—I do ask that we say a prayer."

I bow my head in assent to my uncle's request. We all follow him in genuflecting before the altar, then file into a pew. Kneeling, we fold our hands. And after a brief interlude, Joe begins to chant, then pray.

He begins with Prayers to the Blessed Holy Virgin Saint Mary, Mother of God, from the Coptic Orthodox Agpeya, and while it is not a long prayer, he leads us to repeat it with him a dozen times.

The repetition of the prayer becomes a meditation for me, and I add my own appeals for Ripley and the legacy of our love. Ones that grow so fervent that my knuckles go white as I clench my hands together.

"God works on his own time," I remember my mother telling me.

We sit for a few minutes in silence at the end of the observance, before Joe blinks his eyes and smiles, his kindly face alight with affection.

"Thank you for indulging a man of faith," he says to Cornelius. "Perhaps our rituals are not so foreign to your Catholic ones."

"My mother was Catholic, but I don't consider myself as such anymore."

"A rejection of faith is a form of faith nonetheless," my uncle tells him. "Better than an ignorance of belief."

"Joe," I say. "What I bring before you today is a matter of faith as well." I square my shoulders, taking a visible, audible breath that leaves me a bit self-conscious. "You see, Ripley and I wish to be married, immediately. Cornelius is here as our witness, but so much more."

Joe's eyes widen, and he knits his brows together in a way I've seen in my own mirror reflection a thousand times.

"Leila," he says. "I can't just snap my fingers and make it so. You've had no Rite of Betrothal, and I wouldn't dream of doing this without your father being a part of it."

I'm not surprised by his resistance, of course, but nor will I be deterred. Leaning in, I entreat him with my whole self.

"I know this is irregular, but when I said it was a matter of faith, I wasn't just referring to the Holy Sacrament. I meant your faith in me, in destiny."

Joe considers me for a moment, and I see that I've affected him. His eyes, black as ink, begin to quail.

"Of course I have faith in you, but I can't just . . ." He stops, his nostrils flaring. "Oh, no, you're not?"

"Of course, she isn't!" Ripley says.

I take Ripley's hand and the fierceness of his instinct to protect me seems so very sweet right now. For the flash of an instant, it's as if I can see our prospective unborn child in his face, and it quite nearly takes my breath away.

"I am not with child, Joe. But I want to be," I say. "As soon as earthly possible."

Joe's body settles in relief. "My dear, there's plenty of time for that."

"You see, but there isn't," I tell him, and Joe raises an eyebrow at me as if he thinks I'm rushing this along for my own unwholesome reasons.

"It's not what you think," I say.

"Then what else is it, may I ask?"

"It's a matter of providence! Perhaps Divine Providence, I don't know."

Letting go of Ripley, I put it my hands on Joe's shoulders. Running the fingers of my right hand along the gold chain around his neck, I grasp the crucifix he wears.

"Joe, you're the only one I've ever been able to talk to about Mother. About seeing her after her death. I can't even consider telling Father about any of that. This is why we've come here—to you, and not gone simply to a magistrate. I want Ripley and I to be bound before God, with you as His conduit."

Joe wraps his hand around mine, so that we're clutching the crucifix together.

"Are you saying your mother told you to rush into marriage without even inviting your father to this most important occasion? Because I can't believe she would do such a thing."

"No, not exactly. I am asking you to believe in me, though, as she does—did."

I remove my left hand from his shoulder and put it on top of our jumble of hands, our tangle of unspoken promises.

"Of course I believe in you," Joe says. "But you can't ask me to do such a thing without the proper covenants. Your father and my relationship is strained enough as it is. We've only shared one meal together since your return to Cairo, and he only did that for you."

"He's just afraid of his own pain, is all. I'll make it right with him—you know I will."

Joe bites down on his lip, shaking his head. He breaks from me and turns away, facing the altar.

"No, Leila. I'm sorry, but I will not. Not today. Soon, yes, but not in haste."

"Father Joseph Sarabion Saber," Ripley says from behind us. He comes up close behind my uncle and speaks quietly, just as Joe had done when he led us in prayer. "I understand your reticence. Your stance is right and just—I won't pretend otherwise. But if I can at least help you know what is in my heart, it might soften yours to our predicament."

He walks past him, coming as close to the altar as a lay person should. An image of Mary and the Christ Child looks at us from its place on a long, red velvet curtain, filling me with hope and firming up my resolve. She is with us, I feel.

"I have loved your niece since before we met, before I even knew of her existence," he says. "I loved her as I played as a child, always aware that there was someone who should be playing alongside me. I loved her in every action, every duty I performed, knowing that I was building a character that she could take strength in. I loved her when my mother died, taking comfort in knowing she was waiting for me. I loved her at weddings and births, dreaming of when I could share them with her. I loved her in prayer just now, although if I'm to be honest with you, I was raised with little religion. All of these things I swear to you. As I swear that I feel God has communicated His will to us—all of us here."

I look to Joe and see he is moved by Ripley's words, can feel the verity in them. Can feel what they mean to me. He breathes deeply, his eyes, as long-lashed as my mother's, blinking slowly.

"Perhaps God is communicating His will through me, as well, and He is asking you to wait."

Joe stands up. He turns away from Ripley and takes my hands again.

"For your own good, as your uncle, as one who loves you, I will not rush your nuptials like a permit through a civilian magistrate. I'm sorry. I am. You know I would do anything for you. But anything can mean saving you from your impulses."

I close my eyes tight to collect myself. I think of how Mary must have felt when the angel Gabriel told her not to be afraid. That she had been Blessed. When I open them again, I can see them reflected so clearly in my uncle's. They are greener than ever, as if a bright light has gone on behind them. "Joe, I believe with all my heart that God's hand is in this, and that I must become pregnant."

"Leila!"

Ripley steps between my uncle and me. He faces Joe most admirably, then goes slowly to his knees.

"Father, I came here today because of how I love your niece, and I will leave here, and promise to keep her honor intact until we can marry, because of that same love. Even if I believe with every fiber of my being that we are here today because destiny has brought us to you. Put us in your hands. God is asking of you in this most unusual manner, just as He asked of us, and I will leave it to you to decipher what it is He wants you to do."

Joe stands, frozen before us. It is as if even his heart has stopped beating. Then, with a deliberate, gentle motion, he closes his eyes and folds his hands. Joe prays, silently this time, and for only a few repetitions. When he opens his eyes, he makes the sign of the cross.

Cornelius looks to me and Ripley, widening his eyes, raising his shoulders in question. Every moment feels like an hour, a century, as we wait for this Coptic priest to speak.

"Father," Ripley says. "Do you not hear what we hear? The Lord your God asking for you to honor us with your Blessing?"

Joe's eyes train on Ripley's with great force, like he intends to unearth his soul, bring it out in the open for his inspection. Ripley, for his part, gives him all that he is, as if opening his veins. My uncle's lips quiver, his eyes turn liquid.

"Alright," Joe whispers. "Alright."

There is a long silence between us, until Ripley bows his head and thanks him. I want to wrap my arms around Joe, kissing both of his cheeks, have him accept my burst of affection with his usual delight. But he seems weary, like he has aged twenty years in a few moments' time. What's worse is that I know that, somehow, I did this to him.

"We can iron out the more legal aspects over the coming days," my uncle says. "But at least I can take care of the spiritual ones. As for your father . . ."

"I will take care of Father, and I promise you he will understand. Just as Joseph understood when Mary told him they had been graced by God with a destiny to fulfill. Do you not feel it yourself? That there is something godly in nature at play here?"

Joe nods, his eyes grazing over the three of us.

"Thank you," I tell him. "You won't regret this."

Chapter 26

King and Queen, Man and Wife

"**M**Y LORD," I say, looking down at myself. "If I'd known I would be getting married when I got up today, I would have thought better about what I chose to wear."

My dress is the color of a slice of cantaloupe, made of soft, light cotton. I notice a tiny button missing just above my collar.

"I like your dress," Ripley whispers. "The hue makes you look as if you're blushing."

His own attire is simple and I love it that way: a linen shirt with a waistcoat and trousers the color of milk caramel.

Cornelius, on the other hand, is the only one of us who looks as if he is at least outfitted for some sort of occasion. He's still in the suit Dr. Davies had made for him, and it's becoming harder to imagine him dressed any other way.

"You look like you should be the groom," I tell him.

A boy in robes, a priest's assistant, has come out from behind a velvet curtain. He's holding a stiff jumble of ornate fabrics and two crowns. Joe is right behind him, a brass thurible for the burning of incense in his hands. It dangles at the end of a thick chain.

"We're going to do this right. Or at least as right as we can under the circumstances," he tells us.

Joe wastes no time. He lights the thurible and begins to

chant, as the boy hands the crowns, as well as a small pouch of purple velvet, to Cornelius for keeping. He holds up the first garment, which is bigger than he and looks like nothing short of a royal mantle meant for a queen. It's lavishly embroidered in gold thread and beaded with gems, and I cover my mouth, feeling I just may cry. Wrapping myself in it, I let it swallow my summer dress completely.

"What do you think?" I ask Ripley.

His smile is so candid. "I can hardly think at all."

Next, the boy holds up the second garment that's much the same, only more so. He gestures to Ripley, indicating that it's for his wear, and he steps into it. The garment looks even heavier than mine, like the thickest linen that's dripping wet. For the first time ever, I see Ripley flush with embarrassment.

"You look like a king!" I tell him.

Joe continues to chant the hymn, sung in Demotic Egyptian, and I explain to Ripley and Cornelius that it's the Coptic language, much like Latin is to the Catholics.

"It sounds old, with a rough poetry to it," Cornelius says. "Dr. Davies says it's largely unchanged since Roman times."

Joe places the crowns on each of our heads, and gives a blessing.

"He's saying we'll be the rulers of our household from now on," I whisper to Ripley. "You'll be my king, and I your queen."

For a long time, Joe blesses us, and recites the matrimonial prayers, while the boy chants the hymns. He reads from the Bible, and I glimpse the Demotic script—its entrancing combination of the Greek alphabet and Egyptian hieroglyphs. With everything I have, I wish my father and mother could be here. Not that Mother could appear to me, the way she did at the fortuneteller's flat, but that she could be alive and human and here for me to hold. That Father would burst in, having come all the way from Aswan. But I must believe that in some way, they are here with me. Perhaps through Joe.

And yes, as I look into my uncle's face, I do believe it's true—especially with the way he looks upon us during this sacred ritual. With such love and hope. Despite his initial reservations, he has put his heart and soul into officiating our marriage, becoming the conduit with God that we had been seeking. Just now, he looks down and asks for our hands, meaning for us to exchange rings.

I turn to Ripley, and his face falls.

"I hadn't the chance," he begins to explain, but Joe waves away his concerns. He turns to Cornelius, who hands him the pouch of purple velvet, and produces from it two exquisite rings, ornately engraved and made of rose gold.

"Joe," I gasp. I can feel my nose turning hot and red, as my eyes brim with tears.

"They were your grandparents', if you'll recall," Joe says. "And your great-grandparents' before that."

"Where did you get them?"

"I've kept them with me since your mother died. She would want you to have them."

"Oh, Joe," I say. "Can you not see now that you were meant to marry us tonight? Why else would you have our rings?"

Joe bends down and kisses the back of my hand. He ushers us over and has us sit in two richly carved wooden chairs, our thrones as king and queen, man and wife. He anoints us with Holy oil that smells of musk and minerals.

"Our ceremony is a bit different than your Anglican and Catholic ones," he says to Ripley and Cornelius. "You and Leila will not speak your vows to one another. Your sacred commitments will be given to you by me in the form of Admonitions. But I will recite them in English, so that you can understand every word."

"Thank you," Ripley says.

He turns to me, first, and begins.

"Wives, submit yourselves to your own husbands as you do to the Lord," he reads, translating from Ephesians. "For the husband is the head of the wife just as Christ is the head of the Church. So as the Church submits to Christ, wives must submit to their husbands in everything."

Ripley glances at me, clearly, endearingly, wondering how I feel about such a pronouncement. His Leila, who dresses as a boy to go out into the city, and doesn't think twice about dressing down a man, when he deserves it. But the admonitions are not finished, and Ripley has his own to hear. Joe turns his full attention to Ripley, and I must repress the urge to giggle—with joy, with mischief, with all the love I have in my heart.

"Husbands, love your wives just as Christ loved the Church and gave himself up for her to make her Holy. Husbands ought to love their wives as their own bodies. He who loves his wife, loves himself. After all, no one ever hated their own body, but they feed and care for their body just as Christ does the Church. For this reason, a man will leave his father and mother to be with his wife. They will become one flesh."

He puts the Holy Bible down and continues speaking. It is unclear to me whether Joe is reciting from memory, or giving his own, personal admonition now.

"A husband should never be upset if a wife demands more of his time, for this indicates her love for him. He should enjoy being home with her and prefer her to all others."

He steps back and looks to us both.

"Each should be an example to the other by leading a virtuous life. They should pray together, attend church together, and at home discuss the reading they heard. When they have parties, they should not only invite their friends, but also the poor. For that, too, is the purpose of a union—to do the work of the Lord. A husband and wife should trust each other and consider both their bodies and all their possessions as common property. 'My own' is an abominable phrase that comes from the devil. They should remind each other that nothing in life is to be feared, except offending God."

Joe takes a deep breath and stretches out his hands to us.

"If you fulfill these commandments, the world will bless you in all that you do."

He asks us to kneel and pray, and we slide off the chairs onto the red carpeted floor. I hear Ripley breathing next to me, and can almost swear I can hear his heart beating as well. Perhaps it's the drum of his pulse that I feel as I hold his hand.

"Pray with me," Joe entreats us, as he begins to chant in closing.

I clutch Ripley's hand and pray that he will forever feel the depth of my love, not doubting it for a second, no matter what trials may await us.

When I open my eyes, I feel Ripley's gaze upon me. I want to kiss him badly—even a sweet kiss on his cheek.

"It is done," Joe says, bowing his head.

Ripley leans in close to me and whispers in my ear. "More than anything, I pray that God takes me instead of you. That he lets your heart keep beating. Even if we are destined to live again and again, I want you to live your life—this life that you love. A life with your father, in this city that means the world to you. That is my admonition."

I am left speechless. Humbled and sad and joyful that someone could love me so much. That I love him so that I do not wish any of those things for myself, but for Ripley.

Joe lifts the crowns off our heads and hands them to the boy, blessing them, asking they be admitted into the Kingdom of Heaven. He asks Cornelius to give us a blessing as well, and our friend closes his eyes. "What God joins together, let no one put asunder. Neither living nor dead."

"My husband," I say, my voice soft with awe.

"My wife," Ripley says, strong and even, like an Amen.

ON THE ROOF of our family home a white, billowing bed has been made up. It's for hot days that trap too much heat inside the house for a comfortable night's sleep. A cold sea of stars looks down on us, and there's a soft breeze. Lanterns are littered all over the rooftop and I light them one by one, the flames dancing with the grace of a swan. The plants I've been growing shudder when I come near, as if they, too, wish to offer us blessings.

"Everything about you shouts and screams of life, of forever," Ripley says.

"We are forever."

"What good is forever if this is the only life I know? I won't live it without you."

The specter of my ailment is looming larger as the truth of it sinks in. I hate that he's thinking of it on this night of all nights.

"Don't even say that," I say. "Neither of us knows what the future will bring. We hardly know our pasts, for goodness' sake. That's why I asked Cornelius to leave us with this."

I sit down on the bed, and lift up a pillow, revealing the ancient figure to Ripley. At once, I feel a mighty attraction to it—a lust I'm at a loss to describe. Stronger than I've ever felt, even at the museum this morning. Ripley grips my hands— he feels it, too. I cover it quickly with the pillow again and look away.

"Not yet," I say. "I want to know you here and now, first."

Reaching up, I take the pins from my hair, letting it cascade over my shoulders and fall straight down to nearly the small of my back. He takes a lock of it at my temple, holding it between his two fingers and riding the thick strands all the way down to the end, like he's done it a thousand times.

"I lost my virginity when I was sixteen," he confesses.

"What?"

This is hardly what I expected him to say at such a moment.

"I'm sorry. Our vows today asked for honesty and integrity in all we do."

He tucks my curtain of hair behind my ear, and I raise an eyebrow at him. "Are you thinking I should be surprised at your revelation?"

Because I realize, in just this moment, that I am not.

Ripley shakes his head, not at all surprised that I'm not surprised, and this synergy ignites a spark of joy in me.

"I want to tell you about it, because it means something."

Now I purse my lips and swallow hard, bracing myself. While not surprised at his revelation, I don't exactly wish to hear all the gory details. But it seems important to him, so I do my best not to look as if I've eaten a bug.

"It was a French girl. Older than me by a couple of years. Father and I were spending a few months in France, while he worked with the National Archaeological Museum near Paris. She looked so much like you. She even had green eyes, though not quite like yours, obviously. I knew she wasn't the girl from my dreams, but she reminded me so much of her, of you, and I was so lonely."

"Stop," I say, rising from the bed.

"Leila, please." He shuts his eyes and continues with his story, speaking quickly.

"You see, the French girl told me afterward that she'd made a man of me so that I'd always remember *her* and not the girl I was in love with.

"'I'm not in love with anyone,' I'd told her. I hadn't met you yet, obviously, and had only glimpsed love in my dreams.

"'Don't lie,' she said. 'I know a man in love when I see one. Only now, you'll always think of me.'

"Only I haven't. I've thought of *it*, but hardly given her a second thought. And I haven't been with anyone else since then, either. I want you to know that."

"Ripley," I say.

My voice startles him and he turns around. His throat seizes up on him, stopping my breath cold, and I can hardly blame him. Because here I stand, naked before him, having undressed myself fully as he unloaded his conscience. His gaze drifts down from my face and roams me all over. I almost reach over to take a blanket and cover myself, but manage to hold my courage.

"I didn't know anything could be so beautiful," I hear him say.

Crouching down, I kneel on the floor, as I've rehearsed in my mind. He watches me so intently—the way I watch the night sky when searching for a shooting star.

"Ripley," I whisper. "Undress for me now. Will you begin with your shoes?"

He nods to me, as hypnotized as I am.

"Let me help." I crawl to him and untie his shoelaces, lifting each of his feet and slipping off his shoes and socks, placing them next to me. My breath changes as I look at his bare feet, becoming slower, deeper. They are handsome feet, I think. Strong and supple, as if they spend all of their days walking in the desert sand. It is strange and sublime to serve him this way, to watch every part of him come alive to this intimate performance.

"What would you like next?" he asks me.

I admit I am visited by a loss of composure. My lips quiver

and I have a hard time keeping my eyes trained on him. They want to look at the floor, the flowers, anything but him.

"I'll take off my waistcoat and shirt," he says.

I blink my agreement and pinch my eyes shut for a few seconds of reprieve, then open them again. This time, there's no averting them from Ripley. I look to him, and he to me, and we do it so completely, daringly. Something animal takes hold of him, and he removes his waistcoat quickly, with no ceremony. As for his shirt, that he does gradually, a button at a time, and sloughs off the right, then left sleeve, tossing the garment hard to the floor at his feet. I can't help but pick up his shirt and inhale his scent.

"I'd like you to do the rest," he says.

I put my hand to my mouth, needing a moment. "Wait," I whisper.

"No. I want you to do it now."

"I can't."

"You will, please."

He looks upon me the way he feels, the way I feel—with all the love of the vows we took today, and all the want of a thousand lives.

I rise up and step closer.

"Now," I say.

WHEN WE'RE DONE, we nestle into the covers, wet with each other's bodies. The moon illuminates our bare skin and we turn towards one another, on our sides, looking long into each other's faces—searching for memories we sense only as echoes. I am walking in the desert, I am trudging through a forest, climbing a mountain, running through the streets of a city. He holds a bow and arrow, a mallet, a musket. I wear robes and dresses, he, a suit of armor, or a suit of finery. But always he holds me and only me.

My hand reaches under the pillow and I find Ripley's hand there, too. "Are you ready?"

His eyes glow fiercely, and he kisses me with them open. Our hands go together to the figure. Our fingers grip it. There's no going back now.

"IT IS THE SAME SKY that sheltered us on our wedding night," Nif whispers. "There's LoOanah'a's unblinking eye."

He points up at what is now called Venus, and I touch the tip of my finger to his. That finger, so pale, travels over the veins of my hand, down my arm, and over my breast. "I thought this night would never come."

Our hands, these bodies—new and old.

"I do love your hair like this." I ruffle it, then comb my fingers through, making it smooth again. "Like it's made of straw and sunlight and joy. Your skin," I say, my thumbs caressing the apples of his cheeks. "It doesn't blend with the night, it glows like the moon."

"You are the moon," he tells me.

"Like the god Mazal's wife, whom he set into orbit about him when he became jealous?"

His throat vibrates with laughter. A playful sound muffled by the warm, dry skin of my shoulder, as he kisses me there. "The moon is, was, and ever shall be the poetic figure of eternity. A constant in all our lives."

"What poem would you say about me, if I am the moon?"

He pushes up onto his elbow and gazes at me whole. With every moment, he looks more like the man I knew in the Rah'a.

"Sherin of the Rah'a, you are my serene and sublime fixture in a turbulent universe. One whose love I sought since the birth of the first man, and will stay with me until the last one takes his final breath. If I glow like the moon in this life, it is because I stand in your light, making wishes as people have done for all of time."

I wrap my arms and legs around him. "I so miss your poems and your stories."

"I'll give you another poem," he whispers. "This one raw and vehement. Unbroken."

I have no more taste for words.

IN THE NEXT MOMENT—no, not moment—can't be. As I focus my eyes, I see the moon has moved across the sky, and now looks down slyly at us, peaking from behind a thin cloud that is uncharacteristic for the season. I am coiled around Ripley and we're no longer on the hot weather bed, but some distance away, tangled up in a damp sheet under one of my flowering shrubs. Its powder pink buds strain towards us, but all I can smell is Ripley and me. My body aches in the most splendid way.

"Do you remember?" I whisper.

"Yes," he says. "Do you?"

"Every moment."

"MICKEY," I whisper.

I'm drowsing.

Mt. Baldy hovers outside my window, backlit by a purple blush that tints the night sky. Beneath the tip top of the mountain, it fades to black—black all the way down to the field of fireweed beneath my window. A view that will glow like a swarm of fireflies in the crisp light of dawn.

Only tonight, I swear I see Dr. Neville walk across the field in the dark, pointing to things I can't see.

My dreams are my wings.

It's the last thing I think of as I lose myself in sleep. One door closes, another door opens. Or something like that.

I sit up first, then rise above my bed, looking down upon the sleeping form of a girl. Ever. She is me, Sherin of the Rah'a.

Or Agnes of Rome.

Sayuri of Nagiso

Gabriella of New Spain

Angelie of Niue

Leila of Egypt

Hundreds of other girls.

Slipping easily through the cracked window, I glide down to that field of fireweed. The yellow buds, invisible from the second-floor window of the cabin *he* built, turn to jewels encrusted in the path leading to the Sultan's Palace City. Night becomes day.

My daughter, Calliope, walks with her arm around her husband's waist, lost in her own reveries about this place. A place she's never known, except in her bones.

But she is not who I seek.

I go to Cornelius Michelangelo Neville—Mickey—sinking inside him, as if he swallowed me whole. He gasps, feeling me race through his body. The merging of my soul with his being is a mighty infusion. As if the divine essence of my blood, when mixed with his, makes something akin to magic. A thing beautiful and dangerous, of unimaginable depths . . . like a rough sea.

It makes Mickey stand up tall and clench his teeth. He looks about him with a new clarity—one infused with the ghosts that I see here. They tickle his memories.

You would think it would be easy for me and Nif to communicate when I'm inside Mickey like this, but in a way, it's harder. So close, but unable to touch. Our voices muffled, distant, as if a thick pane of glass separates us.

"What do you think?" Neville asks his son. The pride on his face beams like the sun.

Last time Mickey saw the excavation site, it was what Neville called an "organized mess," with lots of tomb-like holes in the desert floor and only the tops of a few ancient buildings that had been fully exposed.

Now, five years later, with it all mostly dug out of the desert, the Palace City of the Rah'a looks to him like a fantasy kingdom set built for a Disney movie—and he says so. There's a wall around the whole of the ancient city, except for the end part, which backs into a series of dunes that looked a lot shorter before the excavation. Thousands of years ago, they'd been imposing, like the Cliffs of Moher in Ireland. It is a startling visual for me; my one time home exposed, like a time capsule.

Calliope squeezes Mickey's shoulders as they walk up to

the gates. It is so good to feel her touch through him. The gates are every bit as astonishing as when I saw them first, carved with the most fantastic creatures, portrayed in bright colors, some of them sparkling, studded with gems.

Neville walks ahead of us, standing before the titanic effigies.

"The figures on the gate are mostly animal—cat-like beasts with some big Godzilla-style reptiles thrown in. They have different expressions, too, some of them peering down like we're peons and they're gods, others shooting looks of pride or warning."

He walks along the gate as he speaks, pointing at the various monuments.

"The story builds like a drum roll, one that's three dimensional and realistic. Looks like a Goya painting was crossed with a sculpture by Michelangelo, doesn't it? There's little of ancient Egypt's formal symbolism, and it's strange to me that these actually preceded the murals inside the tombs in the Valley of the Kings by several thousands of years."

"The reliefs reach all around the walls," Calliope adds.

Indeed, there are stories of hunts and agriculture, battles and religious ceremonies. Ones telling the history of a people that are no more. My people.

"Why does it look like it was all painted last week," Mickey asks.

"To be honest, we're still trying to figure that out." Neville winks and throws a soft punch. "But if you think the exterior looks good, wait till you see what's inside."

Neville pulls a two-way radio from his belt and tells Jordie Mustafa they've arrived. A familiar voice that's one part horn instrument, one part wheel grinding into gravel comes blasting out of the device, demanding to know if they've finally brought Mickey to see the miracle of what's been done here.

"Dr. Mustafa!" he calls out.

The voice from the radio tells Mickey to call him Jordie.

"*Dr. Mustafa*," Dad emphasizes.

"How about Dr. Jordie? Surely he's now old enough for that."

Neville rolls his eyes and Calliope mouths "It's okay," so, Dr. Jordie it is.

"Wait until you see this exquisite chamber of horrors!" Jordie says before signing off.

All at once, there is an ear-splitting creak, and the gates begin to crank open.

"It's like we're on Skull Island and they're letting in King Kong," Mickey says.

Neville chuckles with a good dose of self-satisfaction and Calliope catches her breath.

"Wish you were here," Mickey whispers. I know he is talking to me, to Ever.

"I am," I say, and Mickey shivers.

Between the enormous open doors stands Jordie Mustafa, whose stature is nothing like King Kong's. His personality is so big that he seems to take up a lot more space than he actually does, though. He runs towards us, stopping sharply, like a hockey-stop, right when he gets close.

"Dr. J!" Mickey says, having settled on the name he'll call him for all of eternity.

"Well, for all the gods of Egypt," Jordie says, peering up at him. "You are a colossus. Just like your father."

Jordie hugs Calliope, then faux karate chops Neville in the arms, performing some Silat moves. Jordie then turns to Mickey in fighting stance, and is greeted by a turning kick, which just misses his head. Jordie is easily able to deflect the blow, and Mickey bows.

"Don't you dare underestimate me," Jordie says.

"Hey, I'm just a thin, white hair away from getting my first black belt."

"And don't you dare mention thin, white hairs in my presence, either."

Jordie grabs Mickey's face between his hands and kisses his forehead hard, like he's stamping him with his signet. "Are you ready to see the home of the gods?"

Mickey informs Jordie that he most certainly is, and the small man turns around with a skip and a jump, spreading his arms wide.

"Mark my words, my dear Calliope—your son was born ready!"

We follow Jordie Mustafa under the arched gateway flanked by two snarling stone tigers dressed in writhing snakes. Mickey fists and unfists his hands, sensing a pricking at his fingertips, a warmth in his left palm.

An open breezeway ushers us in. I remember it well—this one lined every few feet with tall, bejeweled columns carved with faces of gods, and punctuated with celestial bodies—the moon, Saturn, Jupiter.

"Without telescopes, it's not clear to me how the people of the Rah'a even knew what our neighboring planets looked like, but here they are," Neville says.

They step onto the pathway made of large stones and engraved with our language. Mickey stares down at the symbols like they've got something to tell him and only him.

"Exquisite, isn't it? We're on what's called the Path of Sultans."

To our left, past the columns, is a large area with spikes in the ground, chains attached to them, and I feel an ache that almost consumes me. It's a place where slaves were bought and sold, criminals and trespassers punished in a way that would usher in a human rights tribunal today. It was a place where Nif was beaten and shamed. Where he first truly touched me.

I wonder if Mickey knows. If Nif's memories are echoing within him.

"What are those?" he asks.

To the right of the columns is an open arena. There are piles of sand—symmetrical ones—just where the arena curves around the actual palace structure.

"Those are the remnants of a star-shaped sort of protective bubble that kept a large part of the Palace City in pristine condition," Neville says. "We really have no idea how that happened."

"That leads to the Temple of Pallah," Mickey says.

Neville chuckles and blots his forehead with a handkerchief before stuffing it back in his pants pocket.

"I see you have been paying attention all these years. Except you pronounced it as Jordie—Dr. Mustafa—thinks it should be. Pah-luh. I lean towards the 'a' being more of a long vowel . . . like Pay-laah."

He leans wrong, and Mickey's inclination is to tell him so. But he doesn't.

What could he say? That it's a name that came to him like an old phone number rather than something he would have seen on one of Neville's ever-evolving maps of this place.

Another shiver sneaks up on Mickey, warping into a cold sweat.

"You okay?" Calliope asks.

We step onto a draw bridge suspended over a large pit—its walls sculpted and painted, littered with jewels, just like the outer walls. On each side, there are stairs descending into the pit and onto what looks like a floor of washed-up seaweed that's been dried by the sun.

"We think those were some superb gardens," Jordie says. His voice has become quiet and reverent.

Neville puts his hand on Mickey's shoulder as they cross the bridge and step into the actual palace.

"Welcome to Pompeii on steroids," Neville remarks. Calliope pinches him for being disrespectful of the dead here, and he kisses her temple.

Jordie Mustafa, in a low, awed tone, begins his lecture about the Palace of the Rah'a. It's one he's waited a long time to give Mickey, who is hardly paying attention.

Because he's drifting.

For as long as he can remember, he's tried to piece together his father's descriptions of this place. How the bodies had been preserved in such a way that they almost looked like fresh corpses, the ritualistic nature of their deaths, the way this whole city looked like it had been abandoned yesterday.

Every time he thought of it, a new detail would appear, like a puzzle piece.

He knows that when they pass through this entrance hall—grand and wildly colorful—and walk into that very chamber used for judgement, it won't be something like he envisioned it, but exactly as he did. He knows it like he knows the taste of salt that the desert leaves at the edges of his mouth.

"Maybe this is too much for him," Calliope whispers. "There's a lot of death here." She starts to go to her son, but Neville takes her elbow and gently pulls her close again.

"I'm fine," Mickey says.

Nif? I call into every part of this being, but I get no answer. He is here, though. He is awake now.

"Dr. Mustafa and I have a couple of theories on how the exterior portions of the city retained their integrity despite being whipped by the sandstorm to end all sandstorms." Neil Neville watches his son carefully, visibly relieved when Mickey turns to him, appearing to engage again.

"Indeed we do," Jordie chimes in. "When we started excavating, we thought it would be thorny business, given the large air pocket we'd detected over a significant portion of the city. As we began removing the top layers of sand, it was as if the walls of that pocket simply disintegrated, falling to the ground in piles, like sugar. They made a precise star shape where they landed, and some archeologists we've consulted have wondered if it wasn't an artistic sculpture of religious significance. A sort of ancient wonder of physics that these peoples had put up as a tribute to their gods."

"Your mother thinks it's a miracle," Neville says.

My Calliope's eyes of chocolate and violets train on her husband.

"Will I be able to see the bodies?" Mickey asks.

"Indeed you will!" Jordie Mustafa trills.

Neville shoots him a warning look and Jordie shrugs, palms up. He doesn't think the boy needs any coddling and he's right.

"We've decided to keep the bodies here for now, so, yes," Neville says. "It seems right to leave them where they died, at least until we can figure out what happened and how they were able to remain preserved without any detectable process of mummification."

Mickey begins wandering ahead without them. His parents whisper to one another, following behind him quietly from room to room, as he enters and exits the Chamber of Justice without a flinch or a word despite viewing the corpse of a man named Adamen. He'd been grotesque in life, Adamen, having raped and murdered my sweet, young brother, Salan. I feel some satisfaction that he died a ghastly death, with a determined grouping of arrows in his mouth, and three arrows in each eye. He's seated bolt upright in a plain throne that is the Seat of Verdict and should be a sight of horror and fascination for a boy of Mickey's age. Of any age. But Mickey's eyes scarcely linger upon him.

We go by a grouping of cadavers, all shot in the right eye. Shot where they stood. Still, Mickey continues to pay little mind, marching forward with a potent sense of purpose.

Finally, we enter the Sultan's apartments. Where the body of the Sultan was found lying open-eyed and stuffed to the gills with jewels, a dribble of smaller gems having leaked from his mouth.

Mickey looks right where the Sultan's body used to lie.

"Pretty extraordinary, isn't it?" Neville says. "The body we found here—we presume it was the Sultan's—is being studied at the Museum of Cairo. Under high security, of course."

Calliope goes to her son and puts her chin on Mickey's shoulder. He shrugs her off and she steps back, startled. He turns to his parents, his face configured into an expression they've never seen on him. "Get me out of here."

The part he doesn't say out loud, but that I hear because it is said by Nif's soul's voice. That voice says, "Or else." And I cannot understand what it is that is twisting his feeling so.

*

As Night Falls, we breathe together, see together, feel the cool air of the desert tickle Mickey's skin.

"Hey." Neil Neville's voice is clear as bell. He enters Mickey's tent and lies down next to his son, propping his head up on his elbow.

"Hey," Mickey says.

Neville takes a deep breath and expels it through his mouth, his cheeks puffing up like a blowfish. "I know you're a tough kid, it's just . . . maybe we should've waited to bring you through the palace."

"I'm not a little kid anymore, Dad. Death exists. Violent death exists. I mean, Grandpa died a violent death."

"Yes, he did."

Mickey watches his father relive the dark memory—so wicked in its senselessness. A friend in the police delivered the news—his voice shaking with fury and grief. The elder Neville had been knifed on the street by some thug, walking a path he took every day on his way home from his office at the University of Chicago. He'd died with a book of Pablo Neruda's love poems in his hand. A present he'd bought for his wife for no particular occasion.

"Didn't even take his wallet," Mickey whispers. "Isn't that what you said? Just that old locket he always carried around."

Neville runs his big hand through the curly mess of Mickey's hair. "How about we go on a camel ride tomorrow? There's an oasis not that far from here—it'll be fun."

"Dad, you're a terrible camel rider."

Neville rolls his eyes. "We can't all be naturals like you."

Mickey stills. I feel his heart beating, a deep, hollow echo in his chest.

"What about Ever? You and mom haven't given up, have you?"

It's a question Mickey poses often.

"Son, we care a great deal about Ever—always have. But by law, this is none of our business. We have no legal right to—"

"I don't care about legal rights. She belongs with us and not that father of hers."

It's both Mickey and Nif talking, and the tone of voice, the steel behind it rattles Neville. He begins to speak very slowly, with some care.

"The courts wouldn't see it that way. To them, he's a committed father, with a steady job. A lot of kids have it much worse."

"There's something not right about him."

"Mickey, he grew up poor, and had a very serious drug problem—which he's kicked, by the way, and that's no small thing. Look, his experience is very different than yours and mine, you know what I mean?"

Mickey sniffs and falls back onto his back with a thump.

"I'm not trying to lecture you. I'm just trying to give you some perspective. Ever's father . . . he's . . . doing the best he can."

Mickey stares up at the tent ceiling, listening to the shuffle and murmured conversations around the bonfire outside. Usually his favorite part of visiting his father at a dig. But not tonight.

"He's evil," Mickey says.

Neville shuts his eyes tight, pursing his soft lips. The two deep lines between his eyebrows move even closer together, in emphasis, like a pair of bellows.

"We tried," he whispers. "Your mother and I. We tried in every which way to reach out to Hunter, but we couldn't find them."

"What do you mean you couldn't find them? I thought you just said he wouldn't let me talk to her."

"By inference, that's true. Look, they left Nellysford. Not even Hunter's boss at the resort knew where he went. Or wasn't saying."

Mickey sits up lightning fast, as nimble as an arrow shot from a bow. "And you're just telling me this now?"

"Son . . ."

"Dad, he can't just do that! Take her away from everyone who knew her, close down her email address, make her impossible to reach!"

Neville sits up and comes close to his son. He wants to hold him, but doesn't dare.

"Yes, son, he can."

Chapter 27

There Will Be Blood
Cairo, 1902

I AM A WIFE.

A wife to one Ripley Allen Davies.

I say this to myself every morning, after I awaken from a night of love and heavy sleep. I have not slept this well in years. Perhaps it is because my night's dreams have made their way into my days. The good ones, anyway.

And another day begins as dawn breaks in the sky above us. A soft bloom of gold rousing the city. The rooftop garden has become the home of our marital bed. At least for now. And it is my idea of heaven.

Below us, on the street, I hear the sluggish, yet sure-footed steps of a mule, who is being coaxed by his master.

He calls her *Habibti*, "my love" in Arabic, and makes sweet, smacking kissing sounds at her.

I roll over, tangled in our covers, and whisper "Hayati" to my love. That means simply, "my life." Ripley wraps his arms around me and breathes in the scent of my hair. His embrace tells me that his heart is full, but his mind is troubled. I lift up my head and put my face close to his. I can see that, once again, Ripley is not as rested as I. His sleep has been disturbed and full of dreams, too. Not bad dreams exactly, but ones of portent.

"Did you dream of the dunes again, and those images on its cave walls?"

I wipe his damp brow with my thumb, and Ripley takes my hand in his and kisses it.

"I saw the painting in full this time. Simple line drawings like the ones in the caves of Lascaux and Chavet. People and animals. But they seemed out of order. I couldn't quite tell if the people were coming or going. And if they were going, what they were going away from."

"If they're so old, these cave paintings, then coming and going would have been normal for itinerant people."

Ripley shakes his head. "This was no normal sequence of nomadic scenes. I've seen plenty of those. There's something ominous about the way the events are portrayed—with fewer people in each story image."

"If you dream them out of order, then perhaps they began as fewer and grew to many?"

Ripley puts his hand to his skull, as if wiping away the foggy bits of his dream the way one would shine the glass of a window pane.

"Leila," he says. "I think it's time for us to go there."

I turn over onto my back, trying to keep my breath from sounding huffy. Despite everything we have learned about our ancient origins, the death around us—including the specter of my own—I'm happy.

"A dune in the middle of the Sahara somewhere? How on earth would we find such a place?"

"How did we find one another?"

I roll towards him again and run my finger down the line of his neck and onto his breast, right where his heart beats.

"Ripley, I've been thinking. Maybe God means for us to live out our lives, in whatever time we have left, simply as man and wife? We can have our child and enjoy our home. You can work with your father and Cornelius, and I can help.

Is that not better than chasing phantom killers and opaque prophecies?"

"It is better," he says.

A loud clearing of throat announces Ahura, Horus's wife, as she peeks her head up from the upper parlor. Her eyes, warm and animal, like the eyes of a hippo, roll all over the roof garden until settling on us.

"Good morning, Ahura," Ripley says. "Would you be so kind as to give us our breakfast downstairs? We'd like to take it with Cornelius."

Ahura winks and nods, descending back into the house as if dipping her head under water.

CORNELIUS PISSARRO NEVILLE is dressed in work clothes, the sort of sturdy, man-handed attire meant for the physical work of an archaeologist. He and Howard Carter will be spending the day at the museum together. Hardly a more fitting pair. There, they'll clean freshly extracted artifacts in an attempt to decipher clues, puzzle together the stories of Carter's long-dead Egyptian elites.

We've hardly sat down and given thanks, when a hard knock comes at the front door. Cornelius takes a large spoonful of *ful*, like he's afraid it'll be his last. Hani, Ahura's boy, skippers to the door and we hear him unlatch it. Hard stepping comes at us from the entry parlor.

"Lieutenant General Blackwood," the three of us say, in crisp unison.

Our friend bows and asks us to remain seated. Despite the stoicism that he wears as a suit of armor, there is an unmistakable pall of woe about him.

"What is it?" Ripley asks.

"I wish I were here merely to congratulation you on your nuptials," he says with another slight bow. "Your father alerted me to the news with a telegram."

He does not try to hide his disapproval of the way we went about getting married, but at least it doesn't appear that my father rebuked us in his message. Ripley and I both sent our fathers long, impassioned letters detailing, as best we could, why we felt the need to marry before their return. About the mix up of their both being away at the same time, the murders in the City of the Dead, and Ripley's determination to protect me at all costs. Dr. Davies was somewhat understanding in his response, saying that while a man needs to do what he feels he must, Ripley should have at least consulted my father. He did add that I am a fine addition to their family. Perhaps the distraction posed by his hunt for antiquities thieves kept him from dwelling too much on having missed his son's wedding. The telegram Father sent us in response was a bit different in tone, however. It was short, radiating a hurt that wrenched my heart, but at least it was not angry.

"I do congratulate you," the Lieutenant General says, warmth creeping into his tone. "And can think of no two people I've met who seem so naturally suited to one another."

Ripley and I thank him and offer a seat, which he refuses. I tell Hani to fetch more tea.

"I've found the lot of you prefer the most direct flow of information, so I won't dither with words that might make an attempt to soften the news I'm about to relay."

Ripley takes my left hand and Cornelius my right. We look to one another, then back at Lieutenant General Blackwood.

"A young man has been arrested for the murders of Edna Watson and Mohammad Gamal."

It's as if the air has left the room.

"What sort of young man?" Cornelius asks.

"A young man who resides in the City of the Dead."

Cornelius stands, his hands fisted at his hips. "Who but a wretched waif with barely enough to eat would rip apart a pair of lovers for his own amusement?"

Hani brings the Lieutenant General a cup of tea, which he accepts with no enthusiasm.

"It is indeed a cynical move on the part of Cairo constabularies, and not the sort of thing they would normally involve themselves in, but as Edna was a British citizen, it appears they're making an exception. The murders have become quite the diplomatic incident." The Lieutenant General looks down into his tea as if contemplating his reflection. "The more generous way to look at this development is that it at least clears Mohammad and Edna of the moral stain of murder and suicide. By implication, it suggests that the pair had not gone to a hotel together of their own volition, and were taken there, or lured there, by an evil-doer."

Now Ripley stands, as do I, each of us wanting to pick up a plate and shatter it against the wall.

"Don't they care who actually killed them, for God's sake?" Ripley demands. "That killer is essentially being set loose—free to come after more young women in the City of the Dead. Or after Leila!"

"I only hope he comes after me," Cornelius says.

"You should know that the young man in question is insisting on his innocence, not that it will help him," Lieutenant General Blackwood tells us. "He claims to have heard about the carnages, and maintains your friends were felled by one of Mohammad's relatives. A powerful man who moves behind the scenes, and who no one in the Gamal family is willing to betray. Not even Mohammad's parents."

"Just as we suspected!" I say. "And Mohammad's family is using their power to sweep this all under the rug, while hanging their horrors on some poor boy!"

Lieutenant General Blackwood puts his tea down and shakes his head; a rare demonstration of helplessness.

"This is not the only reason I've come here today," he tells us. "I'm sure you've heard, if not felt, the rumblings of unrest among Mohammad's many disciples. He was an inspiration, a symbol of Cairo's future as a seat of power and a place of consequence. Even the poorest Egyptians who shared little in common with a man of his class looked up to him. Looked to him to guide them into the twentieth century as more than bystanders. Now he's gone and a man has been arrested for his murder. They are angry and they don't know what to do about it."

"What do you think will happen?" Ripley asks.

"I think there will be violence in the streets. Tonight there will be a vigil in honor of Mohammad's life. A crowd of those who mourn him will be marching through Cairo, and they will be many. I don't expect that it will remain a peaceful event, a silent march of grief and candlelight. There will be blood. Mark my words."

Lieutenant General Blackwood takes a pleasureless sip of his tea.

"There have been several of those vigils already," I say. "Ripley, Cornelius, and I have been to them, and there was nothing out of the ordinary. Not even right after the news of his killing broke. Surely, rumblings don't have to become rampages."

"Not unless someone wants them to," Cornelius says.

Lieutenant General Blackwood nods. "Young Mr. Neville is quite right. I only wish we knew who that someone was."

"Would it be the killer or someone acting on his behalf?" I ask.

"Could be. Or simply a political opportunist looking to discredit Mohammad's legacy."

Ripley reaches down to the table and fingers his knife. "Is there anything we can do?"

"Stay home."

"You must be joking," I say.

"I'm not. You, least of all, should be out on the streets. And you," Lieutenant General Blackwood says to Ripley, "should stay with your new bride. Both you and Mr. Neville need to be guardians of this household, not running through the streets like adventurers."

"We're hardly adventurers," Ripley says. "Our friends were slaughtered by a fiend whom we believe is the same man who attacked us. He's also the slayer of two young women in the City of the Dead, and . . ."

"And what?" Lieutenant General Blackwood says, in a voice of unforeseen temper. "And the fallen women of Whitechapel fourteen years ago? Is that what you were about to say?"

"No," Ripley says.

"Yes!" I shout. "Damn it—I saw it on your face when we were at that awful hotel where Mohammad and Edna drew their last breaths! When you saw the smear of blood just like the one left by the Ripper in London's East End after he slashed Annie Chapman to bits."

For a moment, I think the Lieutenant General will admonish me for cursing. But he doesn't.

"Lieutenant General, I met the boy. When I was in London a few weeks ago. The boy from Whitechapel who's now a man—the very one, and only one, who got a good, hard look at the killer. Eyes like fire, he told me. Or maybe fire fruit."

Lieutenant General Blackwood's eyes widen, and I watch his shoulders rise.

"Don't be ridiculous," he says. "You seem to be drawing wild conclusions about utterly disparate events. Some from years ago that happened far, far away from here."

"Not everything can be explained in linear time or through rational investigation! Who's to say what's rational anyway? The most rational explanation might just be that—"

"That Jack the Ripper is not only responsible for the Whitechapel murders, but several murders in Cairo at present? Oh, and while we're at it, he may have had a hand in some way of disappearing an entire British regiment in the middle of the desert sixteen years ago?"

The Lieutenant General slams his hand on the table and turns his back to us. I, however, will not be deterred.

"And God knows how many he's killed over millennia." I say it slowly, and with gritty purpose. I want every word to sink in.

"Leila." Ripley pulls me close. "Our apologies, Lieutenant General. Leila's been feeling ill of late."

Lieutenant General Blackwood turns back around. He softens immediately. "I hope it's nothing serious."

"Not really," I lie. Ripley gives me a good, hard look that says *stop it this instant*. I don't want to stop, but I fear I've gone too far. "My apologies. I get cross when I'm unwell."

"There's no need to apologize," he says.

Although he dismissed our notions about The Ripper quite tersely, his eyes delay, studying me. I almost bring the matter up again, but both Ripley's and Cornelius's expressions brim with warning. We may need the Lieutenant General in the near future, and to further strain our credibility with him at this point would be foolish. It's enough what I've already done, though he may forgive it, as I am a woman.

"Are you sure you won't stay for breakfast," Ripley says. "We'd love to have you, perhaps talk about less troubling events."

Lieutenant General Blackwood makes for us a small smile. "I'd very much like to, but I'm afraid we'll have to leave that for next time."

"At least allow me to walk you to the door," Cornelius says, and the Lieutenant General accepts this kindness.

Ripley and I wait until Lieutenant General Blackwood leaves the room before daring to face one another.

"I'm sorry," I say. "I didn't mean to overplay our hand like that. I suppose I was hoping he would be ready to hear more about what has been happening, all the things we've learned." My mind is still spinning, my blood racing. Obviously Ripley was right to diffuse the situation, and not make us look like complete lunatics, but it's so troubling that a man as quick witted and open minded as our older friend will not even entertain our suspicions. And when they're right there before him, too.

Ripley puts his forehead to mine. "He will be ready, and soon, I think. Though not today."

Just then Cornelius rushes back in, his face full of impatience. He's holding an envelope of thin crepe paper, which he shoves at us like it's on fire.

"This was slipped under the door just now," he says. "Only a moment after I'd waved at the Lieutenant General as he got into his carriage."

"Perhaps he forgot to give it to us." Ripley stares at the unaddressed letter. Not even a Christian name on it.

Cornelius shakes his head. "I thought the same thing, and opened the door straight away, but no one was there. And your friend's carriage was already rolling down the street. You have to admit it's strange, at the very least, especially given everything that's been going on."

Ripley takes the envelope and opens it, his eyes narrowing at the script. "It's in Arabic," he says.

I lean over his shoulder and read it once to myself first, rather dazed by the contents. "It reads, 'I can guide you to the dune you seek. But you must meet me tonight at Bawabbat al-Mitwali, when the moon is crowning.'"

"The Bawabbat?" Cornelius says.

"It's the southern gate of the city in Old Cairo," Ripley

explains. "Bawabbat al-Mitwali is what it was called under the Ottomans. You would know it as Bab Zuweila."

"And what about the dunes being referenced?" I say. "Can't mean the ones from your dreams? Not unless you've been asking around about them."

Ripley takes a deep breath and shakes his head. "I've told no one about my dreams. Only us, here in this room."

There is a soft, grim change among us. As if the last bubble of our post-nuptial serenity has burst and we are all three of us exposed again.

"We must go, of course," I say. "No matter what Lieutenant General Blackwood thinks is going to happen tonight."

"You will stay here," Ripley tells me. "You were right about this being our time, and I want you home and content."

"Don't be ridiculous. I was talking nonsense and you know it."

"I won't have you endanger yourself. On this account, our most rational friend was quite right."

"No he was not." I stomp my foot like a child. Can't help it. "And I won't have you endangering yourself without me. That letter is most likely from the killer and you know it!"

Ripley tosses the letter onto the breakfast table and looks me right in the eye. The crimson veins in the deep brown of his irises move like rivers of lava on a volcanic mountain. They are as beautiful and awful as infinity.

"Are you even listening to what you're saying? That you want to accompany me to meet a potential maniac with a penchant for slicing up young women?"

"The letter was written in Arabic," I say. "Which you don't speak or read."

Cornelius comes between us and places a hand on each of our shoulders. "But I do."

"See, Cornelius can come with me."

Ripley tips his head to Cornelius as if this is a done deal.

To his credit, it is obvious to our friend from Senegal that it is not even close to such a thing.

"I will not consider letting the two of you go without me. That's final. And who's to say I'll be any safer in this house, anyway? Particularly with the two of you gone *adventuring*, as the Lieutenant General calls it."

"She does have a point," Cornelius says. "If this letter is indeed from the killer, we should not let him divide us. We are stronger together."

Cornelius breaks away from us and goes to the window, peering out onto the street. It's a bustling day here in Cairo, like every day, and it feels a long time away until we must go out to meet with our ominous correspondent.

"I have an idea," Cornelius says. "The two of you can go to the southern gate and I can follow close behind. I'm an excellent sneak, as you know, and will make sure I'm undetected."

"Undetected, like when we caught you in my father's office?"

Cornelius shrugs. "What you don't know is how many times I'd been in that office before. Just to look at things, hold the artifacts in my hands."

Ripley chuckles at him with more than a hint of skepticism. "Only takes once to be caught."

"Indeed, which is why I'll bring assurance this time. When I follow you tonight, I intend to also be armed, just as you should be Ripley. That way, we can corner the bastard—and keep Leila safe."

Ripley goes to our friend at the window. They are backlit by the sun and look like two young gods in a celestial quarrel.

"I can't allow Leila to be imperiled. I can't. Do you understand that?"

"She'll be imperiled whether she stays here or not," Cornelius says.

"Ripley," I tell him. "It may not be a perfect idea, but I

admit I can't come up with better. Not without asking for Lieutenant General Blackwood's help, and it's unlikely he'd be keen on letting us walk the streets this evening, even with a military escort not far behind. And if we don't go at all, we'll lose a chance at finding out anything about the mysteries we're embroiled in. About our lives—past, present, and future. I'd say it's worth it, don't you?"

"I think we haven't a choice," Cornelius says.

"There's always a choice! But in this case the choice is to risk Leila or do nothing."

"Doing nothing risks me as well!"

I go to the window and stand with the men. Ripley lets his head fall into his hands, and I put my arms around him.

"She's right you know," Cornelius says. "This isn't just about one killer in one time, but likely someone who has perhaps lived as many lives as you. A man who in just one life has killed in the desert, and on the streets of London and Cairo. Staying home tonight will hardly deter him, let alone keep anyone safe. Especially if he suspects that you are like him."

I feel Ripley's body move with his breath—the slow, measured breath of a man of courage. A man who will do what he must. Always has, always will. I wonder how many times he has stood with me facing an enemy, looking the specter of death in the eye. How many times he has vowed to protect me and failed, and how that knowledge must tear at his guts.

"Pray with me," Ripley whispers.

I take his hand, then turn to Cornelius, who offers me his as well. We all pray—believer, agnostic, and atheist. We all pray because that's what we do when it's all that's left to us.

Chapter 28

The Vigil

THOUSANDS OF CANDLES, glowing like a fragile hope. Thousands of hands holding them. Ripley and I join the silent march near the North Gate on Kasaba Street, the only accessible place where Horus is able to drop us off. Hopefully, he will arrive at the South Gate before we do.

The march may be silent of voices, but is filled with the sounds of shuffling feet, many of them bare and whispering across the ground. And it is thick with the weighty breath of an unshakable sorrow.

Cornelius is behind us, within vision. He's dressed in the black robes and turban typical of Cairo's snake charmers and blends in with the common folk of the crowd at first glance.

Ripley has on his person two knives as sharp as razors, while Cornelius has a firearm hidden beneath his robes. I have the men and my wits. I'm dressed as a boy, of course, and try as I might to act as Ripley's servant, attempting to remain a couple of steps behind him at least, but he'll have none of it. He wants his arms around me, protecting me, regardless of if it makes us look strange.

But no one in our immediate vicinity seems to be paying us much mind anyway, and hopefully, he who would pay us mind is ahead of us, waiting at the South Gate, where we will be prepared to take him on.

We are in a crowd as dense as a herd of cattle, and one

getting bigger all the time. Groans bubble up from the crush, as we get pushed and jostled. The candles flicker, the hot wax spills onto knuckles and toes. But we've agreed not to slink into the side streets until we're closer to our destination, wanting to get a read on any disturbances meant to derail the vigil. Each of us has the feeling, deep in our bellies, that our rendezvous at the Bab Zuweila and the potential for eruptions of violence on the main boulevard, are somehow linked.

"May he dwell in paradise!" A man calls from a second floor window above us, and countless *Amens* from the horde answer his blessing.

As we pass a market, a swell of people joins the march, making it more difficult for us to budge outside of what is prescribed by the throng. Ripley pulls me even closer and dares a look behind us.

"Cornelius is farther back now, but he's still within sight," he tells me.

I glance back as well, trying to seem casual about it. I encounter Cornelius's eyes of black oil, and he throws me a terse nod that is of some reassurance.

From in front of us comes a sound like the crack of a whip, causing a current of commotion to frizzle through the mourners. It appears to be nothing but the split of a wooden wheel, but makes a cleft in the spirit of remembrance, bringing more of us out of our thoughts and into an awareness of our tight, suffocating circumstances. The fact of the air becoming heavier and more viscous by the minute.

These physical discomforts prick at us all, and a fight breaks out near the rim of the march. Nothing savage, just a skirmish, but one that causes yet another ripple amongst us, this time forcing a parting of the crowd. Ripley and I are shoved along, unable to effectively defend our position. We, with those in our immediate vicinity, are forced off the main street and onto a narrow side road. One of many in a maze of streets that curl around the larger thoroughfares in Cairo.

"Damn it all," I grumble.

Ripley and I both look for Cornelius, and catch only a bare glimpse of him as we are funneled further away from the march. Not an unexpected occurrence at such a large vigil, but certainly an inconvenient one. Dangerous if we aren't able to right things soon.

"Whatever you do, don't let go of me," Ripley says. "Hopefully we'll be able to double around and catch sight of Cornelius again."

The side streets we've been steered onto are darker than usual, with only a few lanterns lit. Likely, residents who would normally be home to light them are either watching the march or have joined it themselves. The one improvement of our predicament is that the quality of air is better with fewer people about, and gets better still as our splintered faction starts to thin, and people make their way back to the main part of the vigil. At a fork in the road, Ripley and I catch a breath and try to orient ourselves.

"I imagine at this point we may as well head to the South Gate via these smaller veins rather than the main artery," I say. "The moon is beginning to crown."

Ripley looks up at the moon, a little less than half full and resembling a mushroom cap. "We might get there in twenty minutes, assuming one of us knows how to go from here."

"I suppose I could get us there." True, although hardly an assertion that inspires confidence. After sunset, the streets can easily deceive us, and we hadn't planned on going the back way until we were further down the vigil's path.

Ripley peers down one of the slender alleyways. Near empty and full of shadows, it can boast only one glowing orange light at the far end. "Late or no, I don't think we should risk it," he says. "It's bad enough we've gone looking for this maniac, but I'm not going to provide him with his favorite venue for murder by taking a meandering route through darkened streets. Especially when we've lost Cornelius."

A point I can't deny, even if it is largely for my benefit. I know if Ripley were alone, he'd make a go of it.

"Perhaps we should head back the way we came," I say, and this is agreeable to us both, even if it will bring us to the South Gate later than we would like.

I follow Ripley closely as we round the curve, beginning to snake our way to Kasaba Street. The lane we're on has just a smattering of folk. This, of course, makes Ripley stick out even more. He catches the attention of a vagrant with scabbed, boney fingers and one eye sewn shut.

"A coin for a dying man?" the beggar entreats us. Ripley needs no translation of his Arabic and begins digging into his pocket, as if I haven't told him a dozen or more times not to allow himself to get reeled in.

Upon receiving Ripley's offering, the beggar launches into a profuse recitation of thanks, skillfully angling for more. I grit my teeth and kick at a stone, then pinch Ripley's arm to get on with it.

"Sherin," a soft voice calls.

"What did you say?"

The beggar glances my way with some annoyance, then turns his attention back to Ripley.

"Sherin, come here."

A downy smear of white catches in the corner of my vision and I look to it. I watch a cat crawl into a hole at the base of a façade, and I would swear it was the trinket seller's cat. Or one that looks just like it.

"Hurry, Sherin. He's close."

I look to Ripley and the beggar, who are still engaged.

"Sherin," that voice keeps saying. "Please."

The white Turkish cat appears again, scampering towards

the alleyway behind us. He stops and sits, turning back and glaring at me. He's licking his paw, as if he's waiting. I cannot stop seeking him with my eyes, my whole being.

"Ripley," I say. He's wrapping up his business with the beggar, and I turn towards the cat once again. But then the tone of the voice changes abruptly.

"Sherin, it's too late. He's here. Go, go away. Don't let him see you."

The cat begins to run, and I tear away from Ripley and run after him, dashing down the narrow path where the voice appears to be coming from. I can't help myself.

I can hear Ripley call my name, and the quick drum of his footsteps behind me. I round a corner, then veer right when the path splits in two and narrows. I hear Ripley go in the other direction and fear we could lose each other, but I can't think of that now.

"Sherin, no!"

And the voice goes silent.

It is an ill-omened silence that visits me like a slap in the face. I am aware that I'm not alone. I cannot say how, only that I feel the presence of malevolence, bold and sure. The light around me is hardly light at all, just a lantern, the half-moon, and candlelight radiating from behind a small kitchen window. I step into the blue-black recess of a doorway, just to get hold of myself again. There, I press my eyes shut, listening, trying not to breathe quite so hard.

After a silent count to three, I dare to open my eyes, but keep my gaze cast down. At first it is only his shadow that enters my vision. The elongated shadow of a pair of legs in trousers, a hand holding a thin, sharp knife. Then the feet come into view. A dark pair of handsome dress shoes—the kind an Englishman might wear, or a well-to-do Egyptian— step heel to toe on the dusty ground. The cold steel of the blade winks at me in the moonlight. It is darkened and drips with what I know must be blood. When he comes closer, I gasp.

The well-appointed feet come to a halt directly in front of me.

I do not look up at his face. I remind myself I'm clad as a servant boy, a decidedly safer ensemble than a dress once the sun has set on Cairo. If this is the same man who encountered a poor Whitechapel boy in London just after Annie Chapman's murder, and simply walked on, he may see me as hardly above notice.

But he doesn't walk on at leisure like he did back then. It seems a long time that he stands there, as if considering me. Each second moves with the sluggishness of a fly in honey, as I can feel every place where he studies my person—from the top of my muslin-wrapped head, to my shoulders, over my torso, and down my legs. Then, as suddenly as he came into my sights, he turns on his heel and goes on, his pace neither easy nor hurried. I nearly fall to the ground in relief.

"Are you still there?" I rasp into the darkness. "It's me, Sherin."

I hear a grunt coming from further down the way. In my deepest fear I wonder if it isn't Ripley or Cornelius, and I break into a run. As I round the bend, I see him. Lying on the ground, his eyes wide as if straining to stay open. Waiting for me.

It is the trinket seller.

"Who did this to you?" I kneel at his side and put my hand on his cheek. His robes are drenched in blood around his middle from what must be a very large wound. He wets his lips and blinks, turning his head towards me.

"You know him and he knows you."

He says this in the language of my dreams.

The trinket seller's breath is ragged and failing, yet he reaches out and grabs my tunic. The force of it startles me.

He pulls me close, until I can smell his blood. "The Dune you seek is in the southwest of Egypt. Near Libya."

"How is it you know about the dune?"

I search his face for something I can recognize—a glimmer from a past life, perhaps, but the light is poor.

"I have always known you," he says.

The trinket seller coughs, and blood dribbles from his mouth. I can feel the life draining from him, yet his eyes remain alert and determined. "And I will always find you."

It is then he begins to fade.

"Who are you?" I shake him and his eyes roll back into his head. When his focus returns to me, I can see he is further weakened. His expression has changed so much that I hardly recognize him. He begins babbling in Arabic.

"Where am I?" he asks.

I tell him he's in Cairo, near the South Gate.

"Where is the friend in my head? Where has he gone?" He seems bewildered, as if he's just awakened from a strange dream. Even his voice is changed.

"What do you mean?" I ask him. "You had no friend when I found you. What is your friend's name? What is your name?"

But it is of no use.

The trinket seller's eyes look past me. I take his hand and see that it has become heavy. In a couple of moments, I am sure that he is gone.

Meow.

I look up from the dead man, and there sits his cat, the Turkish angora that follows him wherever he goes. The creature looks me straight in the eyes as if he'd smile at me if he could. He steps over his dead master and curls up next to me, rubbing his cheek against my hand.

"Leila!"

"Ripley, thank God!"

He sprints from the corner, all the while admonishing me sharply for leaving him.

"What in the devil happened here?" Ripley asks, as he bends over me. "My God, is that the man who sold Cornelius the statue?"

I tell him roughly what happened up to the point when I found the dying man.

"Good grief! If you heard a voice, you could have taken me by the arm instead of taking off!" he says, in what I hope will be his final rebuke. "I would have gone with you instantly."

"I couldn't stop myself," I explain. "Once I heard that voice, that name, I could do nothing but follow it. I can't say why, I just felt that it was for me and me alone. Like the letter that told us to come to the South Gate. And when I got here, after the killer had gone right by me, the knife still in his grip, this man began talking to me in that language." I reach out and take my husband's hand. "Ripley, he told me where we can find the dune."

Ripley's eyes widen and he searches the man's face much as I did, eager for some clue, a tiny spark of recognition.

"You are sure this was the man who wanted you to meet him, and not the killer who walked by you?" he asks.

"Yes. I'm saying exactly that. I don't think the killer expected me at all. I'm wearing a disguise, obviously, so if he was looking for me he didn't recognize me. But I don't think he was. I think he was looking for this trinket seller right here, and found him."

"He's after the statue," Ripley says.

"I can't think of anything else."

The cat seeks out my attention again, bumping his head against me. He then arches his back and hisses. Not at me or Ripley, but at an unseen foe.

Ripley tears his eyes away from the dead man. He looks

about us with a birdlike attention and steps close to me, putting his hands on my shoulders.

"He's here," Ripley says.

Ripley draws his knives, one in each fist.

"For God's sake, Ripley, at least if you had a pistol! This is madness."

"If I'm going to kill a man, I'm going to look him in the eye," he tells me. "I don't need a pistol."

A small dagger—no bigger than a House Sparrow—flies from out of the shadows, barely missing Ripley's head. I gasp as he dives to cover me with his person when another, this one landing, grazes Ripley's leg.

"Blast!" he grunts.

We land on the dusty ground just as more daggers come, this time from another angle.

"Show yourself!" Ripley calls out. "Or do you hide from men, only daring to face the women you hunt as prey?"

Ripley springs up, breaking the window next to him with his elbow and unlatching the door to an empty house. "Quickly," he says, as another dagger flies through the air.

I do get up, rather clumsily, shaking with fear, as two more daggers hit the stone wall and clang to the ground. Ripley picks them up, then ushers me inside the house.

Once we have taken cover, a quiet descends upon the alleyway, the silence violated only by my heaving, fitful breaths.

"He's still here," Ripley whispers, and I have the same intuition. He's merely waiting, figuring that at some point we'll gain the confidence to leave our hiding place. I feel no such inclination will visit me any time soon. Not with Ripley's propensity for heroic acts, and the killer's appetite for murder whetted with the poor trinket seller.

"Come on," says Ripley, his teeth gritted with menace. His eyes are wide, the whites of them lustrous and wet.

From up the way, rounds a carriage. In a cacophony of

brays and jingles, its horses trot purposefully towards us, and for a moment I think I'm having visions.

"By Jove, it's Cornelius," Ripley cries. And indeed it is, though I can scarcely believe it myself. And what's more, he's commandeered Horus! The Hugheses' man, whose eyes are darting all over the alley, finally lands them on our window, where Ripley is waving his arms.

"Quickly." Horus beckons us, as Simar, his lead stallion, rises up on his hind legs. "The vigil is descending into madness and the police have begun beating the crowds!"

"Both of you, whatever you do, stay down!" Ripley calls to them. "The killer is here and heavily armed!"

Cornelius jumps down form the perch and crouches at the wheels of the brougham.

"I'll cover," he says, holding up his pistol. "You take care of Leila."

Ripley nods briefly at Cornelius, and puts his arm around me, guiding me along. I hate the terror that courses through me as we begin to make our way to the carriage. The way my skin feels cold and my attempts at composure betray me.

A shot reverberates loudly as Cornelius does as he said. No daggers fly at us from the shadows as we make a break for it, and Ripley opens the door to the coach, pushing me inside. The trinket seller's cat, its white fur still raised in alarm, follows, jumping into my arms and giving a snappish *meow*.

"For God's sake, let's go!" I shout.

Horus cracks the reins and gets us moving before Ripley is even properly able to climb aboard. Cornelius jumps onto the coach's step, gripping the handle with one hand and his pistol with the other. A dark figure steps out of a slim footway between two unlit houses, and another dagger flies, hitting the second stallion in the thigh, causing him to reel. It is only due to Horus's expertise with the animals and his lead stallion's headship that we are not knocked over by the creature's panicked movements.

Cornelius fires once again, but cannot land his target, given the jagged movements of the carriage.

In as smooth an exit as we can possibly hope for, we careen out of the alleyway and are able to make way onto less cloistered roads. The injured stallion behaves with impressive discipline, taking us all the way to the island where Ripley used to reside, where the Hugheses' empty home pines for them to return. The animal whinnies as we amble to a stop and Horus jumps down immediately to tend to him. The dagger has sunk into the muscle of his thigh, and rivulets of blood stream all the way down his leg. Horus pets the creature, looking into his eyes, while getting a firm grip on the handle of the knife. He yanks it out and the stallion neighs in shock, but does not panic again. Horus has managed to tame him, speaking softly with a voice of unquestionable authority.

"It is better you spend the night here, surrounded by men of the military," Horus tells us. "Especially with the mayhem going on in the streets tonight."

He's right, of course. The thought of being followed back to our family home, which is not nearly far enough from where The Ripper slayed the trinket seller, gives me a violent chill. We can, all of us, return in the morning when the danger will have abated. At least I hope.

Because it is clear this is no mortal foe with whom we are tangling. This killer is like us, only something more. If only we knew exactly what sort of more. What it is he knows that we do not.

I OPEN MY EYES to the dead quiet of his house—Hunter's, but I'm not allowed to call him that. "It's Daddy," he keeps saying. Dad is about all I can muster, but most of the time I try to avoid calling him anything at all.

The dream—the one that started out so good and turned wicked bad—is still with me, and I rub my eyes hard. Not to get rid of it exactly, but to get some distance from it.

"Just an expression of my subconscious," I say. "That's all."

In it, I was wearing a snug, long dress that fit like a second skin. It was barely the color of a peach. So pretty. I can't imagine ever having a place to wear something like that. I'm happy and as natural as can be in that dress, like it was made for me. And I'm in a place that feels like home, too, looking out at a village of mud brick houses that stands on the edge of a desert. With me is a man. I'm sort of uncomfortable in his company, but at the same time more content than I can ever imagine being—except when I'm with the Nevilles.

And that's when the dream takes a turn. I find myself gone from that home and in a mountain range that's nothing like the mountains of Virginia, or Alaska for that matter. These are craggy and black. As lonely as evil. My wrists are bound with oily leather straps and I'm being beaten by a group of men dressed like gladiators. Rough and tattered, they're like the lone survivors of something terrible—a war, an alien invasion, a zombie apocalypse.

Behind them, the man who was standing with me when I was wearing that peach dress, is watching the goings on. He's big, with black hair that falls to his shoulders. I can tell it pains him to see me like this, but he keeps watching anyway. And my eyes are drawn to his. Startling eyes that look like they're on fire. My father's eyes.

I feel sick.

I sit up, rubbing my wrists. I can still feel echoes of the pain; the way the leather burned against my skin as I struggled. As I was kicked and punched and whipped with belts. Taking a few breaths, I hang my feet over the edge of my bed. I steady myself and look out the window, reassured that I'm here, in Eagle River—not there, in my dream. It's the only time I'm glad to find myself in Alaska and not back in Virginia, where I should be, or Cairo, where I want to be.

There's a deep drawer in the desk Hunter built for me and I glance over at it, feeling that pull again. That's where I keep a bag of pretzel knots, cinnamon gum, a Polaroid instant camera I got for Christmas, and other items he wouldn't give a damn about. Things he'd get bored rifling through, if he ever decided to search my room again. At the bottom of the drawer is an old flannel shirt I used to wear as PJs when I got behind on laundry.

I go to that desk and open the drawer—it's not locked on purpose. I don't want Hunter to think there's some big secret in there, and it's not like he couldn't jimmy it open if it was locked. Plus, since he made the desk, I'm sure he's got a spare key to that drawer.

The flannel shirt is all rolled up and I take it out carefully, placing it on the desktop. Then I listen. There's still not a sound in the house and I'm sure my father's asleep. Otherwise I'd hear the soft murmurs of his radio program coming up from downstairs.

I lick my lips, dry as a cat's nose, and turn on my desk lamp.

Then I unwrap the flannel shirt in the way I always do. One bit at a time, making sure to count to three before I peel away each layer. The rolled-up drawing of the desert that Mickey once made for me is the first thing I see. I smooth the flannel under and around it, before unrolling it. The contents of my secret bundle sit right there at the center of the drawing. I place each item on the lacquered wood: a small map of Cairo, all folded up in a square, a gold locket, a razor blade. And there's one more thing. A brochure for The Putnam School of Virginia that the librarian at the Eagle River Public Library gave me last week. It's a school for gifted kids, she said, and in her forty-two years in and around Anchorage schools, she's never met a kid who was better made for Putnam than me. I pick up the brochure and fan myself with it, then reach over and slide it under my pillow.

"Damn," I say. I shouldn't do this. I want to and I don't all at once. But I know I will.

I hold down the curling edges of Mickey's drawing, and study it for a while. It's definitely the same place as my dream. Not the village part, there are no mud brick houses. The landscape is the same, though. Flat at the outset, but a shelf of dunes in the far background.

Next, I open the map of Cairo. And that is just a map of Cairo, nothing more, but it centers me, makes me feel close to Mickey. I've circled the street where the Nevilles used to live, but I know they've moved since last time they were there. Probably living in that ancient house they'd been wanting to fix up.

Next is the treasure, and looking at it always makes my mouth feel mucky. Sometimes it makes my hands shake, but not now. I found it in our shed, of all places, wrapped in a piece of felt and stuffed into a magnetic key box stuck under a metal work table.

Gold and old. Precious, but sturdy. I take the oval and

unclasp it. On the inside left are two names engraved in cursive. Ripley Allen Davies, Leila Saber-Wellington. Under those is a date, 1902, and there's a large, green gemstone, probably an emerald, just under the numbers. I bet it's worth a fortune. I move the locket this way and that to make the green stone shimmer under the light of my lamp. It's not lost on me that it's nearly the exact color of my eyes.

On the other side is a picture portrait of a young, dark-haired woman who's probably no more than a couple of years older than me. I'd memorized her face long before I ever found her picture in our shed. She's the same girl in the old photograph in Dr. Neville's study back in Virginia. The black and white one from Cairo that had Dr. Neville's great-great grandfather in it. And another boy, too. Handsome as an old-time movie star.

Damn him. My father stole this from the Neville's house—that has to be it—although I can't remember a time when he ever went there. And for all the things my father might be, I've never known him to be a thief, at least not in the time I've been with him. But here it is. He wanted this locket and he got it somehow. Maybe back when he was still using, but then I can't think of why he wouldn't have pawned it for some serious cash.

He's never said a word to me about it being missing from its hiding place, and I guess he can't without tipping me off that he'd pinched it. That's why I'm never giving it back. Although one day, when I see Mickey again—and I will see Mickey again—I'll give it to him. Whoever the girl in the photo is, she seems to mean a lot to the Nevilles.

Last, but definitely not least, is the razor blade. It's clean and shiny. I always put a new one in when I finish. Looking at it makes my heart beat fast, and my breath catch in my throat.

It's time. Get on with it, I say to myself.

First, I get up and go to the stack of vinyl records that my friend Lottie's parents gave us when we first moved here. I pick an opera, The Tale of Tsar Saltan, from the middle of the stack the way someone who does card tricks would do.

"Pick a card, any card," I whisper.

Taking it out of its sleeve, I put it on the antique record player I bought in Anchorage for just pennies. The needle lands right at the start of Flight of the Bumblebee and I turn the volume low. So low I can barely hear it. But it's there.

Leaning back, I roll up the sleeve of my pajama top, folding the purple cotton up tight so that it doesn't come undone. I turn over my left arm, looking close at the run of flesh from my wrist to my elbow. Thin, white lines at the wrist, from back when I was just getting started. They're right where the leather straps would've dug into my skin, and they're starting to fade. I don't want that.

I grab my tissue box from the corner of my desk and set it right in front of me, then I pick up the razor, pinching it between my thumb and index finger. I close my eyes and breathe. I don't have to look to land the edge of the blade right exactly on the top of the first white line, and feel the sting as I drag the razor across the scar, turning it from white to red. Then I do the next line, and the next. Enough to bleed and leave a mark, but not enough to bleed out or anything. Not like I'm trying to kill myself. Just the opposite. This makes me feel alive.

Next to the row of white-turned-red lines on my wrist is a curlicue scar that runs in concentric circles, like on a snail shell. Keeping my eyes shut, I let the edge of the razor land again, giving it the same treatment as the lines.

Then there is a bolt of lightning. I push a little deeper on that one and feel my blood well up and run down the side of my arm, warm against my cool skin. Finally, next to the crease in my elbow are two locked circles with a pearly dot in the center where they overlap. I push even deeper into that one because I don't ever want these scars to fade. They bring me to Mickey somehow, and when the razor blade cuts into my skin there, it actually feels good. So good that my eyes roll back and I almost lose myself to a dream again.

Chapter 29

Monsters
Cairo, 1902

WITH **C**AIRO **U**NDER curfew after the violence at Mohammad's vigil, Ripley and I did not move back into our family home until Father was able to leave Aswan and Alfred Davies returned from Damascus. It has been an awkward adjustment since then, I'll admit. While Dr. Davies has been philosophical about what appears on the surface to be a rash decision made by a love-struck young couple, Father has been frustrated and saddened by our sudden marriage. Not because he disapproves of Ripley, but because, more than anything, he'd expected to be consulted on such an important decision. I can't blame him, and my heart is still heavy over it.

"I do understand love," he said to me, on that first night he was home. "But your mother and I told our parents first— even when we knew they would disapprove of our union."

It was hard to look into his eyes—so sad and cloudy blue.

To add to the whirlwind of our circumstances, Cornelius has been able to arrange for an excellent cover in regards to our plan of traveling to the dunes the ill-fated trinket seller was able to locate for us. The Great Maspero, with his boundless appetite for artifacts, has been convinced by our African friend that the dune and its caves are likely to hold treasure never before discovered. Father, not surprisingly, does not approve of my intention to join on this "treasure hunt," as he calls it, but as a wife belongs with her husband, he has kept most of his grumblings to himself.

As for the plotting of our journey, we've had some luck here as well. Howard Carter has acquainted us with two archaeologist friends of his, who will be traveling by caravan to the region we seek in just a week's time. Naturally, we've arranged to be going with them.

That's why tonight is just for Ripley and me. A time to put away worry and family squabbles. A time to hope and love.

I can't help but admire my husband's handsome profile, and how damned respectable he looks in his evening attire. All black with a crisp, white shirt, fitted to perfection—the gold locket I gave him hanging by chain from his left breast pocket. I love the way his wedding ring glows gold like a crown on his ivory-skinned finger. He taps it impatiently on the rail of our balcony at the Khedivial Opera House, flitting his eyes about the grand structure—all carved wood and lush paint. My husband has acquired for us some tickets to see *The Tale of Tsar Saltan* by Nikolai Rimsky-Korsakov, and we can hardly wait for it to begin.

An attendant visits our box, tying back the heavy, silk drapes which frame it. I look down at the stage and feel like a girl at Christmas. But as the curtain rises and the opera commences, I find my mood changing from one of elation to disquiet. It is not for disappointment at the quality of the production—quite the contrary. The show is excellent and the primo uomo and prima donna are wonderful.

It's that the opera is a telling of the most disturbing Russian fairytale. In it, two jealous sisters, after having been passed over as wives for the Tsar in favor of their youngest sibling, conspire to destroy the new Tsaritsa's life. As a wedding present, the young Tsaritsa had promised her husband that she would bear him a son who would become a warrior-knight.

While the Tsar is away, fighting in a war himself, the black-hearted sisters send him a letter informing him that the child born to his Tsaritsa was not human, but a monster!

The Tsar—clearly a vain and foolish man—decrees that his wife and son will be placed in a barrel and thrown into the sea. Miraculously, they land on the shore of an island, and eventually, the son becomes its prince.

Only the boy laments not knowing his father, and a magical swan turns him into a bumble bee, so that he can fly over the sea as a stowaway on a ship and finally meet the silly, impetuous, and frankly, murderous man.

Flight of the Bumblebee begins to play as the interlude starts, and Ripley touches my wrist, pushing up the sleeve of my new dress of silver, midnight blue, and dusty lilac—the last his favorite color for me. Between his touch and the frenetic rise of the music, I feel as if I might take flight. Though I fear mine would be of the Icarus variety, ending in my destruction. As it has in so many lives before, I imagine. Am I not a monster? Is Ripley not? Monsters that have been cast out over and over again, landing on a new shore, in a new life. Having to begin again, and yet always searching for what was lost. Suddenly, I am aware of being terribly old.

"Maybe we should go," I whisper to Ripley.

"Are you feeling alright?"

I nod.

Ripley asks this all the time, concerned about my heart, mostly, but also eager for a sign that I may have conceived the child we are destined for.

"It may be some time until we're able to indulge in culture and finery," Ripley says. "Are you sure?"

I hate that my husband has endeavored to give me such an ideal evening and I'm wanting to leave early because of my own morose thoughts. I say a small prayer for courage in the face of what may await us in the coming weeks, as we journey to the dunes in the Southwest of the Sahara. That we will, all of us, return safely and with answers to some very ominous questions.

"We should stay."

Ripley and I accept another glass of champagne from a waiter. I nurse it until the opera begins again, and the tale comes to its conclusion. One that feels most unsatisfying. The Tsar is reunited with his wife and son, all goes back to being just dandy between them—even the wicked sisters are given grace—and the son marries a princess.

"So many horrors of human nature and all is forgiven," I say with acid on my tongue.

Ripley leans over and kisses my cheek.

"I would forgive you any horror," he tells me.

SLEEP WILL NOT COME FOR ME, but Ripley is out cold and I can't help wonder what dreams are visiting him tonight. His body seems so heavy and there's a light dew of sweat on his brow. His eyes move rapidly beneath their lids, and the deep and full flow of his breath sounds like something one would hear on a large boat in the middle of the sea.

Radcliffe, which is what we've named the trinket seller's cat, sits up from his place at the foot of our bed, where he has taken to sleeping ever since we moved from the rooftop terrace into one of the bedrooms.

He hisses, hunching his back.

"What's the matter?" I whisper.

He looks back at me briefly, then launches off the mattress and dashes out into the hall towards the stairwell.

"Lunatic cat." Scarcely before I finish my curse of the feline, I hear a ruckus downstairs. I huff and look over at

Ripley. Thankfully, he's doesn't awaken, so I creep out of bed and slip on my robe, eager to get to the bottom of things before that damned kitty wakes up the whole house.

"Radcliffe," I call, as I descend into the parlor. And right there, father pops up from behind his wingback chair, nearly scaring me to death!

"Good Lord," he says, looking rather put out.

"Is that all you have to say, after scuttling about in the middle of the night? You should be in bed."

Father shakes his head and runs his hand through his hair.

"I wish I was, and this was all just some nightmare."

I look about at the shattered vase on the floor, and a bunch of bric-a-brac that also made its way down from the shelves.

"Damn that Radcliffe."

"Radcliffe," Father says. "The cat is a hero."

I bend down and pick up a shard of porcelain. Radcliffe peers at me from the top of the bookshelves with a rather smug look on his face.

"A hero? How is that you figure?"

"My dear, an intruder made his way into the house tonight!"

I look about and yes, of course, I can see that now. The front doors are ajar, the place is in disarray. My heart starts to beat madly.

"The city has been in a state of psychosis of late," Father says. He makes his way around the chair and sits down with a long, frustrated breath. "I came down for a brandy, and here was this man! He stood here, like he owned the place, and with the ancient breastplate from the Hugheses under his arm! I said, 'I say, sir, you are in my home, and that is my property!'"

I go to Father and take his hand. It is cold and trembling.

"What on earth was the breastplate doing here? I thought Dr. Davies had it."

"Well, indeed he did, until this evening when I brought it home. The thief may have followed me from the museum thinking it was one of the Egyptian artifacts being moved from the royal palace. You know how dedicated these antiquities thieves can be."

"Indeed," I say.

"And this thief stared at me with a particularly cold viciousness of the like I've never seen. I can see why Maspero has such an extreme disdain for them now."

Radcliffe jumps down from his shelf and lands squarely in Father's lap. He is immediately rewarded with a good scratch behind the ears. "Your cat, of all creatures, came to my rescue, having knocked over one of your grandfather's byzantine vases. Thank God it was one of those of a lesser value. Anyway, he knocked it right over and onto the man's head! Gave him a good knock on the noggin, he did. The scoundrel seemed a bit dazed and then turned and sprinted out the door."

"With the breastplate?"

"Yes, unfortunately."

"Well, at least you're alright for heaven's sake."

Father shrugs and waves his hand. "Oh, I'm fine, dear. Quite fine. It would take more than a mere antiquities thief to take me down. But I'm rather distressed about the artifact."

I suppose I am, too, given its import in Ripley's and my quest to put together the pieces of our collective lives, but part of me is rather relieved to not have to face looking at it again. "Why did you bring it home from the museum?"

Father's brow knits into a thick line, and I know that look. His lips part as if he can hardly form the words, but then he steels himself and begins talking.

"It would seem Alfred discovered some fresh markings etched into it in Arabic. Turns out they were from a poem your mother wrote just before she died."

"What?"

Father urges me to sit down, but I absolutely cannot. My traitorous, defective heart begins beating erratically again, until I can practically feel it thrumming in every part of my body. I pace all over the parlor, shaking my hands, and kicking aside pieces of vase.

"You see, your mother had started having these frightful notions just before she died," Father continues. "And, well, as to why the Hugheses would inscribe such a thing into that artifact, I can't say. Even stranger to me is that I don't at all remember ever having let Hugh and Clara know just how terrible her end was, dear as they were. *Are*, I mean. I don't think I ever told anyone."

I gulp back a fountain of tears that threatens. "Not even me."

"No, dear. Not even you."

Now I must sit, and do. "What did it say?"

Father swallows hard, and pets Radcliffe, making him purr most volubly.

"Writ with the blood of my daughter's vein, there in the mountains of the slain. Her eyes will live on, though his, like a dying sun, will hunt her."

A dreadful chill sinks deep into my bones. I grip the armrest of my chair, watching my knuckles go white. "What an odd little poem."

"Yes, it is. She was so ill, of course, when she wrote it. Closer to the dead than the living—although she talked of you most often of all on that last awful day."

I take Father's hand again and kiss it. Radcliffe nuzzles his head into Father's belly, and I have the urge to do the same. To curl up on his lap the way I did when I was little. "What did she say about me just before she died?"

"Oh, darling, let's not do this. I hate to think of that day. And your mother, well, she wasn't quite herself as it came to the end."

"She seemed quite herself when I left her that morning."

Father leans back in the wingback chair and looks up at the chandelier as if seeking help from heaven.

"Leila, I've watched people die before. Some go a bit mad towards the end. My father, for instance. Why, he thought he was back in Bombay and began rambling on in Marathi. So, yes, your mother was still herself that morning before you left for school. It wasn't until lunch time, just after she awakened from a nap that she started talking nonsense."

My poor father's shoulders slump. His breath becomes heavy and languorous.

"Daddy, please. I know this is hard for you. We both loved her so. But I do need to know what she said—even if it's nonsense."

Father shakes his head and rubs his chin. He looks over at a picture portrait of Mother on the mantle. It was taken shortly after my birth and she sits with her hair down and such a look of pride, like a dark lioness. "I suppose if we're going to do this, we ought to have that brandy I came downstairs for."

Without a word, I go to the armoire where Father keeps his stash. I pour us each a bit too much and take a deep sniff before handing Father his snifter. He raises an eyebrow at me, but says nothing. I'm a wife now, and by extension, a grown woman.

We go to the sofa, sinking into its many pillows. Father watches the picture of Mother across the room from us, as if she's there, and holds the snifter in his hand, twirling the brandy about. Taking nearly half the glass in one swallow, he closes his eyes.

"'Leila,' she said. The way she spoke your name was like a prayer. She talked of what an old soul you are." Father opens his eyes and looks at me.

"Yes, I believe I am."

"That was when the conversation took a queer turn."

A shiver runs down my spine and my mouth goes dry, prompting me to take yet another sip of brandy. Father does the same, licking his lips in concentration.

"She said she hadn't wanted to tell me. She didn't think I'd believe her. I said I would always believe her and she smiled, petting my fingers." He looks down at his hand as if reliving the moment. "I wished so much that I could close my eyes, and when I opened them she would be just as she was. Jolly and well. Full of life and ideas. You mother was always so full of ideas. And on her last day, in the few, remaining hours, she had a lot of ideas. Only they weren't of her usual sort."

Father gazes at me and touches his hand to my temple. "She feared for your life, she told me. I said, 'My love, you're the one whose life is in peril.' 'You don't understand,' she said. 'Leila won't live to be 18.' 'Stop it,' I told her. 'She's fit as a fiddle.'"

I look away, unable to meet my father's eyes. Afraid they might tell him what my mother knew—or at least suspected. That I would die the same death as she. It's bad enough I denied him my wedding day, but here I've been going about as if everything is just fine, pretending I don't have spells of feeling winded and woozy. Pretending he'll always have me.

"I shouldn't have spoken so harshly to her," Father says. "It's just it was all too much. 'Floyd, please,' she begged me. 'Our daughter's in great danger.' 'Our daughter's in school,' I told her. 'And she's fine.' But she wouldn't stop going on. 'There's a terrible storm,' she insisted."

My whole body stiffens. The storm I so often dream of comes rushing through my mind. The darkness of it, the sand lashing my flesh. Like thousands of tiny needles.

"'It's just a nightmare, darling,' I told her. 'No,' she said. 'The storm has passed. It's the desert that I'm afraid of.' 'The desert can be a menace, certainly, but we spend all of our time here in Cairo,' I said, trying to assuage her. 'It's that place,' she said. Her eyes drifted, looking so far away. I could see the end was near. 'The one of sand and bone,' she whispered. 'It'll kill again if she doesn't stop it.'"

It is difficult not to betray my horror at the words my mother spoke as she lay dying. How badly I wish I could turn back time and be there at her deathbed. To hold her hand, to ask her questions, to understand what it was she was seeing as she slipped further away, closer to the other side.

I don't tell Father this. Instead, I comfort him as we drink our brandies. Sharing such a revelation was painful for him, yet at the same time, I feel it was something of a relief to get it off his chest. His eyes twinkle again, as he leans back and sips his elixir.

"Claret is the liquor for boys; port for men; but he who aspires to be a hero must drink brandy. That's what Samuel Johnson said anyway."

"You've always been my hero," I say. "So Mr. Johnson must be right."

I wish I could summon the courage to tell him about my own precarious health, but I'm no hero tonight despite the brandy. The thought of him being alone, of losing mother and me is too much to bear.

"It's been quite a night," I say.

Father stands up, wobbling.

"I fear I may have had too much to drink."

"You don't say. I think a good, hard sleep is in order for you, so I'll do the honors with the police and summon Cairo's watch in the morning. I'll tell them all about what happened here tonight, as I've had more than enough experience giving such testimony in recent weeks."

Father opens his mouth to put up some resistance, but thinks better of it. The police will want him to visit headquarters in the next day or so and make a statement anyway.

I help Father lock up the house good and tight and settle him into bed. I can hear his light snore begin before I even reach his door to take my leave.

Radcliffe follows, light-stepping with me back to Ripley's and my bedroom. It's coming on three in the morning, a full two hours since I went down to the parlor, but Ripley is still deep in his dreams. His lips are sealed tight and his teeth gritted, as if he is watching something intently. I slip off my robe and climb into bed, wrapping myself around him. Radcliffe jumps up and sits at Ripley's side, placing his paws on his ribs like a sphinx.

"You," I say, rubbing under his chin. "The true hero of the night, and without a nip of brandy."

He watches me, his eyes loving and familiar, compelling me into sleep. I can feel myself falling into another place, and I try to resist at first, I don't know why. Maybe because it feels so strange. Because I'm in Cairo, I'm sure of that, but it is not the Cairo I know. And Radcliffe is there, but he's not a kitty, he's a woman. An older woman with dark skin—only a little lighter than Cornelius's—and long braided hair. I think she knows I'm watching, although no one else seems to sense I'm there.

HER NAME IS AMARINTA, Neville's mother, and she keeps glancing upwards towards the ceiling as if she thinks she'll catch a glimpse of me. I wish I could reach out to her, pull on her braids, do something to spook her. Like old times.

"Lot of spirits in this place," she says.

Amarinta's the only one in the family who doesn't much like the large house in Old Cairo—the one that sat empty until Neil and Calliope undertook its renovation. Looks different then when I lived here—they've made it very modern on the inside, keeping only the historical shell.

"We're inventing a new holiday today," Amarinta says, bumping her hip against Calliope's as she rummages through the spice cabinet. "From now on, every February First shall be called Christpass."

Calliope is cooking an early Passover dinner, and smiles as Amarinta invades her space, as she always does in the kitchen.

"More pepper," Amarinta tells her. She takes another bite of the brisket in gravy. "Definitely more pepper."

"You always think everything needs more pepper."

"Because it does."

Calliope laughs and takes the pepper flakes from her mother-in-law. She dispenses a sprinkling of them into the pot.

"That'll do," Amarinta says. "You should've seen the looks I got on the airplane, putting all those in the overhead." She gestures towards several packages wrapped in themed paper and ribbons—snowmen, Santa, and baby Jesus, of course. "Y'all usually come out to Chicago for Christmas, and brave the cold."

"Well, you could've come to Cairo for Christmas, to brave the heat."

They bicker more like mother and daughter than in-laws, but then Amarinta knew Calliope's mother—her real mother. Me. She held my hand as I gave birth, and continued to hold it as I lay dying. She held Calliope all night long after I had slipped away. I got to watch them at least. Until my new life beckoned. Until now.

"You all do the Hanukkah thing anyway," Amarinta says.

Calliope swats her mother-in-law's behind with a wooden spoon. "We're always with you on Christmas, and you know very well we put up a tree for Mickey regardless of where we are."

Amarinta dips her finger into the mashed potatoes, and suggests they could use more butter and salt. "Well," she continues. "I could have come, but where would I go to church here on Christmas morning?"

Calliope gives her a sardonic look. "There are Christian churches in Cairo."

Amarinta adds pepper and more cream to the potatoes. "Not my kind there aren't."

Mickey and Neville come in from the side porch, deep in a conversation about baseball history—the Cubs and the White Sox being the only real baseball history either of them is interested in. Calliope puts them to work taking the food to the dining room and Amarinta follows along, picking at various elements of the Seder meal—the potatoes, the smoked trout, and the chopped liver.

"Mmm," she hums. "I do like me some liver."

Removing her apron with one hand, Calliope smooths her

corkscrew curls with the other. She comes to the table and asks everyone to join hands.

"Let's take a moment to give thanks for all of us being together."

Amarinta gives a loud "Amen," and Mickey laughs. Neville kicks him under the table.

"We ready, gentlemen?" Calliope asks.

Neville performs a loud clearing of his throat, signaling that, ready or not, his wife should start her short reading before everyone faints from hunger.

"We retrace our steps from then to now, reclaiming years of desert wandering," Calliope begins.

And this, as always, casts a spell over the family. Faces grow serious, and any urge to make light of the reading falls away. Perhaps it is the evocation of a Biblical story, dear to all of them—even a strict man of reason like Neville. Or maybe, it is the reference to desert wandering.

"On this night," she continues, "we ask questions, ancient and new, speaking of servitude and liberation, service and joy.

"On this night,

"We welcome each soul, sharing stories of courage, strength and faith.

"On this night,

"We open doors long closed, lifting our voices in songs of praise.

"On this night,

"We renew ancient hopes and dream of a future redeemed.

"On this night,

"We gather around Seder tables, remembering passage from bondage to freedom.

"On this night,

"We journey from now to then, telling the story of freedom."

They stand in silence, Amarinta with her eyes closed, mouthing a prayer.

AFTER DINNER, they move to the living room, lounging on an assortment of colorful pillows scattered across a low sofa taking up much of the room. A small, pink-needled Christmas tree frosted with fake, gold-dusted snow, sits atop the glass coffee table, presents spilling out from under it.

"Gorgeous!" Amarinta coos, as she snuggles an enormous silk wrap patterned with ancient Egyptian iconography. Calliope tells her she had it made by a popular local designer favored by Queen Noor of Jordan.

Neville stares at the gilded antique frame in his hands, his eyes wide.

"You like it?" his mother asks him.

"Incredible. Dated 1886."

"What is it?" Mickey asks.

"It's an old letter," Amarinta tells him. "Found by a British Lieutenant General in 1905. One by the name of Blackwood. The man who wrote it—his name has been mostly frayed off at the bottom—was apparently the commander of a lost regiment that disappeared in the Sahara not long after that letter was written."

"Minty, you love mysteries even more than Neil does."

Amarinta takes a long, deep glug of her wine. "I do, but I hate to dig, and I hate the dirt. I prefer my mysteries on the page, and told to me by the likes of PD James and Walter Mosley."

"Jesus," Neville says, reading the letter to himself. "Listen to this. 'The contagion is fierce and unmerciful, spreading from man to man like a fire with a wind at its back, and seeming to spare almost no one. Agony and blackened flesh. Some go mad. We will all succumb to it, I fear, and we know we must stop it. We have agreed to destroy any last remainder of this evil, including ourselves.'"

"Good Lord," Calliope says. "That's like a horror movie." She glances over at Mickey, who's deep in thought.

Since their visit to the Rah'a excavation site, Mickey has not been acting like himself, in her estimation. Of course, in my view, he is more himself than he's ever been.

Amarinta takes Calliope's hand. She kisses the top of her head, like she would a child, and they cuddle together.

"We should get into our PJs."

Calliope follows her mother-in-law up the stairs to the guest suite, where they change into the new cashmere tops and lounge pants Amarinta brought from Chicago. She digs a couple pairs of cashmere socks out of her suitcase and tosses one to Calliope. She then slides a painting enveloped in brown paper from behind her headboard and places it on the bed.

"This is for you, kitten."

Calliope bites down, giving Amarinta a wide-eyed smile. She tears off the paper and gasps.

The painting is a desert scene. A blue blood moon at the top, like the eye of a cyclops. It pours down on a landscape of bone-colored sand that seems to go on forever. There is a man, in shadow, standing in the distance. He's draped in a dark tunic that flows to his ankles and carries arrows on his back.

"My God, it's so beautiful. Where is this?"

Amarinta shrugs. "Just an image I got stuck in my head. Made me think of you, so I thought I'd paint it for you."

"Well, you thought right. Thank you, Minty."

Amarinta turns to see Mickey standing in the doorway, like she knew he was there. He goes to his grandmother and wraps his arms around her waist.

"What's that?" he asks.

"Grammy painted me a picture. Looks like something you would make, doesn't it?"

Mickey doesn't respond. He extracts himself from Armarinta, and leans over the painting. His eyes drink it in—every shape and color.

"I thought I'd hang it above the mantle," Calliope tells him.

"Pride of place! I'm honored," Amarinta says. "You like it, Mick?"

Mickey lightly fingers the shadow man's arrows.

"Mickey, your grandmother asked you if you like it."

He tears his eyes away from the canvas. "It's uh . . . yeah, yeah, it's amazing, Grammy."

Mickey shoves his hands in his pockets. He makes his excuses, saying he and Neville are going up to the roof to observe Jupiter and Saturn through his new telescope.

"I brought my oils and pastels," Amarinta tells him, as he turns and heads back downstairs. "We're going to make something this visit."

"Don't mind him," Calliope says. "He's been upset about Ever."

"We all have." Amarinta sinks into a chair that looks like it's made of marshmallows. "You given any more thought to sending him to that school?"

"Putnam?" Calliope shrugs and clicks her tongue. "It's far."

"Not from me."

"It's a two hour flight from Chicago to Virginia."

"Takes a lot longer than that to travel from his school here to that dig you're moving to."

"Not for another year, at least. Besides, Mickey can move with us."

Amarinta rolls her eyes. "A tent is no place for a boy to

live. No place for wife to live either, but we chose it when we married archaeologists. Mickey hasn't chosen anything, and he hates that place."

Calliope turns away and starts picking up the paper wrappings from her painting. "He does not."

"Well, he'd rather come back to Virginia and said so. Besides, that School is just the kind of sweatshop for smarty-pants kids that you and Neil think is *so* great."

"Minty, yes, it's an incredible school for intellectually gifted children. Why do always have to make that sound like it's a bad thing?"

Amarinta puts her finger under Calliope's chin and turns her head from the torn, discarded paper that she's taking the trouble to smooth and fold. "I'm not looking for a fight. I'm proud a place like that wants him so badly. More than anything, I know Mickey wants to go there."

Calliope grips Amarinta's hand, bringing her close.

"You know why, don't you? It's not just because Putnam is Putnam. He's hoping he'll find Ever. And I don't want him looking for a needle in a haystack. Especially since Ever's living with her father now. Minty, I don't like that man, and I don't want my son anywhere near him."

"Alright," Amarinta whispers. She kisses Calliope on the nose. "But you underestimate that boy."

Chapter 30

The Assassins
The Sahara, 1902

WE'VE SET UP CAMP under an endless sky in the throes of a twilight luminous with blood and citrus hues. It consists of one large tent, several small ones, a fire, and a makeshift pen for our animals, which include three goats, a half dozen chickens, and of course, our camels. With the exception of the two archaeologist friends of Howard Carter's, our caravan is made up of tradesmen, a few of them speaking a fair amount of English. Their fine wares wrapped in cotton and burlap, these men will travel on to Oea, after guiding us to the dunes we seek.

The archaeologists—Carter calls them a pair of rogues—are indeed quirky men with odd habits. One is a Frenchman, who has been having loud and obvious trysts with the lead tradesman's servant, as Frenchmen will do. He calls himself Degarmo. The other, a Turk named Mataraci, is an excitable sort, who will eat only eggs for reasons he has not articulated in any satisfactory way. He merely says, "Because they are perfect, and I love them," as if this should explain everything.

"More meat and bread for us," Cornelius pointed out.

These men are on their way to the Nubian pyramids, and will camp with us for a day or two once we reach our destination. Hopefully, we'll have enough eggs.

In our fortnight of travels, I find myself still of a troubled mind. We had a rough start of our journey to the dunes, one made up of distressing news and tender goodbyes. The news was about poor Mrs. Watson, and here I was thinking things couldn't possibly get worse. Edna's mother walked straight into the Cairo jail requesting an audience with the young man accused of murdering her daughter. Such an audience was foolishly, or perhaps cynically, granted. From what Lieutenant General Blackwood told us, she never even uttered a word to the one we know was innocent of the atrocities of which he was accused. She merely placed the barrel of her husband's pistol through the iron bars of the window to his cell and shot him dead, next turning the gun on herself.

So needless, all of it. This cast a most awful mood over our departure, one made worse by the fact that we were not entirely forthright about our plans to our respective fathers. Ripley, Cornelius, and I had agreed to tell Father and Dr. Davies that we were primarily headed to Oea to obtain some fine, second century pottery. A quick stop at a crescent of interesting dunes we'd told Maspero about, and off we would go. Our last dinner with them at the Shepheard, while fine and jovial and filled with wise advice about our travels, was tainted by our deception.

But it was a deception we feel was necessary. If the men knew the extent of the chase we're on, they would certainly do everything to stop us from going—especially Father. Can't say as I blame him. In the event I never see him again, I don't know I'll ever be able to forgive myself for leaving him with so much unsaid between us—especially since he will be the one suffering over unanswered questions. My only consolation is that he will have but a single life to ponder such things. I, on the other hand, may be thinking of them for eternity.

I look over at Ripley, who is in deep conversation with the

Turk, Mataraci. The latter is boiling some eggs over the fire for his supper. Cornelius lies on his back, chewing on a stick of salt-cured lamb and gazing up at the emerging stars. He turns his face to me and I am touched by him in a way that pierces my very soul. Like he is friend, brother, and angel to me all at once.

Seeking out a lesser scene to observe, I find one in Monsieur Degarmo, who is eyeing me with a lecherous gaze that he saves for when he knows Ripley cannot see him. I haven't shared this bit of news with my husband as we have greater things to worry about than a Frenchman's libido, and Ripley would certainly make it his problem. Apart from his natural possessiveness of me, as his wife, his concerns over my health are a constant plague on his mind. And despite doing my best to reassure him, he remains in a state of upset. So, a fight over a woman is the last thing we need. In this spirit, I simply shut M. Degarmo down with look of bored disgust, and am rather amazed that this seems to make him like me all the more. Men!

He pulls a small diary out of his back pocket and gives me a pointed look, before scribbling something in it. Degarmo then tears the piece of paper from the book, crumples it into a ball and tosses it into my lap.

I raise my eyebrow at him and shake my head, flicking it off me. Naturally, he does it again. I know I should probably continue to pay him no mind, but he isn't taking the hint. Plus, curiosity and the monotony of our expedition are getting the better of me tonight. I roll my eyes out of exasperation, pluck one of the crumpled papers out of the sand, and unravel it.

Your eyes beguile me, and I will look into them all the while as—

I crumple it back up immediately and pitch it to the desert floor.

"What's this?" Ripley asks, startling me. I didn't notice him approaching.

He bends down and picks up the discarded note.

"It's nothing," I say, making sure not to look at Degarmo, who I can hear chuckling under his breath.

"It can't be nothing if you look so angry."

I want to tell him everything about that filthy Frenchman, but instead, I bite down on my lip and shake my head. "We'll talk about it later."

My husband appraises me, then starts to open up the paper.

"Ripley, don't!" I say.

"Leila, I'm going to look at it."

And look at it he does, reading every brazen and tawdry word. Ripley's eyes widen, at first with shock, and then utter fury. He says not a word, simply whirling around and lunging at Degarmo, who appears genuinely surprised by his reaction.

"How dare you accost my wife in this way!" he roars in French.

Ripley pins the Frenchman to the desert floor and punches him hard on the cheek.

"Ripley!" I scream.

Degarmo flails his arms and legs like a beetle on its back, but in the end, all he can really do to defend himself is call my husband an impressive string of obscene names. It's when his lewdness extends to actually suggesting that I invited his lust, that Ripley hits him again, then again! The tradesmen gather round, on their faces a combination of excitement and satisfaction. Clearly, they think Degarmo is getting exactly what he deserves.

"Stop it this instant!" I bellow, but Ripley's rage only appears to be escalating.

He brings blow upon blow down upon the Frenchman's

head, as Degarmo tries to shield himself with his arms. But Ripley is too strong and determined.

Thank God for Cornelius, who comes up behind my husband, crushing him in a bear hug and dragging him off the whimpering Frenchman. I say a silent prayer of relief, as I was truly afraid he might kill Degarmo.

"Let me go!" Ripley growls, but Cornelius is not having it. "Now is not the time!"

"Why in the hell not?"

"Because," Cornelius says, straining, barely able to keep Ripley in his grip. "We've got company."

I look about and realize the traders have already dispersed. Their leader, a man named Saad, looks out into the desert eve, where a group of men on their camels is barely visible, backlit by the last pale glow of the departing sun, and a rising moon that is three quarters full.

Ripley extracts himself from Cornelius's grip, shooting one final look of warning at Degarmo. The Frenchman utters a short, punchy series of profanities and crawls to the other side of the fire, where his Turk colleague has sat peeling his boiled eggs, paying hardly any mind to our ruckus.

Cornelius retrieves Ripley's field glasses from his pack and looks out at our approaching visitors. He then hands the glasses over to Saad.

"Kubartu," he says.

"What on earth would they want with us?" Saad asks.

The pit in my stomach wonders the same.

Ripley takes the field glasses from Saad and has a look for himself. "Would you mind telling me what exactly Kubartu are?"

"They are a clan of musicians and executioners belonging to the Wadai," Cornelius explains.

"You can't be serious?"

"I'm afraid he is," Saad says. "They travel in groups of

nine, and it appears these men have at least as many slaves with them."

As the Kubartu come close, their apparent chief, heavily bearded and dressed in fine, red and black robes, comes forward. His eyes scan our camp. Ripley and Cornelius, in turn, scan him.

"Is there something we can offer you?" Saad asks him in Arabic. "Our rations are tight, but we always help our fellow travelers."

The Kubartu's face registers no understanding. He puts his hand to the grip of an iron-tipped cudgel at his waist, but does not pull it from his belt. "Degarmo," he says.

I try to glance casually about the camp, but see no sign of the French archaeologist.

The Kubartu chief signals two of his slaves, who boldly enter our domain and begin searching our tents. The rest of his men make a circle around us, and the tradesmen huddle together, whispering. Ripley's eyes search the perimeter, assessing our situation and our options. Cornelius stares down the chief in warning.

As I get a closer look at the men of this Kubartu clan, I see they wear a variety of weapons: two-edged swords, sheathed daggers, and iron lances, mostly. But all of them, quite prominently, wear the same particularly menacing iron-tipped cudgels at the ready. One of them, a thick, muscular sort with bulging eyes stares at me with a canine interest.

I look at Ripley and Cornelius again. Our African friend has the air of a caged leopard—dangerous, ready to pounce. My Ripley wears no expression at all, and stands with an unsettling calm about him. I wish I could be more composed, but a horrible sense of déjà vu has visited me. I wrap my arms about myself and say a small, silent prayer.

It does not take more than a minute for the Kubartu slaves to find Degarmo, who'd hidden himself in his tent, under blankets. They drag him out, as he curses them in French, and bring him before their master. Hardly a moment later, Mataraci, the Turk, is brought out from his hiding place in the big tent. He is pushed down onto his knees behind the Frenchman, who remains standing, facing the Kubartu who seeks him.

"Degarmo," the Kubartu says.

The Frenchman begins speaking in a Berber dialect. I am able to pick up a few words here and there; something about an insult to the Sultan.

The Kubartu leader listens, letting him say his piece. When Degarmo appears to have exhausted himself, the chief raises his hand in signal. The men surrounding us remove their packs, each of them taking out an instrument—string, percussion, flute. They begin to play an odd, eerie melody reminiscent of a dark fairytale—all high notes with a decidedly unfriendly drumbeat. Degarmo's eyes widen in alarm, his mouth opens, but before he can even make a sound, the Kubartu chief takes the iron-tipped cudgel from his waist and bears down on the man. He hits him square on the head with a sickening crack and I gasp, nearly crumbling to my knees.

"Ripley," I whisper, but my husband shushes me softly.

Quite suddenly, the men playing each begin to take their turns on the Frenchman. One by one, they set aside their instruments, striking him a single, horrible blow with their cudgels. The music dwindles this way, until only the clansman who's taken a particular notice of me is left, playing a slow, steady beat on his hand drum. Finally, he stops playing and places his instrument on the ground. He takes his eyes from mine for only the second it takes him to identify his mark, then he bears down. There is no doubt that Degarmo is dead, although I believe his death would have been sealed with only the chief's single and devastating strike. He lies in a pool of blood, his head barely recognizable, and I feel that I'm going to be sick.

Next, they push Degarmo's body to the side and take Mataraci by his arms, pulling him up to his feet before the Kubartu chief. The Turk begins to ramble, clearly begging for his life, trying to distance himself from whatever the Frenchman has done, but the chief appears indifferent to his appeals.

"Don't move," Ripley says, and everyone turns to him. My mouth falls open in relief, as I see he's holding a pistol, aimed right at the chief.

"If you lay a hand on that man, I'll shoot every one of you."

The Turk begins fervently translating, although it's quite clear that the clansmen understand. One of them rushes Ripley with his bloody cudgel nonetheless, and my husband fires the pistol with a cold confidence, felling him.

"Tell them I don't wish to kill them, but I will if they don't leave immediately. I have an eight round magazine with seven more bullets left, plus two very sharp daggers."

"They'll have to get through me, too," Cornelius says, although his pistol and knives are in his tent. He clenches his fists in fighting stance and Ripley tosses him a blade.

There is a deadly quiet that falls after Mataraci finishes this latest translation. Even the desert seems to go silent of air current, the scuttle of reptiles, and the cawing of night birds.

From behind me, there's a rush, and a moment after, a man's hand covers my mouth. I feel a knife at my throat.

"Let her go!" Ripley growls.

Four large clansmen surround me and my captor, making us invisible to my husband and Cornelius, though they stand only a few paces beyond us. Panic consumes me as my captor then drags me over to their chief, forcing me to my knees, next to the Turk, who has similarly been pushed to the ground. The men take out their instruments and resume playing again. Same terrible tune. My skin grows cold and my limbs stiffen with fright.

"Stop at once!" Ripley roars.

The Kubartu chief pays him no notice at all and firms up his grip on his cudgel. Behind us there's a shot, then another. I hear two men fall, but the Kubartu doesn't even flinch. He raises his weapon, a single-minded killer intent on performing his macabre deed. Ripley and Cornelius are calling to me, and my husband fires his pistol yet again.

I tear my eyes away from the Kubartu chief's awful pose, and search the men standing around us. I find the one who's been watching me, and see an odd look on his face, quite different from the looks of icy resolve on the others.

"Please," I cry out to him. I grab at the amulet dangling at my throat, touching the blood stone at the center. I pinch it between my fingers, hoping it'll give me an idea or, at the very least, courage and peace.

The man's eyes travel down to the necklace and he blinks very hard. His nostrils flare and his lips become a hard, thin line.

"Do you want it?" I say. "You can have it."

The man steps backwards, holding his arms out, as if in offering.

"Hun-dah-un!" He calls out.

My eyes dart back to the chief, who it seems my watcher was addressing. The Kubartu leader is still holding his cudgel high, but has paused—even if for just a moment.

My watcher speaks to his chief in a firm voice, spilling an aggressive medley of hard consonants. I only understand what I think are the words for "lady of life." He points at my neck, and the chief's eyes follow his direction, flickering back and forth between the charm and my insistent gaze.

"Tell him it was a gift," I say to Mataraci. "My husband's

father traded it with a desert tribeswoman long ago. It was a love token for his wife after she bore him a son."

I hope such a story will soften the man, but I worry that somehow this necklace might have belonged to someone he knows and that he might think we've stolen it.

Mataraci opens his mouth to begin translating, but before he can utter a single word, the Kubartu chief falls to the desert floor, lying prostrate before me. His men, even the slaves, immediately follow suit, leaving me and Mataraci kneeling at their center. Ripley, Cornelius, and the tradesmen become visible to us, standing outside of our bizarre configuration. My men are still holding their weapons, clearly as confused as to what is happening as I am. In a flood of relief, Ripley tosses Cornelius his pistol and rushes to me, whereupon I throw my arms around his neck. Cornelius points the gun's barrel at the Kubartu chief, who pays him no mind at all.

The tenor of this strange and wretched evening has changed with a horsewhip immediacy. The Kubartu remain at my feet, mumbling and chanting. Ripley remains at my side.

"What on earth are they saying?" I ask the Turk.

"They are praying to you, Madam."

I turn to Ripley, who shakes his head in puzzlement.

"Can you be more specific?"

Mataraci slumps down upon his heels, taking a handkerchief out of his pocket and wiping the sweat from his brow.

"The prayer is in worship, it appears—honoring you as a lady of life. I can't say as I understand what that means, exactly. And they also ask that you not destroy them with your . . . thought lightning? Something of that nature."

"Thought lightning," I repeat to myself.

"Please tell them that I would like them to get up and talk to me. If they are honest and answer my questions without hesitation, I will spare them my . . . thought lightning."

Mataraci does as I tell him, and the Kubartu stop their prayers. The chief sits up, but does not stand. He keeps his head lower than mine, out of respect for me, I assume, and will not make eye-contact with me now.

"Tell him I'd like them to tend to their dead and wounded. After they are finished, we will sit and talk."

THE KUBARTU are quite efficient in tending to their dead, wrapping them tightly in cloth and laying the bodies at the edge of camp. Even the Frenchman, Degarmo gets this treatment. They seem unsentimental about having lost two of their men, another two having taken injuries—a bullet to the arm and a graze to the neck that just missed his carotid artery. Those men are being tended by the medicine man among them; the one who also happens to have stopped his chief from killing Mataraci and myself, and who is responsible for the strange esteem in which I find myself being held.

Mataraci explains to Ripley, Cornelius, and me that the dead men will be taken to the highest point in the desert that is within a day's travel. Their faces will be exposed to the heavens, and they will be left to the elements. It is their way of honoring the dead, ensuring that they will be taken to the next world fully, if piece by piece.

No offence appears to be taken at Ripley for killing them. Mataraci tells us that, as executioners themselves, they have come to terms with death. Their own and that of others. And they hardly expect for a man or woman sentenced to death by Kubartu to go quietly. On the contrary, they are concerned that they have offended me, and by extension, other supernatural forces which could visit their sultan.

"Good," Ripley says.

When order has been restored, the Kubartu chief has his slaves bring foodstuffs from their supplies. They lay out a bounty of wine, flatbread, cheese, dried nuts, and meats for me, Ripley, Cornelius, and Mataraci to feast upon. A small offering of each is placed to the side, for the gods, I assume.

It is then the Kubartu chief bows his head to me. He sits, once again being sure to make himself appear lower, and closes his eyes. His men do the same.

"Ask him why he killed Degarmo."

Mataraci takes a deep, exhausted breath.

"Oh, I'm well aware," he says. "You see, they were sent by their sultan to kill him. And me, since Degarmo and I were travelling together, although I had nothing to do with any of his antics, I assure you. We thought we'd finally shaken them a good week before we entered Cairo."

"I assume Degarmo molested one of the sultan's wives?" Ripley offers.

Mataraci snickers and takes a bite of an egg.

"Not exactly," he says, through a full mouth. "Although, given time and opportunity, I wouldn't have put it past my dear colleague. No, Degarmo and I were in pursuit of some artifacts related to their local folklore, and he'd climbed Mt. Treya in search of a piece from a particular stone tablet. The mountain is off limits to all but the highest officials, you see, so this was a great insult to the sultan and one he couldn't ignore. Honestly, the sultan probably would have been more understanding if the Frenchman had interfered with one of his wives. In any case, he sent a band of his executioners to hunt us down, sentencing us to death by Kubartu, which I don't think I need to explain after what we witnessed tonight."

I try to dismiss the image of Degarmo's decimated skull.

"Do you have any idea why these men have taken such a peculiar interest in Leila?"

Mataraci shrugs and shakes his head. "I'll ask them, of

course, but my knowledge of their dialect is not as good as I'd like."

"I wish I spoke Berber," I say.

"Oh, it's not Berber, although the languages do share some vocabulary. It's a Tuareg language heavily influenced by what I can only identify as Numidian."

"Numidian," Cornelius says. "Numidian is extinct. Pre-Roman and scarcely attested."

"Not attested doesn't mean not existent," Mataraci tells us. "When the chief was lying down before Mrs. Davies here, he was reciting an ancient poem that has religious significance, especially amongst some of the more obscure desert tribes in their region. 'There is a wind in the desert that speaks of children. Ones here and ones we will make. One day, the desert again will be filled with our numbers. We will be as many as the tiny crystals that lie in these sands.'"

"Oh," I whisper, my own wind feeling as if it has been knocked straight out of me. It sounds like a verse from the song in my dreams, and the one from when I visited Mrs. Watson after Edna's murder. The song she sang in her quavering voice, with her eyes wide.

There is a wind in the desert that bellows; there is a wind in the desert that wails in anguish.

There is a wind that speaks of ghosts and memories; there is a wind that sings your funeral song.

Had the men around us actually sang it, instead of spoken it, I would have recognized the melody immediately.

"Are you alright?" Ripley asks me. I nod and clasp his hand.

"Mr. Mataraci, won't you please ask the chief what this song has to do with me?"

The Turk does as I ask, and the Kubartu chief opens his eyes, but will not look at me. He begins his explanation.

"It's the necklace you're wearing," Mataraci says. "The

symbol on it is inscribed above that poem anywhere you can find it. Mostly, it's been written in caves here and there, with that symbol etched or painted at its start. Maybe on an artifact or an old piece of stone. Ancient graffiti as it were. In any case, what I can tell you is that it's rather arcane."

"My father certainly doesn't know what it means," Ripley says.

"I, myself, have only seen the symbol once. In a cave painting in the dunes you've asked me to guide you to, as it happens. But I have heard other tribesmen, I mean besides the Kubartu, make a reference to such a poem and its symbols. It was once common lore amongst the desert tribes, I think, but lost relevance around the time the Egyptians rose. Some think it was a promise made by a goddess to the people of the desert long, long ago. And, of course, by the time the Egyptians came along, that promise had been fulfilled."

I take a deep breath at last, and put my head upon Ripley's shoulder, fingering the amulet he gave me. "I guess this necklace saved our lives."

"Not quite," Mataraci says.

"What do you mean?" Ripley asks him.

"Wasn't just the necklace, according to the chief here. It was your eyes, too. He said his grandmother had eyes much like yours, only they were blue. Then he used a word I'd never heard before. I have no idea what it means."

I look to the Kubartu chief, my eyes boring into his. I reach out and put my hand on his forearm, hearing gasps from the men around us.

"Nin'ti," I say.

Chapter 31

To the Dunes We Travel

THE KUBARTU call themselves "the nameless ones," as they must do their business in secret, dedicating their lives to death, taking pleasure only in the music they make, and their offerings to the gods. Sufian is the name of their chief and he and I are becoming something akin to friends, if one can even be friends with an assassin.

While I am treated by the clan as a visiting goddess, Ripley has practically become one of the Kubartu, held in special esteem by the chief. Ripley's eyes betrayed him as a Nin'ti, once Sufian got a good look at him, but that's not the sole reason why he's been elevated to such a role. It's not a position I have with them, after all. They revere me, yes, even fear me, although I can't for the life of me fathom why—Mataraci can't even seem to find the right words for their explanation of what my alleged "thought lightning" could be. But despite it all, this strange clan of men would hardly look to me for assistance in the desert. In making the sorts of judgments that will determine whether we eat or go hungry, for instance. Ripley, on the other hand, has become trusted, folded into their decision-making as if he has always been with them.

It's a good thing, too, as Saad and his tradesmen have moved on, no longer wishing to travel with us after what transpired. They were grateful we let them go, as I could have easily insisted they stay, and the Kubartu would have enforced my wishes. With Mataraci able to guide us to the dunes, however, and the Kubartu able to help us survive in the desert, we no longer needed them as traveling companions. We said our goodbyes and they could not get away from us fast enough.

Since then, we have fallen into a new routine. It has not been quite as comfortable traveling with the Kubartu, but it has been more efficient. These are desert survivors who are at home in the harshest of environments, and their ruthlessness brings with it a sense of security with which a caravan of tradesmen—no matter how seasoned in the Sahara—cannot compete.

We travel faster, leaner, stopping less frequently during the day. Our food supply is supplemented not by domesticated animals—except for the hens which were left behind by Saad to lay Mataraci's eggs—but by hunting everything from spiny reptiles to addax. They think nothing of eating beetles and other insects, but fortunately, we haven't had to stoop to such a diet. Only ten days into our travel with the Kubartu, we find ourselves within a week of the dunes.

Tonight, we settle around the fire, as we have nearly every night on our month-long journey. Nights with the Kubartu are surprisingly more pleasant than the evenings we spent with the tradesmen. They play music both before and after we eat, and are eager for conversation. Poor Mataraci must serve as our perpetual translator, but he appears to be deriving some satisfaction from his growing proficiency with this rare dialect. Cornelius, too, is keen to master it as best he can, at least stocking up on a decent vocabulary. Archaeologists are all the same in this regard, I've noticed. No matter how unlikely it is they'll ever again use some small, regional language, they feel compelled to master it nonetheless.

Just now, Cornelius is sitting at the outer edge of the fire, repeating the short phrases Mataraci has taught him.

"Askinwar ti-sek diwan-ah," he says, over and over, trying to get the intonations just right. Something about the making of porridge.

Ripley, despite being an archaeologist in training and lineage, feels no such compulsion. It is, in my observation, because he wasn't born for this work, like Cornelius and Mataraci. His calling is something else altogether. To always take the first step, even if he knows not where he's going, perhaps.

His merely transactional interest in learning this obscure desert tongue doesn't keep him from being able to understand and make himself understood. I love him more for the way the other men look to him as a man of consequence, for the burdens he's willing to bear without complaint. That of a young wife with a bad heart, a dear friend with a thirst for adventure that is bound to get him in trouble, that of life and death over others, if need be. I think of the clansmen he shot in defense of me. His first ever experience with meting out death, yet he did it with a steady hand, like he'd had to make such a split-second decision a thousand times before, and knew well what such a sequence of events would force him to bear in his soul.

"What are you looking at?" Ripley asks, taking a seat next to me. He's just come back from a short hunting run with Sufian, and I can still see the blood under his nails. My husband, it seems, is not only a good shot, but an ace with a simple bow and arrow.

"I'm looking at you," I say.

My watcher, a man I've learned is called Zishan, is drumming a soft, low beat, while another Kubartu, Yahya, twitters on his flute.

"Feels almost as if it's just for us," I say. "The music, the stars, the desert."

"It is," Ripley whispers.

He kisses me; a slow, deep kiss of love and marriage. The sort of kiss that makes me wish we could find a place to be truly alone.

"Anywhere else, I would feel scandalized by such a public display," I whisper, burrowing my fingers into his soft hair, made all the more golden by the unrelenting sun. "But here, now, it feels as natural as sinking into a bath."

Ripley chuckles. "Maybe it's being so far from civilization, or the fact that as de facto mythical creatures, we are awarded a certain latitude to behave in ways that are outside the social norms—ours and the Kubartu clansmen's."

"Mmm," I say. "Just like Sufian's grandmother—the one he claims was a Nin'ti, too. She had many strange habits and was indulged in them, despite being part of a tribe that held stringent, if not odd, beliefs on what is and isn't acceptable behavior. At least according to Mr. Mataraci's interpretations."

Ripley kisses my nose. "She did sound like quite a character. Almost as if she could have been a woman from your mother's family line."

"Hardly!" I say, then pull on Ripley's ear. "That woman seduced a much younger lover quite freely after the death of her husband, and had him live with her without the benefit of marriage. She then took over as midwife and medicine woman for their tribe, even if she had not been schooled a day in those functions. My mother would have never done the former, although she was quite capable of the latter, I admit."

I nestle into my husband's arms and we watch the fire dance. In its illusory flames, I try to imagine what this Nin'ti of the Wadai might have looked like. Her cheeks would be high and prominent, like Sufian's, I imagine. Her skin a polished onyx. But eyes bluer than a bluebell—crystalline.

Ripley and I find ourselves quite naturally fascinated by

Sufian's stories of this woman. Unlike Ripley and me, who had to uncover our extraordinary fate through our own dreams, intuitions, and experiences, Sufian's grandmother had the benefit of being born into a tribe with an institutional memory of the Nin'ti legend. From birth, her eyes had given her away, and her every dream was disseminated, deciphered, and debated amongst their elders.

Then one day, when Sufian was only a boy of eleven, his Nin'ti grandmother packed a small parcel and wandered off. She did not say where she was going or why she felt compelled to go, but before she left, she urged Sufian to become a nameless one.

"I cannot help but wonder if that grandmother didn't dream about us," I say.

"About you and me?"

"Perhaps she knew, or at least dreamt, that if Sufian set off with this band of executioners, he would meet us eventually, perhaps play a role in our destiny."

Sufian sits down with us, and I feel overheard, even if I know he can't understand what we're saying. He brings with him some water and wine, plus a rather delicious block of cheese wrapped in fermented leaves, and some dried fruit and jerky. Cornelius, always hungry, notices the bounty, and manages to tear himself away from Mataraci, who has been captivating him not only with language lessons, but histories of the relics he has extracted from the ground, the water, and the hands of unscrupulous scoundrels.

He joins us, and the Turk follows; a satchel of boiled eggs is tossed into his lap by Zishan. When they have settled in, Sufian begins to speak, slapping Mataraci's back in a crude signal to start translating. He does this all the time, treating the Turk as if his sole purpose in life is providing a line of communication between the Kubartu and their Nin'ti honoraries.

"The chief says we will reach the dunes in three days' time," Mataraci tells us.

Ripley and I both communicate that this is good. The excitement and trepidation I feel at this prospect settles in my stomach, making it difficult for me to eat, even if I am quite hungry. Part of it is not knowing what it is that awaits us there—either in evidence about our past, or in the potential of crossing paths once again with the murderous devil who appears to share our quest in some way. The other part is the exhilaration of what those dunes might mean for our future. I admit that in my hope of hopes, I wonder if there mightn't be a way that my heart could be healed and Ripley and I could live as man and wife for a full lifetime. One made of love and children and impossible undertakings.

"He also wants me to tell you that he will stay with you in the dunes, and accompany you to Oea when you are ready, making sure you arrive safely. The rest of the nameless ones must continue to Faya, to retrieve the body of a clansman's brother and return him to Kanem. He apologizes that they cannot wait, but their journey will be long, as they must travel around what he calls 'cursed mountains,' in order to reach their destination."

"Cursed mountains," Ripley says. He shoots me a look. "Ask him to which range he is referring."

As Mataraci translates, I take several generous sips of the wine. A feeling of profound foreboding visits me, and I wrap myself in a woolen shawl, although the sun has barely set, and it is not yet even cool.

"He says they are some ways to the south of us," Mataraci begins. "They call the mountains cursed because they're thought to be haunted. Black and craggy, made of sand and bone, he says. The black bones of demons."

My heart starts to thunder. I take Ripley's hand, squeezing it hard.

"I'm sure those are just legends," Ripley murmurs.

"He says a couple went into those mountains some months ago, as their caravan waited in the foothills."

"The Hugheses," I gasp, and Ripley brings me closer.

Mataraci raises an eyebrow. "Whoever they were, they made it out, and the caravan made ready to move on to Faya. But that's when the story grows mysterious. Only one from the caravan—the guide our friend here mentioned—ever made it back. He claimed they all became possessed by demons and their flesh rotted off their bones while they were still alive. He was the only one the demons left alone."

"Good God," Cornelius says. "That must be the wretched soul who brought back the artifact. The breastplate with the snake!"

"I thought the Hugheses sent it."

Ripley shakes his head. "They found it, certainly, but they never actually sent it, as they never returned from the desert."

I sit up, extracting myself from Ripley's arms. I turn towards him and sit on my heels.

"Yet they took the time to engrave it with my mother's poem, and insist it be sent back to Cairo."

Ripley takes a deep breath made of more ghastly news. "It was a French officer who found it amongst the things this Kubartu relative, who was behaving like a raving lunatic apparently, had brought with him from the desert. It was assumed he'd stolen it from the Hugheses and murdered them." Ripley swallows hard, and nods in sympathy to Sufian. "He was quickly executed for his alleged crime."

"Father never mentioned any of this," I say.

Ripley finds my gaze again. "It's all terribly upsetting and I know how much you loved them. Leila, I asked him not to tell you."

If I were on my feet, I would certainly fall to the ground. Part of me wants to roll into a ball and weep, while another

part wants to scream—to hold my hand, the one that burns
in the palm, over the fire until my skin blisters and blackens.

"We have to go find them," I say. "Mr. Mataraci, tell Sufian
we must go to these mountains and try to rescue our friends!"

"No!" Ripley says. "Leila, the Hugheses are dead. Even
if they were alive and marooned by their guide, that was
months ago. Months of living alone, with hardly any way to
survive."

"But we don't know that! Not for sure. Good God, Ripley,
this is Aunt Clara and Uncle Hugo!"

Ripley runs his hand through his hair. "Mr. Mataraci," he
says. "Ask Sufian if this clansman's brother, the one whose
body they seek to claim, would have left a British couple
alone in the desert. When he had been charged as their guide
by order of their sultan."

The Turk does as Ripley asked, and Sufian answers, his
voice grave and certain. He speaks as if to me, directly.

"He says once a man is bound in honor by their sultan, he
is bound until death. Not even demons could drive him away
from his duty. If this dead relative said the Hugheses rotted
off their bones, then their bones and nothing else lie scattered
in the sands of those mountains."

"My darling," Ripley says. "I'm so very sorry. You should
know your father did everything he could for them, and if
there was even a speck of dust that could serve as hope they
were still alive, he would have pursued it."

"I know what they meant to you," Cornelius says. "But
the dunes mean something as well, and we must go there.
For Edna and Mohammad, for you and Ripley. Maybe for
all of mankind."

Ripley takes my face in his hands. "If we find the answers
we hope for in the dunes, a place your own mother, from
beyond the grave, told you to go—or even if we don't—I
promise I will take you to those mountains myself. I will

search every corner of them until the Hugheses are found. One way or another, we'll bring them home."

The tears come now, flowing freely down my face. I nod to Ripley, then Cornelius. I know what we must do. I know we must, first and foremost, go to the dunes, but the thought of Clara and Hugo out there, alone, even if they're dead, is almost too horrible to bear.

"You should have told me," I whisper. "You should have told me."

IT'S A DAMN COLD NIGHT. Not so cold that it's the kind of night even Alaskans won't venture out in, but cold enough. I still haven't gotten used to the perpetual arctic chill in the air here and never will. Because it's not just cold in the winter here, when it's actually freezing. It's cold in the spring and the fall, and just barely not cold in the summer. Nice walking weather in July, sure, but never the kind of heat that makes you want to run through a sprinkler.

It's amazing that the old wood-burning stove Hunter fixed up keeps the whole downstairs of the cabin warm without us even having to turn on the heat. But then, it's one of those hundred-year-old numbers he found discarded on a porch deep in the mountains of Virginia. All cast iron with chrome accents and a copper crown at the top, it looks like a work of art, but heats like a sun. I guess back then, when all you had to heat your home was a single potbelly stove, it'd better work. You best be able to boil water on it or fry an egg—dry your laundry next to it.

The door swings open and the polar air barges right in, along with Hunter, who's shaking off the snow.

"Spring storms," he grumbles. He strips down to a t-shirt and jeans, even taking off his flannel shirt. If I weren't around, he'd probably walk around naked.

"Not quite spring yet," I say. "Made some smoked salmon chowder." That's basically Alaskan chili.

I get up and serve us both a bowl, along with a slice of some homemade sourdough bread Lottie's mother gave us. I think she's sweet on Hunter, even if she's a good ten years older. But they're the only single parents in our homeschool cooperative. By single, I mean unattached. Seems hardly anyone is married to the actual father, or in my case, mother, of their children anymore. Except for the Christians. Marriage is just one more of those things that used to be for everyone, but is becoming just for rich people.

I bring the bowls by the hot stove and plop down on a big, fat throw pillow that's almost like a bean bag chair. Lottie's mom made that for us, too. Hunter sits in a wood and leather rocker he made.

"You finish your homework?"

"Always do."

There's a long silence as we eat, which I'm grateful for. When Hunter finishes his chowder, he thanks me, saying it was really good. I'm only half-way done, so he starts rocking in his rocker in that way he does when he's taking pride in something he's built himself. It gets on my nerves.

I mean, I know there's nothing wrong with that. He's an ace builder, and the rocker is styled and handsome. Something he'd charge one of his fancy customers six grand for.

Kind of like our cabin. If it weren't in the middle of nowhere, like in one of the nice neighborhoods in Anchorage, it would be worth a small fortune.

"I was thinking of volunteering at that new drug and alcohol rehab center that's opening up late spring."

Hunter raises up an eyebrow and stops his rocking.

"Volunteering," he says. "That's just working without getting paid right?"

I shrug at him.

"And what kind of volunteering do you plan to be doing at the junkie resort?"

"Aren't you a junkie?" Probably shouldn't have said that.

"I was."

"Mom said those programs tell you that once you become addicted to drugs, you'll always be an addict."

"That's what they say." Hunter shrugs back at me in that one shoulder way of his. "I guess it was true of your mother."

Normally, he says things like that in a purely matter-of-fact way, but this time it's a little like he said that just to twist the knife. Or maybe get back at me for calling him a junkie. Hunter feels he's cured, and that there's nothing that would make him start using again. Nothing a million miles or a million years from here. Mom was never so sure. Whenever the topic of her falling off the wagon would come up, she'd say, "Oh, I hope not. I sure don't want to, Sugar. I need to be here for you. Especially now." By "now" she meant, after we no longer had Granny Dora around.

"You want some more bread?" I ask him. As I reach for the loaf, my sleeve inches up and I watch Hunter's eyes shoot to the fresh cuts on my wrist.

In a snap he goes from being all calm and objective to grabbing my wrist and yanking it so hard that the bread falls out of my hand and I fall off my pillow, going splat on the floor. He startles me so bad I start to shake. Because, for a moment, I see that strange, dangerous part of him that he hides behind acting the fine-looking, quiet type. The part of him Granny Dora saw from the start, but mom overlooked on account of being so in love with him.

"What the hell is this?" he snarls. "I thought you quit doing this back in Virginia. You promised, Ever!"

"I'm sorry . . . I just."

"You 'just' what?"

"It's the only thing that helps me stand it!"

And that's that. The tears start to flow and flow! I hate this!

Hunter gives a "huh" and "ha," nodding to no one in particular, just some invisible force that appears to sympathize with him about what an ungrateful bitch I am. He lets go of my arm and I sit up, scooching back onto the pillow. There's so much salty water on my face that I can't just wipe it with my hands, but have to use my whole arm.

"Can't stand it, huh? Can't stand living in a nice home with good food on the table?" he says. "Instead of a banged up trailer with rusty water and a bathroom that stinks in the summer months?"

"Or living in a nice house in Cairo with people who actually care about me!"

Now I feel terrible all of a sudden. My throat gets sticky and my eyes start to dry. Because I do know that, in his own way, my father cares about me. He spent all that time getting his life together so he could go back and be with me and my mom. And I know in my rational mind it's not his fault Mom had a relapse and did herself in. Somehow it feels like it, though.

"You know, I spent two years apprenticing in Chicago, building stuff for rich assholes practically for free while I learned how to do all this, and do it right."

Oh, God, here we go again. How he moved back to a city he hates, that he and his mother ran away from when he was just a kid my age.

"I bartended nights to pay for a crap basement apartment in an even crappier neighborhood so I could do that, Ever. Got real skills that paid for a good piece of land and fine materials that someone with a lot more money than we got would want for themselves." He leans in, elbows on knees, and looks hard at me with those eyes of his seeming to glow as hot as the embers in our stove.

I bite my lip and squeeze my eyes shut so hard my head hurts. Chicago makes me think of Mickey, whose dad grew up there. And how his grandmother made the best, most buttery lemon bars.

"I just don't understand why we had to move all the way here, and not talk to anyone anymore!" I say that to Hunter, but I'm also asking God. "I keep waiting for it to get better."

Hunter gets up from the rocker and goes to the kitchen, taking his empty bowl and spoon with him. I hear them clang into the sink. He comes back to the living room all calm and collected, at least on the outside. But on the inside, I know there's a storm raging.

"Those people wanted to take you away from me."

"Not away from you—just to be with them. I wanted to go!"

He shakes his head like I'm the most ignorant creature alive.

"You're my daughter, Ever. You don't just get to go wherever you want just because you want it."

"I guess that's a privilege reserved only for you!"

"You're damn right it is!"

"Why? Because you started acting like an adult five minutes ago? Where were you when Mom had to lock me up in a closet with a dog bed and a bag of chips for dinner because she had to work and our front door lock was busted? Where were you after Granny Dora died and we couldn't afford a Thanksgiving turkey?"

"Well, you can afford one now, and with all the trimmings! I don't suppose that matters to you, though, does it? Matters to me. I was lucky to get a peanut butter and jelly sandwich on Thanksgiving when I was growing up, and I wasn't going to raise a daughter the same way! I waited until I'd made something of myself to come back for you!"

I jump up from the pillow, kicking my almost done bowl of chowder aside on accident. Although it probably looks like I did it on purpose and I don't care. I run upstairs, missing my mom even more than I missed her right after she died. When everything was still raw and hopeless and I couldn't believe I wasn't ever going to see her again.

And no, Mom didn't have a nice home like this for me, but things had been getting better. If she hadn't relapsed they would've kept on getting better, whether Hunter stuck around or not. And Mom always understood what the Nevilles meant to me. That it wasn't just about the fact that they had a nice house and traveled the world, and wanted to make me a part of that. It was that I *was* a part of that. I knew it and felt it in every part of my being, and Mom and Granny Dora knew it, too. Even if they didn't understand it. *I* didn't even understand it. Why it never felt weird despite the fact that I was nothing like them at first glance. I wasn't rich, I wasn't black or Jewish, and I probably would have never known who Margaret Mead or Howard Carter or Joseph Campbell was if I'd never met them. But I was one of them from the day Mickey and I were born—on the same day, in the same hospital. And they knew it, too.

IF THERE'S ONE THING I've got to give Hunter, it's that he knows when to back off. He didn't come upstairs after our fight, he just listened to his true crime program on the radio and drank the one beer he allows himself. He's not supposed to drink at all, even though drink, specifically, wasn't really his problem. But he likes to have one beer a day just to prove to himself that he can, and so far, he hasn't ever had more than one. At least from what I've seen. I'll give him that, too.

Around eleven, things go silent in the house and I hear the soft thump of Hunter's panther step on the stairs, then his door closing. By eleven-thirty, I'm at "midnight run."

That's just a small clearing on the banks of the Eagle River, but it's where kids around here go to do all the things Hunter used to do: drink, drugs, and fornication galore. Tonight, there's a group of fourteen to twenty-twos all standing around a bonfire like a bunch of homeless people under a bridge. I only recognize Grace, Lottie's older sister by a year, and she waves me over and hands me a beer.

I take a fake sip, listening to some junior, introduced to me as Will Yazzie, tell a story about his dad getting a grizzly bear high on edibles. I'm fast starting to think this is all going to go nowhere, but then I hear a whoop and guffaw. Everyone seems to perk up, and I turn around to see what they're all looking at. It's Rick Johnson. I should've known.

"Wisconsin!" Yazzie calls out. Most everyone calls Rick Johnson Wisconsin Johnson on account of his grandfather being born in Wisconsin. The fact that it rhymes is an added bonus.

But Wisconsin's okay. He's got one helluva handsome, boyish face and he's almost charming in that way that guys who aren't very smart but who know how to flirt can be charming. And he's been flirting with me ever since my breasts came in.

"If it isn't the green-eyed monster," he says, giving me a wink.

"Hey, Wisconsin. You been working out?"

I'm actually a terrible flirt, but I watched my mom do it to her customers all the time and she got the biggest tips when she complimented them in the form of a question—like she noticed something they did to improve themselves, and gave them the opportunity to tell her all about it.

"Yeah," he says. "I've been upping my game."

I put my hand on my hip and nod the way my mom would have, like I'm saying, *yup, it shows.* And yup, he likes that alright.

"To self-improvement," Yazzie says, and throws Wisconsin a beer. He catches it one-handed, then holds up his other hand. Yazzie throws him a second beer, which he catches *no problemo*, too.

Wisconsin offers me one of his beers, but I pretend like I just got the one in my hand, although I've been nursing it since the last ice age.

He chugs his first in about three gulps, crushes the can, and tosses it in a trash bin that Will Yazzie set up. Even Eagle River's minor juvenile delinquents don't want to trash our pristine natural environment. Then he opens the second and drinks it down by half. He kind of giggles at me, and it actually works on him, but only because he's big and good looking. Otherwise he'd come off like a derp.

I smile and run my fingers through my hair, then sit down on a log just a few feet away from the group. Wisconsin follows me. Grace shoots me a look like *what are you doing?* But it's not like she even cares enough to tell Lottie, and it's not like Lottie would care at all. She'd think it was funny.

On the log, Wisconsin and I talk about public high school, which he started attending just this year, and how much he hates it.

"Some of the people are cool, though," he says, raising his beer can in salute to the tribe of overall disappointments to their mothers that frequent "midnight run." "And the work is way easier than in the co-op. Way more boring, too, and they make us do homework."

He makes like he's sticking his finger down his throat.

"Sounds like it sucks," I say, and we find ourselves totally out of conversation. I mean it's not like he's the type who'd want to discuss the book I'm reading about the evolution of Egyptian Hieroglyphs. Come to think of it, no one around here is that type.

"Hey, you want to walk with me? I don't like to go alone."

And Wisconsin says sure, unlatching the flashlight from his belt and clicking it on. He puts it under his chin and says, "Mwaaaah-ah-ah-ah," like one of those electronic grim reapers that greet you at any self-respecting haunted house.

I feign a proper damsel-in-distress gasp, and he says, "Yeah, right." Then he takes my hand, which I let go limp in his grasp.

We crunch along the bank, which is crusted with slushy ice, and make our way around the curve and into a group of sloping trees. The water burbles gently and I can hear fish breaking the surface and splashing around.

Wisconsin keeps trying to make conversation, which is nice. He tells me he'll be a featured artist in a chainsaw carving demo this summer at the Bear Paw Festival and that he can't decide between doing a *Day of the Dead* type skull, which is his signature design, or a salmon-tailed mermaid, which he thinks would be a big crowd pleaser. I tell him definitely the skull.

"Maybe I'll throw my hat in for the beauty pageant," I tell him. "I think Miss Bear Paw has a nice ring to it."

"No way!"

I laugh and punch his arm. "Yes, no way. I wouldn't be caught dead."

Wisconsin sort of smirks and we go quiet for a minute.

"I think you'd win."

"Hmm?"

"I said I think you'd win. The Bear Paw Beauty Pageant. And by a long shot."

Wisconsin sort of looks down before meeting my gaze again. He laughs a little nervously, but he keeps looking.

My heart is beating so loud and hard that I can practically hear it over the river sounds. I figure this is my chance, but I don't really know how to do this. The only boy I ever think about is Mickey, so I tend to treat the guys I know in the co-op like buddies. I decide to go for the direct approach.

"Um. You want to make out?" I whisper.

Wisconsin looks surprised I said that, so now I start to wonder if I didn't blow it by being too forward. I mean, he probably wanted to do the asking, but he was taking too long and I can't be out all night. And if Hunter gets up to use the bathroom, he'll check on me, I just know it.

"Yeah," Wisconsin finally says. "Yeah, I do."

THE MORNING is dark and cloudy, like a storm is coming, so I have to turn on a lamp to get a good look at myself in my vanity. Not a wink of sleep, and it shows.

Making out with Wisconsin was weird. Like it wasn't really me doing it. It was doubly weird because it was my first kiss and this wasn't exactly what I'd been hoping my first kiss would be. Or who it would be with. But it was practical and I got out of it exactly what I needed.

I hold my hair up and scrutinize the four perfect hickeys on my neck, plus the half of one on that soft space just where my shoulder begins. When Wisconsin started that one, I'd had enough. Plus, I didn't want to give him the wrong idea— like that he could go anywhere beyond my neck. So, I pushed him away.

I didn't think I did it hard, but Wisconsin fell to the ground like he'd tripped over something creepy, like a big vole. His body seized up and his back arched in a way that looked wrong and really uncomfortable.

"What did you go and do that for?" he said, panting like he'd run a mile.

"I just wanted you to stop, okay?"

"Man," he said, still kind of shaking. "You didn't have to tase me. You could've just said stop, you know, I'm not an animal—I know what *no* means."

"No, I mean, I didn't." I take a breath and do a big face-palm. "Look, it was an accident, whatever it was. I don't even own a taser. Maybe you landed on something and it bit you."

Wisconsin shakes his head and gets up, giving himself a once-over and brushing the dirt off his jeans. "Nothing bit me."

It was quiet between us for a couple of minutes as we started ambling back towards the group, but it didn't stay weird for very long after that. Wisconsin doesn't hold grudges, being so damned good natured. He even gave me his jacket to wear and told me to return it "next time."

"Hey, you want to go off-roading this weekend?" he asked me, but I told him I had a feeling my dad wasn't going to let me go anywhere for a while.

We'll see.

I go to my wardrobe and pull out a scoop neck sweater that I usually reserve for late in the spring, when the days are warmer. Then I tie my hair up in a scrunchie. This way Hunter can see just how good Alaska is for me. That there's little to do around here but learn how to drink and screw. Even some of the uber-Christian off-the-gridder kids have lost their virginity. Lottie lost it last summer in a snow bank, which is about the most Alaskan way a girl can lose it.

I swear there are times I think I'm the only virgin I know.

I look back in the mirror and tuck a stray lock of hair behind my ear. Then I put on the jacket Rick—Wisconsin—gave me a few hours ago. Hunter will sure as hell recognize it's not mine and that it so obviously belongs to a boy. And one considerably larger than me. Plus, it says "Rick" in cursive on the lapel, and "JOHNSON" on the back in big, block letters.

I stuff my hands in the pockets and my knuckles crunch

into a paper box. There's a pack of Spirits with three cigarettes left in it, and a box of matches from the Buckshot Pub. I stare at them for a few moments, then pull out a smoke, lighting it without inhaling.

The taste of the smoke is one part gross and one part interesting. Like smoke from a rain-soaked campfire. I watch the red-hot tip glow like iron in a fire.

The palm of my left hand starts to feel warm and I open it up. The center of it looks like it does every other day, but the longer I look at it, the more it starts to burn. I hate it and love it—that feeling. Depends on the day. But right now, I love it, because I haven't felt it in a long time. I take a deep, deep breath and roll the cigarette lightly between my thumb and index finger.

"Mickey," I whisper.

Then I smash the lit end of the cig right into my palm, hearing a strange, wet hiss as it goes out. "Ah." I bite down so as not to make any more noise about it. Damn, it does hurt, but not as much as I thought it would. The pain, the smell of my burnt skin. Something about it feels like home. Feels like Mickey. For a minute there, it's like he's right next to me, and I could turn to him and ask him to hold me. But I don't, and he's not. Instead, I let out a hot breath and I start down the stairs.

Chapter 32

Ghosts of Past and Present
The Central Sahara, 1902

A T LAST we come to the rock dunes. Dunes made of the past—perhaps ours. The dunes of my mother's ghost, and of Ripley's dreams. And mine. They are a few stories tall, maybe four or five, and much like a honeycomb. Red as clay in parts, and yellow like the coat of a lion in others. They are ugly and desolate and beautiful all at once. And feel so very old as to be nearly forgotten. Ripley tells me they were much taller once, many thousands of years ago, but the sand on the desert floor has shifted, likely from a preponderance of sand storms.

"There are more over there," Mataraci says, pointing north to a series of dunes shaped like a crescent. Those are low and have the look of ancient decrepitude.

"No, not those," Ripley says.

He looks up, his eyes meeting the opening of a cave at about the mid-way point to the top of the rock shelf. Its opening is shaped like a pair of hands in prayer.

"Up there," he tells us, and I feel a shiver take me over. A feeling of recall so strong that I have to look away and get busy.

The Kubartu, ever efficient, begin to unload the camels and set up camp at the base of the dunes, and I make sure to be useful. I get the makings of a proper fire assembled and sort through our rations.

Ripley and Sufian get their heads together, while Cornelius runs about exploring our surroundings with the exuberance of a boy.

Once the fire is good and hot, I set water on it to boil. We last filled our water pouches at a well about two days past, and we're running quite low. But both Ripley and Sufian appear confident that we'll be able to find some in this cave structure. Tonight, we shall likely camp outside, as we have every night of our journey, and though I love to look up at the stars, I would like us to find a suitable cave to settle in if we're to be here for a number of days. I feel hope bloom in my chest as Ripley and Cornelius go off to explore the dune formations, several unlit torches tucked into their back pockets. They climb up the dune face and disappear into the cave shaped like a prayer.

"Most of the Kubartu will leave at dawn." Mataraci comes up behind me and ladles some of the hot water into a vessel filled with tea leaves.

"So soon?" I say. "Don't they wish to stay for a few days—just to conserve their strength before their next long journey?"

Mataraci shakes his head. "Do they look as if they need to conserve their strength?"

I glance about at these dangerous, industrious men and must concede that they don't look in the least bit the worse for the wear.

"They are quite eager to take charge of the remains of their clansman's brother," Mataraci says. "For how cavalier they appear to be about death, they take caring for the corpses of the dead rather seriously."

"Perhaps it brings meaning to what they do. Like the way a huntsman might field dress an animal with a certain flare for ritual?"

Mataraci takes an egg from his pouch and peels it. "There's no meaning in what they do. You saw how they finished Degarmo. For what, trespassing? Not on a home, but a mountain that belongs to everyone. He stole nothing that belonged to them or their sultan, yet they turned his head into pudding."

"I'm sorry," I say. "I know he was your friend."

"Degarmo?" Mataraci stuffs his egg into his mouth. "Degarmo was a royal pain, but there was never a dull moment with him, you know?"

I sit on the sandy desert floor and lean against a good-sized rock. Mataraci joins me, but he's no longer interested in conversation. He just prefers my company to that of the Kubartu when Ripley and Cornelius aren't around.

I stare up at the cave where my husband and our friend disappeared and find myself longing for so many things at once. For them to return, for an early dinner, for my mother's laugh and my father's whiskers. For Clara and Hugo and Mohammad and Edna. For sleep. At least that comes.

I'M AWAKENED by a kiss. Groggy, with a crick in my neck, I look up into my husband's face. The glow of the moon surrounds his head, like a halo, and it must be very late or very early.

"Shhh," Ripley says, kissing me again. "I want to show you something."

As I get up and stretch, Ripley tip-toes around the camp-site. A discordant symphony of Kubartu snoring covers the pitter of sounds that accompany lighting a lantern and filling a sack with sundry provisions. I realize I fell asleep without eating supper, and my stomach growls audibly.

Ripley beckons me to follow him and we tread carefully around a debris field of various rocks. Ripley takes my hand and holds up the lantern as we begin to climb the dune face. It's not much of a difficult climb, even in the dark. With the moonlight and the gaslight, it's easy to see the shelf of stone leading up into the caves. One cave in particular is our destination—the prayer cave. Ripley sets the lantern down on the shelf at the base of that grotto and boosts me up and in.

"My God," I say, as I lift up the lantern.

The ceiling is high—very high, like a cathedral's—and everywhere I look I see a twinkling spread of crystals covering the cave walls. They even speckle a series of smooth, giant boulders that protrude from the shimmering rock surfaces, looking almost like sculpture.

Ripley comes up behind me, taking the lantern from my hands, and assuming the lead. "Wait until you see what's deeper in."

As we head towards the throat of the hollow, the interior landscape changes abruptly. Stalactites and stalagmites, all twisted in serpentine shapes, come at us from every which way. They're quite beautiful, making the cavern look as if it's alive and in motion. I reach out to touch one of them and immediately slice my finger, feeling the blood rush down onto my palm. Ripley holds up the lantern to get a good look.

"It's not bad," he says, then takes my finger into his mouth to clean the wound. It stings a bit, but feels warm and good and carnal all at once. My breath hitches, and Ripley looks up at me, taking my finger from his mouth.

"Not yet," he whispers.

Ripley hands me the lantern and bends down, picking me up, and holding me close to his chest. He's warm and heavenly.

"It's a bit tricky from here," he says.

I hold the light out in front of us, but it seems he hardly needs it at all. It's as if he knows this place, its every curve and passage, its every dead end. I rest my head against him, breathing in the cold, mineral smells mixed in with the damp, bittersweet scent of Ripley. Ones imbued with the burnt nut odor of desert travel.

The scent of the air changes when we come upon a sort of room off the passageway. It's fresher, milder in here. He sets me down on a smooth slab of rock and takes the lantern from my hands.

"Look at this." He holds up the light to a wall utterly surfaced with brightly painted scenes. Of a people that are many, but then die off somehow, of battle and hunts, celebrations and offerings—to the gods, I imagine. It shows a people who lived here, and ultimately, shows those people preparing to leave.

"Do you think this was us?" I ask Ripley.

"Yes," he says. "Look up here."

My hand goes immediately to my necklace. At the top of the painting is the exact symbol etched upon it—the circles looped together, with the red stone in the center. "Oh, Ripley."

We stare at the cave paintings for some time, enthralled. Their intricacy and realism, the hope and pain they convey, their strength and resilience. I cannot help but take pride in them. To think that we, Ripley and I, could have been one of these people. That we may have painted these very scenes to let others know of our plight, and give our existence some permanence and meaning.

Ripley feels the shiver move through me, and nuzzles me, moving my hair aside and kissing my neck. Sweetly, at first. Just as a way to touch me while we absorb what this place could mean for us. But it's been too long since we've been skin on skin, and a simple, single kiss in the dark becomes many kisses, warm and wet. Hands running over each other's bodies, under our clothes. Low, deep breaths come faster and faster, and our passion loses all tenderness.

Ripley lays me down on the flat slab of stone. He is patterned in shadows from the gaslight and I watch him the whole time. We are old, animal, ancient together. We are the wild wind of the storm in my dreams—tearing at one another, making to possess each other whole.

As Ripley and I begin our return to camp, I cannot help but feel that we're being watched. Ridiculous, as the sun hasn't even peeked a tiny bit over the horizon, and the caves are as quiet as a chapel. Still, it's a feeling even more prevalent than when we were in Thebes months ago and felt we were being stalked.

The warnings of getting here before *he* does, whoever *he* really is, must have something to do with my suspicions, and I calmly remind myself that these dunes were as empty, when we arrived, as the many tombs Howard Carter and his ilk have uncovered in the Valley of the Kings. No litter from a previous camp, no evidence of an arrival of anyone other than ourselves. Not to mention that we are, quite literally, in the middle of a vast, merciless desert. I want to ask Ripley if he has felt the same inklings as I have, but change my mind when I glimpse his face. He smiles at me with all the tenderness he shed back in the cave of paintings, and my heart beats faster, grows warmer with his attention.

As we approach camp, however, we must once again put away our stolen newlywed pleasures. Sufian is up, although it is still pitch dark, and has already made plenty of tea. The rest of the Kubartu are quietly packing up camp. Only Cornelius is the same—curled up near the fire and asleep, oblivious to the rest of us.

Ripley gestures to Sufian, communicating with him in that way that seems to work for him just fine, and the Kubartu chief returns his question with a series of gestures and single words. Ripley asks Sufian about Mataraci, who is nowhere in sight, but the man seems to have no idea where the archaeologist has disappeared to. His eggs and his things are still here, so perhaps he was having a difficult time sleeping and went for a walk.

"Good grief," Cornelius grunts. "Can you keep it down? It's the middle of the night."

"It's just before morning, actually, and you had no problem sleeping through Sufian and his clan clanging about. But here we whisper a few words and now you're up all of a sudden?" Ripley says.

Cornelius looks about and moans.

"Do you know where Mataraci went?"

Cornelius scratches his head and sniffs hard. "How would I know that when I've been asleep?"

A mad rush of embarrassment and fury hits me as I wonder if it mightn't have been Mataraci's eyes that I felt upon me and Ripley. Although he has not exhibited the same lecherous qualities that his late companion did, I wouldn't put it past him to intrude upon a young couple's privacy either. As outraged as I am at the prospect of such lewd behavior on the part of our Turkish fellow traveler, part of me feels a bit of relief, too. Better that it be Mataraci.

Sufian barks a series of phrases—without even his hand gestures this time—and Cornelius stands up to stretch.

"Didn't quite catch that," I say.

Cornelius yawns and rubs his eyes. "I think he wants Ripley to go hunting with him."

"Again?"

Ripley is already packing up the bow and arrow the chief gave him, and stuffs our full sack of provisions—the ones we didn't touch, as we were otherwise engaged—into their hunting pouch.

"Leila, we're out of meat," Cornelius says. "I don't know about you, but if I have to eat another piece of jerky I'll lose my will to live."

Chapter 33

Spirits and Demons

WHILE I WAS not happy to see Ripley go off with Sufian, and, unlike Cornelius, would prefer a meal of jerky and nuts to some roasted reptile, I do find myself craving an hour's peace. With Cornelius having taken the lantern and gone to have a look at the cave paintings Ripley discovered, the Kubartu busy getting ready for their departure, and Mataraci still wandering about the dunes somewhere, I have it.

The sky is blue and blank, the air as still as a crocodile on the bank of the Nile. It is an eerily beautiful morning here in the middle of nowhere, and I wish to get a better look at it.

Not far beneath the cave Ripley and I explored is another grotto, this one with a roundness to its entrance, like an open mouth. It's recessed onto a small ledge that's hardly two yards above the desert floor, so it's easy to get to. I tuck a couple of torches into my belt and a box of matches, then I gesture to Zishan that I'll be back soon.

The aura of familiarity that has walked with me since we arrived hangs heavy in the air once I am standing at the actual entrance to the cave. I light one of my torches and toss it inside to get a look without actually going in yet.

The cave is a simple one, with none of the crystals or rock formations of the cavern Ripley and I explored, but it's huge, and seems a perfect place for us to set up camp for the remainder of our time here. However long that will be. I can imagine a fire in the center, and our comforts arranged in a way that's almost homey.

That fire in my mind seems so real as to be roaring right there, in front of me. I step tentatively into the cave, but not too far. There, on the edge of the spectral fire stands a boy. Barely there, but enough that I can see his curly, dark hair that falls about his shoulders.

"Salan," I whisper.

A groan escapes my lips and my palms smack up, digging into my eyes. I start to weep, crumbling to the ground, captured totally by a sense of grief so great that I cannot make a word or coherent sound. And then, like magic, the grief is gone. I can feel the blood leave my tear-soaked face as I sniff and blot my nose with the skirt of my dress. The cave is empty, the fire of my imagination is no more. The boy is no more. The word I had spoken—the boy's name, I think—eludes me. It sits on the tip of my tongue for a moment, and then it's gone, too.

For a few, long minutes, I rest on my heels, recovering from this fleeting madness. More than a memory, more than a delusion or a vivid dream. It was as if I had stepped back in time, and was the girl I had been. Someone intimate, yet a stranger to me.

The torch I tossed into the cave is still burning brightly, and I crawl towards it. Taking it by the stick end, I hold it up, trying to conjure the vision of the fire once more. I do not want to be struck by the pain again, the almost unbearable notion of that child being dear to me and then being gone forever, but it feels so important. Like a key to our very existence, Ripley's and mine. At the very least a key to one of the doors we must unlock.

But this time, it is just me and the cave.

I hold the torch up high, moving to my right and my left,

getting a glimpse of what look like a series of passages at the back of the cave. Teetering to a stand, unsteady at first, I test my legs. They seem fine. While the last thing I want to do is encounter a colony of bats or other creatures of the dark, I do feel compelled to get a closer look. They could lead to another cave painting or be strewn with artifacts from these long lost people.

As I step closer, I do indeed see something. It's not in the dark holes of the entrances to one of these passages, but on the ground. There's a shoe, rather, a short boot, just like the ones Mataraci wears, and I rush over to it, my body in alarm before my mind can catch up and make sense of what is in front of me.

Because there I see that it is Mataraci. I can tell by his clothes, even in the low light of the torch.

"Mr. Mataraci," I say, but he doesn't move.

I crouch next to him and touch his shoulder, shaking him. That's when I notice his eyes are open, giving a cold stare into what was pitch darkness until I came over with firelight. I put my hands on his chest, feeling for a heartbeat, or any motion. It's there I encounter a sickly, wet patch on his clothing.

"Damn," I say. "Damn, damn, damn!"

I don't have to hold the torch over his wound to know he's been gutted. I don't have to ask myself who could do such a thing, let alone wonder who it is that comes up behind me. I can see his shadow in the glow of my torch. Lean, tall for an Arab, his hand gripping something. He lifts it up, and I wait to feel my skin tear and my blood rush out of me, emptying onto the floor of this cave like Mataraci's. Instead, a cotton cloth smothers my nose and mouth and the smell of ether takes me into the black.

I AWAKEN to find myself blindfolded and tied up, hands behind my back, ankles crossed. I don't know where I am, but I'm sure it's not where I found Mataraci. The smell is different—less desert and more calcite. Must be an enclosed space, perhaps deep in the dunes. I catalog all of this with a peculiar detachment, even if I am well aware of the danger I'm in.

I would be tempted to call out—for Ripley, for Cornelius, or Sufian—but I'm not alone. I hear the shushing sounds of a light breath. He's close. Reflexively, I swallow to cleanse the bile from my throat, and it seems so loud, crackling in my ears. Damn it, I feel sure I've alerted my captor to the fact that I'm awake!

Maybe I should say something, but I can't think of what. I could ask him why he's here, or to loosen my bindings, but I don't see where that will get me. I wonder if this is how Mohammad and Edna found themselves? Did he immobilize them with ether and bring them to that dismal hotel? Did they wake up, like I have, unclear as to why they were taken, or what was next?

My muscles tense. They ache like I've been clenching them for a long time. Perhaps all the time as I lay unconscious. The ground is hard, with lots of tiny pebbles, and my shoulder hurts. Gently, I roll onto my stomach, where it's not much better, but at least it's different. That's when a whistle pierces the air, and my sense of detachment becomes one of revulsion.

Clear. Perfect in pitch. Like a long-practiced habit. One unsuitable to a situation like this. What kind of monster would whistle as he prepares to butcher a young woman?

I know the song, too. That's the most horrible part. It puts a pit in my stomach, made greater by the knowledge of whose lips it is flowing through. It's the song of my dreams, of Mrs. Watson's bedroom. A melody as much a part of the desert as the pitter-pat of rain on a London street. And I know it is as old as time. At least as old as my time on this God's earth.

There is a wind in the desert that speaks of eternity.

As the murderer whistles, prickles of fear come at my scalp, traveling down my spine, and eliciting a cold sweat. After, comes the strongest notion of precognition that I've had yet. Even surer than when the specter of the boy appeared by the fire. The one whose name comes back to me now—Salan.

All at once, I feel distant, different, and very much alive. It's unthinkable to me that my heart is defective and will ever stop beating—either in the clutches of this abomination or in the inevitable course of my mother's ailment. For the first time, at least in this life, I feel infinite. My fear abandons me again, just as my grief for Salan did along with my vision of him just a few short hours ago.

The longer I have been in the desert, I realize, the less I have felt like Leila Saber-Wellington, Leila Davies, or just Leila. The more I am drawn into my past—whatever that is. The more I know that the man who killed Mataraci and countless others—from the night women of Whitechapel to the poor waifs from the City of the Dead – is part of that past. He has been with me from the start.

That man stops whistling. I hear him scoot closer, but not close enough to touch me, I think.

"Who are you?" he asks me in Arabic.

"I'm just a wife and a daughter," I say. "I've lived in Cairo most of my life. My father—he's English, though. He could give you money, if you're looking to escape the authorities. Think of how easy it would be to disappear in the middle of the Sahara and never return to Cairo again."

I hear him slake his thirst, loudly, as if he wants me to hear it and be painfully aware of my own. But then he puts a sponge to my lips, squeezing it, allowing me plenty of water. It is an eerie gesture of kindness that I am almost tempted to refuse.

"I don't want money," he says. His voice is smooth and fashionable.

"What do you want?"

"What my dreams have promised me."

This chills my blood and makes my throat go dry as bone again.

"What is that?" I rasp.

"You."

I CAN SEE THEM as clearly as I could the bottom of a cold, shallow stream. Mickey and his grandmother. It is like heaven to be in their presence, even if I cannot reach out to them. I long for the day when Ever and I, in her strong, young body, can actually be in their company. A day I can share with them, rather than follow them in a dreamscape.

"Your mother's worried about you." Amarinta swipes her flatbread through the chickpeas, tomato puree, and long pour of hot sauce she's piled on top of her koshary.

It's Mickey's favorite dish, and they're at his favorite restaurant—a local fast food diner which serves only one dish and it happens to be the best dish in town.

"I'm not as big a fan of Cairo as your parents are, but I do love the food." This time Amarinta loads up on a heaping spoonful. "They could serve this in something other than a plastic tub, though. Ambience. This place could use some ambience."

She peers up at the lime green florescent lights that beam down on the metal tables, giving the place a bit of a "Blade Runner" look.

As for Mickey, he just moves his food around like he's contemplating making something out of it. He watches the rice and pasta group together, the chick peas tumble off the spoon, the tomato sauce, lentils, and onions flow with a gooey elegance like hot lava.

"I love the desert," he says, like he hasn't heard a word she said. "I never want to leave it."

Amarinta flags down a young Egyptian boy and orders the only other thing on the menu—rice pudding. Aromatic, rich, and creamy as crème anglaise, and also the best in town. Worth the crappy ambience, she grumbles to herself.

"And yet you keep begging your parents to send you to that school in Virginia. Is it because you're afraid of that place?"

Despite the non sequitur, Mickey knows exactly which place she's talking about. He looks up at her, pushing away his half-eaten tub, and shakes his head.

"The Palace City? Not exactly."

"What exactly is your problem with it then? I mean, apart from the weird wax museum mummies. And don't say 'nothin'' because we both know that's a load of horse shit."

Mickey sits back and folds his arms across his chest. The thing about his grandmother is that there's no messing around. She asks, you answer, and whatever you say, it's okay. The only thing that's not okay is not answering.

So, he takes a deep breath and places his elbows on the table. Amarinta does the same, going nose to nose with him.

"I don't know," he says. "It's just that when we went there that day, it all seemed so real."

"Like you knew those people, and could see yourself there."

Mickey nods, looking into Amarinta's big, black eyes. Black like a tuxedo jacket. "Yeah, I could see myself there."

His grandmother takes his hand and squeezes it. "You'll make a great archaeologist one day. Like your daddy, and granddaddies. You've got that kind of an imagination. It's a gift. Like you. You're a gift."

Mickey looks away. He watches a kid, probably the son of the owner, balance a long, tin tray filled with rice puddings, and dispense them onto several tables, including their own.

"Grams?"

Amarinta ladles up her rice pudding and closes her eyes, chewing. "Hmm?"

"Where did you see that desert landscape you painted for mom?"

His grandmother shrugs. "You didn't seem to like it very much."

"No, I liked it. It's just that I'd seen it somewhere before."

"Wouldn't be the first time you and I got the same idea without talking about it."

Amarinta puts her empty rice pudding container aside. She gestures to Mickey's, and he pushes it over to her.

"We've always had something special, haven't we?" she says.

Mickey nods. "Will you tell me about the Nin'ti again? Dad thinks it's just a myth."

"What do you think?"

"I don't know. Mom thinks there's some truth in every myth. Do you think it's possible that certain people could be born over and over in different times and different places? I mean, I know there's nothing like that in the Bible, and I'm not trying to be disrespectful."

Amarinta raises an eyebrow in that way she does, then licks her lips. A second empty rice pudding container gets set aside, piled on top of the previous one.

"A lot of things have been cut out of the Bible over the centuries. It was inspired by God, but it was edited by man."

Mickey laughs. "You think the Nin'ti were in the Bible once?"

"How would I know?"

Mickey rolls his eyes and pays for their meal. He holds out his arm and his grandmother takes it, tossing the scarf

Calliope gave her over her shoulder. Outside, it's hot as blazes, dry as dust. Amarinta squints and wrinkles up her nose. She hates the smell of Cairo.

They walk to the Coptic district, which isn't far, and it's doable in the heat. It's her favorite part of Cairo—in truth the only part she really likes. Her late husband's grandfather had contributed significant funds to the founding of the Coptic Museum there, in 1908, a few years after he'd converted to the faith.

And that's where they go—to walk past the Coptic Museum. It's a sandy colored place, beautiful with an intricately carved facade. It's got a courtyard, the way lots of the lovely, old Cairo buildings do. Amarinta stands outside, admiring it the way an English Lord might admire the property of his ancestors.

"Our souls are deathless, and ever," she says. "When they have left their former seat, do they live in new abodes and dwell in the bodies that have received them? I myself (for I well remember it) at the time of the Trojan war was Euphorbus, son of Panthous. Recently, in Juno's temple in Argos, Abas' city, I recognized the shield which I once wore on my left arm."

"Who said that?"

"Ovid, right around the time our Savior was born."

"What does that have to do with the Nin'ti?"

Amarinta shakes her head. She strolls up to the sculpture of a lion and pets his head like he's her own. "Nothing much. Just illustrating how the idea that some of us could have lived before is a concept that's been around for a long, long time."

"Like the legend of Nin'ti."

She makes like she's scratching behind the stone lion's ears. "And according to that legend—at least what your father and grandfather could scrape up of it—the Nin'ti do tend to gravitate to certain places for a while. Often living several lives in a particular vicinity, among very specific people."

Mickey nods. "Makes sense if they're trying to solve a mystery. How else could they figure anything out and break their curse?"

"You think it's a curse to live so long?" Amarinta laughs. "I guess it can be. But don't you forget that a curse is also an enchantment. Grimm's fairytales have long told us as much."

"A Nin'ti's life doesn't sound like much of a fairytale."

Amarinta looks up into her grandson's face. She pinches his chin and looks deep into his eyes. "It's a story of two souls bound by eternal love. And eternal love is eternally complicated."

Mickey scrunches up his face.

"Eternal love? Dad never said anything about that."

"Hmm." Amarinta smiles and gives him a wink. "I must be reading too many romance novels."

Chapter 34

The Storm in His Soul
The Dunes in the Central Sahara, 1902

"**L**EILA!" I hear Ripley call my name, and at once, a violent sense of vertigo comes over me.

I am in a very dark place. Darker than the eyes of a raven or the petals of a hellebore.

My heart is beating fast. I know I was in one of the grottos with the killer. He told me I was promised to him, and I told him nothing. I closed my eyes and retreated into what I thought was sleep, so that's where I must be.

Dreaming. The glow of a torch casts a yellow light over the dark, shadowy stone of a passage, and I take in the smell of this place—one that is infinitely pleasing to me. Infinitely familiar, anciently so.

"Are you here?"

At once, I am privy to the vestiges of Ripley's memory. I can see the wallpaper in his mother's bedroom. One of violets and lilies of the valley, where the woman who gave him this life spoke her last words. And I see a gazelle. Sufian carried it back to camp on his shoulders after Ripley had shot it with a bow and arrow. He marveled at how natural such a weapon felt in his hands. I hear Ripley calling my name again, tearing from cave to cave. I see Cornelius and Sufian splitting up from him to search for me, while the remaining Kubartu and their slaves surround the dunes.

I feel as if we are treading water in the midst of a sea that is miles deep, with an untold legion of monsters beneath our feet. Or just one.

"He's quite sane," I tell Ripley. "But in his soul is a storm the likes of which we cannot imagine."

The darkness that surrounds me begins to change, becoming thinner. It lightens like the dawn. The torch falls to the ground and extinguishes, leaving only a tendril of smoke curling up from its burnt end.

"Where are you?" Ripley says, but it's not clear whether he's talking to me, or someone else.

Sheer images flash before me, but I forget them easily, except for one. That one keeps appearing, but in pieces, like a puzzle. I see a moon, some ripples of sand, a strange, wildly colored palace of a kind—all of these fill in, as the pieces start to stay, becoming whole, obscuring the dark passage entirely and taking me in, bit by bit, until I am a part of that vista.

"I see you," Ripley says. "Those eyes of fire that know me. That hate me."

He does not sound like Ripley anymore.

"You took your time," another voice says. "And I will take mine."

"Ripley, no!" I call to him.

But it is too late.

In the span of a single breath, I am not in my dream anymore. The strange mirage that had swallowed me whole is gone, and I am on the ground, just as I was before. My hands are tied behind my back, and as I move my head from side to side, my blindfold slips, freeing my left eye. Not that it does me much good. There's so much smoke in the air, and my eyes are tearing up something fierce. My throat burns.

Blinking hard, I lift my head, focusing on the smears of grey rock with ribbons of red about me. Everything is so blurry and dark, lit only by the light of the offending fire.

The grotto I'm in is bigger than I envisaged it, easily able to fit two carriages and their corresponding horses. My captor has moved me into a hollow within this cave. Further away from his camp and its fire, but close enough that I am not too cold.

I roll to my other side, and as my eyes adjust, they focus on a sight I cannot make sense of at first. To my left, is a jumble of red and black robes. As I squirm nearer for a better look, I notice I've gone into a puddle, and try to fidget back, whilst lifting up my head for a better view. A waft of sweat and animal musk, plus the scent of herbal tonics—the kind desert men rub into their beards and hair—visits me, and my heart sinks in my chest. He's lying still, his blood spread beneath him like a blanket! "Sufian," I whisper. He doesn't stir, but I do see that he's breathing.

"You're awake." I hear that melodic voice, smooth as wet clay. It seems to come from everywhere.

"And you're a murderer," I say. "A Ripper."

He emerges from behind a substantial knot of rock and goes to the fire, his bare back to me, his legs wrapped in loose trousers. There, he ladles up water from his bucket, and drinks it.

A chuckle, one of genuine amusement, rattles the whole of his torso.

"Murderer is much too formal a moniker, and Ripper is far too theatrical for my tastes," he says. "Please, call me Ata."

"Mohammad's cousin," I whisper, and Ata nods.

He has black hair, like Mohammad's, and as he angles just slightly to his right, I glimpse the side of his face replete with the dark, heavy brow and prominent bones of the Gamal family. He's wearing the ancient breastplate stolen from our home in Cairo! It hangs from a strap around his neck and is tied with a leather belt around his middle. He wears it like it was made for him, and watching him makes me sick.

Ata takes another ladleful of water and disappears back behind the rock from which he came. I hear a splash and a cough, then a low grunt in a distinctive pitch. "Ripley!" I cry out. Every part of me wants to scream.

My husband does not reply to me. I can hear short huffs of his breath, like he's fixed his mouth closed.

"Oh, she'll hear everything," Ata says to him. "I'll make sure of it."

I hear him slide his dagger from its sheath and a gut-wrenching terror seizes my entire being.

"To hear something, but not be able to see it," Ata says. "That's a powerful thing. I heard my brother get killed by a hippopotamus when I was a boy of nine. They have an iron-lock bite that's double the power of a lion's, you know. I closed my eyes tight, but I swear I could see it. The beast threw him in the air and caught him again, then shook him like a dog with a rag doll. I remember every moment like it happened only seconds ago."

Ata seems to savor the memory. Yes, the violence of it, but also the grief.

"You have my pistol," Ripley tells him softly. "You could just shoot me."

"No!" I shriek. My head falls upon the rough, hard ground and I feel a tremendous urge to bang it there over and over again.

Ata breathes deeply, like he is readying himself for a long meditation. I can hear the whistle of Ata's blade as he whips it through the air.

"That would hardly be sporting, as you British say."

"Because killing defenseless women with that dagger, as you did, is so sporting," Ripley says through gritted teeth.

"It's more than sporting, my friend," Ata whispers. "It is . . . significant."

"Ripley!" I call out. "Oh, God, run, Ripley, please!"

I hear a thin, high sound, like metal upon metal, and my gut twists again. Ata is sharpening his weapon.

"You don't like it do you?" Ripley asks him. "When she calls my name? Did it bother you when Edna called Mohammad's? No, I didn't think so. Not like this. You want her to call *your* name."

A quick shuffle is followed by a cracking sound. Ata has struck him, hard! Ripley spits and I wince as I imagine his blood and saliva hitting the floor.

"I've been dreaming about you," Ata says. "At first I thought it was Allah who wished me to find you and kill you for his glory, but then I realized that it was me."

"So you think you're Allah?"

That earns Ripley another blow, and I can't stand it anymore. I curl up and bury my face in my knees to try and stifle the cries that threaten. I don't want my husband to feel my pain in addition to his, or for Ata to get pleasure from it.

"Leila, my wife. You know she's very ill," Ripley says.

Ata says nothing, and the air becomes very still.

"It's her heart. Same thing that took her mother. Whatever you want to do, I don't think you want her to die. Not here. Not today."

I hold my breath as I hear Ata place his dagger on the ground. There's a rustle, like he's removing something from his clothes. His footstep is light as he makes his way over to the back wall. That is where there's a small hole which lets in the light. I know it because Ata told me. He described the way the light cut in from the outside like a knife-edge, illuminating a debris field that looks to have been made by whomever had forged the opening. He thought it was ages and ages ago. Ata walks about there, and I hear him kicking aside some stones. I think he's bending down to collect others.

"I want only the very smooth and the very jagged," he

says. There is a clinking sound as he drops them one by one into something—perhaps a bag or canister.

"Please, sir," I call out. "You say I was promised to you, so take me. Take me away from here to be with you. Just don't hurt Ripley."

"Leila, stop it!" Ripley says.

Ata ignores us both, grunting as he lifts up what sounds like a sack of these rocks. One that must be bulging like a gourd.

"Ah!" he shouts, as the heavy sack slices through the air, bearing down onto the fire, which explodes with some force, and sends hot embers into my field of vision. The realization of his intention to use this barbaric weapon on Ripley crashes though me. It is an evil I can scarcely fathom! I hear him walk towards my husband, slow and sure, picking up his dagger along the way, talking to it, calling it his friend. My teeth start to chatter and my palm burns like hellfire.

"For God's sake," Ripley says. "Whatever you do to me, don't make her listen. Cut out my tongue if you must, but don't let me make a sound. It will kill her."

There is a strange, long pause between the two men and my shoulders begin to quake. Something has changed, and I hate that I can see nothing, do nothing. Only imagine, just as Ata had while his brother was slowly slain by a beast.

"Your eyes," a voice quite different from Ripley's says. "Yellow and orange like a dying star, they seem a reluctant tribute to the fiery sunsets of the desert."

I know whose voice it is, I do. Strong and formal. Inclined towards poetry, even when facing death. It is nearly as old as life in the desert. It is Nif's.

The brilliant sun of late morning gushes onto our kitchen table. Seems almost like a message from God, just like the piece of paper that's come in from the mail.

That, I'm holding in my hand, blinking my tears away and glancing up at the mountains like they're co-conspirators of mine. The paper is thick and the color of real cream, like stationary from a British period drama. It even smells of everything I've been hoping for.

"Way to go," Hunter says.

He's got a super pleased look on his face, like when he finishes building something beautiful that he knows nobody could get in just any furniture store.

"The headmaster, this *Dr.* Titus Tuttle, says you scored one of the highest scores in their history on that test they made you take."

I pinch my lips together to stop them from trembling so much. "I just never thought they'd want someone like me."

Hunter tips his head and folds his arms across his chest. I can almost see the chip on his shoulder.

"Well, it's a school for intellectually gifted young people, or so they tell us," he says. "Best one, too, according to them. Doesn't say anything about having to be rich, and they are letting you go for free."

I run my fingers over the seal stamped at the top of my acceptance letter. It reads The Putnam School at the top.

Beneath that is shield with a fish, a lion, and fleur-de-lis. *Cognito, ergo sum,* which means, "I think, therefore I am," is written in a blue ribbon at the bottom, and it makes me so happy just to see it.

"Thank you," I whisper.

"I'm just looking out for what's best for you," Hunter tells me, all while looking out the window at what he loves, what he thought was best for me until last spring.

I fully admit my role in his change of mind. Coming home with a neck full of hickeys was like drawing first blood. Over the next few weeks, a quiet rage came over my father, scaring me, if I'm to be honest, and making me doubt my big plan to make him turn on Alaska and let me go back to the mainland.

He didn't ground me or anything, the way I thought he would. The way any normal father might do. He didn't even say anything much about my hickeys, but damn, the look in his eyes. The way he spoke to me in a low, even voice that might've only been a three on the Richter scale, but felt like a warning that the Big One was coming.

"So, when do I leave? End of summer, I guess." I try not to sound so chipper about getting away from here.

"We leave," he says.

"We?"

"You're all of fifteen, almost. I'm not letting you go alone."

"Well, I mean, it's a boarding school."

I give him a disinterested shrug, like his stalking me to my new school is no big deal.

Hunter leans in and puts his elbows on the table. "We go together, or we don't go at all."

"I thought Alaska was your dream place. I mean, you built our house here, and you do so well with your business."

Hunter now shrugs, same way as I did. "Getting back to you was my dream, too."

I don't know what to say to this, as my father's not the sentimental sort, so I focus back on my acceptance letter, taking it in both hands. I try to chase away the dread of continuing to live in the same zip code as Hunter. I'll still be boarding, according to my scholarship, so at least there's that.

"The Putnam School in Natural Springs, Virginia," I say. "Resort town's a funny place for a school like that. You'd think it would be in New York or Boston, not nestled at the foot of the Allegheny Mountains."

"I know a little bit about these resort towns," Hunter tells me, and I bet he does. He'd been working at Winterglen when he got back in touch with my mom, and Natural Springs is only a couple of hours in the other direction. Might as well be another planet from the patch of the Old Dominion I grew up in.

"A lot of fancy people visit the Home Hearth Resort," he continues. "Convenient to visit their kids, too—a little golf, a little skeet shooting, a little pretending they give a shit. Basically, it's a small town full of rich tourists and resort workers. Not much else, except for The Putnam School for Intellectually Advanced and Gifted Students."

And that's really what all this is about, and I know it; getting me to a small place without trouble. Not that I can blame him. Only a couple months after the hickey incident, Rick Johnson was found near the banks of the river with his guts cut out. That hit hard, and for one crazy minute there was this voice in my head that told me Hunter had something to do with it.

When the police came to our house interviewing everyone in the area, Hunter told them how he couldn't help thinking it could've been me out there, and that got me thinking about things from his perspective. Like maybe I shouldn't be entertaining dark fantasies about my father being a psycho killer just because I can't stand living with him. It's not like he's ever hit me, or even my mom during their worst, drug-fueled fights.

And the fact is, it could've been me on the banks of that river. I think of when Wisconsin Johnson and I wandered away from "midnight run." If some maniac sicko had come and attacked us, nobody would've even heard us scream.

Poor Wisconsin. After I gave him back the jacket he lent me on the night we made out, he kept trying to ask me out for real, and yes, I still feel terrible for leading him on like that, especially after what happened to him. But he was way too old for me, and I never thought he was the serious type, which is why I picked him for my show and tell with Hunter. I mean, Wisconsin had been blessed with boy band looks and was always making out with girls. But then there he went leaving notes for me, and bags of peanut M&Ms on our doorstep. I never expected that.

And I'll never forget that he gave me his jacket to wear that night we sort of got together. It was decent of him, considering how cold it was, and that he thought I tased him when he couldn't get past first base with me. That jacket's the same one he died wearing. Rick stitched on the front, and JOHNSON in big letters on the back on top of a map of Wisconsin.

Even all these months later, no one in all of Eagle River can figure out why someone would want to hurt Wisconsin Johnson—and by now, we would've heard if he'd been up to something stupid. Around here, everyone knows if you've got an enemy, or if you do things that might make you an enemy. And all Wisconsin ever did was drink beers after school and practice his woodwork. Not even all the girls he hooked up with held it against him that he spread himself around. They all figured that a guy with his looks deserved a selection. Especially since he was so damned nice all the time.

"I hear they're going to have an *in memoriam* exhibit about

Rick Johnson at the Bear Paw Festival," I say, apropos of nothing but what's been going on in my own head. "His dad's entering the chainsaw carving demo using Wisconsin's Day of the Dead design. The one he was going to make last year."

"Hmm?"

"Rick Johnson, the boy who was murdered last spring."

"That kid who was buying drugs?"

"Nobody said he was buying drugs. They just found him dead for no reason at all."

"There's always a reason," Hunter says.

"Well, Rick was okay," I tell him.

Hunter picks up my acceptance letter from The Putnam School, and folds it back up nicely, slipping it into the thick, creamy envelope it came in.

"You want to go out and celebrate? We could go to the Moose's Breath and get some pizza and chowder."

"Sure," I say.

I CAN THINK of about a hundred things I would've rather done than spend the evening at a pub with my father. What with his usual flashes of anger, the digs at my ungratefulness, and the secret thoughts that go through his mind and hover unspoken between us, creating long silences that used to be uncomfortable, until they became our standard operating procedure.

But there was none of that tonight.

Hunter and I ate our five-meat pizza and played pool. We "shot the shit," as he likes to say, and actually had a decent conversation.

"What's that?" he asked, when he caught me doodling on my dinner napkin.

"Just some hieroglyphs I'm practicing. Um, for my history lessons." I was quick to add the last part, as hieroglyphs connect to Egypt, which connect to the Nevilles, which makes him *mad*.

"The lotus and the eye of Ra," he said, pointing at my drawings. "What, you think I don't have any interests besides carpentry?"

I must've given him a look.

"I was in the gifted program at my school, too," he told me. "Until, well, until it all went sideways for me."

I did not know that.

"The eye of Ra is something to do with the sun god, right? And symbolizes authority and protective powers. And the lotus? That's also associated with Ra, but another god, too. Something starts with an N . . ."

"Nefertum."

"Nefertum. God of healing, medicine, and beauty."

Strange to hear him talk like that. Smart, like a man of interests. Mom never did, and half the time looked at me like I was an alien when I tried to talk to her about what was going on in my head. What made me curious, and came so easily to me, but made no sense at all to her. But she was also proud of me, and I guess she was right when she said I was more like my father than I realized.

The high of getting into The Putnam School, and on a full scholarship, took Hunter and me through the first good time we've ever had together. Probably because my applying to Putnam was the first thing we've ever done together, for a common goal. And I'll admit, when Putnam sent me an invitation to apply, I didn't think there was any way Hunter would let me do that. To my surprise, he was not only impressed that my AMP scores could get their attention, but seemed to think giving it a try couldn't hurt.

Now here we are.

I look out my window, my former escape hatch, and watch the sun start to set over the mountains. It's 11:14 pm in the land of the midnight sun. And 9:00 am in Cairo.

"You're a fool, Ever," I say, but I sit down at my desk anyway. I take out some college ruled paper and a pen, writing *Dear Mickey* at the top. *I hope you get this. Doesn't seem like you got any of my other ones.*

It's not that I expect the American Embassy to act as a mail carrier for American citizens abroad, but I figure it's worth one more try. I'm going to pray harder on this one than on any of the other letters I wrote to him.

I have some great news. I'm coming back to the mainland, and I'll be back on the grid.

Right then, I hear a laugh bubble up from downstairs, and put down my pen. It's a woman's laugh, which is weird.

I get up and sneak out my door, tip-toeing to the bannister that overlooks our living room. There, rolling around next to our pot belly stove, half-naked, are Hunter and our waitress from Moose's! She's got her tight jeans on, but no top at all, like the hippie girls in the 1970s *Playboy* magazines that Lottie's grandfather keeps stuffed under his bathroom sink.

I hurry back to my room and shut the door, and I don't even know why I bother to be quiet about it, because it's not like Hunter seems to care if I hear him or not. I mean, he's got to know I'm not asleep, since my light's still on, and the sun's barely over the mountain.

I get it, okay, I'm not the only thing in your life. And I'm fine with that, by the way.

But it's like, I don't know. It's almost like he wants me to be jealous.

That's a strange and ugly thought, and it gets me thinking about how he was practically gloating when he told me about Mickey's parents selling their house in Charlottesville and that they're probably never coming back there again. That's probably why he let me apply to Putnam at all.

I sit back down and crumple up the letter I started, then I pull out a new piece of paper.

Dear Mickey, I write.

I'm sick of wishing and waiting.

I love you. More than anything in this world or any other.

I don't even bother to sign my name. If he gets it, he'll know who it's from. I just needed to put it out there.

Because maybe if I do, then somehow, soon, we'll find each other again.

Chapter 35

Invincible
The dunes of the Central Sahara, 1902

"**W**HO GOES THERE?" I whisper. Cornelius comes to me, and I feel the heat of his torch near my cheeks. For the first time in hours I get a wonderful, joyous look at the face of someone I love.

"Thank God!" Cornelius exhales. He kisses my forehead hard with relief.

"Ripley. He's in there with that monster who killed Mohammad and Edna!"

My sobs break through with complete abandon. I can't even form the words that would give voice to what I've been hearing. Hard blows and other clamor, yes. But the worst is the silence after. Ripley's unwillingness to cry out.

"I'm here," Cornelius whispers. "Everything will be alright."

Cornelius strokes my head, running his fingers through my hair. He swallows hard, and kisses my forehead again, but gently this time. Then he stands.

"Untie me."

A grotesque guttural noise—from Ripley—comes from the grotto, and I want to scream!

"Stay here." Cornelius's chest rises and falls, as he fists his hands up tight.

"Not without me! You can't!"

He shakes his head and bends over me. Quickly, he takes out his blade and slices through the ropes tying my wrists. "You can untie the rest yourself, but stay put. I have a killer to dispense with, and I can't be worrying about both you and Ripley while I do it."

Turning away, he runs into the belly of the grotto, leaving me alone to more frightful noises. Thumps like flesh against bone, smothered moans. But there is no time to think on them. I sit up, dizzy after having been supine for so long, and work to untie my feet. It's a stubborn knot, better suited for a knife's edge, and I struggle to loosen it with my trembling fingers.

Quite a commotion interrupts those ghastly, hateful sounds, allowing me a breath, a rest of heart and soul, even if only for a moment.

"Let's see how you do against a man who isn't tied up," I hear Cornelius say.

I scoot towards the grotto. The ground is coarse and sharp bits of rock cut at my clothes. My ankle bones rub together with a wet burning pain. But I lose all thoughts about my discomfort when I inch past the rock wall and the grotto becomes visible to me.

Because there hangs Ripley in the most gruesome state! He's naked, except for his cotton briefs, and his hands are bound at the wrist and hooked over a spike pounded into the cave wall!

A whorl and a lightning bolt have been carved into his chest, and blood streams down the length of his body. Where there is not blood, there are terrible welts. Only my husband's face remains untouched—flushed and damp with sweat. His head hangs to the side, resting on his shoulder, his eyes are barely open.

A loud crash shocks me, and I look to find just what made the dreadful welts upon Ripley's body. His back is to me—my captor's—and from a rope, he dangles the sack that's stuffed to density with stones, and looks like a hornet's nest. Swinging the sack above his head, he and Cornelius circle one another, until our friend rushes him, dagger in hand.

"Watch out!" I call, as The Ripper brings the sack down, walloping Cornelius in the hip, and dashing him to the ground!

Cornelius grunts in deep agony, and I can only hope his bones haven't been shattered. He squirms along the ground, sitting himself up, and I'm reassured that he appears to be able to move his legs.

As for Ata The Ripper, there is a sinister order in his comportment. His hair is wet with exertion, but neat. His posture upright, proud. But he is breathing hard. He swings his sack again, only Cornelius is able to roll out of its way, before it comes down right where his head would have been. Our friend gets back on his feet, and dives for the sack just as our foe aims to swing it again. And yes, thank heavens, he's able to grab it, getting a good hold on the rope and yanking hard. The Ripper loses his composure and goes tripping over him, stumbling past the demolished fire and knocking his head into the cave wall.

"Sherin."

That voice. I look up and see Ripley, his head upright now. His eyes bore into mine, the streaks aflame, and the red rushing like rivulets after a storm. They seem so close, though he's on the other side of the grotto.

He is not the Ripley I know. The one of late nights and archaeology, loving words, and poor attempts at verse. He still looks like that man, my husband, but he is someone else. Someone I know in my bones. He says the name again, my name, in a voice as sure and olden as a yew tree.

"I'm coming."

Cornelius and The Ripper are now fighting hand to hand,

moving about the grotto in a rough, ferocious dance. I'm able to turn my gaze from them to start to loosen the knots at my feet again, but I cannot ignore my husband's eyes! They draw me in, making me watch them as I labor with my bindings. Those eyes drop away from mine, and he looks past me, urging me to do the same.

I turn about, following his gaze, and find it trained on The Ripper, who is fresh from his tussle with Cornelius, hunched, blood dripping from his head wound. He's making his way back towards the remains of the fire!

Cornelius scans the ground for his knife, still wavering as he stands, clearly favoring his right leg. It's then I notice just what The Ripper is up to, what Ripley—Nif—is alerting me to. Near a pail of water is a pistol—Ripley's pistol!

"Cornelius, the gun!" I cry out.

But it's too late. The Ripper takes the firearm in his hand, and aims it at our friend. He holds it weakly, and staggers a few feet closer, then fires.

I shriek like a banshee as Cornelius stumbles back! For a moment I expect him to fall, but then I realize that he's not been hit at all. The Ripper, enfeebled, missed his target entirely, and is gearing up to try again. He holds up the pistol once more, trying to keep it straight.

"Don't! Stop it!" I cry, as I'm finally able to free my legs. I kick off my bindings and get up on my feet, then run to insert myself between the fighting men and Ripley's battered form. The Ripper stalls for a mere moment, his eyes seeking me out.

But it is moment enough, for Cornelius dives to the ground and scoops up his blade. He throws it, piercing The Ripper's thigh, and making him fall down on one knee. The pistol discharges again, missing Cornelius once more, thank the Lord!

"Cornelius, get away from him!"

He does not, but nor does he come at our foe, which

I feared he might do. His eyes widen, the whites of them bright like stars, and he bites down. It's then I see what he sees. Sufian! Sufian, whom I'd presumed to be very near dead, has come up behind The Ripper! His turban is gone, and his long, oiled hair falls past his shoulders. Though his robes are wet with blood and he is noticeably weakened, his movements are determined as he raises up his arm, cudgel in hand, and strikes down upon the evil man's head.

The Ripper, however, does not fall! Instead, he turns, seeming at once confused and filled with rage. His eyeballs shake and his teeth gnash. He starts to mumble in Arabic, cursing the sun, the moon, the desert most of all.

I hear Cornelius's labored breath, and something between a hum and a snarl emanates from Sufian's throat. I smell the blood and sweat of murderous abuse all around me, and spin around to Ripley. He hangs there, still as a sleeping household, and I start to go to him.

But The Ripper's pistol discharges again, startling me, making the whole of my body jump up. This time, his bullet finds Sufian's shoulder. The Kubartu leader drops to the ground, a small smile painted upon his face. A smile that grows wide as he begins to chuckle. He glares at The Ripper and tosses his cudgel—I watch it roll across the floor.

"You, I would hunt down and kill for myself," he says in his language. I recognize every word, as if I've known the tongue all my life.

Blood streams into The Rippers eyes, and he blinks them forcefully, holding the pistol straight this time.

"No!" I shout, and The Ripper tips his head, as if he's forgotten I am here. He angles towards me, the snake on the breastplate entrancing me, bringing to mind images of terror and anguish. Betrayal. I see myself being drowned, and beaten, violated. I feel every blow, hear every ugly word. It is me, it is not me, it is then, it is now.

"Mine," he says. "Forevermore. I will take you with me this time."

"Never," I say.

A dark, violent current begins to take me over. It is a murderous thing that flows through me, like nothing I have ever felt—not even when I touched the ancient statue. It seems to come from the earth, infusing me with its power, and tempting me with its use. The ground beneath us shakes in a tremor, the air feels angered and alive. It's so potent—at once dangerous and dreadful, yet I feel invincible. It could take us all down, the dunes crumbling to nothing, our bodies bursting into a million little pieces.

"Sherin," Nif says. "Bring it upon me."

No.

"Look at me."

But I can't.

"Give me what you cannot bear."

I try to stop it, but I can feel some of the flow leaving me. "No, Nif don't!"

The current within me begins to feel less savage. It lessens enough for me to take notice of what is around me. From the corner of my vision, I see a dark movement.

"Nif?"

But it is Cornelius. He comes up behind The Ripper and raises Sufian's cudgel high. He bears down on the monster with all the force the Kubartu could not summon. Once again, I hear the sickening crack, as I did when Degarmo was felled. The Ripper falls to the ground, finally, but Cornelius does not stop. He strikes him over and over, until there is no doubt that the man—I can barely make myself call him that—is most certainly dead.

The deadly current that has been surging through me dissolves at once, and it is as if an anvil has been lifted from my soul.

"R-Ripley!" I cry out, and scurry towards my husband.

Cornelius pulls his knife from The Ripper's thigh and helps me take my husband's bleeding, battered body into my arms. Cornelius cuts him down, and we ease him to the ground.

He still breathes. His eyes are open. He is still the other one. The love I feel for him is beyond any sense of mind. It spills out from me with a power much like the current that struck terror in me only minutes ago. Only it is all goodness.

"I'll be waiting for you," he says.

"No, God, please no. You can't leave me! It wasn't supposed to be like this."

"It's been like this many times."

I know he's right.

"Go look at the dunes," he whispers. "They glow with the majesty of the sun. You'll remember."

"I don't want to remember," I say. "I want you to stay with me."

"Do you hear the wind?"

I don't care about the wind, I want to tell him. But then I do hear it. My heart slows, not beating quite so hard, and I listen. Such a sweet, familiar sound.

"It sounds like the belly of a conch shell, doesn't it?"

I nod that yes, it does.

He closes his eyes, and blows the air softly from his lungs. When he opens them again, they're different. Not as vivid, more of the earth than the heavens.

"It's alright," Ripley says.

And it is Ripley again. I'm so happy I forget to breathe. My husband raises his hand, and touches his finger to my jaw. "This is our place, in these dunes. It's always been our place."

I shake my head and sniff back my tears, smearing them on the tattered sleeve of my dress. "I'm the one who should die first. I'm the one with the bad heart."

"No," Ripley says. "You have things to do yet."

I bend over to kiss him, and I do so with everything I have. As if my kiss alone will be the beacon that will bring us back to one another. I keep my lips on his even after I know that he's gone.

CORNELIUS AND I take Ripley's body to the cave anointed with our age-old paintings, and the symbol on the necklace my husband gave to me. I feel so empty of life that my every step is a labor, and yet, I want to do this more than anything for him. For the one I will see again soon, I hope.

We lie him down on the smooth, flat, slab of stone where Ripley and I loved one another just this morning. There, we wipe down his battered body, cleaning him, honoring him. Then we dress him in fresh clothes—a soft, well-beaten tunic from Sufian's stores. I chose a deep red one tied with a leather belt. He looks fine, ready for his journey.

I kiss Ripley's sweet form everywhere—his face, his breast, his hands and feet. I pray, and I pray, and I pray. I hope it does some good.

Cornelius wanted to take him with us, wrap his body in linen, saturated with scented oils, and carry him to Oea. But he belongs here, in our place.

"I must go attend Sufian," Cornelius whispers.

Sufian, who is made of survival, lives. Zishan, the Kubartu medicine man, believes he will recover from his wounds, though they are grave, and we will care for him all of the way until we can get him a real doctor—which he will undoubtedly refuse, anyway.

"I'll be there soon," I say.

Cornelius leaves me with my husband, and I place my

hands over his heart. My tears fall all over his chest, and my voice echoes in the chamber as I sing the song Edna's mother sang in her bed, the song I hear in my dreams, the *Songs of the Desert Wind*. I sing all of the verses of love and destiny, as I hold up my torch to our paintings, and once again follow the story of our ancient journey.

But when my eyes find the last of the images, my song becomes stuck in my throat. For there, in smoky black, as if made by fire, are two new illustrations. In a place that had been blank just minutes ago, are the lightening bolt and whorl that were carved upon Ripley's flesh by Ata the Ripper! I lean closer, shivering as if a cold wind has blown through my clothes, and reach out to my husband's body. Slipping my hand beneath his burial robes, I place my fingers upon his wounds, tracing the lines of his scars. Reading them like hieroglyphs.

"My God," I whisper.

On the ground, just beneath the images, is a red porous rock. I take my hand from Ripley's chest and pick it up, putting it to the cave wall. Before I write what must be written, I say a prayer. It's not for me, but for the one who will come here seeking answers one day. In my next life, or the next one after that. I pray they will find the strength to do what must be done, in the only hope of stopping what draws nearer with each of my lives. Then I write.

And when I emerge from the dunes, the sun is setting. It does indeed grace us with such majesty, as Nif told me. The way he told me when we were dying together for the first time, and how he told me today before he entered infinity again.

And yes, I remember now. I remember everything.

Chapter 36

Birthday
Oxfordshire, England, 1903

"ROSIE-POSEY," I sing. "Both truths and roses have thorns about them." That's what Henry David Thoreau said, and likely a quote Ripley would be burbling at our baby girl right now, if he were here.

Little Rose cries with such fury—a face as red as a cherry pepper, her tooth-poor mouth open wide enough to swallow a crab apple whole. I am full of fury, too, though my fury is a bit more complicated than teething pain. And I keep mine inside, mostly. Burning and festering as my heart continues to wither and weaken.

Fury at the monster who murdered my husband. A man whose face I barely got a glimpse of, before Cornelius bashed it in until it could hardly be called anything but a bloody porridge. Fury that my father couldn't live to meet his granddaughter. Mowed down by a carriage as he hurried home to me from a night of cards and whiskey at Lieutenant General Blackwood's place, a much-needed reprieve from grief. It has been nothing but death it seems. Deaths of people, of dreams, but not of memories. I have hundreds of lifetimes of those, and they are difficult to make sense of. It's hard for me to think about anything but the memories most close to me. The ones I made in this lifetime, with Ripley.

There's a light knock at the door of Rose's nursery, and I

know it is Imogen even before she peaks in her head. Aunt Imogen knocks with the tips of her fingers, and says "who-who," like an owl, before she enters any room.

"He's returned," she says, then clears her throat as a way of registering her displeasure.

Imogen makes a beeline for Rose, her most favorite thing in all the world. She scoops her up from my arms and coos at her. Rose sputters and looks about, confused at the amendment of her circumstances. At least she stops crying.

"Cornelius!" I say.

My dearest friend gales into the room, and I would, if it weren't for Aunt Imogen's pucker, throw my arms about him.

"I'll leave the two of you," Imogen says. "Rose could use a nap."

She leaves almost soundlessly, giving a cool nod to Cornelius, as he bows.

"I've missed you," I say.

"I don't think your aunt has."

"She just needs to get used to the idea of you, that's all."

Cornelius lifts an eyebrow and chortles. "The idea of her widowed niece married to a penniless African with a penchant for digging up old things?"

I start to giggle, too, but my breath becomes shallow and I sink into the chase lounge. "Sorry, Rose was up all night, so I'm a bit knackered."

Cornelius shakes his head at me, and joins me on the lounge. He takes a tendril of hair that has come loose from my braid and tucks it behind my ear.

"Don't," he says. "I know it's not Rose—not with how everyone in this house is fighting over who gets to hold and feed her. You don't look well."

"Oh, thank you so much."

"Dark circles under your eyes. You're even managing to look pale." Then he smiles and holds my cheek, rubbing his thumb at my temple. "Somehow you're still more beautiful than any woman I've ever known."

Cornelius takes my hand and kisses it. I look him in the eyes, wishing so many things were different.

"I'm sorry for hijacking your life like this," I say.

"You've done nothing of the sort. I would do anything for you, and Ripley, and Rose."

Cornelius looks out the window and onto the gardens. There is Imogen holding Rose and showing her all the flowers I've planted. She glows like a new mother.

"You'll have to claw that child out of her hands," he says.

"No, you'll have to."

"Well, as your husband and executor of your will, I'll have that obligation."

Tears sting my eyes. It's been happening to me more often of late. "I keep telling myself I'll see him soon, but then that means I won't be with Rose. I suppose I take comfort that our baby looks so much like him. That Ripley and I, who we have been in this life, will live on in her." I pick up the photograph of Rose we had taken just a few weeks ago. "Of course, she hardly looks like me at all."

"She has your mouth."

I lick my lips, tasting the rouge I've painted them with. My feeble attempt not to look like death today.

"She's a good egg, you know."

"Little Rose is more than a good egg. She's almost better than you."

"My aunt—Imogen I mean. She's a good egg and she'll get used to you. She'll even forgive you for taking Rose to Niue. And once she does, she'll treat you like family. Give her a year after I'm gone. Don't give up on her."

"Don't say that."

"I'm just being realistic."

"Yes, but don't say it. Let's enjoy the time we have."

Cornelius leans his elbows on his knees, one of those definitive looks on his face.

"If you love her, I will make myself love her."

"Atta boy," I say, and he laughs.

"How's Alfred?"

A woeful breath escapes from him as he leans back and looks up at the ceiling. His eyes follow the fairytales Imogen had painted up there for Rose—*The Little Mermaid, Thumbelina, The Princess and the Pea.*

"He's still grieving very badly," he whispers. "Drinking more than he should. More than anyone should." Cornelius turns his head to me and furrows his brow. "He could use a little girl like Rose around, you know," he says.

"Seems everyone can." I take Cornelius's hand and place my head upon his shoulder. Such strong shoulders he's got, made even stronger by his work with Howard Carter. "You know what Ripley—Nif—said to me in my dreams. My father's kin, the Ogdens of Niue, must raise her. He was adamant about that. And my mother—my mother thought my getting to Nuie, if I could, was of the utmost importance. It was the last thing she wrote to me."

"But you're not going to Nuie."

"No, but Rose is the next best thing."

Cornelius squeezes my hand and looks into my eyes, almost as if I'm a real wife to him. "I would like the honor of raising Rose myself."

"I know you would, but you have other obligations. Besides, the Ogdens have never been able to have children of their own. Rose will be such a blessing to them, and can carry on their work for the London Missionary Society. Imogen, well, her son is grown, and you'll have children soon enough, and they'll need you."

"I'll never stop loving her," he says. "And I'll always be there if she needs me. I'll never stop loving you."

It's difficult for me when Cornelius says such things. He's so open and strong with me about what's in his heart that I can't help but admire him for it. One of many things that make me cherish him.

"Thank God she'll have you," I say. "And that I have you, and Alfred has you. You've been a second son to him, and he depends on you completely now that Ripley's gone."

Cornelius tears his eyes from mine and does his best at a smile.

"Yes, well, let's get on to something a little brighter, shall we? Your birthday, for one."

"Eighteen," I say. "In two days' time."

"Leila."

"You know what my mother said on her deathbed. That I won't see my eighteenth birthday."

Cornelius glances out the window at Rose and Imogen again. My aunt is now dancing with her, bringing her into the maze.

"Nothing is set in stone," he says.

"Perhaps you're right. Penny, after all, is making sponge cake with tutti-frutti icing. Should be marvelous."

"Nothing the English cook is marvelous."

My dearest friend takes a gander around Rose's nursery: the big white wood crib and tea table, the rocking horse, the dollies all about. It's like he's viewing an alien landscape. I suppose it is, to him. Cornelius is much more comfortable around the rubble of history—age-old homes, ruins, pyramids. It feels right to me that he will take possession of my family home in Cairo once I'm gone. I like to imagine him raising a family there, passing it down to his children.

Cornelius turns to me and our eyes find one another's again.

"Don't leave me," he says.

I DID NOT have much of an appetite for dinner, mostly piddling around my plate, moving my beef and vegetables about. At least Cornelius and Aunt Imogen managed to have a decent conversation. They talked of what made up an ancient Egyptian garden, and which of those plants might grow here. Quite an improvement over the usual uncomfortable silences.

Imogen gifted me with some volumes of ghost stories: "The Signal-Man" by Dickens, which I didn't have the heart to tell her I've already read, "The Open Door," by Charlotte Riddell, and "The Body Snatcher," by Robert Louis Stevenson, which I've also read. I've lost my taste for ghost stories entirely, since my life has become a spirit tale. But Cornelius has picked up where I left off, tearing through every saga of the unnatural that I've hidden in my secret library. The one where I also keep the scrapbook Edna gifted me, hiding it from Imogen's curious eyes. The book is now almost full, and Cornelius and I have poured over it at least a hundred times, adding bits of information we may have neglected. He will take it back with him to Cairo after I'm gone, and enlist Lieutenant General Blackwood's help in our puzzle, and that gives me confidence in the future. That Ripley and I, in whatever form we are born next, might come upon the clues we've assembled, and finally be able to unlock the mystery our Nin'ti fate has entrusted with us. One that involves not only the fates of those we love, but of humanity itself, and will bring with it war and disease, unleashing an unthinkable evil. A force I had but a taste of as it demanded my whole being, whispering to my every cell that we are meant to come together.

Tonight, I'm tired, so tired. I crawl into bed, and retrieve the letter Ripley once wrote to me. It was for my sixteenth birthday, nearly two years ago to the day. I was in London, and he was in Cairo. We were not yet even married.

You're as captive to me, as I am to you, and while you would have given yourself to me, had I asked, I do not take your heart or your body lightly. It is everything to me.

I read it over and over until I start to fall into a gentle sleep. It is for me a step from one world into another, only this time, things feel different. Leila's body, my body, is sluggish and frail. A heart that once beat with such fervor now stammers and falters. Then stops.

And at once, I am free.

"Nif!"

The stars whir around me. The blackness and the light.

"Where are you?"

I hear far away whispers—Cornelius giggling with Rose on his lap, Imogen telling her late husband's photograph all about her day, Alfred Davies pouring himself yet more gin and raising a glass to Cairo—her living and her dead, Claudia Ogden singing to herself as she toddles along the rocky beaches of Nuie.

Then the strange and anxious words of a mother in Moscow.

"It's like they're on fire," she says. "His eyes. When he looks at me, it's not a look of love like the other mothers get from their children."

"He's just an infant," a man tells her. "Barely over a year old."

"He's a demon!"

"Stop it!" he shouts and slaps her.

And then I feel the draw. A magnet, a cyclone, the voice of God commanding me. The spark, then explosion of conception, and I fall, as if I'm dropping from the top of the sky to the pit of the earth.

"Sherin!" His soul's voice calls me. My Nif.

"I think I know!" I call back. "We must find our way back to Cairo!"

But he's gone and I continue to fall.

Thank you for reading **Of Sand and Bone**.

If you enjoyed the story, please take a moment to leave a starred review on Amazon or the platform of your choice. Reviews from readers like you not only let we authors know what we're doing right, but draw others to their next great story adventure!

JOIN ME ON SOCIAL MEDIA!
No politics. Just a great conversation.

Twitter: @vicdougherty
Instagram: victoria_dougherty
Facebook: @victoriadougherty.author
YouTube: youtube.com/victoriadougherty
Podcast: www.anchor.fm/victoria-dougherty
Web: www.victoriadoughertybooks.com
COLD Blog: www.victoriadougherty.wordpress.com

VICTORIA DOUGHERTY is the author of three acclaimed Cold War historical thrillers, *The Bone Church*, *The Hungarian*, and *Welcome to the Hotel Yalta*. Her epic historical fantasy series, including *Savage Island*, *Breath* and *Of Sand and Bone* are her newest works of fiction. Readers and reviewers have called Ms. Dougherty's fiction "breathtaking", "mesmerizing", and "genre-defying."

Her blog—COLD—features her short essays on faith, family, love and writing. WordPress, the blogging platform that hosts some 70 million blogs worldwide, has singled out COLD as one of the Top 50 Recommended Blogs by writers or about writing. Ms. Dougherty's new podcast, also called COLD, has been praised by listeners as "the storyteller's church."

I WANT TO THANK my husband and children for their love, patience and support, my friends for their perpetual willingness to help, and most of all my readers. I say with complete confidence that I have the best readership on the planet. You all are interesting and interested, bottomless in your curiosity, and always up for challenge! A very hearty thank you goes out to Laura Drew and Chris Bell, my gracious and hugely talented exterior and interior book designers, Alex Eckman-Lawn, my brilliant illustrator, Faith Moore – the best editor I've ever worked with, Janet Margot, friend and queen of all things book and story, and all of my glorious friends in the writing community. Without you, none of this would be possible.

Victoria's Newsletter is Smashing!

Emails are boring. Mine aren't. Signup today for Cold Readers Club and get your weekly dose of dangerous women, hot-blooded warriors, and white-knuckle storytelling (random bad-assery included for free).

To join, go to www.victoriadoughertybooks.com and click "Get in Touch" at the top of the page. Then click the "Signup for Newsletter" button at the bottom right of the page.

OTHER BOOKS BY VICTORIA DOUGHERTY

Breath

Two souls. Infinite lives. A quest across history.

In the ancient past, in the now lost Kingdom of Rah'a, a young woman named Sherin finds herself in mortal peril after her family succumbs to a deadly contagion to which she is immune. Alone and afraid, she is cast out into the desert in search of a safe haven.

But the plague continues to ravage her region, forcing survivors to band together. Some form haphazard tribes, others violent gangs. Through her wits and courage, Sherin captures the attention of two very different men: Nif, a desert warrior who leads a nomadic tribe, and Roon, a powerful soldier for the crumbling sultanry.

As cannibalism, torture, thievery, and war blight the region, alliances shift and terror reigns. Despite all of this, Sherin finds herself falling deeply in love with one of her suitors, sensing a mystical energy between herself and the man to whom she is so passionately devoting herself.

The forces of destruction enveloping them, an extraordinary destiny begins to unfold before the lovers, ensnaring them in a fate that traps them in an endless cycle of death and rebirth. It will propel them through history, from the earliest of civilizations to the present day, where they must struggle to save humanity from the same fate that befell their ancient civilization, or risk losing one another forever.

www.victoriadoughertybooks.com

Savage Island: A Breath Novel

Some people fall in love. Others fall through time.

The island of Niue, 1944. On this remote island, deep in the South Pacific, about 1,500 miles from its closest neighbor, it hardly feels like a war is on. Angelie, a 17-year-old Australian girl, is waiting out the war on the island, where warm tropical winds blow through her hair almost as gently as native islander Will Tongahai's eyes graze her body.

But the arrival of an African archaeologist and his German consort unsettle the inhabitants of this tranquil isle, and Angelie begins to wonder if the war hasn't finally reached their shores.

As Angelie and Will are drawn to the suspicious pursuits of the new visitors - an ancient statue, a fantastic myth - a series of vivid dreams about deserts and long forgotten prophecies ensnares them. The lovers discover that their destiny, one forged thousands of years earlier, is not only bigger than their prospective future together, but makes a mere world war look like child's play.

What readers are saying about *Savage Island*:

"I love the author's way with words and her ability to wrap you into her story and entangle you in its threads. I'm going to be breathless with anticipation for the next installment of Breath."

"There are worlds within worlds [in this book], and time and space have no true meaning. Only the language of love."

"From the moment I opened its pages, I fell into an otherworldly, enchanting time and place that felt dreamlike and mesmerizing"

www.victoriadoughertybooks.com

The Bone Church

In a time of danger and distrust, two lovers seek redemption…and a way back to each other.

What readers and reviewers are saying:

"In this case heavy is good, very good." Back Porchervations

"The Bone Church, by debut author Victoria Dougherty, is possibly one of the darkest and most sophisticated historical novels you'll be able to put your hands on." Mina DeCaro, Mina's Bookshelf

"This novel has it all…an addictive jaunt into a world of paranoia, deceit, distrust, and then the ultimate betrayal. I really, really, really loved this book!" Lit Bitch

"This FIVE STAR Cold War thriller is so highly recommended I would say beyond all doubt this would be declared the thriller novel of the year." —Amazon reader review

The Hungarian

Grinding her old life beneath the heel of her Dior stiletto, Lily puts her new one on the line, surrendering to fate, love and for once, events bigger than herself.

What readers are saying:

"Absolutely brilliant, and readers will never regret getting it. I think it's one of the very best of its genre that I've ever read."

"Weighty, philosophical, poetic, with great knowledge of the literature and history of the Soviet Bloc."

"The heroine is fantastic and the story fast paced with lots of action."

"History and intrigue. Couldn't put it down."

www.victoriadoughertybooks.com

9 781955 039086